The
GOVERNESS
of
Highland
HALL

Center Point
Large Print

**This Large Print Book carries the
Seal of Approval of N.A.V.H.**

The
GOVERNESS
of
HIGHLAND
HALL

CARRIE
Turansky

CENTER POINT LARGE PRINT
THORNDIKE, MAINE

This Center Point Large Print edition is published
in the year 2013 by arrangement with WaterBrook Press,
an imprint of the Crown Publishing Group, a division of
Random House LLC, New York.

The text of this Large Print edition is unabridged.
In other aspects, this book may vary
from the original edition.
Printed in the United States of America
on permanent paper.
Set in 16-point Times New Roman type.

ISBN: 978-1-61173-932-9

Library of Congress Cataloging-in-Publication Data

Turansky, Carrie.
  The Governess of Highland Hall / Carrie Turansky. — Center Point
Large Print edition.
    pages cm
  ISBN 978-1-61173-932-9 (Library binding : alk. paper)
     1. Large type books. I. Title.
PS3620.U7457G68 2013b
813′.6—dc23
                                                    2013030009

This book is dedicated to my husband, Scott Turansky, whose love and encouragement have freed me to write the stories of my heart.

You are the inspiration for every hero I write.

Many waters cannot quench love;
rivers cannot sweep it away.
If one were to give
all the wealth of one's house for love,
it would be utterly scorned.

—Song of Songs 8:7

Blessed are the pure in heart,
for they will see God.

—Matthew 5:8

One

October 1911

Berkshire, England

Julia Foster lifted her gaze to the clear October sky as a lark swooped past. Her steps slowed and her thoughts took flight, following the bird as it dipped into the golden trees beyond the meadow. If only she could fly away, back to the familiar life and cherished friends she had left behind in India. But that dream would have to wait.

She shifted her gaze to the country lane rising before her. Around the next bend she would see Highland Hall. At least that was what she remembered, but twelve years had passed since she had attended a charity bazaar at the large estate before her family left for India. What if she had misjudged the distance or the time it took to walk from the village of Fulton to Highland Hall? She quickened her pace. It wouldn't do to be late for her ten o'clock appointment with Mrs. Emmitt, the housekeeper.

When she reached the top of the rise, she spotted an expensive-looking navy-blue motorcar with a black roof pulled to the side of the lane. A tall man, who had discarded his jacket and rolled up the sleeves of his white shirt, stood over the open hood. He reached in and pulled on something, then bent lower and scowled.

She considered walking past since they had not been introduced, but her conscience would not allow it. Stopping a few feet away, she cleared her throat. "Excuse me, sir. Do you need some assistance?"

He turned and glared at her. "Assistance?" His dark eyebrows rose to a haughty slant. "I suppose you know something about car engines?"

Julia lifted her chin, suppressing the urge to match his mocking tone. "No sir. But I'm on my way to Highland Hall, and I could ask someone there to come and help you if you like."

He huffed, grabbed the rag lying on the car's running board, and wiped his hands. "It won't do any good. No one there knows a blasted thing about cars." He tapped the gold Highland insignia on the door.

Julia stepped away, more than happy to leave the brooding chauffeur behind.

"Wait, you say you're headed to Highland Hall?"

She turned and faced him again. "Yes, I have an interview with Mrs. Emmitt." Perhaps if he knew she might soon be working for Sir William Ramsey, the new master of Highland Hall, he would treat her with a little more respect.

He narrowed his deep blue eyes and assessed her. "An interview? For what position?"

She looked away, debating the wisdom of continuing the conversation with a man who wasn't civil enough to introduce himself.

"It's all right. You can tell me." He nodded to her, obviously expecting a reply.

"If you must know, I'm applying for the position of governess."

A look of disbelief flashed across his face and the scowl returned. "You look too young. Do you have any experience?"

She straightened, trying to add another inch to her petite stature, but she was still at least a foot shorter than he. "I've been teaching children for nine years."

"Really? Did you begin teaching when you were ten?"

She clenched her jaw. Was there no end to the man's rudeness? "No sir. I was eighteen. And if you'll excuse me, I must go, or I'll be late for my appointment." She turned and strode away.

"There's no need to rush off in a huff." He caught up with her. "I didn't mean to insult you."

"I'm not insulted, just intent on being punctual." She cast him a quick side glance. "I don't have the time or luxury to stand by the roadside and fiddle with car engines."

He grinned and then chuckled.

Heat flashed into her face. Infuriating man!

How dare he laugh at her. She hurried on, not giving him the satisfaction of a reply.

"Well, pardon me."

She sent him a withering look and walked on so quickly she got a stitch in her side.

With his long legs, he had no trouble keeping pace. "You certainly have spirit. I like that."

She gulped in a big breath and spun toward him. "You, sir, are entirely too familiar and too rude for words!"

His jaw dropped, and he stared at her, wide-eyed.

With her face burning, she marched away. She'd only gone a few steps before regret overtook her. *Forgive me, Lord. I should not have spoken to him like that. But he was so ill mannered I couldn't help myself.* She sighed and lifted her eyes to heaven. *I'm sorry. I know that's not true. You're faithful to give me the strength to control my tongue if I will only ask. But please, Lord, could You make him forget what I said? Or at least let me have little contact with him at Highland?*

She doubted that last part of her prayer would be answered. While Highland Hall was a large house, the staff probably saw each other throughout the day.

What a terrible way to start off. No doubt he'd tell everyone she was hot-tempered and not worthy of the position of governess. And that was assuming she got the job. And she must. Her father's illness had stretched on for months, forcing them to leave India and return to England. Now that he was unable to practice medicine, her parents depended on her for support. She must not let them down, no matter how humbling or difficult the job might be.

The lane curved to the right, and Highland Hall came into view. Julia's steps slowed as she took in the lovely grounds and large house. It looked more like a castle, standing four stories high at its tallest point, with a wide lawn and curved, gravel drive leading to the front door. It was built of sand-colored stone, and though some sections had turned yellow and gray with age, it still looked sturdy and imposing. A tall, round turret stood at the right corner, and an arched portico stretched halfway across the front of the house.

Oh Lord, that house is worth a fortune, and the people who live there are definitely used to a different life than I've lived. How will I ever fit in?

She shook her head, then straightened her shoulders. There was no time to fret, not if she wanted to make a good impression and arrive at the appointed hour. She made her way around the side of the house, following the directions Reverend Langford had given her.

A broad-shouldered man wearing a brown cap and tweed coat pushed a wheelbarrow toward the greenhouse. He stopped and nodded to her. "Can I help you, miss?" He looked about thirty-five and had a kind, honest face.

She returned his nod with a slight smile. "I have an appointment with Mrs. Emmitt."

He pointed to a door tucked in a corner at the back of the house. "Just ring the bell there, miss, and someone will be along to help you."

She thanked him and crossed the rear courtyard. Pulling in a deep breath, she smoothed her hand down her cloak and skirt and checked her hat. Everything seemed to be in place. Lifting her hand, she pressed the bell while her stomach fluttered like a nervous bird.

Only a few seconds passed before the door opened and a plump young woman with rosy cheeks and bright blue eyes greeted her. She wore a white apron over her dark green servant's uniform and a white cap. "How can I help you, miss?"

"I'm Julia Foster. I'm here to see Mrs. Emmitt."

"Very good. Come this way." She started down the steps and smiled over her shoulder. "I'm Lydia, one of the housemaids. Are you here about a position?"

"Yes." Remembering her encounter with the brooding chauffeur, she decided not to add any more details. As they reached the bottom step, the heavenly scent of baking bread and roasting meat floated toward her. She breathed deeply, savoring the smell. Her empty stomach contracted, reminding her that she had walked off the simple breakfast of porridge she'd eaten at seven.

Lydia led the way past the kitchen. Julia glanced through the doorway and saw two young women and a man in a white chef's jacket chopping vegetables at the table in the center of the room. He said something to one of the women, but his French accent was so strong Julia couldn't understand him.

"You'll want to mind your p's and q's with Mrs. Emmitt," Lydia said, continuing down the hallway. "She's a stickler for proper manners and such. But you're smart-looking. That should help it go well for you."

"Thank you," Julia murmured, though she wasn't sure that was the right response.

"This is it." Lydia stopped in front of a closed door. "Mug's parlor, at least that's what we call it." She grinned and nodded. "Go on, then. Give it a knock, and good luck to you."

Julia nodded to her, sent off one more silent prayer, then rapped on the door while the maid disappeared into another room.

The door swung open, and a stern-faced woman who appeared to be about sixty looked out at her. She wore a plain navy-blue dress with a cameo pinned at the high neck and a set of keys clipped to her waistband. Small, wire-rimmed glasses perched on the bridge of her nose.

"Good day, ma'am. I'm Julia Foster."

"Come in. I've been expecting you." She motioned toward the straight-backed chair by the fireplace while she lowered herself onto the settee. "Do you have your letters of reference?"

"Yes ma'am." Julia took the letters from Reverend Langford and Lady Farnsworth from her handbag and gave them to Mrs. Emmitt.

The housekeeper pursed her lips and read Lady Farnsworth's letter first. "She says your family has been acquainted with hers for many years."

"Yes, my father served as her family physician since the time of her marriage to Lord Farnsworth."

"I'm not sure what that has to do with you." Mrs. Emmitt opened and read Reverend Langford's letter next, her stern expression never softening. "It says you've been out of the country for twelve years. Is that correct?"

Julia nodded. "Our family has been serving in India since 1899 with the London Missionary Society."

Mrs. Emmitt's nose wrinkled slightly as her gaze dipped back to the letter. "You were a teacher there?"

"Yes, we opened a home for girls and ran a medical clinic for the village."

Memories of India came flooding back—the overflowing marketplace, heavy with the scent of spices, the magenta flowers climbing the stone wall surrounding their home, the colorful embroidered saris of the women, and the beautiful dark faces of their girls . . . her students and the flowers of their ministry.

"Miss Foster?"

Julia blinked. "I'm sorry, what did you say?"

"How do you intend to teach the social skills our young ladies need to learn to enter society when you've been raised in"—she looked at Julia over the top of her glasses—"such a heathen environment?"

Heat infused her cheeks. "I was raised in Fulton by loving Christian parents who passed on their godly values and manners. I attended the village school until age twelve, then my mother taught me at home until I was fifteen. My training continued under my parents' guidance when we traveled to India. My experiences there have given me unique opportunities to see God at work in the world and to interact with all types of people."

Mrs. Emmitt took a handkerchief from her sleeve and dabbed her nose. "Yes . . . all types of people." She folded the letters and handed them back to Julia. "We've had a difficult time finding a governess. There are few qualified candidates in the area."

Julia wasn't sure what to say to that remark, so she kept silent.

Mrs. Emmitt sighed and gave a resigned nod. "Sir William has two children. His son, Andrew, is nine, and his daughter, Millicent, is six. Andrew will most likely be going away to school within the year, but he needs someone to help him prepare. Millicent has poor health. She needs careful attention and should not overexert herself."

Julia nodded, her hopes rising. Did this mean Mrs. Emmitt was satisfied with her qualifications?

"The children's mother passed away three years ago, which may be the reason Andrew has had such a difficult time."

Julia tensed. A difficult time? What did she mean?

"Sir William is also the guardian of his two young cousins," Mrs. Emmitt continued. "Miss Katherine Ramsey turns eighteen next month, and Miss Penelope is fifteen. The girls have been raised here at Highland, and it's been quite an adjustment for them to grieve their father's death and see the estate passed to their second cousin once removed." Mrs. Emmitt sent her a pained look. "It has been an adjustment for us all."

Julia swallowed, trying to take it all in. "So I would be teaching Sir William's children as well as the two young ladies?" Reverend Langford hadn't mentioned Katherine and Penelope. No wonder Mrs. Emmitt wanted to know if Julia was prepared to teach social skills. Katherine was old enough to be presented at court and take part in the London social season.

"That's correct." Mrs. Emmitt nodded. "You would oversee all four, following a program for their education and training set out by Sir William."

Julia had never taken part in the season, but her mother had, and she could probably advise her on how to help Katherine prepare.

"If that's agreeable to you, I will take you to meet Sir William, and he can finish the interview." Mrs. Emmitt stood and waited for Julia's reply.

"Yes ma'am, I would be happy to meet him." Julia rose.

"Come along then." Mrs. Emmitt left the parlor and led the way up the stone staircase, past the green baize door, and into the great hall.

Julia's eyes widened as she gazed up at the beautiful carved ceiling that arched high overhead. Richly colored tapestries and paintings of distinguished people hung on the paneled walls. Were they the past owners of Highland? A large fireplace with an elaborate marble mantle stood in the center of the wall on her right, and opposite that, a grand oak staircase rose to an open gallery one floor above.

Mrs. Emmitt glanced over her shoulder. "Don't dawdle."

Julia dropped her gaze and hurried after the housekeeper. There would be time to take in the splendor of the house after she spoke to Sir William—if she got the job. A shiver of anticipation raced down her arms.

A stout butler in a neatly pressed black suit, white shirt, and black tie stepped forward to meet them. A touch of silver in his dark hair gave him a distinguished appearance. His excellent posture and calm expression announced he was a man of dignity and authority.

"Mr. Lawrence, this is Miss Foster. I am interviewing her for the position of governess. Is Sir William available to meet with her?"

Mr. Lawrence looked Julia over and gave a curt nod. "I'll see." He stepped through a nearby doorway, and she heard him say, "Miss Foster, the woman applying for the position of governess, is here to see you, sir."

"Who? Oh yes. Have her come in." Sir William's voice seemed to carry a note of irritation.

Mr. Lawrence stepped out the door and nodded to them. Julia took a deep breath and followed Mrs. Emmitt into the room. Bookshelves lined the wall on the right, and opposite the door, three tall windows looked out on the side gardens. In the corner a man sat at a beautifully carved desk with his back to them. He put his pen aside and turned to face them.

A shock wave jolted Julia. Her eyes widened as she stared at the man she'd met on the lane, the man she supposed was the chauffeur. Her stomach tumbled to her feet, and her hopes fell with it.

"Miss Foster, please take a seat." Sir William stood and nodded toward an overstuffed chair. His gaze shifted to the housekeeper. "That will be all, Mrs. Emmitt."

The housekeeper stiffened. "Perhaps I should stay and—"

"That won't be necessary." His steady gaze made his meaning clear.

Mrs. Emmitt gave a curt nod, then turned and left the room. The butler followed.

Julia swallowed and sank into the chair.

"So, Miss Foster, you've come seeking the position of governess for my children and my two cousins?"

"Yes sir." Julia clasped her hands in her lap, her face burning. "But first, I must apologize for the way I spoke to you earlier this morning on the lane. I'm sorry. I had no idea . . . I thought you were the . . . chauffeur."

"There is no need to apologize. I should have introduced myself."

"Yes sir, that would have been helpful." *And it might've kept me from making a fool of myself and jeopardizing my chances at Highland.*

He sat opposite her. "So tell me why you believe you're qualified for the position of governess."

Was he truly going to give her a chance, even after all she had said to him on the lane? She gathered her thoughts and looked into his eyes. "Since I was fifteen I've assisted my parents, teaching and training the young girls who came into our care in our mission work in India."

"India, you say?"

"Yes sir. Our family served there for the last

twelve years. My father is a physician, and we ran a medical clinic and a home for girls who were orphans or those we were able to buy out of . . . difficult situations."

He frowned slightly. "What kind of situations?"

She hesitated, trying to remember exactly how her parents explained it. "It's hard to speak of, sir, but some girls are sold by their families to serve in Hindu temples." She looked down, her cheeks warming again. "It's a very heathen practice that takes away a young girl's innocence and purity."

His expression sobered. "Rescuing girls caught in such circumstances is commendable. What was your role there?"

"The girls lived with us at the mission station. I helped oversee their care, education, and upbringing. I also assisted my father in the clinic and helped my mother with all the practical aspects of running our home and the mission."

"That sounds like quite an undertaking."

"It's important work, sir. I felt privileged to do it."

"You seem quite committed." He hesitated a moment. "May I ask why you decided to leave?"

"My father's health has been declining for quite some time. It reached a crisis three months ago. He needed more medical care, so we decided to come back to England."

"Has he improved since you returned?"

"Not as much as we had hoped. He is confined

to his bed most days." She looked away and tried to swallow past the tightness in her throat.

His expression softened. "I'm sorry to hear that. Perhaps with more rest and good care he will recover."

"That is our hope and prayer." She pressed her lips together for a moment, and then lifted her gaze to meet his. "And that's why it's so important that I find a position nearby, one that allows me to help support my parents and makes it possible for me to visit them on my afternoons off."

"I see." He stood and walked over to the desk. "Give me a moment, please."

Her heart pounded, and she clutched the folds of her skirt. Had she said too much? She closed her eyes.

Please Lord, move his heart. Give me a chance to help my parents and serve this family.

William shuffled through the papers on his desk, turning the decision over in his mind. Miss Foster had experience as a teacher, but she had worked under her parents' guidance in India. Could she handle these new responsibilities on her own? She was obviously much younger than past governesses, but none of them had lasted more than six months. Perhaps age was not the most important factor to consider. He'd had a devil of a time finding someone suitable in London, and it had been even more challenging since he'd come to Highland.

He also had to think of his young cousins. They needed someone who could help them complete their education and guide them in finding suitable husbands so they could take their place in society. Was Miss Foster up to the task?

He tapped his fingers on the desk. It was hard to discern a person's character by her appearance, but Miss Foster made a good impression. Her clothing was simple, neat, and modest. She was slender but seemed healthy, with a fair complexion and a rosy tint to her cheeks.

But was she trustworthy? That was the most important question. There didn't seem to be any guile in her blue eyes, but he had been fooled before, and with very painful results.

He clamped his jaw and banished those thoughts. Turning from his desk, he faced Miss Foster. "Thank you for waiting."

She opened her eyes and looked up at him, her expression hopeful. Had she been praying? He supposed that might be her habit, coming from a religious family. Well, a little piety might be good for his cousins.

"I've decided to offer you the position."

Relief flashed in her eyes. "Thank you, sir."

"But it will be on a trial basis. One month seems like an adequate time to judge if this is the right decision."

"A month, sir?"

"Yes. I want to be sure you can carry out your

duties and handle the children and my cousins. Are you agreeable to that?"

She glanced away for a moment and then looked back at him. "Yes sir. I'm willing to accept the position on a trial basis."

"Good. Mrs. Emmitt will inform you about the children's needs and routines."

Lawrence walked into the room. "Mr. Bixby is here to see you, sir."

Sir William nodded. "Have him wait. We're almost finished here."

"Yes sir." Lawrence hesitated, and a pained expression crossed his face. "I'm sorry, sir, but I thought you should know Master Andrew has taken a fall."

William's heart lurched. "Is he hurt?"

"Just a small bump on the head. Mrs. Emmitt had him lie down, and she put some ice on it."

"How did it happen?"

"He pulled a chair over and was climbing up to open a cabinet in the pantry. It appears he was trying to help himself to another piece of cake."

"Blast! Where was the nursery maid? Isn't it her job to keep an eye on him?"

"Yes sir. It is."

"Well, she is failing miserably. This is the third time this week she's let him get into mischief. Tell Mrs. Emmitt I am not pleased. She's to speak to her and be sure it doesn't happen again. Andrew is to be sent to his room, and he's not to have anything to eat until dinner."

"Yes sir." The butler turned and left the room.

"Excuse me, sir, but will you speak to Master Andrew about the incident?"

William frowned at Miss Foster. "I hadn't planned on it. And why should I? Don't you think that punishment is sufficient?"

"Perhaps, but how can a child learn from your discipline unless you discuss the offense and explain what is expected of him?"

"That, Miss Foster, is why I'm hiring a governess. It will be your duty to supervise and train the children."

"But isn't it a parent's responsibility to bring up his children in the nurture and admonition of the Lord?" She rose from her chair. "How can you carry out that duty when your message is relayed through a butler or even a governess?"

He inhaled slowly. Did this slip of a girl really think it was her responsibility to instruct him in his role as parent? "I have always worked through my staff to care for my children, and I plan to continue to do so. If you want to fill this position, you need to put aside your modern child-rearing philosophies and accept my traditional methods."

"My philosophies are not modern, quite the contrary. They're biblical. And—"

He raised his hand. "Miss Foster, do you intend to argue with me before you've even begun your first day of employment?"

Her eyes widened, then she dropped her gaze. "No sir. I'm sorry. I spoke out of turn."

"Yes, you did." He straightened his jacket, regretting his tone. He hadn't meant to sound so harsh. "However, I'm willing to overlook it. Will you be able to start tomorrow?"

She looked up. "Yes sir."

"Report to Mrs. Emmitt at eight in the morning. You may go."

Julia walked out of the library and into the great hall, her heart beating hard and fast. Mr. Lawrence stood by the door, a disapproving frown on his face. He'd obviously heard everything she'd said. One more mark against her. A rotund gentleman in a black suit waited with him. He brushed his finger across his thick silver moustache and shifted his black leather case to the other hand. Mr. Lawrence showed the man in and announced him to Sir William.

She slowly crossed the great hall, taking time to look at the portraits and beautiful furnishings. Was this the type of home her grandparents owned? Had her mother grown up surrounded by wealth like this until she had decided to marry against her parents' wishes? That decision had caused a huge uproar, and Julia's grandfather had cut her parents off completely.

But her parents' love and shared faith had carried them through those difficult times. After Julia's family traveled to India, her mother's sister, Beatrice, shared their letters with Julia's grandmother, but they were always kept secret from Julia's grandfather, who had never forgiven his daughter for marrying a young, middle-class doctor. Julia had never met her grandparents, or anyone else on her mother's side of the family, and she doubted she ever would. Her domineering grand-father had forbidden it, and no one in the family dared to go against his wishes . . . except her parents.

She approached a beautiful marble sculpture on a pedestal. The peaceful expression on the woman's face drew Julia closer. Who could she be? Leaning toward the statue, she peered at the inscription on the small brass nameplate.

"Miss Foster!"

She jumped at the butler's sharp tone and stifled a gasp. "Yes sir?"

"The staff do not use the front entrance unless they are greeting guests or accompanying the family out of doors."

Julia's gaze swung toward the front door. "Oh yes, of course."

"The staff exit downstairs, through the kitchen or at the end of the lower hall."

She nodded. "Yes, I came in that way."

"And that is where you will exit." He nodded toward the other end of the great hall. "Mrs. Emmitt asked that you see her on your way out."

"I'll look for her downstairs. Thank you." She walked at a comfortable pace through the great hall, taking in a few more glimpses of the paintings and crests carved into the molding above the fireplace. Such splendor! What would it be like to be surrounded by such beauty every day? Certainly much different from her simple life at the mission station in India or her parents' rented cottage in Fulton.

As she reached the end of the hall, she turned and looked over her shoulder. Highland Hall was a large and impressive home, but wealth and prestige didn't always bring happiness. She didn't have to look any further than Sir William Ramsey to see that was true.

"I'm sorry I don't have better news for you." Mr. Bixby, William's solicitor, shifted in his chair. His moustache twitched, and he grinned slightly. "I'm afraid these death duties will be the death of us all."

William turned his brooding gaze on the solicitor. "I don't see the humor in it."

The little man immediately sobered. "Forgive me, I was hoping to offer a little levity."

William grimaced. "It's all right. It's not your fault the government is trying to choke the aristocracy out of existence."

The solicitor bobbed his head. "Exactly. It's dreadful. These inheritance laws have made it almost impossible for families to pass on their estates intact. Perhaps Parliament will repeal them."

"I doubt it. The government will become dependent on the funds, and there will be no turning back."

Bixby clicked his tongue. "I suppose so, but not everyone can comply. Some families have had to sell their estates and settle in town."

William scowled and walked toward the window. He'd come here to escape London. All the gossip and social wrangling was enough to turn a man's stomach. Selling the house in London seemed preferable to auctioning off a chunk of his newly inherited estate. But when they had prepared to move to Highland, his sister, Sarah, pleaded with him to keep the family home in London so they could return a few times each year. He hated the idea of disappointing her. With her crippled hand and arm, happy childhood memories were one of Sarah's few comforts.

"Perhaps the funds from the sale of your business interests in London could cover the duties?"

"I've set those aside for the repairs that need to be made here at Highland. We can't let the house fall down around us." William returned to his chair opposite Mr. Bixby. "My late cousin, Randolph Ramsey, was not the best manager of his finances or property."

"I see." Mr. Bixby stroked his chin. "Then you'll have to come up with the funds another way."

"How long do we have before the payment must be made?"

"I can slow things down a bit, but I'd say the first of March at the latest."

Four and a half months? What did the government expect him to do? Wave a magic wand and double his bank account?

"Perhaps the estate can bring in more income. There is the rent you receive from your tenant farmers, and you have a fine herd of sheep, large orchards, and acres of grain."

"I've only been here three weeks. I've just begun to get my feet under me. I have no idea if we're maximizing our income."

"Well, I'm afraid you'll have to do something. They'll tack on a very steep fine if you don't pay on time."

William growled under his breath. "All right. I'll meet with my overseer and see if we can increase our income over the next few months."

Mr. Bixby stood. "Very good. I think that's your best option."

William rose from his chair and pulled the cord to summon Lawrence. When the butler appeared, William shook hands with Mr. Bixby and bid him good day. The butler showed the solicitor out.

William returned to his desk, where a stack of repair estimates, bills, and letters needed his attention, but he struggled to regain his focus. He had no idea overseeing a large estate would be this difficult. It made his former position in London—running his family's import business—seem like a holiday.

When he first heard he had inherited Highland Hall and his late cousin's title as baronet, he had been thrilled with the prospect of leaving London and settling in the country as master of his own estate. Had he made a mistake? Perhaps he should not have been so quick to sell his business interests to his younger brother, David.

Well, it was too late to change course now. He must find a way to restore Highland to its former glory, even if it drained his bank account. Perhaps then he would be respected as master of a fine estate rather than pitied for—

He clenched his jaw and banished those thoughts.

Turning, he looked up at the large painting of Randolph Ramsey, the former master of Highland, hanging above the library fireplace. Why had his cousin ignored the needed repairs on the house and property? He'd never confided in William about his financial struggles. Was it the strain of running the estate that had driven his cousin to an early grave?

Or was it something else?

Two

Julia folded her brown woolen shawl and laid it on top of the other clothing in the leather trunk. Glancing around the small upstairs bedroom of her parents' cottage, she looked for anything else she might want to take to Highland. Most of her possessions had been packed away and left in India, with the hope she would return. She closed her eyes and sighed, her heart aching at the thought of remaining so distant from her beloved friends and the ministry there.

No, she must refocus her mind. There was no reason to feel sorry for herself. The Lord had answered her prayers and given her a good position with a fine family. The salary would help her parents, and more important, she would be close enough to see them every Sunday afternoon.

She crossed the room to her dresser and gently ran her fingers over the top of the framed photograph of her parents, her brother, Jonathan, and herself, from a happier time. How different her father looked, so strong and vibrant, very little like the pale, thin man who rested downstairs. Her mother also looked older after all that had happened to them in the last few months.

Julia lifted her gaze to the small oval mirror above the dresser and checked her reflection. She didn't see many signs of change, but her usually bright blue eyes had dimmed, and the slope of her shoulders was more pronounced. Well, it couldn't be helped. Life had taken an unexpected turn, and she had to carry on the best she could.

She lowered her gaze to the other photograph on the dresser. The seventeen girls who lived at the mission station, her students, surrounded her in the picture. How she loved them and missed them. Little nine-year-old Sarita, wearing a bright smile, stood beside her in the center. Mondulai stood next to them with her arm looped through Julia's. She was a wonderful assistant, and though she was only nineteen, she had stepped into the role of teacher when Julia had to leave.

With a whispered prayer for her parents, her brother, and her dear girls, Julia placed the photographs in her trunk. They would be a comfort and reminder that she only had to be separated from those she loved for a short time.

"Julia, dinner is ready," her mother called from the bottom of the steps.

"I'll be right down." Julia added her Bible

and journal to the trunk, then lowered the lid.

Her mother greeted her with a caring smile as she entered the kitchen. She had prepared three dinner trays, which sat on the small wooden table. "Did you finish packing?"

"Yes. I'm all done." Julia leaned in and kissed her mother's cheek. "Dinner smells wonderful."

"Thank you, dear." Her mother handed her a tray. "Would you take this to your father?"

Julia nodded and carried it to the parlor where her father rested in a bed near the fireplace. Her mother followed with the second tray.

He looked up from his book and smiled. "Ah, Julia, what are you bringing me tonight?"

"I believe it's a lovely lamb stew." She settled the tray on her father's lap while her mother adjusted the pillow behind his back.

"It looks delightful." He shifted his gaze to his wife. "Thank you, Mary. You're a fine cook."

"You haven't tasted it yet, Phillip."

"After thirty-three years of enjoying your cooking, I'm sure it is delicious."

Her mother patted his cheek. "You're a dear man. You always have been." She returned to the kitchen to bring out the last tray.

He watched her go, a misty look in his eyes. "Your mother has borne this all so well."

"She's a brave woman."

He shifted his gaze to Julia. "And so are you."

She took his hand. "You're the brave one."

A warm light filled his eyes, and he shook his head. "I appreciate what you're doing for us. I know it's not your first choice to leave home to work as a governess."

Her throat tightened. "It will be fine. I'm thankful they've agreed to hire me." She pulled up a chair next to him and sat down.

"You'll do well at Highland. They'll hate to see you go when the time comes."

She glanced away and reached for her dinner tray.

Her father frowned slightly as he watched her. "Julia, you did tell them this is temporary, didn't you?"

She looked up as her mother returned, but she did not meet her father's gaze. "I meant to, but the whole experience was so . . . unsettling. Before I knew it, the interview was over, and the butler was showing me out."

Father looked at her over the top of his glasses. "Honesty is an important foundation for all relationships. You don't want to mislead them."

"No, of course not. But I'm not sure I need to tell them right now. Sir William made it clear there is a one-month trial period. He may not keep me on after that."

"All the more reason to tell him we plan to return to India as soon as my health improves."

That was her father's plan, but the longer his health remained unchanged, the less likely it seemed it would happen. Julia exchanged a glance with her mother.

Her father sighed. "I know what you two are thinking."

"And what is that, dear?" Her mother's expression remained serene.

"That I'll not be able to go back."

The slightest hint of pain appeared in her mother's eyes then quickly faded. "That decision is in the Lord's hands. We're trusting Him to direct us."

Her father's sorrowful expression eased. "Of course. You're right, dear." He focused on Julia again. "But my illness must not keep you from returning to India, if that's what you truly want."

They'd talked about this many times. He knew how much she loved teaching in India and that she longed to go back, but how could she leave her parents when her father was so ill? Who would care for them if she left the country? Jonathan attended medical school in London and needed more training before he could begin his own practice and assume some of the responsibility of caring for their parents. "I'm content to wait for the Lord to open that door at the right time."

"Are you, my dear?" Concern filled her father's eyes. "Can you accept this position at Highland and see it as God's will for you at the present?"

Julia looked toward the window where the fading sunlight painted the sky soft shades of peach and gold. After living in India for twelve years, it felt more like home than England. But her parents needed her here. The only answer was to surrender and allow God to choose . . . and for now the choice was clear.

She turned back to her father. "God has guided me to Highland. My present and my future are safe in His hands."

Her father patted her knee. "Very good, my dear. With your mind set like that, He will bless you and take care of everything. I'm sure of it."

Julia nodded, but she wished her heart felt as strong and certain as her words. For her parents' sake, she must cast off her homesick thoughts of India and make the needed adjustments to her new life at Highland.

"Shall we pray?" Father reached for her hand.

She clasped his warm, rough fingers in her own and then took her mother's hand on the other side. Lowering her head, she listened while her father offered a simple prayer of thanks for the day, for Julia's new position, and for their meal.

Tears burned her eyes. This is what she would miss most—more than the fragrant jasmine flowers, the chatter of the girls at play, or the heat of the Indian sun on her shoulders. How would she find the strength and wisdom she needed without daily interaction with her parents? All of her life they had trained her to trust God. Well, the time had come for her to step out, exercise her faith, and find her peace and security in Him alone.

The next morning Julia arrived at Highland Hall promptly at eight. Mrs. Emmitt met her at the back door and asked her to wait in her parlor while she finished speaking to the maids. Julia paced the room and repeated one of her favorite verses. *God is our refuge and strength, a very present help in trouble.*

Mrs. Emmitt arrived and gave Julia a summary of the two younger children's activities and preferences and told her a bit more about Millicent's health issues. Julia nodded, trying to remember everything. The housekeeper didn't mention Katherine or Penelope, which seemed odd, but Julia decided to wait and see how the day unfolded.

Finally, she followed Mrs. Emmitt up the backstairs past the main floor and up to the first floor above.

"Your room is the second door on the left." The housekeeper nodded toward it. "I'll have the footmen bring up your trunk."

"Thank you." Julia slowed, expecting to be shown into her room, but Mrs. Emmitt continued on.

"The nursery and schoolroom are across the hall." She motioned toward a door on the right. "The children's maid is helping them dress and prepare for the day. The family and staff gather for

Scripture reading and prayer in the great hall at nine o'clock. You'll be introduced to everyone at that time. Then you'll return with the children to the nursery for breakfast and lessons."

Julia nodded, pleased to hear Sir William was concerned about the spiritual needs of his family and staff. Her thoughts shifted back to the children's schedule. "Do the children eat luncheon with their father?"

"No, you will supervise their meals in the nursery."

Julia hesitated. "All their meals?"

"Yes. Sir William believes—"

A high-pitched scream came from the other side of the nursery door.

Julia gasped.

Mrs. Emmitt stiffened, then jerked open the door.

"Andrew, please!" The maid chased the boy across the room. Freckles covered his face, and his bright red, wavy hair glowed like a flaming torch as he ran past. He raced behind the table, clutching a gold-and-black stuffed tiger. He dodged the maid, eluding her grasp, and turned over a child-sized chair.

Millicent stood in the corner, tears flowing down her pale cheeks. "He's got my tiger!"

Mrs. Emmitt drew herself up, her eyes blazing. "Andrew Ramsey, stop this immediately!"

The boy darted a gleeful look at the housekeeper, then dashed into the closet and slammed the door.

The young maid, her face flushed and her blond hair coming loose from her cap, hurried back to Millicent and knelt beside her. "It's all right, Miss Millie. Please don't cry. I'm sure he won't tear the head off Tiger."

"Ann, what is going on?" Mrs. Emmitt glared at the maid.

"I'm sorry, ma'am. Master Andrew is . . . having a difficult morning."

"That's no excuse for letting things get so out of hand." Mrs. Emmitt marched to the closet and twisted the knob, but the door was locked. "Master Andrew, come out at once!"

"No! I'm never coming out!"

"That's nonsense. You can't spend the day in the closet."

"Yes, I can!"

"Very well. Then you'll have no breakfast, and I shall have to tell your father you are misbehaving again."

Julia and the maid exchanged a glance. Would that motivate the boy to obey? Apparently not, because the door remained closed.

Mrs. Emmitt spun around and faced Ann. "I have a mind to dismiss you on the spot!"

The maid's eyes widened. "Oh no. Please, ma'am. I'm sure he'll settle down and be out in just a minute."

"He'd better be!" Mrs. Emmitt snatched a watch from her skirt pocket and checked the time. "You have twenty-five minutes to finish dressing the children and bring them downstairs. If you fail in that duty, you will pack your bags and leave this house today. Do you understand?"

The color drained from the maid's face. "Yes ma'am."

Mrs. Emmitt sent Julia a stern glance. "Perhaps Miss Foster can help you get the children under control." She strode out of the room and closed the door with a loud bang.

Julia swallowed and turned to the maid. "I'm so sorry. What a difficult way to begin the day. I'm Julia Foster, the new governess."

Tears gathered in the young woman's eyes. "My name's Ann Norton, and I'm ever so glad you've come. I've only been in service here a week, and I've had a dickens of a time trying to manage these two wild ones on my own." She nodded toward Millie. "Spawn of the devil, if you ask me."

Julia stifled a gasp. "We mustn't speak about the children that way." She glanced at the little girl, who watched them with wide blue-green eyes. Her tears had slowed, but she still breathed in jerky sobs.

"You're right, of course. But I've never seen such disobedient and unruly—"

"Please, I must insist on it."

The maid sighed. "All right." She placed her hands on her hips and glared toward the closet. "We've got to get that boy out here and dressed." She walked over and tried the doorknob again. "Andrew, Mrs. Emmitt is gone. You'll not be punished if you come out now and finish dressing." Ann bit her lip and waited, but the door did not open. "Miss Foster, your new governess has arrived, and she's brought you a treat."

Julia shook her head. "We mustn't lie to the children to convince them to obey."

"What kind of treat?" Andrew's muffled voice came from behind the closet door.

Julia opened her mouth, intending to explain she hadn't brought him anything, but the maid cut her off. "It's something delicious, and if you come out now you can have some before we go downstairs."

The door creaked open about a foot, and the boy peered out. "I don't see any treats."

Julia stepped forward. "You're right, Master Andrew. Ann was mistaken."

He started to pull the door shut, but Julia grabbed hold and kept it open. "I didn't bring treats today, but if you settle down and get dressed, I'll tell you about the time a real tiger came calling at our house."

He snorted and tossed Millie's stuffed tiger on the floor. "There are no tigers in England, except perhaps in the zoo."

Millie ran forward and snatched the stuffed animal. She gathered it into her arms and sent her brother a hateful glare.

"You're right," Julia continued in a calm voice. "But I'm talking about my house in India."

His green eyes lit up. "India? Like *The Jungle Book*?"

"Yes. You've read it?"

He shook his head. "Mrs. Lambert, our governess in London, started reading it to us, but then we had to come here." He scowled, his expression looking very much like his father's when she met him in the lane yesterday morning.

"It's a wonderful book," Julia continued. "Perhaps we can find a copy and finish reading it."

Ann placed her hand on Andrew's shoulder and guided him away from the closet. "Yes, maybe Miss Foster can read it to you after breakfast, but first we must get dressed."

"I want to hear the tiger story." Millicent walked toward Julia. She was a lovely child, with long, wavy red hair flowing over her shoulders and a few pale freckles scattered across her nose and cheeks.

Julia smiled. "Let's obey Ann and finish dressing, and I'll tell you the story while I fix your hair."

Millicent held out her hand to Julia. That simple offer of trust warmed Julia's heart. She grasped the girl's hand and led her to the dressing table.

Fifteen minutes later the children stood by the door, neatly dressed, hair combed, and ready to go downstairs.

"There now, you look very nice." Ann straightened Andrew's jacket and gave him a pat on the shoulder.

Julia nodded her approval. "Andrew, since this is my first day, I'd like you to escort me downstairs and show me how everything is done."

The boy's face brightened. "All right. I can do that."

Julia took his arm, and he led the way out of the nursery and down the hall.

A young woman met them in the gallery. She wore a dark blue dress with little adornment, but it looked well made of expensive material. Her dark brown hair was pulled up in a simple style. Kindness flowed from her brown eyes. She sent Julia a shy smile and slipped both hands behind her back. "Good morning. I'm Sarah Ramsey, William's sister."

"This is our new governess, Miss . . ." Andrew looked up at Julia.

Julia smiled and gave her name. "I'm happy to meet you, Miss Ramsey."

"Oh, please, call me Sarah."

Julia nodded. "As you wish."

The sound of conversation in the great hall on the floor below drew Julia's attention and she glanced over the banister.

"We had better go down," Sarah said. "My brother likes everyone present at nine o'clock."

Andrew tugged Julia toward the stairs.

She held him back. "When a gentleman walks with a lady, he keeps her pace in mind, especially indoors." She spoke to him in a low, gentle tone so no one else could hear.

He nodded and walked slowly, looking like a perfect little gentleman.

Sir William stood by the large marble fireplace in the great hall, watching them descend the stairs, his expression unreadable.

At the bottom, Julia hesitated. Should she stand with the servants, who waited on one side of the hall opposite Sir William, or should she join him?

Sarah leaned closer. "Your place is with the children."

Julia nodded her thanks and followed Sarah, Millicent, and Andrew toward the fireplace. Sarah walked with a slight limp, and Julia wondered if she had suffered an injury.

Across the hall the servants lined up in what appeared to be the order of their rank. At the head of the line stood Mr. Lawrence, the butler, then Mrs. Emmitt, the housekeeper. Next to her stood the French chef she'd seen working in the kitchen, wearing a white chef's coat and dark trousers, then two tall footmen dressed in formal livery. Next came five maids, including Lydia, the young woman she'd met when she first arrived at

Highland for her interview. Lydia sent Julia a slight nod and smile. Three young kitchen maids, who looked like they were no older than fourteen or fifteen, came next. The gardener, who had directed her to the back door yesterday, and his two young assistants held their caps in their hands as they waited at the end of the line.

It was a large staff, and she imagined there were many others who worked for Sir William outdoors, managing his horses, cows, sheep, orchards, and crops. That was quite a responsibility to oversee so many people and such a large estate.

She glanced at Sir William, noting the lines of strain around his eyes and the stiffness of his posture. Once again she pondered how wealth and possessions didn't guarantee a carefree life. She must pray for him and do all she could to ease his concern for his children.

William pulled his watch from his vest pocket and scowled when he saw the time. He did not intend to wait all morning for his two young cousins to appear. On the opposite side of the great hall his butler, Lawrence, met his gaze. He glanced toward the staircase with a question in his eyes.

William blew out a breath and tried to restrain his growing irritation. "Mrs. Emmitt, do you know why Miss Katherine and Miss Penelope have not come down?"

"No sir. I'm sorry. I do not. I've been a bit preoccupied this morning." She narrowed her gaze at the new governess who stood beside William with his children and his sister. The housekeeper turned to one of the maids. "Lydia, did you wake the young ladies this morning?"

She bobbed a quick curtsy. "Yes ma'am. Miss Katherine sent this note."

A ripple of surprise crossed the servants' faces as the maid took the note from her apron pocket and passed it to Mrs. Emmitt. Lawrence cleared his throat and flashed a warning glance down the row. The servants all lowered their gazes to the floor.

Mrs. Emmitt snatched the note from Lydia's hand. "Next time you will give me any messages immediately."

"Yes ma'am." The maid's lower lip quivered, and she dropped her gaze.

Mrs. Emmitt walked across and handed the note to William. "I'm sorry, sir." She softened her tone. "Lydia is new and just getting used to the way we do things at Highland."

"I'm sure she meant no harm." He took the note and unfolded it.

Dear Cousin William,

We are not feeling well. Please excuse us for not coming down this morning.

Your cousins, Katherine and Penelope

Heat surged into his chest. *"Not well," my eye! They'll be perfectly fine by the time they want to go riding or call on a friend this afternoon.* He stuffed the note in his pocket. This would not do. Morning Scripture reading and prayer were not optional. Everyone needed to fall in line, even his young cousins.

He looked up and straightened his shoulders. "Very well, let's begin. This morning, before I read our passage of Scripture, I would like to introduce our new governess, Miss Julia Foster." He nodded toward her.

Her soft blue eyes lit up, and a slight smile tucked in the corners of her mouth.

An unsettling awareness traveled through him. He shook it off and shifted his gaze away. "She is originally from Fulton but has recently returned from India, where she and her family were engaged in mission work. She will be overseeing the education of the children and the young ladies."

Andrew squirmed on his left, and William placed a firm hand on the boy's shoulder. Andrew stilled and looked up. William squeezed his son's shoulder, hoping to press in the point. "I expect you all to cooperate with her and give her the respect due her position."

Nelson, the first footman, looked Miss Foster over with a slight smile and an unmistakable gleam in his eye.

William frowned and made a mental note to speak to Lawrence about it. Relationships between the staff were discouraged, and he would not put up with any of the men bothering Miss Foster.

He cleared his throat and opened his Bible. "This morning our passage comes from Galatians, chapter five, verses thirteen and fourteen. 'For, brethren, ye have been called unto liberty; only use not liberty for an occasion to the flesh, but by love serve one another. For all the law is fulfilled in one word, even in this; Thou shalt love thy neighbor as thyself.'"

He closed the Bible and waited a moment, hoping the words would sink into his servants' minds. "Let us pray. O gracious heavenly Father, help us guard our hearts and minds from sinful thoughts and actions, and remind us of our responsibilities to diligently serve others and love our neighbor." Someone snickered, and he looked up.

Nelson grinned at one of the young kitchen maids, and she returned a shy smile.

William narrowed his gaze at them. They immediately sobered and looked down. He paused a second more, then added, "We ask You to watch over our household, keep us safe from harm, and lead us in the way everlasting. Amen."

Lawrence nodded to the row of servants, dismissing them.

William tucked the Bible under his arm. "Miss Foster, will you wait a moment, please?"

She looked up. "Yes sir."

"Mrs. Emmitt," William called.

The housekeeper stopped at the foot of the stairs. "Yes sir?"

"Would you please look in on my cousins? Apparently, they aren't feeling well, and I'd like to know if I should send for the doctor."

Mrs. Emmitt nodded. "Of course, sir. I'll see to it right away."

"And would you also inform them Miss Foster has arrived and arrange a time for them to meet with her . . . before they go riding or engage in any other activities."

"Yes sir." Mrs. Emmitt climbed the stairs, followed by Andrew, Millicent, and Ann, the nursery maid.

He nodded to the governess. "Miss Foster, I'd like to introduce my sister, Miss Sarah Ramsey."

"Miss Foster and I met on our way down this morning." Sarah turned to the governess with a warm smile. "We're very grateful you've come to Highland. We hope you'll be happy here."

"Thank you. I'm looking forward to getting to know the children and the young ladies."

At the mention of their cousins, Sarah's smile faded. "I believe they will benefit greatly from the guidance of a governess."

"I hope I can encourage their love for learning

and help them develop their character and gifts."

"Yes." Sarah smiled at William and tucked her arm through his. "That's exactly what they need, isn't it?"

William nodded. "Character development is key for anyone's education."

Miss Foster looked up at him, and he couldn't help noticing her soft blue eyes and the sweet openness of her expression. "Will there be anything else?" she asked.

A warning flashed through him, and he broke his gaze. "No. That will be all."

Three

Mrs. Emmitt strode down the first-floor hall, her mind spinning with all that needed to be done that morning. They were expecting a delivery from the grocer, and he would need to be paid. The gardener must be told to bring in fresh flowers for the dining room, and she had to speak to Lydia about her having held on to that note. But first she must check on Katherine and Penelope. She doubted the girls were truly ill. This was probably another example of Katherine's silent rebellion.

Ever since Sir William, Miss Ramsey, and the young children had arrived at Highland, Katherine had stubbornly resisted Sir William's authority, and Penelope simply followed her sister into whatever mischief she created.

She knocked on the elder sister's door, then pushed it open without waiting for an invitation. The curtains were closed, but a faint light filtered through a slight gap in the middle. "Miss Katherine?"

The girl rolled over on her bed and squinted up at her. "What . . . what do you want?"

"Your note said you were ill. Sir William is concerned and asked me to look in on you."

Katherine tossed the blankets aside. "Why would he do that? I doubt he truly cares." She swung her legs over the side of the bed and slowly sat up.

"Shall we send for the doctor?"

"Of course not. I'm perfectly fine . . . I'm just extremely tired of my stuffy cousin ordering me out of bed at an ungodly hour."

The housekeeper held back her frown. "I'm sorry, miss, but Sir William believes the family and staff should be present for Scripture reading and prayer."

"Well, I won't be ordered around like some feeble-minded servant."

Mrs. Emmitt stifled a gasp. *Ungrateful girl! How could she say such things?* She had always been fond of Katherine, but her behavior these last few months was stretching that fondness to the limit.

Katherine's haughty expression faltered. "I'm sorry. I didn't mean it like that." She walked to the dressing table and picked up her hairbrush. "It's just not right for him to come here and change everything. He's not my father, and he shouldn't try to take on that role."

"I don't believe that is Sir William's intention."

54

Katherine's father, Sir Randolph, had been a kind man and always fair to his staff, though they all knew he gave too much time and attention to shooting and fishing and not enough to managing Highland or his family.

"It's bad enough that Cousin William has inherited our estate, does he have to treat me as if I have no brain and no say in my own life? I'm almost eighteen. I should be able to decide when I rise and how I spend my day."

Mrs. Emmitt crossed to the windows and opened the curtains. Light flooded the room. "Sir William believes it's his responsibility to watch over you."

"Well, I don't agree." She pulled a brush through her long honey-blond hair, frowning at her reflection. "He's a gloomy, overbearing man, and I have no intention of letting him run my life."

It was time to put a stop to this. Mrs. Emmitt straightened her shoulders. "Sir William asked me to tell you that Miss Foster, your new governess, has arrived."

The brush stilled, and Katherine's eyes widened. "My new . . . what?"

"Your governess. Surely, Sir William told you he's been looking to fill that position."

"Yes, but I had no idea that he'd found someone."

Mrs. Emmitt nodded. "Miss Foster came for an interview yesterday and started this morning.

You and your sister are to meet with her before you go riding or engage in any other activity."

Katherine glared into the mirror. "I won't have it! Penny and I are not children. We don't need some grim-faced old spinster hovering over us and filling our days with boring lessons and tedious conversations."

"Miss Foster is not—"

"I don't want to hear any more." Katherine tossed the hairbrush aside. "Send Lydia up. I want to dress, and as soon as I do, I'm going to speak to my cousin."

"Yes, miss." Mrs. Emmitt turned to go, though she wished she could stay and box the girl's ears. Katherine needed to accept Sir William's authority and the new governess. Her stubbornness and rebellion wouldn't change any of it.

When Mrs. Emmitt reached the door, she looked over her shoulder. "I know this has been a difficult time for you, but I believe Sir William has your best interests at heart. Perhaps you should—"

Katherine's blue eyes flashed. "I won't be bullied by him just because he is master of this house!"

William glared at the headline on the front page of the *Times*: "Parliament Debates Raising Death Duties." A burning sensation rose in his throat. How could they even consider it? What would happen to the empire if all the great estates were taxed into ruin? He supposed his assessment would be even higher now. Would he be able to pay it, or would he be forced to sell Highland and return to London?

The library door swung open, and Katherine marched in, followed by her younger sister, Penelope. Both girls were dressed in riding clothes. "Cousin William, we must speak with you." Katherine's heightened color and tone warned him he was in for a confrontation.

"Please, come in." He rose and motioned for them to take a seat.

Penny started to sit, but Katherine jerked her sister's arm to keep her standing. "There's no need for us to be seated. This will only take a moment." Katherine raised her chin. "Mrs. Emmitt informed us that you've hired a governess, and you expect us to be under her supervision."

He nodded. "That is correct."

"I can understand why you would want a governess for your children. They're at an age when they need someone to watch over them and give them daily lessons, but Penny is nearly sixteen, and my eighteenth birthday is only a few weeks away. Surely you don't think we still need a governess."

That was exactly what he thought, but it was obvious he needed to offer his opinion carefully. "I believe Miss Foster can be a great help to you and your sister." He glanced at the younger girl.

Fifteen-year-old Penelope was several inches shorter than Katherine, with a round face, reddish brown hair, and blue-gray eyes. She shifted from one foot to the other and watched her older sister with an uneasy expression.

Katherine's eyebrows rose. "Who is this *Miss Foster?* I've never heard of her."

"She's a very capable young woman who has traveled extensively. I believe she is eminently qualified since she's been a missionary teacher in India for nine years."

"A missionary?" Katherine rolled her eyes. "Really?"

Heat surged through William. "Yes, a little piety and spiritual instruction might benefit you both."

Katherine huffed. "Our spirits are perfectly fine, no thanks to you."

"That's enough!"

Katherine pulled back, then straightened her shoulders. "Father may have appointed you to be our guardian, but we don't intend to bow and scrape before you simply because you've inherited our home."

Fire flashed through William. "Now listen to me, young lady. While you are living in this household, I will decide what is best for you, including whether or not you will have a governess. And that decision has been made. You will be under Miss Foster's supervision twenty-four hours a day until you marry or leave this house to live with another relative. Do you understand?"

Katherine's face flamed bright pink and her nostrils flared.

Penelope reached for her sister's arm. "Kate, please, let's not argue about this. Perhaps we should meet her. I'm sure we can come to some sort of agreement."

Katherine pulled away, tugged the hem of her jacket back in place, and glared at William. "You may have authority over me now, but you won't for long. I'm going to London in the spring for the season, and I expect to make a good match and marry within the year."

William raised his eyebrows. "Oh really?" He didn't envy the man she would wed. She might be clever and pretty, but she was also willful and stubborn, and she reminded him very much of his late wife, Amelia.

"Our family is well respected," Katherine continued. "I shouldn't have any trouble receiving a proposal."

William crossed his arms. "And who will be paying for your time in London?"

Katherine's haughty expression faltered. "Father left you his entire estate. Surely that obligates you to pay for our expenses."

"The financial situation your father has left me in is precarious at best. There are stacks of bills and lists of repairs that need to be made." Both girls' faces registered surprise, and he felt a twinge of guilt for sharing the news in this way—but it *was* the truth. "Even if the funds become available, I have no desire to spend that much time in London. Who will escort you?"

A hint of panic flashed in Katherine's eyes.

"I will escort Katherine to London for the season." Lady Louisa Gatewood walked into the library, looking regal in a royal blue dress and large hat decked with several ostrich feathers. She crossed the library toward the girls.

"Oh, Aunt Louisa." Penelope hurried to meet her mother's sister. She clasped her hand and kissed her cheek.

Katherine nodded to her aunt, then turned a smug gaze back on William.

William gave the woman a brief nod. "Lady Gatewood, it's a pleasure to see you again."

She looked down her nose at him. "I wish I could say the same."

He clamped his mouth closed, though he would've loved to tell her exactly how he felt about her unexpected visits, but he was too much of a gentleman. The fact that she had lived at Highland for several years after her first husband's death seemed to make her think she could walk in unannounced at any time. He was thankful she had remarried and now had her own home a few miles away.

"Cousin William has hired a governess for his

children, and he insists we must be under her supervision." Katherine looked expectantly at her aunt.

"A governess?" Lady Gatewood's expression brightened. "Why that might be just the thing you need."

Surprise rippled through William. This was definitely a first. The girls' aunt hadn't expressed her approval of anything he'd done since he arrived at Highland.

Katherine's eyes widened. "Aunt Louisa, how can you say that? You know I'm almost eighteen. I shouldn't have to report to anyone."

Lady Gatewood touched Katherine's cheek. "You and Penelope have not had the benefit of your mother's guidance these last few years. I've tried to help, but with all the traveling we do, I haven't been able to devote adequate time to your preparation."

"But must we really have a governess?"

"She can help you polish your skills so you'll be ready for the season." Lady Gatewood turned to William. "That is, if the woman is qualified."

William opened his mouth to answer, but a sudden wave of doubt hit him.

"Well, don't just stand there gawking. Does the woman have social skills and understand how things are done in London?"

His mouth snapped closed. *Infernal woman! Why was she always putting him on the spot like that?*

Katherine huffed. "How could she? Miss Foster is a former missionary. She's been out of the country for years. What would she know about society or the season?"

Louisa Gatewood shifted her gaze back to William. "I would like to meet this Miss Foster and judge for myself if she is the right person to train my nieces."

William shook his head. "I'm sorry. That decision has already been made."

She pursed her lips. "So I'm not allowed to meet my nieces' governess?"

"No, of course you may meet her. I simply meant I've already judged her adequate and hired her." He would not mention the one-month trial period. That would only weaken his position.

The woman locked gazes with him. "My brother-in-law may have named you as the girls' guardian, but I don't intend to let Katherine launch into her first season without proper guidance and preparation. She must shine like a beautiful jewel to make the best match and secure her future."

As much as he hated to admit it, Lady Gatewood had a point. Seeing his cousins happily married and settled in their own homes was a responsibility he took seriously. What if Miss Foster was not able to teach the girls the social skills they needed? Had he made a mistake by hiring her so quickly? But what choice did he have? It wasn't as though he had other applicants who were more suitable.

He nodded to Lady Gatewood. "I'm sure Miss Foster would be glad for your help with their preparations."

The girls' aunt pulled back, her eyes widening. "You're suggesting I assist the governess?"

"Well, if you want them to *shine like beautiful jewels,* then yes, you might want to consider working with the governess and giving your nieces a bit more of your time and attention."

"Well, that's a very unexpected suggestion."

Penelope took her aunt's hand again. "It's a wonderful idea. You know everything there is to know about London society. You will help us, won't you?"

Lady Gatewood sent him a scornful glance, then sweetened her expression as she focused on the girls. "Of course I will. But first we must meet this Miss Foster and see for ourselves what she's like." She sent William a final disdainful look as she turned away and shepherded the girls out of the library.

He watched them go, then walked to the window and stared out at the fading autumn colors. Would Miss Foster have enough confidence and strength of character to deal with the girls' aunt? He certainly hoped so.

His thoughts shifted back to earlier that morning in the great hall, when he'd seen Miss

Foster come down the stairs with the children. It had stirred him in the most unusual way. He wasn't sure if it was her winsome smile or the caring manner in which she guided the children. She was spirited. He'd discovered that through their conversation the day they met, but she also seemed to possess kindness and genuineness that pleased him. She would be good for the children.

And he didn't intend to let Lady Gatewood—or anyone else—make him send her away.

Four

The midday sun filtered through the nursery window, casting a warm light across the book in Julia's hands. On the other side of the table, Andrew sketched wolves and snakes on a drawing pad as he listened to her read aloud from *The Jungle Book*. Millicent leaned against Julia's arm and gazed at the pen-and-ink illustration of Mowgli holding a blazing branch while the wolves gathered around him.

Julia turned the page and continued reading. "'Good!' said Mowgli, staring round slowly. 'I see that ye are dogs. I go from you to my own people—if they be my own people. The jungle is shut to me, and I must forget your talk and your companionship.'"

Millie looked up at Julia. "Why does Mowgli have to leave the jungle?"

"Shh!" Andrew glared at his sister. "Stop asking so many questions."

Millie stuck out her lower lip. "I just want to know why."

"Be quiet! Let her go on and you'll find out."

Julia closed the book, keeping her finger in it to mark her place. "Andrew, it is not kind to speak to your sister in that manner. Please apologize."

"Why should I? She's the one who keeps interrupting the story."

"Even so, your impatience is not helpful."

He crossed his arms and glared toward the windows. "I don't see why I should say I'm sorry when I'm not."

"You do not need to feel sorry to apologize. You simply do it because it is the right thing to do."

He set his jaw and continued to scowl.

"Very well, I'm afraid we will have to put the book away." Julia rose from her chair.

"No!" Andrew jumped up. "We have to find out what happens to Mowgli."

"Then you must do as I asked."

"Oh, all right. I'm sorry."

Julia shook her head. "An insincere apology is no better than none at all. You must acknowledge what you've done wrong and sound like you truly mean it."

His expression eased, and he blew out a deep breath. "I'm sorry for my impatience and rude manner."

Julia nodded. "And you must ask for her forgiveness."

Andrew sent her a quizzical look.

"Asking forgiveness is an important part of a

sincere apology." Had no one ever taught the children these most basic skills? How could that be?

She motioned to Andrew. "Go ahead."

He sighed but finished his apology with a note of sincerity. Millie accepted it, and Julia nodded her approval and sat down. She opened *The Jungle Book* and started reading again.

The nursery door opened, and an elegantly dressed middle-aged woman wearing a large feathered hat entered, followed by two young women dressed in riding clothes. The two girls must be her new charges, but who was the older woman?

"Miss Foster?" The woman crossed the nursery. "I am Lady Gatewood, and these are my nieces, Miss Katherine and Miss Penelope Ramsey."

Julia rose. "I'm pleased to meet you."

The shorter girl sent her a slight smile while the taller girl lifted her chin and glanced away.

"I understand you are the new governess."

"Yes ma'am."

"And you will be helping Katherine prepare for the season?"

Julia nodded. "Sir William has asked me to oversee both young ladies as well as his children." She glanced at Andrew and Millicent. The two watched the scene wide-eyed.

Lady Gatewood lifted her chin, ignoring the children. "You have only six months to help Katherine prepare for her presentation at court and first season. That might seem like a sufficient amount of time, but there's much to be done."

Katherine gazed at Julia, her expression disdainful.

"Both girls will need lessons in French, conversation, a bit of history and literature, art appreciation, dancing, and general knowledge about social etiquette. Penelope is too young to attend many of the social events, but she can begin preparing along with Katherine."

Julia's stomach tensed. Her knowledge of the fashionable London season was limited at best. How would she ever meet Katherine's needs and this woman's expectations?

Julia met Lady Gatewood's gaze. "I am prepared to teach most of the subjects you mentioned, but it would be best to bring in someone else to teach dancing and social customs for the season."

Lady Gatewood's dark eyebrows drew together, then she sighed. "Well, at least you're honest enough to admit your shortcomings." She glanced away. "I was not blessed with children, but several of my friends have prepared their daughters for their presentation and the season. I can ask them to recommend a dancing instructor. And I suppose I can teach the girls what is expected of them during social engagements."

Relief flowed through Julia. "Thank you. That would be most helpful."

"I am not doing it for your benefit, Miss Foster. My nieces' futures are at stake. With the memory of my dear sister to guide me, I intend to do all I can to prepare them for a happy future." She tipped her head and smiled at the girls. "Now, I must be going. Lord Gatewood and I have dinner guests arriving in a few hours."

Penelope kissed her aunt's cheek. "Thank you, Aunt Louisa. Dancing lessons will be divine. We're ever so grateful."

"Dancing is important, but you must apply yourself to your other studies as well. No man wants a wife with an empty head."

Penelope smiled and nodded. "I will. I promise."

Lady Gatewood turned to Katherine. "And you, my dear, will be the focus of my attention these next few months."

Katherine leaned toward her aunt and brushed her lips past her cheek. "Thank you for stepping in to save the day."

"Of course, dear. That's what I do best." Lady Gatewood crossed the room to leave, and the girls followed.

Julia stepped forward. "Excuse me, Miss Katherine? Miss Penelope?"

The girls stopped and turned while Lady Gatewood sailed out the door.

"I'm almost finished with Andrew's and Millicent's lessons. Shall we meet for our studies at eleven?"

Katherine sent her an unconvincing smile. "As you can see, we're riding this morning."

"Very well. One o'clock then. Shall we meet in the great hall?"

"Unfortunately, we have an appointment at the milliner's this afternoon in Fulton."

Julia frowned slightly. "What time is the appointment?"

"Not until three o'clock," Penelope said.

Katherine sent her sister a glare.

"Very well," Julia continued. "I assume someone is driving you to Fulton. That takes ten minutes at the most, leaving you plenty of time to meet with me before you go."

"I'm sorry," Katherine said, though she didn't sound the least bit apologetic. "We must change after riding, and we don't expect to have luncheon until one-thirty, so we won't be able to meet with you today."

"All right. Let's plan to meet tomorrow morning, directly after breakfast."

Penelope opened her mouth to answer, but Katherine gripped her hand. "That's simply not possible. Our neighbor, Lucy Chatsford, has invited us to call on her tomorrow morning."

"Miss Katherine, your cousin has hired me to give you instruction on several subjects, and your aunt has just added more. It is impossible for me to fulfill their wishes if you will not make time for your studies."

"We were not informed of your arrival until this morning. Our schedule has been set for some time. Perhaps we can discuss it on Friday morning." Katherine turned and strode out the door without waiting for an answer.

Penelope blinked, looking torn. "Sorry," she whispered, then hurried after her sister.

"Of all the imperious, uncooperative—" Julia clamped her lips together, barely able to restrain the rest of her sentence. Only the knowledge that the children were listening allowed her to keep her peace.

"They never do what Papa says." Andrew picked up his pencil and began sketching again with quick, rough strokes. "They're so mean. I hate them."

Julia lifted her trembling hand and tucked a strand of hair behind her ear. "Andrew, you mustn't speak of your cousins like that."

"Why not? It's true."

Millie bit her lip and looked up at Julia. "Why don't they like us?"

Julia laid her hand on Millie's shoulder. "It has nothing to do with you, Millie. They're obviously preoccupied with their own concerns."

The little girl sent her a quizzical look.

"That simply means they think of their own wants and desires first, rather than considering how their actions and words will hurt others."

Andrew ripped a sheet of drawing paper off the

pad. "I say they're horrible, and I'm glad we rarely have to see them."

Julia sighed and sank into her chair. If only she could say the same.

The next afternoon Julia took Millie's hand and led her across the back courtyard. "It's a lovely day for a walk. Andrew, will you show us the way to the gardens?"

"Follow me," he called over his shoulder as he raced down the gravel path.

Millie sighed. "He always runs ahead."

Julia laughed. "My brother used to do that as well."

"You have a brother too?"

Julia nodded. "Jonathan is in school in London. He's studying to become a doctor."

"Do you miss him?"

"Very much. I hope he'll visit us at Christmas, but we'll have to wait and see."

They followed Andrew through an arched stone gateway and into the gardens. Julia's steps slowed as she took in the magical setting. Neatly trimmed hedges and a high stone wall enclosed the garden. Gravel pathways bordered with perennial flower beds crisscrossed the close-clipped sod. A small pond with a fountain stood in the center, surrounded by a few late-blooming roses. "Oh, it's lovely."

"Look at these." Millie bent and picked up a

handful of blooms. She held them up to show Julia. "I love purple flowers."

"I believe those are asters."

Millie smiled.

Andrew kicked a small stone down the path. Julia and Millie followed at a safe distance. As they rounded the hedge at the corner, Sarah Ramsey came into view, sitting on a wooden bench with a book in hand. She looked up and greeted them with a timid smile.

"Hello, Aunt Sarah." Andrew ran toward her.

Millie scampered after him.

Julia greeted Sarah and then turned to the children. "I'd like you to find five signs of autumn."

Millie bit her lip and a slight frown creased her forehead.

"Consider it a treasure hunt with a prize for your best efforts," Julia added.

The children hurried off.

"Would you like to sit down?" Sarah asked.

"Thank you." Julia settled on the bench beside her. "It's a beautiful day, isn't it?"

Sarah nodded and looked up at the clear blue sky. "Autumn is my favorite season."

"Mine too, although I'm also very fond of spring."

Sarah smiled and looked down at her book again.

"What are you reading?"

"*Pride and Prejudice.* It's one of my favorites. Have you read it?"

Julia smiled. "Several times. I've always admired Elizabeth Bennett."

"Oh yes. I like Lizzy too. And Mr. Darcy is an interesting character. There is so much more to him than it seems at first." She looked down and turned the page. "I was just reading the scene where Lizzy walks to Netherfield."

Julia caught sight of Sarah's right hand, and her reply stuck in her throat. Sarah's fingers were small and misshapen, and her wrist bent at a severe angle. Julia's thoughts flashed back through the past two days. Each time they'd met, Sarah had hidden her hand behind her back or in the folds of her skirt, and she walked with a slight limp.

Sarah looked up, and her gaze connected with Julia's. She must have read the sympathy in Julia's eyes, because her cheeks turned a deep shade of pink and she slipped her hand under the book.

If only she could assure Sarah she wasn't bothered by her handicap. She'd certainly seen much worse at the medical clinic in India. But unless Sarah spoke of it first, it wouldn't be proper for Julia to mention it.

She shifted her gaze to the flower beds and prayed her friendship with Sarah would grow and that someday they would speak freely about matters that were close to their hearts. Until then, Julia would show Sarah the kindness and acceptance she deserved.

"This seems to be the problem, sir." Clark Dalton, Highland's head gardener, tapped the pipe running down the far wall of the greenhouse. "There's a leak at the joint, which lowers the pressure and prevents the sprinklers from reaching the plants on the outer edges."

William leaned closer, surveying the old pipe. "It looks like we're losing quite a bit of water."

"I'm afraid so, sir. I noticed these loose floorboards this morning. Seems the water has been dripping down and rotting the wood."

"It's probably been going on for some time then."

Dalton gave a sober nod. "I thought the warmth of the summer season had lowered the water level and caused the pressure to drop." He clicked his tongue, looking chagrined. "I'm sorry I misjudged the situation."

William straightened. "It's all right, Dalton. It's an easy mistake to make. I appreciate you bringing it to my attention." The gardener seemed to be an intelligent and respectful man, about the same age as William, though he had a stockier build and deeply tanned skin.

Dalton's father had been the head gardener until his death last year. The son had been promoted, and now he oversaw two other young men, caring for the greenhouses and grounds as well as the kitchen gardens and flower gardens.

"I've sent a message to Harold Bradley in Fulton," Dalton continued. "His father helped build the greenhouse and install the pipes. I thought he might be able to help."

"Very good. Let me know what he says."

"I will, sir."

William heard voices in the garden behind the greenhouse. He looked up and spotted Andrew and Millicent running down the garden path. Millicent bent and scooped up a brightly colored leaf, adding it to the collection in her hand. It was good to see them outdoors, enjoying the fresh air and sunshine in such a happy and carefree manner. Miss Foster sat on a bench nearby, watching the children and conversing with his sister, Sarah. It pleased him to see Miss Foster there.

Perhaps she could draw Sarah out and become a companion for her. His sister needed something beyond her books and needlework to occupy her time. He had hoped she would take on the role of mistress at Highland, but she'd always been shy and lacked confidence. He supposed it was because of her withered hand and arm.

It was such a shame. She had a kind heart and pleasant features, though her manner of dress and hairstyle were simple and unadorned. He doubted she would ever marry, since she barely spoke to any of the guests he invited into their home. But that was all right. He loved her, and she would always have a home with him.

He shifted his gaze back to the pipes. "I hope Bradley can repair it. If he suggests replacing the system, you must speak to me first. We need to solve the problem in the most economical way possible."

Dalton continued to stare out the greenhouse window as if he hadn't heard a word William said.

William followed his gaze to the young ladies seated in the garden. Did he have his eye on Miss Foster? Had he made her acquaintance? Irritation buzzed along his nerves. "Dalton, are you listening to me?"

The gardener jerked his gaze back to William and blinked. "What? I'm sorry, sir. I didn't hear what you said."

"Obviously." He scowled at the gardener. "If you expect to remain employed at Highland, you'd best keep your mind on your work and not on the feminine forms in the garden."

Dalton's ears tinged red. "Yes sir."

William finished his instructions to the gardener and left the greenhouse. The children's laughter echoed back to him as he passed under the archway in the garden wall and walked toward the house.

So Miss Foster had attracted the attention of at least two of his staff. How many others had their eye on her? He huffed as he strode across the back courtyard. If one of those men wooed her, she would most likely accept his proposal and resign her position. If that happened, he'd have to start his search all over again.

What an unhappy turn of events. Here he'd finally found a governess who had a sensible head on her shoulders, and he might lose her before the one-month trial had even finished. That's what he got for hiring a young woman who was so attractive.

But he didn't like the idea of losing Julia Foster, not to Dalton the gardener, Nelson the footman, or anyone else.

Clark Dalton lowered his head and leaned on the wooden greenhouse shelving. What had he been thinking? If he was going to hold on to his position, and he must, then he'd best keep his head down and his eyes on the seeds and soil, not on Miss Sarah Ramsey.

Father, help me rein in my thoughts. Don't let me wander off the path You've marked out for me.

Caring for the gardens and grounds was in his blood. He'd been raised at Highland and learned those skills at his father's side. But it was a solitary life, working from sunrise to sunset with only the plants and trees as his companions. He did oversee two younger under-gardeners, but both were merely boys. They had little schooling or interest beyond their daily duties, while he longed for intelligent conversation with someone who could discuss books, politics, faith, and life past the gate at Highland.

From the first time he had seen Miss Ramsey walking in the garden, his heart had been drawn to her. The kindness in her eyes and her gentle smile impressed him deeply. Now he watched for her every day. What would he do when the cold weather arrived and her walks in the garden ceased? How would he catch a glimpse of her?

With a heavy sigh, he pulled his gloves from his jacket pocket and tugged them on. Maybe the coming change in seasons was for the best. Perhaps it would give his heart time to realize what a fool he was for thinking—

"Excuse me, Mr. Dalton?"

He pulled in a sharp breath and turned.

Miss Ramsey stood in the greenhouse doorway, her soft blue shawl draped around her shoulders and her book in her hand. "I'm sorry to disturb you."

"No, miss. It's all right. You're not disturbing me."

She sent him a sweet smile. "I thought you should know the arm of the bench in the garden has come loose."

He stared at her a moment, taking in the loveliness of her face and form. Her soft pink cheeks, so much like rose petals, and her lovely brown eyes like those of a newborn calf.

Her smiled faded. "Mr. Dalton, are you all right?"

He blinked and straightened. "Yes, miss. I'm

fine. I'll see to repairing the bench right away."

"Oh, there's no need to hurry." She glanced around the greenhouse. "I'm sure you must be very busy taking care of all these flowers as well as the estate grounds."

"Highland is a large estate, but I'm grateful for my work. I enjoy it very much."

"I can see why. It's all so lovely." She glanced out the greenhouse windows to the garden beyond. "Our home in London doesn't have much of a garden. If we want to enjoy time outdoors, we must to go to a park."

He nodded, enjoying the sound of her voice.

"So you can see why I've been so eager to spend time in the garden."

"You're wise to take advantage of it now. The temperatures will be dropping soon, and when it freezes, that will be the end of most of these flowers until next year."

"Except for those you have in the greenhouse." She smiled and shifted her gaze to the blooms around him.

"Yes, miss, that's true." He turned and scanned the rows of plants and flowers he tended year round.

"The roses are beautiful." She leaned forward and sniffed a deep red bloom. "Their fragrance is heavenly."

He pulled his clippers from his back pocket, snipped the rose stem, and held it out to her.

She hesitated, her gaze darting from the rose to his face and back to the flower.

His heart sank like a rock tossed in a pond. What a fool! Someone of his station should not offer a rose to the mistress of the house! It was too forward. "I'm sorry, miss. I meant no offense."

"You haven't offended me. It's a lovely gesture. It's just"—she tucked her book under her right arm and reached for the rose with her left—"I have a bit of a problem carrying things sometimes."

He studied her, not understanding.

She slowly withdrew her hand from the folds of her skirt and held it out. "I don't have full use of my right hand and arm, and sometimes that makes it difficult to . . ."

His heart clenched. Had she been injured? Did it still cause her pain? "It's all right, miss. I'd be happy to cut and carry a bouquet for you." He turned back to the roses. "Which color do you prefer?"

"I like them all, but I suppose the pink are my favorite."

"Pink it is then." He clipped several roses, some buds that were just beginning to open and some in full bloom. After he had cut at least a dozen, he turned and showed her the bouquet. "How does that look?"

"Beautiful." She smiled, warmth filling her soft brown eyes.

His chest swelled and filled with delight.

"Come with me, miss, and we'll add some ferns to your bouquet."

She nodded and followed him out the door at the far end.

"Ferns grow best on the shady north side." He knelt and clipped several fronds, adding them to the roses.

"How did you learn so much about plants?"

"I've worked in the gardens here at Highland since I was a boy. My father was head gardener for almost thirty-five years." He stood and faced her. "He passed away last year, and I took his place."

Sympathy filled her eyes. "I'm sorry for your loss. Is your mother still living?"

"Yes. She and my niece live with me in a cottage here on the estate."

Sarah nodded, a question still flickering in her eyes. "So you're not married?"

"No, miss. I've not been blessed with a wife—not yet." He held her gaze a moment longer.

Her cheeks turned pink, and she looked away. "Forgive me. I shouldn't have asked such a personal question."

"I don't mind. Not at all." He shifted the bouquet to his right arm and held out the elbow of his left. "May I walk you back to the house?"

She nodded, a hint of a smile on her lips as she slipped her hand through his arm, and together they walked down the path toward the house.

Five

On Friday, Ann Norton hurried down the back servants' stairs, carrying Andrew's and Millie's boots in one hand and Miss Foster's in the other.

"Mind you don't drop dirt on those stairs. I've just swept them." Lydia stood guard at the bottom, her broom still in hand.

"Sorry." Ann placed the boots in her apron and lifted the corners, hoping to catch any mud that might fall off, though most of it seemed to be caked on the boots like glue.

Lydia grinned and waved away her warning. "I was just teasing. It's all right. Don't get your apron dirty on my account. With everyone tromping up and down the stairs, I'll be sweeping them again in an hour if Mrs. Emmitt has her way."

Ann returned Lydia's smile, her heart lifting. Lydia was a gem. She often had a kind word or smile while most of the other servants treated Ann with cool disdain or suspicion. She had no idea why. She didn't want to take anyone's position. All she wanted was to hold on to her job as nursery maid.

Life in service at Highland was not easy, especially dealing with Sir William's children, but it was a far sight better than the backbreaking load she'd carried at the farm where she'd grown up as the second of eleven children. She had no desire to go back to caring for her nine younger siblings or to receiving the brunt of her father's drunken rages.

Juggling the boots, she pushed open the heavy door to the back courtyard. Warmth and sunlight streamed down on her head and shoulders, making her smile. Cleaning boots was a dirty job, but it gave her a few minutes outdoors to breathe in the clean, cool air and enjoy a bit of sunshine.

She took a rag and small brush from her apron pocket and settled on a nearby bench. Footsteps approached, and she lifted her head.

Peter Gates, one of the young grooms, crossed the courtyard toward her.

Ann's heartbeat quickened. "Morning, Peter."

He grinned, his golden-brown eyes and tousled blond hair making him look ever so handsome. "Good morning to you, Miss Norton."

She laughed softly. "You've no need to call me that. I'm just Ann to my friends."

He flashed another smile. "All right. I'll call you Ann then." He sat on the bench, just on the other side of the children's boots.

A slight niggle of worry fluttered through her stomach. What would Mrs. Emmitt say if she stepped outside and saw her talking to Peter? The housekeeper had given a strict warning that maids should not become too friendly with any of the men who worked at Highland or delivered goods to the house. But how would she ever find someone to marry if she didn't at least share a smile and a bit of conversation?

"Sir William should hire a hall boy to take care of jobs like that." Peter motioned toward the boots in her hand.

"I don't mind. It gives me a break from the children and a bit of time outdoors."

Peter glanced up, squinting at the sun. "I suppose that's true. Still, a pretty girl like you shouldn't have to brush the mud off anyone's boots."

Warmth flooded her face as she continued buffing the boots with her rag.

He tipped his head. "Whose boots are those?"

"Oh, these are Miss Foster's. She's the new governess."

Peter grimaced. "She's making you scrub her boots?"

"No. I offered."

He shrugged slightly. "I suppose she is above you."

"Yes, she is, but she's been very kind to me and the children. I like her."

"Well, don't let her take advantage of you. She may be the governess, but she's hired to work for Sir William, just like you. She shouldn't be giving you all the dirty jobs."

Ann thought about that for a moment. "She asks me to care for their shoes and clothing and clean up after them, but she treats me well."

"That could just be her way of getting you to do her bidding." He nodded toward the boots.

Ann's hand stilled, and she bit her lip. Was Julia only being kind to get her way? Did she just pretend to like Ann so she could use her as her own servant?

Peter slid off the bench and stood in front of her. "You need someone to watch out for you and be sure no one takes advantage." He reached out and gently touched her cheek. "I've never seen anyone quite so lovely."

Her heart hammered in her throat, stealing away her reply.

"Maybe tonight, after the children are asleep in bed, you could come down to the stable, and we could—"

"Ann?" Julia stepped out the back door and crossed the courtyard toward them.

Peter dropped his hand and stepped back.

Ann jumped to her feet, dropping the boot. "Yes?"

Questions filled Julia's eyes. "The children will be joining Miss Ramsey for tea. They need to change and be down in the drawing room in twenty minutes." She glanced at Peter and then back at Ann. "Can you clean those boots later?"

"Yes. I'll come right now." Ann snatched up the boots.

Julia stood by, waiting and watching Peter with a serious look.

Ann's face burned as she hurried toward the back door.

"I'll see you later, Ann," Peter called.

But she didn't turn back or answer, no matter how much she wanted to.

The scent of freshly cut pink roses added a pleasant, subtle fragrance to the drawing room where Julia sat, overseeing Katherine and Penelope's afternoon lessons. Sarah had also joined them and sat in the corner, embroidering a delicate floral pattern on a pillow cover.

Julia nodded to her younger student. "Penelope, please translate the verb *dire*."

She squinted, then replied, "To say or to tell?"

"Yes, very good." Julia shifted her gaze to Katherine. "Please conjugate *dire*."

The older girl glared at the book, tossed it aside, and rose from the settee. "Why must we learn to speak French?"

Julia pulled in a slow deep breath, praying for grace and patience. After only a few days of teaching the girls, she had discovered they were reluctant students at best and distracted and disagreeable at worst. "You must master French because both your aunt and your cousin have asked you to."

"But it's such a tedious task. I doubt I shall ever use it."

"A knowledge of French will be helpful when you go to London for the season," Julia added, hoping that might perk Katherine's interest.

"Why? I'm not going to marry a Frenchman!"

Penelope giggled. "Are you sure? What if he was terrifically handsome and extremely wealthy?"

Katherine lifted her chin, a resolute look in her eyes. "The man I marry will be wealthy, but he must be a titled Englishman. I've no intention of traveling to the Continent."

"Not even for a grand tour?" Penelope leaned forward, a teasing light in her blue-gray eyes.

Katherine huffed and crossed her arms. "Cousin William would never pay to send us on a grand tour no matter how much we begged him."

Penelope leaned back. "I suppose you're right, but you might take a wedding trip to France after you marry."

A slight smile lifted Kate's lips. "Yes, perhaps I will."

The girls were forever discussing what eligible men Katherine would meet in London and how soon she would receive her first proposal after she had begun the round of balls, dinners, and garden parties. Julia usually tried to cut those conversations short, but today the topic seemed worthy of delaying their French lesson.

Julia closed her book. "Deciding whom you will marry is one of the most important decisions of your life. Choosing a husband should be based on his character, manners, and spiritual maturity rather than his nationality, title, or wealth."

Penelope's eyes widened, and she stared at Julia as if she had never considered those qualities as necessary in a future spouse.

Katherine lifted her chin. "Of course the man I fall in love with will have noble character."

"I hope so," Julia added. "Your future happiness depends a great deal on your husband's choices and disposition."

"His position in society is more important," Katherine added. "I won't consider marrying a man unless he is in line to inherit his father's title and wealth."

Julia shook her head. "A loyal, hardworking, middle-class man might make a much better husband than a wealthy, titled gentleman if he is willful and selfish."

Katherine turned and glared at Julia. "What makes you an authority on choosing a husband? You've never been married."

Sarah's hand stilled, and she looked up at Julia.

Pain lanced Julia's heart, and she shot a heated

glance Katherine's way. "No, but I was engaged."

"Really?" Penelope's eyes brightened. "What happened?"

Julia's face flamed. Oh, why hadn't she kept silent? "It was several years ago."

"Please, tell us," Penelope begged.

Pride tugged at Julia's heart, urging her to keep the painful story to herself. But sharing it might help the girls make better choices and avoid regrets and a broken heart.

Sarah sent Julia a compassionate look.

"All right. I'll tell you. But you must keep it in confidence and not pepper me with questions until I'm done."

Penelope nodded, barely able to keep her smile at bay.

Katherine also nodded, her expression softening.

"When I was twenty-two, a young man came to join our missionary work in India. His name was Richard Green."

Penelope sighed and leaned back in her chair. "Was he incredibly charming and wonderfully handsome?"

Julia lifted her finger and sent Penelope a warning look.

"Sorry." She regained her composure and focused on Julia again.

"Richard Green was tall and handsome, but more important, he had a sincere faith and a desire to spread the gospel. Those were qualities I had always hoped for in a husband.

"But he had a difficult time adjusting to life in India. His efforts to learn the language did not go well, and he often asked me to act as his translator. He became very attentive, and we soon formed an attachment." Her throat tightened, and for a moment she could not continue. She looked down and smoothed her hand over her skirt.

"What happened?" Katherine asked.

"My mother was concerned and warned me that things seemed to be progressing too quickly. But my father felt we knew Richard well, since we shared daily ministry, meals, and conversation. He seemed sincere, and my father had no objection. So when Richard proposed, I accepted."

Penelope clasped her hands below her chin. "How exciting. Were you certain he was the man you wanted to marry?"

"I thought so at the time."

"Did you love him?" Katherine's gaze grew more intense.

Julia swallowed. "Love is more than a fleeting emotion. It's a choice you make based on many things."

"But did you feel a special connection with him?"

"Yes. I believe I did."

Sympathy filled Penelope's eyes. "What tore you apart?"

"One day Richard became very ill. For two weeks I stayed by his bedside, caring for him night and day. His life hung in the balance, and though my father is an excellent doctor, we had no idea if Richard would survive."

Penelope gasped. "Oh no. He didn't die, did he?"

"No, he recovered. But the illness shook his faith deeply. As his health returned, so did his desire to go back to England. Within a month of his recovery, Richard told my father he had been mistaken about his calling to India. He wanted to return to England as soon as arrangements could be made."

Penelope leaned forward. "Why didn't you go with him?"

The betrayal hit her again, stealing her breath for a moment. "He didn't ask me."

"The coward!" Katherine crossed her arms and glared toward the bookcase.

"What did he say?" Penelope asked. "How did he break the engagement?"

Julia had no trouble recalling the painful words. They seemed branded in her memory. "Only that he was sorry, and that he should not have proposed when he wasn't sure he would stay in India. Then he asked me to return the ring." Though five years had passed, Richard's decision still stung. Her affections for him had dimmed, but the feelings of rejection remained.

Penelope's eyes widened. "Did you give it back?"

Julia nodded. "It was a family heirloom that had belonged to his grandmother. It wouldn't have been right to keep it."

Katherine's eyes blazed. "Dreadful man! I would've refused to return the ring and sold it! Then I would've told him I hope your ship sinks in the Indian Ocean and you die a painful death by shark attack and drowning!"

Julia smiled, remembering she'd felt much the same way, though she'd tamed her response for her parents' sake. Still, it did her heart good to hear Katherine take up her cause. Perhaps she and Katherine had more in common than she'd first believed.

William strode through the great hall, his mind on the new electrical generators he'd read about in the *Times* that morning. Bringing electricity to Highland would be a great improvement, but he doubted he could afford it in the near future. If only he could pay off the death duties, then he could continue to update the house and make sure it would be in good condition for years to come.

He heard voices from the drawing room, and his steps slowed.

"Was he incredibly charming and wonderfully handsome?" Penelope's voice drifted past the half-open drawing room door.

Who was she speaking to? Had Katherine been slipping out to see a young man without his permission? He scowled and shook his head.

"Richard Green was tall and handsome, but more important, he had a sincere faith and a desire to spread the gospel."

William's scowl faded. It was not Katherine, but Miss Foster who spoke. He stepped closer.

So the spirited Miss Foster had been pursued by one of her associate missionaries. That did not surprise him, but his scowl returned as he listened to the rest of the story.

Heat surged through William's chest. What kind of man made an offer of marriage without being certain of his intentions? It was shameful and dishonorable. He sincerely hoped he never met Richard Green. If he did, he would have difficulty restraining his desire to flatten the man.

"May I help you with something, sir?"

William spun around and met the sober-faced gaze of his footman, Nelson, who carried a silver tea tray. "No." He lowered his voice and stepped away from the door.

"Miss Foster asked that the ladies be served tea in the drawing room at four. Will you be joining them?"

William hesitated. He understood the sting of betrayal all too well. Could he sit with Miss Foster and not reveal that he had overheard her conversation?

His decision took only a second. "Yes. I'll take tea with the ladies."

"Very good, sir."

He had nothing to fear. In the past three years since his wife's death, he had become accustomed to hiding his true feelings from everyone. Even his closest friends did not suspect he suffered from a bitter wound every time he thought of Amelia and each time he laid eyes on his children, whose features and coloring reminded him so vividly of their devious and unfaithful mother.

Six

A bright red leaf fluttered past Julia's shoulder and landed on the emerald grass next to the pathway cutting across the parkland. The bright contrast between the two colors made her smile. How she loved these cool, crisp autumn days, with the scent of burning leaves in the air and a brilliant blue sky overhead.

She clasped Millie's hand and strolled back toward the house at an easy pace. Ann walked beside her. As usual, Andrew ran ahead, bounding across the grass like a wild pony.

Ann shook her head. "Master Andrew never slows down."

"He does have a wonderful supply of energy."

"It's hard to imagine him as the future heir of Highland."

"He has time to prepare."

"And he'll be needing every minute of it."

Julia's heart ached as she watched him. Poor boy. She tried to give him some time outdoors each day and balance her instruction with words of praise, but others were not so kind. Someone was always telling him to settle down and behave like a gentleman. It grieved her to recall the thoughtless comments she had heard spoken about him in the servant's hall.

Just this morning Mrs. Emmitt had scolded him severely for running his hand along the paneling in the hallway. Why did she have to be so harsh? He was only nine years old. How could she expect him to always walk through the house in a dignified manner and never touch the wood-work?

Ann sighed. "I'm not sure how I'll keep him out of mischief this afternoon while you're teaching the young ladies."

Julia sent her an encouraging smile. "I'm sure you'll do fine." But keeping Andrew out of trouble each afternoon was a challenge for Ann, and it often reduced her to tears. Julia wished it wasn't so, but she could not be in two places at once. Millie could sit quietly and play with her dolls while Julia met with the older girls for their lessons, but Andrew could not. He needed more activity, something that would capture his interest and challenge his skills.

If only there was a man who would teach him the skills and foster the qualities that helped turn a boy into a man.

"Papa!" Millie dropped Julia's hand and dashed down the path. Andrew darted across the grass, headed for his father as well.

Julia's heart lifted as she followed the children to meet Sir William. Surely seeing their father would brighten their day.

He greeted the children with a nod and slight smile, but he did not embrace them.

"Look what I found." Millie held out a shiny stone she'd picked up on their walk.

He clasped his hands behind his back, giving the stone a brief glance. "Very nice." But his words did not carry much enthusiasm.

Why was he so reserved around the children? If only he would lean down, examine the treasure more closely, and share Millie's excitement. Didn't he realize how much they longed for a gentle touch and an encouraging word?

Andrew looked up at his father. "We've been on a walk all the way to the sheep pens and the stream."

William frowned slightly and shifted his gaze to Millie. "Really? You walked that far?"

She nodded, her smile and sparkling blue-green eyes reflecting her pleasure. "I petted two sheep with very soft wool."

"And after she dropped her special rock into the pen, I climbed over the fence and got it for her," Andrew added with a proud grin. "Miss Foster says I am to always be her protector—like the knights of old."

William lowered his dark eyebrows and frowned at the boy's arm. "I suppose that's how

98

you tore the sleeve of your jacket." He pointed to a small rip near the elbow.

Andrew's smile wilted, and he lowered his chin. "Yes sir."

"You must learn to take better care of your clothing." William turned to Ann. "Take the children inside and repair Master Andrew's jacket."

"Yes sir." Ann bobbed a quick curtsy. "Come along, children." She led them off toward the house.

Julia clamped her mouth closed and marched after the children. *Dreadful man!* He'd stolen the joy out of their day with his brooding scowl and disheartening words.

"Miss Foster, I'd like to speak to you."

Did he intend to scold her as well? If he did, she might very well tell him exactly what she thought of his critical, hands-off attitude toward his children. She turned and faced him. Lifting her chin, she returned his steady gaze. "Yes sir?"

"Were you not informed that Millicent has fragile health, and that she's not to overexert herself?"

Julia gave a slight nod. "Mrs. Emmitt mentioned concern for her health."

"Then I must ask why you felt it appropriate to take her on such a long walk."

Heat infused her face. "We go for a walk every day after luncheon. I believe they have strengthened

Millicent and been even more helpful for Andrew."

"But it's at least a mile to the sheep pens."

"Yes sir. I believe it is."

"And that's all you have to say?"

"No sir. I chose the sheep pens as our destination because I read the Twenty-third Psalm to the children this morning. Andrew mentioned you owned a fine herd of sheep, and he seemed quite interested in them. So I promised the children, if they worked hard and finished their lessons before luncheon, we would walk down to see the sheep after."

"But that distance is too far for Millicent."

"I don't think so. You see, I've been increasing the length of our walks each day. I'm always careful to let Millicent set the pace, and we stop and rest if she appears tired."

"So you allow a six-year-old to determine your activities, regardless of whether they are detrimental to her health or not?"

"No sir. I try to take into account her abilities and desires, and then use my best judgment. You'll remember my father is a doctor, and I've grown up assisting him in the clinic."

He huffed a laugh. "So now you consider yourself an expert on health as well as child rearing?"

"Not an expert, but a keen observer and a concerned and loving governess."

He stared at her for a moment, then shook his

head and strode a few paces away. "You are quite a puzzle, Miss Foster."

"A puzzle, sir? In what way?"

He turned back. "You're certainly not afraid to speak your mind—and very boldly I might add."

"I've been taught to be honest. I have no use for pretension or falsehood."

"But you seem to have little concern that I am your employer, and you are still working under a one-month trial."

The reality of her situation sent a tremor rushing through her. "If you feel I've been disrespectful, I apologize."

"Not disrespectful, but I do sense a challenge in your words."

"Then you are correct. As governess, I must speak up for the children when there is a need."

"And you feel there is a need now?"

She swallowed. "Yes sir. I do."

His dark eyebrows dipped again. "You find me lacking in fulfilling my fatherly duties?"

She hesitated, pushing down her fears. Honesty was a virtue, but rudeness was not. Surely there was a way she could state her case without offending him. "I believe there is more you could do for the children."

"And what might that be?"

"I believe investing a little more time with them each day would pay great dividends in their character and happiness."

"I'm not accustomed to spending time with children."

"I understand, but it is a skill that can be learned like any other."

He clasped his hands behind his back and looked off to the distant hills, his eyes shadowed by his brooding expression. "I do want what's best for my children, but I can make no promise to change my habits." His expression eased, and he gave a slight nod. "But I'll consider what you've said."

"Thank you. That's all I ask."

Lawrence stepped out the front door and looked her way, a frown darkening his brow.

Julia pulled in a quick breath, remembering her afternoon plans. "I'm sorry, sir. Would you please excuse me? I am supposed to meet with the young ladies at two o'clock. Lady Gatewood is joining us."

"Very well." His eyes shone with a hint of amusement now. "We mustn't keep Lady Gatewood waiting."

She suppressed a smile, then looked up at him. "No sir, we must not."

"Go on then." The corners of his mouth lifted in the slightest smile.

She bit her lip and hurried back toward the house. Had that actually been a look of acceptance, even approval in his eyes?

Lawrence stepped toward her as she

approached the house. "The ladies are waiting for you in the great hall."

For a moment she thought he might invite her through the front door, but he did not. She sighed. Some of the rules that separated her from the family seemed so senseless. "Please tell them I'll be there directly."

He nodded, stepped inside, and closed the door after him.

Julia glanced over her shoulder as she hurried around the corner of the house. Sir William stood on the path where she had left him. He appeared to be watching her, but his hat shaded his eyes, and she couldn't be certain.

She had taken quite a risk in challenging him like that. But it had been worth it if the conversation prompted him to give the children more of his time and attention.

Every child needed to know he was loved by his father. And didn't every father want to sense his children's admiration and affection? It seemed the natural order of things. But for some reason, it wasn't true for Sir William, Andrew, and Millie. Her heart ached as she considered all that was lacking in their family.

Oh how she longed to see things change for them.

William entered the great hall, his mind still on the conversation with Miss Foster. Were her concerns valid? Had his lack of involvement with his children put them at a disadvantage? He had given them a large, beautiful home and provided for all their physical needs. But in Miss Foster's mind, that was not enough.

She had no idea the struggle he faced or why he kept his distance from the children. But he could never tell her that every time he saw them, their likeness to their mother slapped him in the face. And once again he saw himself as the man who was not enough to satisfy his young, impetuous wife.

It was bad enough that he wrestled with these painful memories. He must not let his negative feelings hurt his children. He might not show it in a way that pleased Miss Foster, but he loved Andrew and Millie, and he wanted them to have a happy childhood.

"William, I must speak to you." Lady Gatewood strode toward him across the great hall. Katherine and Penelope stood together at the bottom of the stairway, their gazes following their aunt.

The muscles in his neck and shoulders tightened, but he forced his expression to remain neutral. "Lady Gatewood." He nodded to her. "Good afternoon."

"Shall we go in the library?"

Her question pulled him up short. Why did she always seem to forget this was his house? He should be the one to invite her into his library, not the other way around. But he forced that thought away and motioned toward the door. "After you."

She swept into the library, her teal-blue dress swishing as she rounded the corner. Stationing herself in the center of the room, she turned and faced him. "Both girls will need a new wardrobe for their time in London. Of course, Katherine's needs will be greater than Penelope's, since this is her first season. But if we are going to work with the best dressmakers, we must get started right away."

William stifled a groan. "I'm not sure that's going to be possible."

She pulled back. "Not possible? What do you mean? It's your responsibility to see that they are properly dressed when they're presented to society."

He narrowed his eyes. "I am well aware of my responsibilities."

"Katherine must have a fetching wardrobe to secure the attention of the right young men. She simply can't take part in the season without the proper clothing."

"Then perhaps she should not go to London this year."

Lady Gatewood's eyes widened. "Surely you jest."

"Not at all. Your brother-in-law left the estate in a very difficult financial situation, and the death duties have made it much worse."

"Oh dear." She lowered herself onto the settee.

"I knew Randolph did not give enough attention to managing his finances, but I didn't realize it was that bad."

"It's been a disturbing discovery for me as well."

"Surely there's enough money to pay for Katherine's needs for the season."

"I'm looking into ways to increase our income to pay the duties, but I'm not certain I'll be able to manage it." He glanced away and steeled himself for her reaction. "I may have to sell Highland."

Her face flushed as she rose to her feet. "But this house has been in the family for four generations!"

He focused on her again. "I will do everything I can to keep the estate intact, but in the end, I may not have a choice."

Lady Gatewood strode across the room, dissatisfaction hovering around her like a dark cloud.

He rubbed the bridge of his nose where a headache had just begun. He hated the thought of selling the estate. But breaking it up and letting it go piece by piece would be even worse. Would he end up losing it all and having to return to London?

Lady Gatewood faced him again. Her expression eased, and a new light shone in her eyes. "What if you were to marry?"

He released a harsh laugh. "That's impossible."

"Not if she were a lady with wealth and position. Her fortune might secure Highland for you and future generations."

"I have no intention of marrying again."

"Why not? You're still young, and it would give you a companion to share your life."

He glared at her. "Marriage did not suit me."

"I'm sorry to hear it." But her words held little true sympathy, and her expression made it obvious that the gossip about his wife had spread from London to Berkshire.

Heat rose up his neck and burned through his face. "Finding a wife worthy of that role is impossible. The qualities of honesty, loyalty, and faithfulness are far too rare." But as soon as the words left his mouth, a vision of Miss Foster rose in his mind.

Honesty and loyalty were apt descriptors for her. She seemed to be one of the few people in his life who was not afraid to tell him the truth. But what did that have to do with him? He could never become involved with a governess. It wasn't done. The society gossips would have a heyday if he chose that route.

He closed his eyes and forced the thought of her away. No matter how tempting it might be to forget issues of class and wealth, it was not an option he could consider. He had been humiliated when word of his wife's unfaithfulness spread throughout London, and he would not be scorned and ridiculed for marrying beneath him. That kind of misstep would make him and his children outsiders from society forever.

Seven

Lifting her skirt slightly with one hand, Julia carried the tray down the servants' steps.

"Miss Foster, there's no need for you to bring that tray all the way down to the kitchen." Nelson watched her descend the stairs with a teasing smile. "Just ring for me next time. I'm always glad to help." He took the tray from her hands.

"I don't mind." She looked past him down the hallway. The low curved ceiling, plain beige walls, and dim light were a stark contrast to the beautiful architecture and furnishings upstairs. "I came down to speak to Chef Lagarde."

"He's in the kitchen, but beware. I just heard him let loose a string of French you wouldn't want to translate." He winked and grinned, obviously hoping for a response.

She averted her eyes and stepped to the side.

He matched her movements and blocked her path. "Just let me know what you need." He lowered his voice and leaned closer. "I'll be more than happy to supply it."

"No, thank you." She stepped around him. *Cheeky man!* It was a good thing Ann usually brought their meals upstairs. Julia was glad she didn't often have to deal with Nelson.

The scent of fresh baked apple tarts filled the air as she rounded the corner and entered the warm kitchen.

Chef Lagarde stood at the large table in the center of the room, hovering over Betsy, the petite, red-haired kitchen maid. "I said to chop *zee* onions, not mince them!" He grabbed the knife from her hand and whacked a second onion in half. "Like *ziss!*" Laying his hand over the top of the knife, keeping the point down, he swiftly chopped the onion into neat, square pieces. "There! That is how it is done." He passed her the knife. "Now you do it."

The kitchen maid bit her lip, looking uncertain.

"Go on!" He waved his hand. "I cannot stand and watch all day. I have to make *zee* dinner!"

"All right." The girl grasped the knife, whacked the onion with surprising energy, and chopped it into a tidy pile, perfectly mimicking the chef's actions.

Julia pressed her lips together to hide her smile. *Good for her!* It must take a great deal of courage to work with such a forceful, exacting man, let alone try to understand what he is saying with that strong French accent.

Chef Lagarde looked up. "Ah, Miss Foster, what brings you to my kitchen?"

"Thank you for the delicious luncheon. Master Andrew and I enjoyed it very much. But I'm afraid Miss Millicent is not feeling well today. Would you be able to provide some broth and toast for her instead?"

"Of course." He issued brisk orders to another maid who stood at the sink, washing a large pot. She set it aside and hurried off to follow his instructions.

"So, how are things going with *zee* children?" The chef scooped a pile of chopped carrots into a large bowl along with the onions.

"I think we're getting along very well."

He lifted one eyebrow. "And Master Andrew? He is . . . yielding to your . . . instruction?"

Julia smiled. "He is energetic and has a strong will, but he is learning to tame those qualities. I'm sure they will serve him well, and he'll make a fine master for Highland someday."

"Ha! You are very clever I think." He speared a chunk of celery with the end of his knife and scraped it off into the bowl.

Julia smiled. "I'm not sure about that. But I do enjoy teaching the children. It's wonderful to watch them grab hold of a new concept or tackle a challenge and master a new skill."

"And *zee* young ladies?"

Julia hesitated. Her sessions with Katherine and

Penelope were not going as well, but she did not want to speak ill of them. "They're coming along. I believe we are learning to understand and appreciate each other."

"*Bien*! Those two have much to learn. They need a guide and teacher."

Betsy looked up and grinned, her green eyes shining. She obviously agreed with the chef on that point.

The clatter of feet in the hallway drew everyone's attention. Ann rushed past, covering her mouth and stifling a sob as she fled up the stairs.

Mrs. Emmitt followed and strode into the kitchen, her face red. "Miss Foster, come with me."

"Of course." She glanced at the chef.

He glared at the housekeeper and shook his head. "Go on. I will send up Miss Millicent's tray when it is ready."

"Thank you." Julia followed Mrs. Emmitt to her parlor. Ann had obviously done something to upset Mrs. Emmitt and received a scolding. And now Julia would hear about it.

The housekeeper pulled the door closed and turned to Julia. "Did you see Ann run past?"

"Yes, she looked quite upset."

"I saw her take the children's laundry outside earlier. When she didn't return in a reasonable amount of time, I decided to investigate." She

111

pursed her lips. "And it's a good thing I did!"

"What did you find?"

"Sheets on the line, flapping in the breeze, and an empty laundry basket!"

Julia's breath caught in her throat. "Where was Ann?"

"I searched the courtyard and garden and finally found her in the stables with that scoundrel of a groom, Peter."

Julia's heart sank. "Oh dear."

"Thank goodness I got there when I did."

"They weren't . . ." Julia's face flushed.

"No, but they were carrying on a very intimate conversation. I warned her when she was hired that Highland maids were not allowed to have followers or fraternize with the men on staff. I won't stand for that kind of foolishness!"

The memory of Ann and Peter together in the courtyard rose into Julia's mind. She hadn't said anything to Ann at the time, and she regretted that now. Perhaps she could've prevented this scolding if she'd spoken up. "I'm sorry, Mrs. Emmitt. I'll speak to her right away."

"I hope so." The housekeeper scowled at Julia as though she were the one caught in the stable. "As nursery maid, she is under your supervision. You must see that she obeys the rules. If I catch her with him again, I'll send her away with no reference."

"I understand."

"Make sure that Ann does as well."

"Yes ma'am."

Mrs. Emmitt pulled a handkerchief from her sleeve and patted her glowing cheeks. "Such behavior will not be tolerated. Not at Highland." She nodded to Julia. "You may go."

Julia walked to the door, then looked back. "Thank you for not dismissing her. I know she values her job."

"Then it had better not happen again. I will not be so lenient next time."

"Yes ma'am." Julia hurried up the backstairs, her mind churning. She could not allow Ann to lose her position over this foolish lapse of judgment. In the last few weeks, they had grown closer, and Ann had told Julia about the struggles she'd faced at home on the farm. Julia was determined to watch out for her friend.

She must find Ann and help her calm down, then make sure she knew how important it was to follow Mrs. Emmitt's rules. She checked the nursery and found Andrew sitting at the table drawing and Millie resting in the chair with her doll on her lap. "Has Ann come in?"

Andrew looked up, a slight frown on his face. "Yes, but she left right away."

Millie clutched her doll to her chest, her eyes wide. "She was crying. What happened?"

Julia crossed to Millie's chair and gently laid her hand on the girl's shoulder. "It's nothing for you to worry about, dear. I'll find her." She sent

Andrew a pointed look. "Please stay here and play quietly. I'll be back in a few minutes."

He gave a slight nod and returned his attention to his drawing. For once both children seemed to sense the need to obey her instructions, so she left them and set off in search of Ann. A few seconds later she knocked on Ann's bedroom door, then opened it without waiting for her reply.

Ann stood by her bed shoving clothing into her small carpetbag.

Julia gripped the doorknob. "Ann, what are you doing?"

"She's going to sack me. I know it. I might as well pack my bag and be off."

"No, she's not going to dismiss you."

"But she said she will if I so much as look at Peter Gates again. And I can't promise that. I won't!"

"Mrs. Emmitt doesn't allow staff to seek each other out or spend time alone. You know that."

"But I like Peter—very much. And he likes me. It's not fair that we're not allowed to be together."

"I know you're upset, but please just sit down a moment."

The girl pulled in a shuddering breath and slowly sank down on the bed. "All right."

"I know you care for Peter—"

"Oh, I do, so much."

"But you must think this through."

"I have, night and day! I can't stop thinking

about Peter. He's the most wonderful boy—"

Julia laid her hand on Ann's arm. "What I mean is you must be very certain before you make a choice." How well she knew the consequences of not doing so.

"What choice? I have no choice!"

"Yes, you do. You have a good position here. And you told me you don't want to go back home."

"No, I don't." Ann looked down and fiddled with the hem of her apron. "Peter says I'm the kind of girl he hopes to marry someday."

Julia tensed. "Are you sure he's worthy of your affection?"

Ann looked up and shrugged slightly. "How am I to know when we're only allowed a few stolen moments together?"

"The fact that he is talking to you about marriage when he hasn't actually proposed does not speak well for him."

"It does show he's serious."

"Perhaps. But coaxing you to meet him in the stable—when he knows it could cost you your job—makes me doubtful of his character."

"But he says the sweetest things and makes me feel so special."

"Sweet words are no replacement for a life-long commitment. If he truly loves you, he should do what's best for you, not just what makes him happy."

Ann nodded slowly, her eyes reflecting a hint of doubt. "Oh, Julia, what should I do?"

"Only you can answer that question."

"But if it were you, what would you do?"

Julia thought for a moment, wanting to give her best advice. "I suppose I would pray and ask the Lord to guide me. And while I waited for His direction, I would obey Mrs. Emmitt's rules and make every effort to do my job to the best of my ability. But above all else, I would guard my thoughts and hold on to my heart."

Ann heaved a heavy sigh. "I'm not sure I have the strength to do all that."

The memory of her own broken engagement filled Julia's mind and sent a shiver through her. "Giving your heart away before you are certain of a man's character and commitment is dangerous. You must discern his true intentions, or you'll pay a high price."

William pushed aside the books and papers on his desk in the library. "Let's spread out the map and take a look." He had put off discussing his financial troubles with Gordon McTavish, Highland's steward, as long as he could. He hated to spread the news among the staff, but it was time the steward knew that the future of Highland was uncertain.

"Very good, sir." McTavish unfolded the map of the estate. "What was it you wanted to discuss?"

William scanned the map, then looked up and met McTavish's gaze. "If I had to let some of it go, which portion do you think would bring the highest price?"

"I'm not sure that's possible, sir. I don't believe the estate can be broken up. At least that's what Sir Randolph told me."

"It wouldn't be my first choice, but the government has placed a heavy tax on all inherited property. I must pay it on time or face some steep fines."

"What I mean to say, sir, is that you may not have that choice. From what I understand, Sir Randolph's grandfather set things up legally so the estate has to be passed down or sold intact."

An unsettling wave traveled through William. "But surely there is some way to sell a portion of the land if we have no other option to raise the funds."

McTavish rubbed his gray beard, looking doubtful. "Maybe your man of business could find some way around it, but I'm not sure it would be wise. You'd definitely see a drop in your income if you break up the estate."

William huffed and scowled at the map. "What about this grazing land? Do you think we need all of it?" He pointed to the top left corner of the map.

"That could bring a high price, but it includes the estate's water access." McTavish shook his head. "You don't want to let that go."

William studied the map again. "What about this forested area? Do you think we could sell it, or is there a possibility of selling the timber?"

"It shelters your game, and we use that timber for making repairs to the cottages and outbuildings."

"And this area?" William pointed to the lower right section.

"That's your hay and grain fields, mostly barley and oats."

William nodded. "And we need that to feed the animals."

"Yes sir. We've had a decent crop this year, and I intend to sell the excess. I expect you'll receive that income at the end of the month."

William looked up. "How much will it be?"

McTavish stated the amount, and William's hopes deflated. It would only provide a small portion of what was needed to pay the death duties.

"Can you think of any other way we could bring in more income, even temporarily?"

McTavish narrowed his eyes and studied the map. "I'm not sure what it would be, sir. I like to think we're managing the property well and making the most with what we have."

William's shoulders sagged. "Yes, of course. I'm sure you are."

"We try to do our best for you, sir. Our very best."

William nodded. "Thank you, McTavish. I appreciate your work." He folded the map and handed it back to his steward, and along with it went his hope that he would find an easy solution to his financial problems.

A sick feeling of dread filled him. If he ended up losing Highland and returning to the city, people would consider him a failure—the baronet who had squandered his family's estate in less than a year.

What would he do? Who would help him carry this load?

Sarah walked into the library, intent on finding her missing copy of *Pride and Prejudice*. Perhaps she had left it behind last night when the family had gathered here after dinner.

William sat at his desk in the corner with ledgers and stacks of papers spread out around him. He turned toward her, a brooding frown creasing his forehead.

"I'm sorry to disturb you. I was just looking for my book."

He sighed and shifted in his chair. "It's all right. I'm glad for an interruption."

"You don't look very glad." She approached his desk. "What is it, William? What's wrong?"

He motioned toward the papers on his desk. "I never expected running the estate would be this difficult."

She placed her hand on his shoulder. "I'm sure you'll do wonderfully. Just give yourself time to learn what's needed."

"But that's the problem. I only have until March —at the latest—to straighten out the financial situation and pay the death duties. And then there are the issues with the tenant farmers."

"What issues?"

"McTavish says two of them are behind on their rent, one because of a health issue, and the other because of laziness or mismanagement. I must decide if we should extend the grace period or ask them to leave."

"I see."

"And Lawrence wants to hire a hall boy and add more kitchen staff, and then there are the repairs to the house and other buildings."

"That is a lot to consider, but you did an excellent job managing our family business in London after father's death. I'm sure you'll do just as well with Highland."

His worried expression remained unchanged. "If only I'd had more time with Cousin Randolph. Or if I could find someone who was skilled in land management to discuss these matters with me."

Sarah bit her lip. Randolph's death had been quite unexpected. He'd become ill following a hunting trip to Scotland and died a week later. His sudden passing had been a shock to his daughters as well as to William and Sarah. "I wish I could be of more help, but I know nothing about finances or running an estate."

He reached for her hand, his frown easing.

"Please don't worry. The last thing I want to do is trouble you with all of this."

Sarah sent him a tender smile. "I'll pray you find someone to encourage you and help you sort things out."

He rose and leaned closer to kiss her forehead. "You're very kind. And I appreciate the thought, but I'm not sure who it would be."

"I'm not sure either. But the Lord can provide what's needed if we trust Him."

William looked back at his desk, doubt shadowing his eyes again. "Yes, I suppose He can, though there is no guarantee He will."

Sarah's heart ached as she studied William's troubled expression. The losses and sorrow her brother had suffered the last few years had challenged his faith. He continued to attend church, lead the family in prayer and Scripture reading each morning, and pray at meals, but she sensed he struggled to believe God truly cared and would intervene on his behalf.

Well, she would offer sincere prayers that God would meet her brother's needs, and do so in a way that would help him believe again.

Julia descended the main stairway, pausing on the landing to examine the large painting that hung on the wall. The size alone made it remarkable, but the subject was even more impressive. A regal-looking knight in a heavy suit of armor rode a handsome white horse. The details, especially those of the horse, captured her attention. Such power and beauty.

"That's King Charles I. Painted by Van Dyck in 1633." William did not look the least bit pleased as he mounted the steps and joined her on the landing.

"You don't care for the painting?"

"Oh, it's fine. Very nice actually." He frowned slightly as he surveyed the king's portrait. "I was just contemplating its value."

Julia smiled. "I'm not sure why that would displease you. Van Dyck is a well-known artist. It must be worth a great deal."

"I'm sure it is." The defeat in his voice surprised her.

She shifted her gaze from the painting to William. The painful look in his eyes stirred her heart. It wasn't her place to do so, but she couldn't help asking a question. "Is something troubling you, sir?"

"It's nothing." He looked away.

But she couldn't ignore his weary, troubled expression. "I'm sorry, sir, but I don't believe that's true." She waited a moment more, then gently added, "If you choose to tell me, you can be certain I'll keep it in confidence."

"I don't want to burden you with my family's problems."

"It's never a burden to listen to a friend."

He studied her. "So we're to be friends now?"

Her cheeks warmed. "I hope we will be." She checked his expression, hoping she had not offended him.

His gaze was steady and unreadable, but he didn't reproach her.

"When burdens are shared, they grow lighter," she said with a slight smile.

"Is that from Proverbs?"

"No, it's something my father often says."

William gave a slight nod, his expression easing. "He sounds like a wise man."

"He is, sir, very wise indeed."

William glanced around, looking as though he wanted to say more. "Come with me."

Her heartbeat quickened as she followed him down the stairs, across the great hall, and into the library.

"Please." He motioned to a chair, and she took a seat. He walked to the fireplace and turned toward her. "I'm facing some very difficult choices concerning the future of Highland." The muscles in his jaw tensed and rippled.

"Go on, sir."

"I never expected to inherit this estate. We all thought when my cousin Randolph passed away that it would go to my elder brother, Nathaniel, but he died unexpectedly in a carriage accident two years ago."

Julia's heart clenched. "How terrible. I'm so

sorry." William had lost his wife and his brother within a year of each other.

"Thank you." William looked away and cleared his throat. "When Randolph died and I learned I would inherit Highland, I was told the estate was burdened by financial difficulties. But I didn't realize how serious they were."

Julia nodded, encouraging him to go on.

"That is only part of the problem. The house and grounds are in dire need of repairs." His pensive expression deepened into his familiar frown. "Then there is the matter of the death duties."

"I'm sorry, sir. I'm not familiar with that term."

"They're taxes assessed on inherited property."

Julia nodded and clasped her hands in her lap. "Are you considering selling the painting to pay off the debts and expenses?"

"I wish it were that easy. I'm afraid the sale of the painting would only bring in a portion of what's needed."

"I see."

"The truth is, I'm not sure how I'm going to pay for it all." He huffed and turned away. "I'm sorry. I'm not sure why I'm telling you this."

His honesty and vulnerability warmed her heart. "I'm honored that you would."

He turned back, his gaze intense again. "I've sought the advice of my solicitor as well as McTavish, and neither of them have an answer to the problem."

"It does sound like a challenging situation."

He sighed and lowered himself into the chair opposite her. "Yes, *challenging* is putting it mildly."

"Have you prayed about it and asked for guidance and provision?"

Surprise registered in William's eyes. "Do you think God cares about such matters?"

"Of course. He cares about every concern we carry on our hearts."

"Yes, I suppose prayer wouldn't hurt, especially since so many people's jobs are at stake if we must sell Highland."

"Do you believe it would really come to that?"

"I'm afraid it's a very real possibility if I can't find another answer."

The desire to help Sir William burned in her heart as a prayer formed in her mind. *Surely, Lord, You have a solution for this problem, or at least some wisdom or encouragement I could share to ease his troubles and give him a bit of hope.*

"Miss Foster?"

She glanced back at him. "Yes?"

"I must find another way to raise the funds we need."

She nodded. "I have an idea. Perhaps it's from the Lord, or perhaps it's from my own upbringing."

"What is it?"

She hesitated. Would Sir William welcome her

input when it would take her across the boundaries of power and position that separated them? Her desire to help him pushed her fears aside, and she lifted her gaze to meet his. "When our family lived in India, I learned a great deal about managing our household and the clinic with efficiency and economy."

He nodded. "Please, go on."

"Perhaps I could assist Miss Ramsey in her duties as mistress of the house, and together we could find ways to reduce your expenses."

He sat back and sighed. "I'm afraid my sister is mistress in name only. Mrs. Emmitt and Lawrence run the house as they did for my late cousin, since he was a widower."

Julia's thoughts traveled back to the day in the garden when she'd first seen Sarah's crippled hand. But that didn't seem like reason enough to prevent her from stepping into the role as mistress of Highland. "Miss Ramsey is an intelligent and capable person. Surely she could take on those duties."

"My sister has many fine qualities, but our parents . . . did not encourage her. Mother didn't expect her to marry or run a household, so she never taught her those skills. Now she lacks confidence and feels she's unqualified."

"Is she aware of your financial troubles?"

"Yes. I spoke with her earlier today, though I hate to trouble her."

Julia thought for a moment, then looked up. "What if I helped her learn the skills she needs to move into her position as mistress? Overseeing purchasing and planning menus with simplicity and thrift could save you a significant amount of money over time, especially with a house and staff this large."

He thought about it for a moment, then nodded. "It's a place to begin."

"Yes sir. It is." She met his gaze with a slight smile, then sat quietly, considering another idea. "Perhaps contacting an art dealer to appraise your paintings would also be wise. Then you will be able to judge whether selling some of them is the best course of action."

William nodded. "Yes, we must consider all our assets as well as doing what we can to run Highland efficiently."

"Very good, sir. I believe you are on the right path."

He stood and extended his hand to her, his gaze warming. "Thank you, Miss Foster."

Her heartbeat fluttered. She took his hand and rose from her chair. "I'm happy to be of service."

His gaze settled on her while her pulse raced. She broke eye contact and slipped her hand from his. *Foolish girl! You must not let yourself think you read anything except gratitude in his eyes.*

Eight

Sarah took Julia's arm as they descended the main staircase, then leaned close enough to whisper in her ear. "I'm not sure I'll be able to face Mrs. Emmitt. She's so stern."

Julia smiled and patted her hand. "You'll do fine. I'm sure of it. Just remember the points we discussed."

Julia's encouragement helped, but even so, Sarah couldn't still the tremor traveling through her. She disliked confrontation and tried to avoid it wherever possible. It reminded her too much of growing up in a home where her father displayed a fiery temper whenever he was challenged, and her mother showed her disapproval with critical words.

Sarah bit her lip. "I'm afraid Mrs. Emmitt won't be pleased to hear what I have to say."

"Of course not. She's been in charge since Katherine and Penelope's mother died, and she hasn't had to answer to anyone."

"I imagine she'll turn several shades of purple when I ask to look over the household accounts and adjust the menus."

"Perhaps, but you are her employer. She must listen to what you say and learn to work under your supervision."

They reached the bottom step, and Sarah looked across the great hall to the painting of Lady Eden Ramsey, the last mistress of Highland. Lady Eden's deep brown eyes and the confident tilt of her chin made her look so elegant and self-assured. Sarah released a soft sigh. How could she ever step into her predecessor's shoes? Even challenging the housekeeper about her duties made her tremble to her toes.

Sarah tucked her withered arm into the folds of her skirt and turned to Julia. "Mrs. Emmitt knows much more about running Highland than I do."

"That may be true now, but you can learn what's needed, and I promise I will be at your side each step of the way."

Sarah's throat tightened. "Thank you, Julia. I appreciate it so much. I feel more confident with you here to guide me."

"I'm glad to help."

"I've never had a sister, but if I did, I hope she would be very much like you."

Julia smiled, her blue eyes glowing. "That's a sweet sentiment. I've also wished for a sister."

"You have a brother, don't you?"

"Yes, Jonathan and I have always been close, but I believe the relationship between sisters is quite different from that of a brother and sister."

"Yes, I suppose that's true. But I adore my brothers. I don't see my younger brother, David, as often as I would like. He's very busy with his business in London. I'm closer to William. He has always been so thoughtful and kind. He never makes me feel like a burden."

"You could never be a burden, not to Sir William or anyone else."

Sarah's heart warmed, and comfort flowed through her. "You're just as kind as he is."

The butler and footman stood near the front door. Lawrence addressed the younger man in hushed tones, then crossed the hall toward Sarah and Julia. "May I help you, Miss Ramsey?"

She glanced at Julia, then straightened. "Yes, Lawrence. Will you please ask Mrs. Emmitt to meet us in the drawing room?"

His dark eyebrows rose slightly. "Is there something I can help you with?"

"No, thank you. I'd like to speak to Mrs. Emmitt."

He nodded and strode off.

Sarah clutched Julia's hand. "I'm so glad you're with me. That took all my courage."

"You did very well." Julia sent her a confident smile. "You'll be a fine mistress for Highland."

Julia took a sip of tea and glanced around the drawing room while Sarah and Mrs. Emmitt continued discussing changes to the menu. So far the housekeeper hadn't expressed resistance to the changes, but her heightened color and grim expression made her true feelings clear.

Sarah set her teacup aside. "I'd like to work with you to plan the menu for the servants and the family each week. I also want to review the items you'd like to purchase before the orders are made."

"But I've always seen to the purchasing and menus." Mrs. Emmitt pulled her handkerchief from her sleeve and dabbed her nose. "I know the dishes the young ladies like, and I also know what Chef Lagarde needs for his recipes."

"I understand, but we want to use more produce, fish, and game from our own land, and that will require changing the menus."

Mrs. Emmitt puckered her lips as though she'd been sucking on a tart lemon. "So we're to eat like poor tenant farmers, then?"

"No." Sarah glanced at Julia.

Julia smiled and gave a slight nod, urging her on.

"We simply want to be more economical with our food purchases and meal planning."

"Chef Lagarde is not going to like these changes. And I'm the one who has to deal with him."

"I understand it may be difficult for a time, but

Sir William and I would like to live more simply. Times are changing, and we must change with them. We see no need for six-course dinners with four types of wine." Sarah shifted in her seat. "In fact, we see no need for wine at all."

Mrs. Emmitt's eyes grew as round as two boiled eggs. "You're doing away with the wine?"

Sarah nodded. "We'd like to be served Highland's own cider and water with our dinner. Sir William won't be taking brandy after dinner either, or any other alcohol. There's no need for it."

"Are you quite sure?"

Sarah nodded. "Yes, so please tell Lawrence he's not to make any more purchases for the wine cellar until he checks with Sir William."

Mrs. Emmitt stared at Sarah in stunned silence. "Do you understand?"

The housekeeper closed her eyes and looked as though she were swallowing a bitter pill. "Very well. I'll speak to Mr. Lawrence and express your wishes to Chef Lagarde."

"We . . . I mean, I can speak to him if you like."

"No, miss. That won't be necessary. I'll tell him."

"Very good. After you've spoken to Chef Lagarde, we can meet again to discuss next week's menu."

"Yes, miss."

Victory flashed in Sarah's eyes. "Thank you, Mrs. Emmitt."

The housekeeper stood and shifted her stern gaze to Julia. Her silent message was as clear as the spiteful look on her face. *You are responsible for this, and I won't let it pass.*

Julia pressed her lips together and looked away.

Sarah smiled at the housekeeper. "Thank you for taking time to meet with us."

Mrs. Emmitt gave a stiff nod. "Of course." She stood and left the room.

Sarah watched her go, then turned to Julia with a bright smile. "We've won our first battle."

Julia laughed softly and rose from her chair. She gave Sarah's hand a squeeze. "You did an excellent job." She opened the drawing room door, and they walked out together.

"I thought she would eat me alive when I said there'd be no wine at dinner."

"She was quite shocked."

Sarah mimicked Mrs. Emmitt's startled expression, and both of them broke out in laughter again.

Lydia came around the corner, carrying a neatly folded pile of linens, and almost ran into Sarah. Her eyes widened, and she bobbed a brief curtsy. "I'm so sorry, miss. I didn't expect to—"

"It's all right, Lydia." Sarah's eyes twinkled. "We're the ones who should apologize. We were just celebrating a victory and not paying attention."

Lydia grinned. "Here's to your victory then."

●　●　●

A few minutes later Julia and Sarah walked under the arched entrance to the garden. A chilly wind blew past, swirling around Julia's ankles and sending a shiver up her back.

She glanced at Sarah. "You did wonderfully with Mrs. Emmitt, but we don't have to see the head gardener today if you'd rather not."

"No, I'm fine." Sarah smiled. "In fact I'm rather looking forward to it. Mr. Dalton is a kind, sensible man. I'm sure he'll be much more agreeable to our ideas than Mrs. Emmitt." She wrinkled her nose at the mention of the surly housekeeper.

Julia nodded. "I'm sure you're right about that."

"So you've dealt with Mr. Dalton?"

"I've greeted him when we've seen him working in the gardens. He's always been polite to me and friendly to the children." She thought for a moment. "Once Master Andrew's kite was stuck in a tree, and Mr. Dalton climbed up and set it free."

"Yes, that sounds very much like him." Sarah smiled again.

Julia studied Sarah and pondered her response. She seemed very familiar with Mr. Dalton. But she did spend a lot of time in the garden, or at least she had during those first few weeks of October, until the weather cooled and the autumn rains began.

Sarah lifted her hand over her eyes and scanned

the garden path. "I don't see Mr. Dalton. Perhaps he's in the greenhouse." She set off in that direction, and Julia followed. They rounded the corner and spotted him trimming the hedge.

He looked up when he saw Sarah, and his smile spread wider. He set his hedge clippers aside, removed his hat, and nodded. "Good afternoon, Miss Ramsey. Miss Foster." He focused on Sarah again. "How are you today?"

Sarah's cheeks turned rosy pink as she returned his greeting. "Miss Foster and I have something important we'd like to discuss with you. Could you take a few moments with us?"

"Of course. My office is just this way." He motioned down the path past the fountain and greenhouse. He and Sarah set off together, discussing how the temperature had dropped in the last few days and the changes that had brought to the garden.

Julia followed, watching their interaction. They seemed quite comfortable together, as though this was not their first conversation. Was there a friendship—or perhaps even a romance—developing between them? Julia smiled. Wouldn't that be lovely for Sarah?

But she quickly reined in her thoughts. She knew very little about Mr. Dalton, and she had no idea if he was a worthy suitor, especially since Sarah had such a tender heart and little experience with men.

It would be highly unusual for a woman from an aristocratic family to become romantically involved with a member of her staff. A head gardener like Mr. Dalton was a step above a footman, but he certainly didn't have the same position in society as Sarah and William.

Memories of the Indian caste system, which created such a huge gulf between the classes, came to mind. Her father had often spoken out against it, explaining that God created all people equal. The Christian faith seemed to be breaking down some of the longstanding cultural barriers in India, but it was still difficult for those of different castes to marry.

Though the English liked to think of themselves as more civilized than the Indians, she wasn't sure it was true. Marrying someone from a different class was still difficult here. Her parents' situation came to mind and, with it, all the heartache their decision to marry had caused in her mother's family.

They reached the gardener's office, and Julia put those thoughts aside. Mr. Dalton showed them in and offered them each a plain wooden chair.

He remained standing by the door. "Now, how can I help you?"

Sarah settled in her chair, then looked up at him. "My brother and I would like Highland to be more self-sustaining. We're hoping you can help us find ways to grow more of our own produce."

He nodded and rubbed his chin. "We could expand the kitchen garden, but that won't give you anything more until next spring and summer."

"What about the greenhouse? Could we grow more food there?"

"I do grow a few vegetables during the cool months. Perhaps I could increase those." He frowned slightly. "Though I'm not sure they're crops you and your family would want to eat. They're simple fare: turnips, radishes, cabbage, and the like. Not the usual dishes served on your table."

"I'm sure they're nourishing, and that's what's most important."

"Very good, miss." He smiled, appreciation glowing in his dark brown eyes. "I save seed each year, and I have plenty on hand. I can start some more plants today."

"Wonderful." Sarah sent Julia a bright smile, then turned back to Mr. Dalton. "I'm so pleased. And I'm sure Sir William will be as well."

"I'm glad to be of service to you . . . and Sir William too, of course."

Nine

Mrs. Emmitt took the key to the store closet from the chain at her waist and inserted it in the lock. She listened for the click, then tugged on the handle to be sure the door was secure. No need to create temptation by leaving it open so anyone could stop by and help themselves. Unfortunately, not everyone was as trustworthy and loyal as she.

Twenty-seven years she had been working in this house, first as a housemaid, then as lady's maid for Eden Ramsey, the late mistress of Highland. These last six years, since Lady Ramsey's death, she had been housekeeper, in charge of all the female staff and equal in authority with Mr. Lawrence to oversee the running of Highland and carry out her duties as she saw fit . . .

Until today.

Her stomach twisted as she recalled her meeting with Miss Ramsey and Miss Foster. Even after all these years, after all she had sacrificed, she was still no more than a hired servant—she had no real control over the running of the house.

Creating menus was *her* responsibility, as was purchasing food and household supplies. Miss Ramsey ought to be asking her opinion and looking to her for guidance, not the other way around.

It wasn't right!

Mr. Lawrence strode down the hall toward her. "Mrs. Emmitt, might I have a word?"

She noted his frown, and a burning sensation rose and singed her throat. "I am not in the mood to hear any more bad news today."

"Then we had best discuss this behind closed doors."

She set her jaw and followed him down the hall and into her parlor. After she closed the door, she turned to face him. "Well, what is it?"

"I'm afraid Lydia is spreading rumors and upsetting the entire staff."

"Why did I hire that girl? She's been nothing but trouble since the day she arrived. What did she say this time?"

"Only that Sir William is considering selling Highland."

Mrs. Emmitt gasped. "Foolish girl! I've a mind to find her right now and shake her until her teeth rattle."

Mr. Lawrence held up his hand. "There'll be no need for that. I've taken care of it."

"Start from the beginning, and tell me what happened."

"We were in the servants' hall, having tea, when she announced she'd heard Sir William was thinking of selling the estate. I was so startled I nearly choked on a biscuit."

"I can imagine. I'm sure the others were upset as well."

He nodded. "I told them not to discuss it, then I called Lydia out of the room and reprimanded her for making up a story."

"I hope that put an end to it."

He clasped his hands behind his back. "I am sorry to say it did not. She insisted she was only passing on what she'd heard from Agnes, the dairy maid."

"Oh, for goodness' sake! What would a dairy maid know about such matters?"

"I have no idea. But Lydia seemed quite convinced it was true."

Mrs. Emmitt heart lurched. "You don't think she's right, do you?"

Mr. Lawrence straightened, looking offended. "Of course not. Highland has been in the Ramsey family for four generations. Why would Sir William want to sell the estate?"

"I don't know, but stranger things have happened."

"Sir William left his business dealings behind in London and moved his family here. Why would he do that if he intended to sell Highland?" Mr. Lawrence shook his head. "There can be no truth to it—none at all."

Mrs. Emmitt lowered herself into her chair, her thoughts tumbling over one another like water rushing down a rocky stream. It had better not be true, or they would all be out of a job. Where would she go then?

"No need to worry, Mrs. Emmitt. That rumor will go no further. I've settled the matter with Lydia."

She sighed. "I'm afraid that's not our only problem."

"Has something else happened?"

"Miss Ramsey met with me this afternoon, and she brought Miss Foster with her." She pursed her lips and sent Mr. Lawrence a meaningful look.

"What did she say?"

"Miss Ramsey wants to control the household purchases, and she intends to make changes to the menus for the staff and family."

"Really? She seems as timid as a mouse. I can't imagine her taking all that on."

"Well, she's not afraid to speak up now." Mrs. Emmitt sniffed and took her handkerchief from her sleeve. "It's that Miss Foster. She's the one stirring up all this trouble."

Mr. Lawrence sent her a skeptical glance.

"It's true," Mrs. Emmitt wiped her forehead. "Miss Ramsey has barely spoken a word to me since the day she arrived. And now, all of a sudden, she waltzes in with that governess at her side and wants to turn everything upside down."

"And you believe it's because of Miss Foster's influence?"

"Of course. You should've seen the way she nodded and urged Miss Ramsey on during our meeting." She paused and lifted her finger. "And wait until you hear this."

He cocked his head.

"There's to be no more wine served at dinner or after and none purchased without Sir William's permission."

The butler's eyes widened. "That's most unusual."

Mrs. Emmitt sat back and glared at him. "None of this happened until Miss Foster arrived."

"I don't know that you can blame all the changes on the governess."

"And why not? She's been raised by radically religious parents and spent the last twelve years in a heathen culture. Why else would Miss Ramsey want to do away with wine and simplify the meals?"

He clasped his hands behind his back again, looking grim. "It's certainly not the way we've always done things at Highland."

"No, it is not." She stared into the fire, turning the issue over in her mind. Perhaps it was time she found a way to be rid of Miss Foster.

...

Julia looked to the top of the grand staircase where Katherine and Penelope waited. Sarah stood beside Julia at the foot of the stairs, watching her cousins with a hint of amusement in her eyes.

Lady Gatewood waited on the lower landing, her gaze focused on her two nieces. "During the season there will be many occasions when you will walk down a stairway to make an entrance into a ballroom. This is an important opportunity to catch the attention of everyone in the room. If there is a butler or footman present, always wait to be announced. Then you must descend slowly, displaying the utmost poise and grace."

The girls exchanged uncomfortable glances. Katherine tapped Penelope's arm. "You go first."

"Why me? You're the one who's making her debut."

"But you're the one who needs the most practice. Go on."

The younger girl huffed and rolled her eyes. "All right." She straightened the sash on her dress, then sent her sister a haughty glance. "At least I'm not afraid to try." With that Penelope plodded down the stairs, looking a bit like a tired workhorse.

Sarah leaned closer to Julia. "Oh dear, she won't make a very good impression that way."

Julia agreed, but she couldn't very well correct

Penelope. Lady Gatewood had taken charge.

"No, no, please stop," Lady Gatewood called. "That will not do. You must *float* down the stairs, as though you were carried on a cloud."

Penelope scowled at her aunt. "How in the world am I to do that?"

"You must bend your knees slightly to absorb the shock of your descent, and then you glide along, keeping your head erect and your shoulders level. Like this." Lady Gatewood demonstrated by lifting her chin and gliding down a few steps while the girls watched.

"She looks more like an actress on stage than a debutante arriving at a ball," Sarah whispered, a merry twinkle in her eyes.

Julia nodded slightly and lifted her hand to hide her own smile. Katherine glared at them from the top of the stairs. Julia sobered. Sarah lowered her gaze, but her faint smile remained.

Penelope tried again, but her second attempt looked more awkward than the first. "This is ridiculous. It feels so unnatural." She stomped down the last few stairs and joined Julia and Sarah at the bottom.

Lady Gatewood sighed and waved her hand. "Never mind, dear. We'll keep practicing. You have two more years before your presentation." She looked to the top of the stairs. "Your posture and carriage should show an attitude of inner confidence and a bit of mystique. All right, Katherine, shoulders back, chin up, and remember, a lady has only one opportunity to make a first impression."

Katherine stiffened and lifted her nose so high she couldn't possibly see where she was going. Julia held her breath, hoping she wouldn't fall. Lady Gatewood continued calling out a series of suggestions, but they only seemed to confuse Katherine. Her face grew pink, and her expression hardened.

Sarah leaned toward Julia and whispered, "Poor girl. I'm afraid she looks a bit like a giraffe with her neck stretched out like that."

Fire blazed in Katherine's eyes as she reached the bottom step. "How dare you stand there and laugh at me."

Sarah's eyes widened. "Oh, Katherine—"

"I saw you whispering."

"I didn't mean—"

"Of course you did. You meant to humiliate me in front of my aunt and sister."

"No, I didn't, but it was thoughtless of me to make light of your efforts. I'm sorry." Sarah sent a worried glance Julia's way. "I'm sure with all the effort you're putting forth, you'll do very well when you go to London for the season."

Katherine spun around. "What would you know about the season? You were never presented to the king and queen or took part in any of it. Your *deformity* kept you out of society."

Sarah gasped.

Katherine hardened her expression. "You know nothing about courtship or marriage, and you probably never will, so that gives you very little room to laugh at me."

The color drained from Sarah's cheeks.

Fire flashed through Julia. "Katherine, stop! You may not speak to your cousin like that." She stepped closer to Sarah.

"I quite agree." Lady Gatewood joined them. "Ladies of good breeding—especially members of the same family—do not criticize each other in public. It's unseemly."

"They don't laugh and try to embarrass each other either." Katherine lifted her chin. "But we might as well get these issues out in the open."

"What issues?" Lady Gatewood looked from Sarah to Katherine.

Katherine narrowed her gaze at Sarah. "I know how she and her brother feel about us."

"What do you mean?" Sarah's voice came out choked and breathless.

"You were more than happy to inherit Highland and take over all that should have been ours, but Penelope and I are an unwelcome burden."

Sarah shook her head, pain and disbelief shimmering in her eyes.

"Well, you needn't worry. By this time next year I expect be married and established in my own home, then you and your brother will be rid of me."

Tears pooled in Sarah's eyes. She lifted a

trembling hand to cover her mouth and hurried away.

"Sarah, wait," Julia called. But Sarah disappeared through the doorway at the end of the hall without looking back.

Julia spun toward Katherine, her heart pounding. "She never intended to hurt you. You've misjudged her and been thoughtless and unkind."

"You're just as bad, smirking and making fun of us."

Julia didn't flinch as she met Katherine's haughty glare. "You cannot excuse your behavior by pointing your finger at someone else."

"I am very tired of your self-righteous attitude. You're just as human and sinful as the rest of us, and you've proved it today."

A hot reply rose in Julia's throat, but before she could speak, William strode into the great hall, his dark eyebrows knit together.

"What is going on?"

"Nothing!" Katherine turned on her heel and rushed up the stairs.

Mrs. Emmitt slipped behind a large column in the upper gallery as Katherine stormed past. The girl was so furious she didn't see her, but Mrs. Emmitt had overheard everything.

Katherine jerked open her bedroom door, strode in, and slammed it behind her.

Mrs. Emmitt shook her head, her own anger simmering. Poor girl. She was still grieving and struggling to accept the changes that had swept through the house following her father's death. She hadn't always been this fractious. It was only in the last few months since her world had been turned upside down that she'd become sullen and difficult.

Today's confrontation certainly had not helped. What right did that governess and Miss Ramsey have to mock the girls' efforts to prepare for the season? Of course, she didn't approve of Katherine's response, but being the brunt of jokes and laughter cut to the heart. She knew that all too well.

She started down the hallway, then stopped. Perhaps these insults could be turned into an opportunity. She knocked on Katherine's door and leaned closer to listen for her response.

"Go away. I don't want to see anyone."

"It's Mrs. Emmitt." When she heard no more protests, she opened the door and stepped inside.

Katherine stood facing the tall window, staring out at the gray November afternoon.

"I'm sorry to disturb you, miss, but I saw you go past. Is there anything I can do to help?"

Katherine sniffed and brushed her hand across her cheek. "Not unless you know of a way to get me out of this house."

Mrs. Emmitt crossed the room and stood beside

Katherine. "Some things may have changed, but this is still your home, and your wishes should be honored."

"If only that were true." Katherine tugged off her gloves and tossed them on the dressing table. "I'm afraid my cousins care very little about me or my wishes. Look at the goose of a governess they hired!"

Mrs. Emmitt's pulse jumped. This could be just the opening she hoped for, but she must tread very carefully. "I know you haven't been pleased with Miss Foster."

"That is an understatement. She has made my life miserable. Not only must we rise early for morning Scripture reading and prayer, but we have to waste our days poring over dreadful French texts, reading boring history books, and discussing other topics that I have no interest in whatsoever."

"That does sound like quite a change from your usual routine."

"You haven't heard the half of it. She also requires us to read classic novels and memorize long sections of poetry. But worst of all, she insists we analyze Bible passages and look for modern applications. It's ridiculous!"

"I'm sorry, miss. I know you're not used to such demands."

"I most certainly am not."

"Have you spoken to Sir William about it?

Perhaps he's not aware that Miss Foster's lessons have become a burden."

Katherine released a mocking laugh. "I doubt that would matter to him. He's probably very glad she has us under her thumb."

"Oh, I'm not so sure about that. He hired her with the understanding that she would have a one-month trial . . . and that time has almost past."

Katherine turned to Mrs. Emmitt, a spark of interest in her eyes. "Really?"

"Yes. He wanted to make sure she could handle her responsibilities before he made a final commitment."

"Do you think he might dismiss her if I told him how difficult she's been?"

"I don't know, miss. But I think it's important to let him know how she's treating you."

"I don't think my disapproval would be enough reason for him to let her go. How has she been getting along with Andrew and Millicent?"

"Sir William is not pleased that she takes them on long walks every day, even when the weather is questionable."

"That's hardly reason enough to let her go."

"No, especially when it's difficult to find a qualified governess."

Katherine narrowed her eyes. "It would have to be something more serious for him to consider dismissing her."

Mrs. Emmitt nodded, barely able to hold back her smile. "I believe you're right. He would only let her go if there was a good reason—a very good reason indeed."

Sarah fled through the music room and ran out the side door, Katherine's hurtful words echoing through her heart. A cold wind whipped around her ankles and tugged at her skirt as she hurried along the side of the house. Heavy clouds blanketed the sky, threatening rain. She wished she had brought her shawl, but she could not go back now, not with her hot tears ready to overflow.

Lifting her skirt to avoid the puddles, she hurried past the back courtyard and stepped under the arched entrance to the garden. She lifted her gaze, and her steps stalled.

Cold, rainy weather had kept her inside for three days, and she had no idea a frost had crept in and stolen all the vibrant flowers, leaving only wilted, brown remains. Their branches lay on the ground now, shriveled and lifeless.

She turned away, her heart aching, and looked toward the greenhouse. Raindrops splashed at her feet and drummed on the glass roof and windows. She ducked her head and hurried on.

Pushing open the greenhouse door, she slipped inside. No one was about, but roses still bloomed in sturdy pots on the pebble-covered shelves. She inhaled slowly, savoring their beautiful scent, but it couldn't banish Katherine's painful words from her mind . . . because they were true.

She would never know what it was like to fall in love and marry or have children and grow old with a husband and family who loved her.

Sagging against the greenhouse wall, she finally let her tears fall, releasing all the hurts and disappointments she had kept locked away for so long.

"Miss Ramsey?"

Sarah gasped and turned.

Mr. Dalton stood in the aisle, a pot of geraniums in his hands. He searched her face, his concern clear.

"I'm sorry. I didn't realize you were working in here." She bit her lip and turned to leave.

"Please, there's no need to go." He reached for her arm. "You're safe here."

His gentle words and touch undid her. She lifted a trembling hand to her mouth as another round of tears overflowed.

"Here you go." He took a neatly folded handkerchief from his pocket and handed it to her, then waited while she wiped her eyes. "When you're ready, I hope you'll tell me what's upset you."

She released a shaky breath and refolded the handkerchief. "It's nothing, really. I'm afraid I'm just feeling sorry for myself."

Frowning, he set the pot aside. "Why don't you

tell me, and I'll be the judge of that." Mr. Dalton had always been kind and caring, but his confident tone and protective manner surprised her. Perhaps she could confide in him.

She lifted her gaze to meet his. "My cousin Katherine misunderstood something I said, and I'm afraid I hurt her feelings." She relayed what had happened in the great hall, stopping short of sharing Katherine's final remarks.

He cocked his head. "And that's what made you cry?"

She lowered her head, her face warming. "Well, that's not all of it."

"You've come this far—you may as well tell me the rest."

She slowly lifted her head. "She said I knew nothing about the season, courtship, or marriage . . . and I probably never would . . . because of my deformity."

His face darkened, and he huffed. "I know Miss Katherine has a quick temper, but I had no idea she could be so unkind."

"It's been difficult for her to lose her father, then see my brother inherit Highland."

"Still, that's no excuse for her to lash out at you."

"I suppose." She slipped her withered hand into the folds of her skirt. "But she's right. My parents sheltered me and kept me out of society. I have few acquaintances outside our family, and sometimes I feel as though life has passed me by." The pain went much deeper, but that was all she had the courage to say.

"Maybe your parents did limit your friendships, but the Lord is sovereign over all that happens. He has a plan and purpose for each of us that no one can alter."

Pain flashed through her, and she lifted her shriveled hand. "You think He planned this for me?"

His expression remained calm and thoughtful. "I know He lovingly designs each of us, and He allows our challenges and limitations, though they may seem unfair. He also gives each of us gifts and talents as He chooses. And He uses them all —the limitations and the talents—for our good and the good of others . . . if we allow Him to."

She looked at her withered hand, then slowly shook her head. "I'm sorry, Mr. Dalton, but I don't see what good has come out of this for me."

He studied her for a moment, not seeming the least bit ruffled by her disagreement. "I can think of three blessings that have come from it, and I'm sure there are others."

"Three blessings? What would they be?"

"Well, first, though you come from an aristocratic family, facing these challenges has given you a humble heart. And because of that, you treat others with kindness and respect, and you're not ashamed to share a confidence with a gardener."

The tension in her shoulders began to fade. "Yes, I suppose that's true."

"You're also compassionate and understanding toward others, especially those who've been hurt. You see the pain they carry, and you want to help them."

She gave a slight nod. "I know life can be difficult, and that gives me sympathy for those who suffer." Her heart warmed, and she sent Mr. Dalton a tremulous smile. "And what is the third blessing?"

His deep brown eyes glowed. "If you'd done the season when you were eighteen, I'm sure you would've received a proposal and married soon after. If that had happened, you wouldn't have come to Highland, and I never would've met you." His gaze faltered for a moment, then he looked into her eyes again. "That would have been a terrible loss to me."

She stilled. Was he saying . . . ? Did he mean he cared for her, not just as a friend, but as a man loves a woman?

He watched her a second more, then his countenance fell. "I'm sorry, miss. I should not have spoken to you—"

"No, it's very sweet of you, really. It's just that—"

"You've no wish to hear anything like that from a gardener."

"Oh no, that's not what I was going to say." She

155

bit her lip and glanced over her shoulder toward the house. "I'm afraid my brother would be upset if he knew you were speaking to me like this."

"I respect Sir William as master of Highland, but it's your opinion that matters more to me."

Sarah's heart pounded so hard she could barely breathe. Should she encourage him and risk displeasing William? Would she be inviting more disapproval and rejection if she did? But if she didn't encourage Mr. Dalton, would she always regret that she hadn't had the courage to follow her heart?

She swallowed and looked up. "I'm honored by what you've said."

"So you've no objection to me making my feelings plain?"

She lowered her head and smiled. "No. I have no objection."

He released a deep breath. "Thank the good Lord above." Then he reached for her crippled hand, lifted it to his lips, and kissed her cool, withered fingers.

Her throat tightened, and she blinked back happy tears.

"Perhaps I could call on you this evening."

She froze as the reality of her situation set in. "I . . . I must speak to my brother first."

Mr. Dalton tightened his hold on her hand. "But shouldn't I be the one to speak to him?"

Her heart warmed, quieting her fears for the moment. "Yes, but the time must be right."

"You'll let me know when I should come?"

She nodded. "I'll send a note or meet you here tomorrow afternoon."

"I'll be waiting." He turned to the nearest rosebush and clipped a long-stemmed pink rose. "Take this with you as a reminder of what we've said to each other today." He gently ran his hand over hers as she took the rose.

A delightful shiver traveled up her arm. She slipped her hand away. With a tremulous smile, she said good-bye and hurried back to the house.

Ten

Julia knocked on Sarah's bedroom door, but there was no answer. She turned and scanned the hallway. Where could she be? She had searched the house and asked Mrs. Emmitt and Mr. Lawrence, but no one had seen Sarah since she'd run out of the great hall.

Julia clenched her hands, recalling the way Katherine had lashed out at Sarah. If that young woman didn't have a change of heart very soon, Julia would have to speak to Sir William. Perhaps he could exert some influence over his willful young cousin.

The sound of approaching footsteps caught her attention, and she turned.

Sarah climbed the stairs carrying a beautiful pink rose.

Julia hurried to meet her. "Are you all right?"

She looked up at Julia. "Yes, I'm . . . fine."

"Truly?" Julia searched Sarah's face, surprised by her calm expression. "I'm so sorry about what Katherine said."

"It's all right."

"Well, if she doesn't make amends soon, I'll speak to Sir William."

Sarah's eyes widened. "Oh no, please, I don't want to cause anymore strife."

"But she shouldn't be allowed to speak to you in such a disrespectful way. Sir William wouldn't approve, and if I allow it to go unchallenged, then I am at fault as well."

"But she's young and upset by all the changes we've brought to Highland. We mustn't be too hard on her."

"That's very kind of you, but Katherine must learn to control her temper and give others the benefit of the doubt. Can you imagine what would happen if she had that kind of outburst in London?"

Sarah sighed. "I suppose you're right. I know it's important to resolve our differences, but must we involve William?"

Julia searched Sarah's face. Did compassion prompt her request, or was she simply too timid to confront her strong-willed cousin? "I suppose I could speak to her again after she has had time to settle down."

Sarah's expression warmed. "Yes. I think that's best."

But doubts swirled through Julia's mind. Katherine barely tolerated sitting through their daily lessons. How could Julia persuade her to listen to correction about her faults without involving William? And would that really be enough to restore Katherine and Sarah's relationship?

"I'm sure it will all be fine. And don't worry about me. I've had a nice walk in the garden and a good talk with Mr. Dalton." She smiled, then she lowered her gaze to the rose in her hand.

Julia studied Sarah, questions rising in her heart.

Sarah sniffed the rose and glanced at Julia. "What is it?"

"I'm sorry. I'm just surprised you've chosen the head gardener as your confidant."

Sarah glanced down the hallway. Leaning closer, she whispered, "May we speak in private?"

Julia nodded, then followed Sarah into her bedroom and closed the door.

Sarah placed the rose on the dressing table and turned to Julia. "I told Mr. Dalton what happened with Katherine, and he was such a comfort. He challenged my thinking about my hand, but he was also very kind and fiercely protective. He said . . . he has feelings for me."

Julia blinked. "Really?"

Sarah nodded. "He wants to call on me properly."

Julia hesitated, uncertain if she should encourage her.

Sarah bit her lip. "Oh, say something, Julia! Do you think I would be foolish to allow it?"

"Not if you're certain he has good character and honorable intentions."

"I believe he does, but we've only known each other a short time."

"Perhaps you should find out more about him before you move ahead."

"How would I do that?"

Julia's mind spun, then she lifted her gaze to meet Sarah's. "I've often seen Mr. Dalton at church on Sunday. Perhaps Reverend Langford could tell you more about him."

"But if I speak to Reverend Langford, he'll want to know why I'm asking, and I'd have to tell him the truth. I couldn't lie to a minister."

"No, of course not."

Sarah's eyes lit up. "I know. You could ask him."

Julia blinked. "Me?"

"Yes, you're very discreet. And if Reverend Langford asks why you're inquiring, you can just say a friend wants to know."

Julia hesitated, trying to think through Sarah's request. "I'm not sure that's wise. He might not give me the information unless I told him the real reason."

"Oh, please, you mustn't do that. I don't want to hurt Mr. Dalton's reputation or cause gossip. Promise me it will remain a private matter between us."

"What about your brother? Surely he should be

the one to make inquiries about Mr. Dalton and help you decide if he is a worthy suitor."

"I'll speak to him about it as soon as you bring me a good report from Reverend Langford."

Julia bit her lip. Could she leave and go into the village without Sir William's knowledge or permission? What would he think of Sarah's request?

Sarah reached for her hand. "Please, Julia. Will you do this for me? I have no one else I can trust." The longing in Sarah's eyes tugged at Julia's heart.

"All right. Ann is watching the children, and Katherine and Penelope are in no mood for lessons. Nor am I."

"Oh, thank you!" Sarah hugged Julia. "I'm so grateful."

"Let's wait until you hear what the reverend has to say before you get too excited."

Sarah nodded, but her eyes sparkled with a joyful light. "I'm sure it will be a good report."

Julia checked on Ann and the children, then put on her hat and coat and headed down the backstairs. The scent of roasting chicken floated in the air as she passed the kitchen. Chef Lagarde's commands to his helpers almost drowned out the clatter of dishes being washed in the sink.

Julia hurried down the hall. Things were always humming downstairs at Highland. It was quite a contrast to the cultured and peaceful atmosphere upstairs.

Mrs. Emmitt stepped out of her parlor. Surprise filled her eyes. "Miss Foster, where are you going?"

Julia's stomach tensed. "I'm just going into the village."

"At this time of the day? Shouldn't you be with the young ladies?"

"I have a brief errand for Miss Ramsey. I'll take the governess cart and be back within the hour."

"An errand? What kind of errand? Surely she could send one of the footmen."

"No, she asked me to go. It's a private matter."

Mrs. Emmitt pursed her lips. "Very well. But hurry back. It makes no sense to send you to the village when you should be teaching the young ladies."

Julia didn't want to argue, so she didn't answer.

"Well, go on then. You're only wasting time standing here."

Julia nodded to her and hurried off. In matters of the heart there was no time to waste.

Mrs. Emmitt watched Miss Foster leave through the doorway at the end of the lower hall and smiled. This was perfect. With the governess out of the house, she could speak to Sir William without interruption. She hurried upstairs and crossed the great hall. With any luck she could get rid of the thorn in her side and take back her rightful place.

Mr. Lawrence stood at the bottom of the oak staircase conversing with Nelson the footman. He looked up and met her gaze. "Mrs. Emmitt? Is everything all right?"

"I need to speak to Sir William. Is he in the library?"

"He is. But is there something I can help you with?"

She glanced at Nelson and then Mr. Lawrence. "No, thank you. There's something I want to discuss with Sir William."

Mr. Lawrence frowned, obviously perturbed she would not explain herself. But it was not possible with Nelson standing by.

"Very well." He entered the library and announced her, then ushered her in.

Sir William sat at his desk with a book in his hand. He turned as she entered. "Mrs. Emmitt, what can I do for you?"

"I'm sorry to disturb you, sir, but I must speak to you about Miss Foster."

He shifted in his chair, and a slight line creased his forehead. "Is there a problem?"

"Yes, I'm afraid there are quite a few. And with her trial coming to an end soon, I thought you ought to know."

He studied her, his eyes clouding slightly. "I'm surprised to hear it. I had the impression she was doing very well."

A tremor passed through Mrs. Emmitt. She had better tread carefully, or she might end up on the wrong side of the issue. "Well, I don't like to bring you a bad report, but I'm afraid Miss Foster is not getting along well with the young ladies."

"I realize my cousins are not happy about having a governess, but I hoped they would become accustomed to it in time."

Mrs. Emmitt shook her head. "There is contention between Miss Foster and the young ladies every day, and she's become quite forceful in her dealings with them. I'm not comfortable with it, not at all."

His frown deepened. "Forceful? What do you mean?"

"She's very strict, and her expectations for their lessons and behavior are impossibly high. If they question her, she becomes angry and tries to control them with harsh words or mockery."

Sir William rose from his chair. "I find that hard to believe. My sister spends a great deal of time with them, and she's never mentioned any of this."

"Miss Foster would never show her true colors in front of Miss Ramsey."

"So you're saying this is going on behind closed doors?"

Mrs. Emmitt swallowed and nodded. Katherine had promised to back up the story, but what if she changed her mind? Mrs. Emmitt wanted to be rid of the governess, but she didn't want to lose her position over it. "The young ladies have no respect for her, none at all."

"And you believe Miss Foster is at fault, not the girls?"

"It's not a question of fault, sir. I'm afraid Miss Foster is simply too young and inexperienced to handle the position. Her temperament and disposition are not what they seem. I don't believe she is able to give the young ladies the education and guidance they need."

"I don't understand. You were the one who brought her to me. You gave me the impression she was well qualified and had good references."

She gave a curt nod. "Yes sir, I did. And I'm sorry for it now. I should've looked into her background more carefully before I brought her to you."

He clasped his hands behind his back and paced to the window.

Moisture gathered on her forehead as she waited. Had she convinced him? Perhaps she should try a different route. "Sir, I've worked here many years, and I'm very fond of the young ladies. They've been through a very hard time these past few months. I don't like to see them unhappy."

"None of us want that," he said, still facing the windows, his voice as cool and chilly as the weather outdoors.

"Their father entrusted them into your care. You must do what's best for them."

He turned toward her, his expression steely. "I understand my responsibilities toward my cousins, Mrs. Emmitt. I'll look into it."

"Thank you, sir." She nodded to him and walked out of the library. Now she must let Katherine know the plan had been put in motion. If everything went as she hoped, Miss Foster would be gone soon and things could finally get back to normal.

William paced the length of his library and back, brooding over his conversation with Mrs. Emmitt. A dull ache began to pound at the base of his skull. Could it be true? Was Miss Foster harsh with the girls, bullying them when no one was there to see it? She was spirited and spoke her mind, but could she really be that devious?

No. It didn't make sense. This was probably just a case of Katherine and Penelope's trying to discredit Miss Foster by complaining to Mrs. Emmitt. They hoped he would dismiss her, and they could be out from under her supervision. No doubt the housekeeper felt loyalty to the girls, and that was why she brought their complaints to him.

But what if it were true?

He stopped by the fireplace and stared into the flames. He had been fooled before by a woman, and the results had been disastrous. His wife's duplicity flooded his mind, and his chest tightened. Amelia had always been a perfect lady in public, but at home, in private, her true character had driven a stake through his heart.

Surely, Miss Foster was not cruel and deceitful like Amelia, was she?

Doubts swirled through him. It wasn't just Katherine and Penelope who needed his protection. He had placed his children under Miss Foster's care. He must not be fooled again. The price was too high.

He would have to confront Miss Foster and find out if there was any truth behind these complaints. If so, he would put things right for his children's sake as well as his cousins'.

William strode out of the library and mounted the steps. As he passed down the hallway, voices in the nursery drew his attention. He stopped by the door and leaned closer to listen. Perhaps he had come at the right time to learn what truly went on in the nursery between Miss Foster and his children.

"This is how Robin Hood took his stand against the wicked Sheriff of Nottingham!" His son's voice rang out from beyond the nursery door.

"Andrew, come down this minute!"

William frowned. That was not Miss Foster's voice.

"Off with you, you wretched scoundrel!" his son shouted.

"Andrew, stop! You're frightening your sister."

"No! You'll never capture me alive!"

"Please be a good lad and climb down before you break something or hurt yourself."

Enough! William pushed open the door and glared at the nursery maid. "What is going on in here?"

Andrew froze where he stood on the window seat, a toy sword raised high. "Papa!"

The young nursery maid's face turned as pale as her white cap. "Sir." She bobbed a quick curtsy, reached for Andrew's hand, and tugged him down off the window seat. Millicent stood by her dollhouse in the corner, watching them with wide blue-green eyes, her doll clutched to her chest.

"Where is Miss Foster?"

"I believe she's gone to the village on an errand." The maid's voice trembled slightly as she spoke.

He huffed. "And this is what happens when she is away?"

"I'm sorry, sir. Master Andrew was just acting out a story Miss Foster read to the children this morning."

Andrew dashed over to the table and lifted a book for him to see. "It's the *Merry Adventures of Robin Hood*. Have you read it, Papa?"

"No. I have not." William scanned the room, trying to discern if this was an actual problem or just a bit of childish behavior on his son's part.

A few toys were scattered on the table, but everything else looked in good order. He turned to the maid. "When will Miss Foster return?"

"Within the hour, sir." The maid placed a hand on Millicent's shoulder.

"All right." He relaxed his posture and shifted his gaze to Andrew. Perhaps Miss Foster's absence was for the best. "Collect your coat and hat, Andrew. We're going for a walk."

A smile burst on his son's face. "Really? I've been longing to go outdoors, but Ann doesn't like to take us without Miss Foster."

"Help Andrew dress for our walk," William said to the maid. "Then send him downstairs to meet me. And please tell Miss Foster she is to see me as soon as she returns from the village."

"Yes sir." The maid bobbed another quick curtsy, relief evident in her expression.

Five minutes later his son came bounding down the stairs, wearing a wool cap and coat and sturdy leather boots. Nelson opened the front door for them, and William and Andrew set off across the park, following the gravel path.

"So, Andrew, do you often disobey your nurse and climb on the furniture?"

"No sir. I try not to."

"But you did today."

"Yes sir." He scuffed his boots in the gravel. "I was so tired of being in the nursery. We usually go for a walk after luncheon, but it's been raining for three days, and Miss Foster said we couldn't go out. And then today we had to stay in again because she had to go to the village and do something for Aunt Sarah."

"Her errand is for your aunt?"

Andrew nodded and hopped over a puddle. "I'm so glad you came. I hate staying inside all day."

A smile tugged at William's lips. He couldn't help it. He'd been much like Andrew when he was a boy. Though he'd learned to discipline himself and attend to his duties, there was nothing he loved more than tramping through the woods or hiking across the fields. Even these cool autumn days didn't keep him indoors if he could help it.

"So, do you like Miss Foster?"

Andrew wrinkled his nose. "She's all right."

William thought for a moment, wanting to phrase his question carefully. "How does she handle things when you disobey?"

"She doesn't smack me the way Mrs. Lambert did."

William stopped. "Mrs. Lambert smacked you?"

Andrew squinted up at him. "Yes sir. She said it would drive the foolishness from my heart." His son looked down, kicked at a stone, and sent it flying. "But I'm not sure that's true."

"So, what does Miss Foster do when there is a need for discipline?"

"She usually has me sit in the blue chair."

"The blue chair?"

"Yes, the one in the alcove in the upstairs sitting room."

"How long does she make you stay there?"

"She says I may come back when my heart has changed and I'm ready to talk to her about what happened."

"So it's up to you how long you sit in the chair?"

"Yes sir." He bent and picked up a stick at the side of the path.

That didn't sound like very severe discipline. His own nanny had been a gentle, indulgent woman, but his tutor, Mr. Burton, had often used a wooden ruler to slap his hands when he'd been slow to answer or disobedient. "Has Miss Foster ever been rough with you or Millicent?"

Andrew rolled his eyes. "Millie never gets in trouble. All Miss Foster has to do is look at her, and she bursts into tears and begs to make things right."

"So Millicent is never sent to the blue chair?"

Andrew twisted his lips and tapped the ground with the stick. "She had to go there once when she wouldn't eat her luncheon."

"Does Miss Foster insist you eat all your food?"

"Not all. But we must try a bite of each thing on our plate."

"And Millicent wouldn't do that?"

Andrew shook his head. "No, and she cried buckets when Miss Foster sent her to the blue chair. But a few minutes later she came back and hugged Miss Foster and said she was sorry."

William frowned slightly. "That was all the discipline she received?"

Andrew looked up and grinned. "When it was teatime, I had cake and sandwiches, but she had to eat her leftover food from luncheon."

William chuckled. "I suppose she ate it then."

"Yes, all the potatoes and some of the peas and lamb."

"And what about your schooling? What happens if you don't understand your lesson or you give the wrong answer?"

Andrew shrugged. "If I get an arithmetic problem wrong, I have to do it again until I get it right. Miss Foster says we must master our studies, and our mistakes help us learn the right way to do our work."

"But what if you don't know how to do it?"

"She will always show us if we ask, but we still must do the work ourselves."

"What if you become distracted or you're slow to finish an assignment?"

"She won't read aloud or take us on a walk until we're done with our lessons."

William nodded. It all sounded reasonable. No doubt Miss Foster found it easier to work with the children than his two cousins. Could she be kind and sensible with Andrew and Millicent but harsh and mocking toward Katherine and Penelope? That seemed unlikely, but he supposed it was possible.

Katherine could raise his ire in two seconds with her sharp tongue and stubborn ways. Did Miss Foster respond in a similar fashion when Katherine challenged her authority? Was she able to control her temper and accomplish her tasks with the girls? Those were the questions he still needed to answer.

At least Miss Foster seemed to handle his children well. He smiled, thinking of the clever ways she motivated them to obey and do their studies.

Andrew skipped ahead, swinging his stick as though it were a sword. His happy, carefree expression lifted William's spirit. His son needed an intelligent and caring governess, someone strong enough to help shape his will but not damage his spirit. Miss Foster seemed to fit the bill, but he would need to spend more time with the children to be sure.

When he lived in London he used to see the children every day after tea for an hour. But since Amelia's passing it had been too painful, and he had let the children's hour fade from his routine. Perhaps it was time to begin again. Then he could watch Miss Foster interact with them, observe their behavior, and hear more about their schooling.

He chuckled to himself. Wasn't that exactly what Miss Foster had asked him to do?

Eleven

Julia removed her hat and coat and hung them on the hook in her room. She took a quick glance in the mirror and shook her head. Taking some hairpins from her dresser, she tucked a few strands back in place, then checked her reflection once more. Her cheeks were flushed from her ride to the village, and her eyes glowed with the knowledge she'd gained in her conversation with Reverend Langford.

Sarah would be pleased to hear that the reverend considered Mr. Dalton a good man, wise and spiritually mature. He also reported he was loyal and caring toward his mother and young niece. But sharing that news with Sarah would have to wait until this evening, when the children were safely tucked in bed. It was almost four, and Ann and the children were waiting for her.

A knock sounded at her door, and she hurried to answer.

Nelson stood in the hall wearing a slight smile.

"Sir William wants to see you in the drawing room."

Her stomach fluttered. "Sir William?" Why would he call her downstairs?

"Yes. The young ladies and Mrs. Emmitt are already there." Nelson's expression turned smug. "You'd best be prepared for battle. They don't look too happy."

Julia swallowed as her mind raced ahead. Was she being summoned to help resolve the issues between Sarah and Katherine? If so, why would Mrs. Emmitt be there? What did she have to do with it?

A tremor raced up her back as she followed Nelson downstairs and into the drawing room. William stood by the fireplace, his expression sober. Penelope and Katherine sat on the settee facing him, while Mrs. Emmitt stood behind the settee where the girls were seated.

William turned to Julia. "Come in, please."

Julia nodded to the girls and Mrs. Emmitt and then William. "You wanted to see me, sir?"

"Yes. Your one-month trial has come to an end, and there are some matters to discuss before I decide if you are to continue in your position."

Julia's heartbeat sped up. "Oh . . . well, I've become very fond of the children, and I believe the young ladies are making good progress." She tried to infuse her voice with confidence, but it wavered slightly.

"Unfortunately, Katherine and Penelope are not happy with your interaction with them."

Julia shot a quick glance at the girls. Katherine lifted her chin and looked away, her expression stony. Penelope lowered her head and stared at her clasped hands. "I'm sorry to hear that. I know the transition has not been easy for them. Is there a specific problem you'd like to discuss?"

"I believe it's more your general manner of dealing with them that is in question."

Julia lifted her hand to her heart. "My general manner? I'm not sure I understand what you mean."

William motioned to Katherine. "Please explain your concerns to Miss Foster."

Katherine focused her cool gaze on Julia. "Penelope and I are not accustomed to being berated and cruelly treated, and we won't stand for it any longer."

A tremor shot through Julia. "As your governess, I must correct you at times, but I don't believe I've been cruel, and I certainly would never berate you."

"But that's exactly what you've done." She elbowed her sister. "Isn't that right, Penny?"

The younger girl looked up. "Well, she does correct us during our lessons."

"Of course she does. That is her job." William's frown deepened. "What we are trying to ascertain is how she treats you when correction is needed."

Penelope bit her lip. "I know we try her patience some days."

"Why do you say that?"

"Sometimes she excuses herself and says she must go pray for a few minutes before she can continue."

Katherine's eyes flashed, and she glared at her sister.

"Go on. What else does she do when you or Katherine have been difficult."

Katherine sprang from the settee. "I'll tell you what she does. Yesterday she grabbed my arm and shoved me into a chair!"

Julia gasped. "I never did such a thing! Why would you say that?"

Katherine turned to her sister. "You were there. You saw it. Tell them."

Penelope stared at her sister, her mouth hardening.

"Penelope, did you see Miss Foster push your sister?"

She lowered her gaze and shook her head. "No sir. I did not."

Katherine huffed and scowled at her sister. "You know it's true. You're just afraid to say it."

"I am not! I did not see her push you, and I won't say it just to please you." Penelope shifted and looked up at William. "When we need correction, Miss Foster usually quotes a Bible verse and explains what we ought to do."

178

William narrowed his gaze at the girls. "I don't see anything wrong with that, do you?"

Katherine jutted her chin forward. "It's her manner that is upsetting. She instructs us to be humble and teachable, yet she is harsh and says the most unkind things."

William lifted one eyebrow. "Such as?"

Katherine's face flushed, and she sat down again. "I don't know. I can't remember. But I am very tired of her demanding we rise so early and follow the schedule she has set for the day. She is a member of the staff, and we should not have to adjust our lives to fit in with her wishes."

William sighed. "Katherine, we've already discussed this. Miss Foster's schedule was created so she could teach my children as well as you and your sister. Rising early to be present for Scripture reading and prayer is a good way for you to start the day. That is my request as well as Miss Foster's."

"I don't agree, but that is not the point. She is strict and spiteful, and I suspect she treats your children the same way when no one is looking."

Fire flashed through Julia. "That is not true! I've never been unkind to them. Ask Ann or the children if you must."

William held up his hand, obviously intending to calm the situation. "I already have, and I'm quite satisfied with the answers I've received."

He shifted his steely gaze from Katherine to the housekeeper. "I believe I understand the situation now. Mrs. Emmitt, before you go, I'd like you to assure me that from now on you will only report what you've seen yourself and not rely on secondhand stories."

Mrs. Emmitt's cheeks flushed and she pursed her lips. "Very well, sir."

"You may go."

She gave a curt nod and strode toward the door, looking as though she would boil over at any second.

William turned to his younger cousin. "Penelope, I appreciate your honesty. Thank you. That takes courage. You may go as well."

She gave him a slight smile, then rose from the settee and left the room.

William crossed and stood in front of Katherine. "I'm very disappointed by what's happened here today. I believe you owe Miss Foster an apology."

Katherine's nostril's flared. "I don't owe her anything."

The muscles in William's jaw jumped. "You will apologize to Miss Foster, or I will cancel the dinner party next week."

Katherine gasped and jumped up. "You can't do that! It's my eighteenth birthday. That dinner has been planned for months."

"I most certainly can, and I will if you don't settle the matter now and promise me there will be no more false accusations."

Katherine turned her glare on Julia, the message

clear: *This is your fault. I wish you had never come to Highland.* Tears flooded her eyes. "How could you be so cruel?"

Julia gasped and stared at Katherine.

"Don't try to blame Miss Foster. You brought this problem on yourself. But if you will admit your accusations are false and apologize, then your dinner party may go on as planned. If not, you will be spending a very quiet birthday alone in your room."

Katherine's expression crumbled, and she sat down again as she lifted her hand to shield her eyes from them.

Julia's heart softened as she watched her—caught in her own lie, humiliated, and obviously still grieving. "Perhaps Katherine needs some time."

William's gaze shifted to Julia. She sent him a slight smile, hoping he would understand she was ready to forgive and would carry no hard feelings toward Katherine.

His tense expression eased. "I suppose that's true."

"Perhaps she could write a letter of apology. That's an important skill to learn, and it would allow her time to compose her thoughts."

William thought for a moment, then nodded. "Yes, a letter of apology is an excellent idea." He shifted his gaze to Katherine. "Are you willing to do that?"

She shrugged one shoulder, her expression still sullen. "I suppose."

"The letter must be sincere and well written, and there is one more thing I would like you to include."

Katherine frowned. "What?"

"An invitation for Miss Foster to be a guest at your birthday dinner."

Julia froze, and her gaze flashed to Sir William.

Katherine's eyes widened. "But that's not possible. The guest list is—"

William held up his hand to silence her. "I'm sure there is room to include Miss Foster, and after what went on here today, I believe it's important for you to offer a gesture of good will as well as an apology."

Katherine rose from the settee, her hands clenched at her side and her face flushed. "May I go?"

"Yes, but Miss Foster must receive your letter tomorrow morning before nine o'clock when we gather in the great hall."

Katherine's defiant gaze darted from William to Julia, then she turned and left the room.

Julia released the breath she had been holding, but her stomach remained in a tense knot. "I'm so sorry. I wish there was some way—"

"Please, there's no need to say any more about it."

"Do you think she'll write the letter?"

"I doubt she would give up her dinner party just to make a point . . . especially one based on a lie."

"Yes, I suppose that's true." She studied him, her stomach easing. "I'm grateful for the way you handled the situation. You showed a great deal of wisdom."

He gave a slight nod, and his face flushed slightly, as though he was surprised by her praise. "Katherine is headstrong. I'm afraid she's destined for trouble unless she learns to be honest and more caring toward others. Prompting her to include you in the dinner should help her move in that direction."

Julia nodded, though she wasn't sure the dinner invitation would draw her and Katherine any closer.

William's gaze lingered on her, his expression warming. "My children seem to be doing very well in your care. Andrew's behavior has improved, and Millicent hasn't had any issues with her health since you arrived. I'm pleased."

"Thank you. I believe we are making good progress."

He nodded. "My cousins will come around in time."

"I hope so." She hesitated, her stomach tensing again, but for a different reason this time. "Sir, there is something else I should tell you."

"What is it?"

"I should've given you this information during my interview, but I was a bit flustered, and I wasn't sure what the outcome of the one-month trial would be." She swallowed, reluctant to continue.

His dark eyebrows lowered. "Go on."

"I am very fond of the children, and I'm grateful for this position. But if my father's health improves and he regains his strength, our family plans to return to India."

His face fell. "You would leave us?"

Her breath caught in her throat.

He grimaced and held up his hand. "I'm sorry. That was not what I meant to say."

But the vulnerability of his comment pierced her heart. Suddenly, the truth rushed through her. She did not wish to leave him or the children, but the time might come when that was necessary. It would be best for her to prepare him—and herself—for that possibility.

She looked up. "I believe we have a calling from God, and if He answers our prayers and restores my father's health, then we must follow that call back to India."

"You speak of *we* as if that tie to your parents is the only claim on your heart."

"I know of no other claim . . . except that of my commitment to the Lord, and it is He who called us."

His expression turned brooding. "Very well.

Thank you for the warning." Sarcasm laced his words, but she heard the hurt beneath them.

She bit her lip, trying to think of a way to ease his mind. "Sir, I have no idea what the future may bring. I pray my father's health improves, but even then, we would have to raise the necessary finances and make the arrangements. It would be several months before we could leave. I'm sure you would have time to find a replacement."

"Finding a replacement is not the point."

"I'm sorry. I don't mean to disappoint you."

"I am not disappointed. It's simply time consuming to find a decent and sensible governess. I've no desire to start that process again."

Her heart dropped. Was that the only problem—finding someone decent and sensible to replace her? She schooled her expression and pressed the hurt down deeper in her heart.

"I'm finished discussing this. You may go." He waved her away as though she were no more than an irritating fly.

She gave him a slight nod, then turned and strode toward the door, leaving him there to brood alone.

The next morning William glared out the library window as rain splattered against the glass. The darkening sky cast gloomy shadows around the room, while the wind blew around the casings with an eerie whistle.

Blasted storm! He would have to send a note to McTavish and postpone their meeting to inspect the stable roof and discuss the needed repairs. No one should be climbing ladders in weather like this. It also meant he would have to stay in and spend the rest of the morning finishing the work at his desk.

With a weary sigh, he focused on the ledger, but the numbers blurred before his eyes. He hated being cooped up indoors almost as much as his son did. Thoughts of Andrew quickly turned to thoughts of Miss Foster. He shoved his ledger aside and rose from his chair.

Would she actually leave them and return to India? She said she would give him several months' notice, but one month or six, he didn't like the idea of her sailing off across the ocean. The whole thing left him feeling very unsettled.

Of course he admired her determination and commitment to her faith. But did that mean she had to leave Highland? Couldn't she stay and serve God by helping him care for his children and cousins?

Miss Foster didn't seem to have a problem with leaving—no hesitation, no regret. Well, she was made of sterner stuff than he had realized.

Not many men or women of his acquaintance would be willing to leave the comforts of England for the challenges of missionary life in a foreign country, especially not the life she had described:

caring for poor villagers and rescuing girls from lives of abuse in heathen temples. He sighed and shook his head.

How could he resent her for desiring to go and do such important work? Caring for his two children and preparing his cousins for the season wasn't nearly as significant as her life in India.

He crossed to the window and stared out through the drizzling rain. He had to admit he'd been wounded by her announcement. How quickly she had become an important part of their lives. He had come to depend on her for more than just overseeing the children and his cousins. Their discussions in the evenings had been stimulating, especially as she related stories of her experiences in India and how they had shaped her faith. She brought her spirituality into her everyday life in a way that intrigued and challenged him.

If she left, it would mean another loss for him and his children, but he did want what was best for Miss Foster. She deserved that, even if it meant freeing her to travel halfway around the world . . . leaving him and his family far behind.

Twelve

Julia ran her hand down her dress's silky lavender sash. "It's so lovely." She looked up and smiled at her reflection in Sarah's bedroom mirror. The lavender underdress was partially covered by a sheer plum overdress decorated with sparkling silver beading. And from each fluttering sleeve hung a shimmering plum tassel—the perfect finishing touch to the exquisite evening gown.

"The dress is pretty, but you are the one who looks lovely." Sarah stood behind Julia, a happy light in her eyes as she gazed into the mirror.

"Thank you, Sarah. I don't know what I would've worn tonight if you hadn't let me borrow this dress."

"I'm happy to do it. The color is perfect with your dark hair and fair complexion. It looks as if it were made for you."

"You're so kind."

"Well, it's true. And I'm sure you will outshine Katherine and every other lady at the table."

Julia shook her head and stepped away from the mirror. "I have no desire to outshine Katherine or anyone else."

This was the first time she had been invited to dine with William and his family and guests. Just the thought of it made her stomach quiver. Her conversation skills and table manners would carry her through the evening, but what would William think when he saw her dressed this way? Would he be pleased?

Sarah adjusted a pin in her hair, a merry light still shining in her eyes. "We have fourteen guests tonight, and three of them are eligible bachelors—four if you include my brother." Sarah tipped her head and smiled at Julia. "Perhaps one of them will want to become better acquainted with you."

Julia's cheeks warmed, and she laughed softly. "I'm sure the gentlemen attending tonight's dinner would not be interested in a former missionary who now works as a governess."

"And why not? Missionary and governess are both noble occupations."

"Perhaps, but I am sure they would all consider me a middle-class spinster."

"No, you're much too young to be considered a spinster."

"I'm almost twenty-eight and well past the age when most young women marry."

Sarah's expression faltered. "You are younger

than I am by two years, and I don't consider myself too old to marry."

Julia reached for Sarah's hand. "Of course not. Love can come at any age. But my circumstances are different from yours. I doubt I will ever marry."

"Why would you say that, Julia?"

"My broken engagement has taught me many lessons."

"Such as?"

"The pain of a broken heart is not easily mended. When Richard Green returned to England and left me behind, taking all my dreams for marriage and family with him, my confidence was shattered, and a cloud of despair settled over me for several months. My parents counseled me to forgive him and accept the Lord's will in the situation, but I couldn't seem to release the hurt or anger. Finally, one morning, the Lord broke through my gloom and spoke to me very clearly."

"Really? What did He say?"

"I didn't hear an audible voice but sensed a very clear impression in my heart. He asked if I was willing to release all my sorrow and pain and let Him carry them for me. Would I let Him safeguard my heart and trust Him with my future?"

Tears glistened in Sarah's eyes, and she tightened her hold on Julia's hand.

"He was so tender and kind I couldn't say no. So I gave it all to Him. It was a costly, painful offering, but with acceptance came peace and the release of my sorrows."

Sarah brushed a tear from the corner of her eye. "How wonderful to hear from the Lord like that and receive His comfort, but I hope you won't give up on the possibility of love and marriage. You would make a wonderful wife and mother. You do want to marry, don't you?"

Julia swallowed and looked away. Of course, that was what she had always wanted, more than anything else. But it seemed the Lord had closed that door and was directing her toward a single life where she would use her skills as a teacher to serve Him and help others. Still, the desire for love and marriage and her own children hadn't vanished from her heart, especially since she had come to Highland. She pushed those thoughts away and adjusted her sash. "How are things going with Mr. Dalton?"

Sarah's smile returned. "We see each other often in the greenhouse or his office . . . but we haven't spoken to William yet."

Julia turned to Sarah. "Do you think that's wise?"

"I'm not sure. My feelings for Mr. Dalton grow stronger every day, and I hate to keep our courtship a secret, but my brother is very traditional and not one to go against social customs."

"I'm sure your happiness means more to him than what others think."

"I hope so, but I'm afraid when he hears about it, he'll be upset and say something harsh to Mr. Dalton."

"What if you spoke to him first, without Mr. Dalton being present. That would give him time to consider the situation before he meets with Mr. Dalton."

"I know I should, but I'm not sure how I'll find the courage to do it. William has always been my protector, and I don't want to go against his wishes."

Julia reached for Sarah's hand again. "Do you love Mr. Dalton?"

"Yes." Her dark brown eyes glowed with warmth. "I believe I do."

"Then don't let fear of your brother's disapproval steal your chance for a future with Mr. Dalton. Gather your courage and speak to your brother soon."

Tears glistened in Sarah's eyes. "Oh, Julia, you are such a dear." She squeezed her hand. "Thank you so much."

Julia smiled and had to blink away the moisture in her own eyes. "Please, there is no need to thank me. I feel blessed to find a friend like you."

Sarah laughed softly and stepped back. "Look at us. We will go down to dinner with red eyes and glowing noses if we aren't careful." She took two handkerchiefs from the top drawer of her dressing table and handed one to Julia.

Julia wiped her eyes and looked in the mirror

once more. Catching Sarah's reflection, she smiled. "You look very pretty, Sarah. I believe our conversation has put some extra color in your cheeks."

Sarah dabbed her nose. "It's your skill with arranging my hair that makes the difference."

"That and your new confidence and lovely smile."

Sarah pulled open the top drawer of her dressing table. "There's one more thing you need." She took out an amethyst necklace and held it out to Julia. "This was my mother's."

"Oh no. I couldn't."

"Please." Sarah placed the necklace in Julia's hand. "It would make me so happy to see you wear it."

Julia examined the silver filigree with tiny diamonds and teardrop pearls surrounding the oval amethyst. "It's the most exquisite necklace I've ever seen."

Sarah smiled. "It always makes me feel like a princess when I put it on."

Julia held it out to Sarah. "You should wear it tonight."

"It doesn't go with my dress." Sarah took a long strand of pearls from her drawer. "I'm going to wear these." She slipped the necklace over her head. "There, how does that look?" With Sarah's glossy brown hair and fair complexion, the pearls were a perfect choice.

"You look beautiful."

Sarah smiled her thanks. "So you'll wear the necklace?"

"Do you think Sir William would mind?"

"Not at all. He'll be pleased."

"All right, if you're sure." Julia fastened the necklace and adjusted it to center the jewels.

"That looks perfect." Sarah checked her hair and smoothed her hand over one section. "Are you ready to go down?"

"Yes, thanks to you." Julia took one last glance in the mirror and gently touched the amethyst necklace. "I do rather feel like a princess in a fairy tale." If only there were a handsome prince waiting to meet her at the bottom of the stairs. She quickly banished that thought.

"All right then. Let's go enjoy the evening." Sarah looped her arm through Julia's, and they set off.

William walked down the stairs and met Lawrence in the great hall. "Is my tie all right? Nelson nearly gagged me when he tied it, and I'm not sure it's even." William lifted his chin and faced the butler.

Lawrence narrowed his eyes. "I'll adjust it for you, sir." He gave one side a tug. "There, now it's even."

"Thank you." William straightened his jacket and glanced around. "So, is everything ready for dinner?"

"Yes sir. We're awaiting the arrival of your guests." The butler glanced up the steps. "And the ladies of the house, of course."

William smiled. "Yes, the young ladies often like to make a special entrance, but I'm not sure why Sarah isn't down yet." A flash of purple in the gallery above caught his eye. He turned and looked up. Sarah and Miss Foster descended the stairs. As they reached the lower landing, Miss Foster came fully in view, and his eyes widened.

She wore a stunning purple gown dotted with silver beads that sparkled in the gaslight. Her dark brown hair was fashioned in a much more elaborate style than she usually wore, and around her neck hung his mother's amethyst and pearl necklace. The transformation was . . . amazing.

She smiled at him, her blue eyes sparkling. "Good evening, sir."

William swallowed and nodded.

"Doesn't she look lovely?" Sarah prompted.

"Why . . . yes. You look very nice, Miss Foster."

She looked down, her dark lashes fanning against her flushed cheeks. "Thank you."

"Lady Gatewood has arrived, sir." Lawrence pulled open the heavy oak-and-glass door leading to the entrance hall.

Louisa Gatewood waltzed in, removed her cape topped with a white fur collar, and handed it to one of the footmen.

"Good evening, Lady Gatewood. It's good of you to join us."

"Of course. I wouldn't miss my niece's eighteenth birthday dinner." She scanned the room and her forehead creased. "Where is Katherine? She ought to be here to greet her guests."

Sarah glanced toward the stairs. "I'm sure she and Penelope will be down soon."

Lady Gatewood ignored Sarah and shifted her severe gaze to Miss Foster. "It is your duty to see that the girls are ready for an important dinner like this. I don't understand why you've come down without them."

Miss Foster's face paled. "I'm sorry. I didn't think—"

"Yes, that is the problem."

William stepped forward. "See here, there's no need to scold Miss Foster. The girls have a maid to help them dress, and they are old enough to be aware of the time."

"Of course they have a maid, but they also have a governess, and it is her duty to prepare them for social events." Her gaze shifted from Julia to William. "And I might add, I am quite surprised that Miss Foster has been—"

William had heard enough. "Please, Lady Gatewood, I am certainly capable of overseeing my own household. I do not need your instruction or permission to choose my dinner guests."

Lady Gatewood's mouth tightened. "There's no need to take offense. I simply wanted you to be aware of how things are done at Highland."

Heat flooded William's neck and face. The woman's audacity was unbelievable. He'd had more than enough of her meddling in his family's affairs.

Miss Foster looked up at him. "I can go check on the young ladies if you would like." Her expression and tone gave no hint that she had been slighted, but the color staining her cheeks made it clear that Lady Gatewood's comments had hit their mark.

Sarah turned toward the staircase. "It's all right. They're coming now."

"Miss Katherine Ramsey and Miss Penelope Ramsey," Nelson announced from the gallery, and they turned to watch the girls descend the stairs.

Katherine appeared first, wearing a dark red dress decorated with black lace and beads. The silky material and slim silhouette made her look quite grown-up. Two large feathers had been pinned to the back of her hairstyle. He thought the feathers looked rather ridiculous, but he had seen many women wear them in London. Katherine gave a well-practiced smile as she reached the lower landing.

Penelope came down next, wearing a jade green dress with a fringe at the hem. With flushed cheeks and a pretty smile, she looked eagerly around the group, obviously hoping for their approval.

Their aunt greeted each of them with a kiss on the cheek and compliments on their entrance. Sarah joined them, but Miss Foster hung back, a touch of unease in her expression.

No doubt Lady Gatewood's thoughtless words caused her hesitation. *Irritating woman!* He wished he could ban her from the house, but she was the only close connection his cousins had with their mother's side of the family.

It was unusual to include a governess in a dinner party like this, but why *shouldn't* Miss Foster be invited? She had many admirable qualities, and she was certainly prettier than any of the other women attending the dinner. If it were up to him, he would seat her in the place of honor on his right and see that she enjoyed the evening. But he had not thought to check the seating arrangements, and they could not be changed at this point.

He would have to look for some other way to support Miss Foster and see that she was treated well and enjoyed the evening.

Ann held her breath and crept down the back-stairs. If she could just get past Mrs. Emmitt's parlor and the kitchen, then she should be able to sneak out the back door without anyone seeing her. Mr. Lawrence and the footmen were upstairs in the dining room, preparing to serve dinner, so she shouldn't run into them.

She slipped her hand in her apron pocket and wrapped her trembling fingers around the note Peter had given her that morning. He had passed it to her when she had gone out back after breakfast to put Andrew's broken stool in the burn barrel. Just as she turned around to head back to the house, Peter stepped out of the stables and hurried across the courtyard toward her.

"Meet me tonight," he whispered, then pressed the note into her hand and jogged back to the stables.

The sweet sentiments he had written melted her heart like wax before a flame. And though it was risky, she made up her mind to find him as soon as she could get away.

And why shouldn't she? Julia had borrowed a lovely dress and gone to dinner with Sir William and his guests. She wouldn't be back for at least two hours, and the children were fast asleep. No one needed her, and no one should care if she enjoyed a little time with Peter.

Conversation floated out from the kitchen where Chef Lagarde directed his helpers in the final dinner preparations.

Ann pressed her back against the wall and stole down the hall. Biting her lip, she slowly pushed open the heavy back door, thankful it was well oiled. The cool evening air washed over her warm cheeks, and she released the breath she had been holding. Overhead a full moon bathed the courtyard in silvery light. Keeping to the shadows, she made her way around the side of the house, careful not to topple the milk crates stacked near the alcove.

A cat howled. Ann slapped a hand over her mouth to stifle her own startled cry. She counted to ten, placed her hand over her heart, and tried to calm her racing emotions. It was all right. No one would see her. She would make sure of it.

After a few more seconds, she crept toward the stable, where a light glowed through the window and flowed out under the large, wooden sliding door. Peter waited for her there. Her heartbeat sped up, not in fear, but in anticipation of seeing him again.

A footstep crunched on the gravel behind her. Her heart jumped to her throat, and she froze.

A hand wrapped around her arm.

She gasped and tried to pull away, but the man grabbed her other arm.

She screamed and flailed about, trying to break free.

The stable door flew open. Peter burst out, his eyes blazing. "Let her go!"

Julia adjusted the napkin in her lap and took a small bite of the roasted potatoes. They tasted fine, but she had lost her appetite. With a sigh, she set her fork aside. She had come down to dinner hoping she would be welcomed like the rest of the guests, but Katherine had seated her at the far corner of the long table, next to Lady Mildred Covington, the mother of one of Katherine's closest friends. The elegant, silver-haired woman hadn't spoken one word to her since they had been introduced. Instead, she had directed all her conversation to the gentleman on her left. Lady Mildred's elderly husband sat across from Julia. He had nodded to her a few times, but conversation was impossible since he was quite deaf. The only saving grace was that Sarah sat beside her at the end of the table.

Julia leaned forward slightly and looked to the opposite end of the table, where William was enjoying a lively conversation with Miss Theresa Farmington on his left and Dr. Matthew Hadley on his right.

William looked up and glanced Julia's way. Their gazes held for an extra second. A slight line creased the area between his dark eyebrows.

Julia looked away and sat back, hoping he had not read the disappointment in her eyes. She appreciated the invitation to dinner and the chance to wear Sarah's lovely gown and necklace, but clothes and jewels could not erase the huge chasm that separated her from the other guests at the table.

Three seats down, on the opposite side of the table, Lady Gatewood smiled at her eldest niece, who was sitting across from her. "Katherine has made wonderful progress in preparation for the season. I'm sure she'll be well received in London."

"Thank you, Aunt Louisa. Your guidance has been very helpful." Katherine turned to her sister. "Isn't that true, Penelope?"

Penelope nodded and tried to smile, but she had just taken a big bite and was chewing furiously.

Lady Gatewood sent Penelope a disapproving glance.

The critical words Lady Gatewood had spoken earlier rose in Julia's mind, turning her stomach into a churning stew.

Sarah leaned toward her. "Is everything all right? You've barely touched this course."

"I'm sorry. Everything is delicious, but I'm already full."

Sarah squeezed her hand under the table. "There's just one more course. Then perhaps we can enjoy conversation in the drawing room with some of the other guests."

Julia nodded and forced a smile.

Lady Covington looked across the table at Lady Gatewood. "I was so sorry to hear the Hartfords will have to sell Pipewell Hall. It's such a lovely home."

Lady Gatewood's eyebrows rose. "Really? I hadn't heard."

"Yes, Rose Hartford told me about it herself this very morning. They'll have to move into town and live in their London house year-round."

Lady Gatewood cringed. "Oh dear, how dreadful. Why do they have to sell?"

"After Reginald's father died, the upkeep and expenses became too much for them."

Lady Gatewood sighed. "What a shame. How terrible for Rose and Reginald."

"Yes, this puts their oldest son Charles in a very awkward position this season. I'm afraid he'll have a difficult time finding a bride, considering his reduced circumstances."

"Yes, how true." Lady Gatewood sent a pointed look William's way. "An aristocrat with no land drops to the very bottom of society. It reflects poorly on the entire family."

William's face reddened, and he stared at his plate.

Julia's heart went out to William. Did Lady Gatewood or any of the other guests know about his financial struggles? What would they say if they did?

Mr. Lawrence walked into the dining room carrying a small silver tray. He leaned down and spoke to William in a hushed tone. William nodded, and both he and the butler looked her way.

Julia stilled.

Mr. Lawrence approached. "A message for you, Miss Foster."

"For me?"

Mr. Lawrence nodded and extended the tray toward her.

"Thank you." She picked up the envelope and immediately recognized her mother's hand-writing. A cold wave of dread flooded her, and she turned to Sarah. "Please excuse me."

Concern flashed in Sarah's eyes. "Of course."

Clutching the envelope, Julia rose from her chair and walked into the great hall. Her fingers trembled as she tore open the envelope and took out the folded note.

Dearest Julia,

Your father has taken a turn, and his condition has become much more serious. I've sent a message to London and asked Jonathan to come home. I believe you should also come as soon as possible. Please do not delay.

All my love, Mother

Julia pressed her lips together and lowered her head. *Dear God, please have mercy.*

William strode into the great hall. "Is everything all right?"

She lifted her head. "My mother has asked me to come home." Her throat swelled, and she could not continue. She passed him the note.

His dark eyebrows knit as he read the message. "You must go at once."

"May I take the governess cart?"

"No. I will drive you."

"But what about your dinner guests?"

"I'm sure Lady Gatewood will be more than happy to take charge." He looked toward the dining room. "I'll make our excuses, then get the car. Collect your coat and whatever else you might need, and meet me out front."

Julia nodded, gratefulness rising to fill her heart. "Thank you."

His serious expression eased, and he nodded to her. "No thanks are needed. I'm glad to help."

Thirteen

Light from the open stable door flooded the back courtyard. Clark Dalton squinted at the squirming maid who wrestled against him.

Peter Gates ran toward them from the stable. "I said, let her go!"

Clark dropped his hold and pulled in a ragged breath as he recognized the young woman. "Ann! What are you doing sneaking around out here?"

Her wide-eyed gaze darted from Peter to Clark. "I'm just—"

"There's no need to answer him." Peter moved to Ann's side. "Why did you grab hold of her like that?"

Clark met Peter's hard gaze. "I couldn't tell who it was in the dark. I thought she was a thief."

Peter scoffed. "Oh yes, she looks like a thief, doesn't she?" His accusing frown deepened. "And why are you lurking about the courtyard?"

"Some of my tools have gone missing from the

greenhouse, and I've been hoping to catch whoever stole them."

"It's not me!" Ann's voice rose to a panicked pitch. "I've no reason to take gardening tools."

Clark huffed and straightened his jacket. "I suppose not. But you've still not explained why you're out here at this time of night."

Ann shot another anxious glance at Peter, and her chin began to tremble.

Peter slipped his arm around her shoulder. "We've no need to explain anything to you."

So he hadn't found his thief, but he had stumbled on two sweethearts meeting in secret. "What would Mrs. Emmitt say if she knew about this?"

Ann gasped. "Oh please, don't say anything to her. She'll sack me for sure."

"You ought to have thought about that before you came down."

"Nothing's happened!" Peter dropped his arm from Ann's shoulder. "We've done nothing to be ashamed of. You've no call to report us to anyone."

Clark folded his arms and looked from Ann to Peter. This put him in a difficult spot. He knew what it was like to keep his feelings hidden. It was past time to bring his secret courtship with Sarah into the light, but she had asked him to wait a few more days. Why hadn't she spoken up? Was she ashamed of him or afraid her brother would dismiss him and cast her out?

He could find a new position if he had to. But if it came to that, would Sarah be willing to give up her home and family and go with him?

He looked Peter in the eye. "You should not go on meeting in secret. If you're sincere, go to Mr. Lawrence and ask for permission to court Ann openly."

"I can't do that! I'd lose my job."

Ann gasped, and tears flooded her eyes.

"I'm sorry, Ann. I do care for you, but I can't go to Mr. Lawrence."

"But I thought you loved me."

"I do . . . but I can't risk losing my position and being sent off without a reference. I've only been here a short time. My dad would never let me come home. He'd disown me if I lost this job."

"Oh, Peter!" Ann burst into tears and ran back toward the house.

Clark's spirit sank as he watched her jerk open the back door and duck inside.

Peter glared at Clark. "Now look what you've done! Why couldn't you leave us alone?"

"Because it's not right. If you're not planning to marry the girl, then you ought not to be leading her on."

Peter took a step toward Clark, his eyes blazing. "I've had enough of your pious talk." He jabbed his finger into Clark's chest. "You've no right to say anything to me. I know what you've been up to with Sarah Ramsey. She might be a cripple, but she's—"

Clark grabbed his shirt and yanked him up. "Don't you dare say another word about Miss Ramsey!" He gave the boy a fierce shake. "Do you hear me?"

"Put me down!"

Clark released him and sent him scrambling back. "If you say anything to anyone about me and Miss Ramsey, you'll regret it."

"You're in no position to be making threats." Peter turned and stormed off toward the stables.

Clark closed his eyes, his heart pounding in his chest. If Peter Gates knew their secret, how long before Sir William found out?

William peered through the windshield and guided his car down the narrow lane. It was barely wide enough for them to get by, but he had come this far and he would deliver Miss Foster safely to her door.

She leaned forward. "My parent's cottage is just up ahead on the left."

He rolled to a stop in front of the thatched-roof home with whitewashed walls and neat black shutters. Soft light glowed in the two front windows, issuing a warm welcome.

Miss Foster reached for her satchel at her feet.

"Let me get the door for you." He left the motor running while he circled the car and opened her door. "I'll drive on and find somewhere to park. I don't want to block the lane." He offered her his hand.

She took it and climbed out. But rather than turning toward the house, she looked up at him. She tightened her gloved fingers around his. "Thank you, sir. Thank you for bringing me home."

He stood very still, gazing down at her. Silvery moonlight highlighted the soft curve of her cheek and the slight dip above her full, upper lip. He swallowed and forced himself to focus on her eyes again. "It's no trouble at all. My only regret is that it could not be for a happier occasion."

She shivered and slipped her hand from his. Her blue wool scarf had come unwrapped. He reached out and gently tucked an end around her neck and over her shoulder. "Now, hurry inside before you freeze."

"Yes sir." She sent him a brave smile, then walked toward the house. When she reached the door, she stopped and looked over her shoulder.

The sweetness of her expression moved him in ways he didn't understand. He nodded to her and walked back to the car.

Had that been affection he had seen reflected in her eyes, or simply gratitude? He shook off the question. Surely it was just the emotion of the evening stirring them both in unusual ways.

He must not think there was anything more to it. The inclination to trust his feelings had cost him dearly in the past, and he did not wish to travel that painful path again. But this time it was not Miss Foster whom he feared could not be trusted—it was more his own failures as a husband and father that made him hesitate. His skills in family relationships were definitely lacking. Miss Foster herself had said as much.

No, he must not consider the possibility of anything more than friendship with Miss Foster.

A few minutes later, with the car safely parked at the end of the lane, he knocked on the cottage front door and waited with his hat in his hands.

Julia answered and ushered him inside. He glanced around the cozy kitchen and parlor, where flames crackled and glowed in a stone fireplace. A middle-aged woman with kind eyes and a gentle smile approached from the parlor. She wore a simple dark blue dress and looked very much like an older version of Julia.

"Mother, I'd like you to meet Sir William Ramsey, baronet of Highland Hall. Sir William, this is my mother, Mary Foster."

Mrs. Foster sent him a bittersweet smile and offered him her hand. "I'm very pleased to meet you, Sir William."

"The pleasure is mine. Your daughter has spoken very highly of both you and your husband."

"Thank you for bringing Julia home. It will be a great comfort to have her here, even for a short time."

"She may stay as long as you need her."

Mrs. Foster's serene expression faltered. "That's very kind of you, but I don't want to keep her from her duties at Highland."

"We have come to rely on her, but there's no need to make a decision about that tonight. How is Dr. Foster?"

Tears glittered in Mrs. Foster's eyes. "He has a fever and troubled breathing as well as a terrible cough. I'm afraid he seems to be fading. I wasn't sure about contacting my son and Julia, but as I prayed about it, I felt the Lord impress that need on my heart."

He nodded. "Would you like me to send for our physician, Dr. Matthew Hadley? He happens to be having dinner at Highland this evening. I'd be happy to drive back and take the message myself."

Mrs. Foster glanced at Julia and then turned back to him. "Thank you, Sir William. We would appreciate that very much."

"I'm glad to do it, and I insist on paying the fee for his visit."

A knock sounded at the door. "Excuse me." Mrs. Foster stepped away.

"Thank you," Julia said softly. "We're indebted to you for your kindness."

Mrs. Foster pulled open the door and gasped. "Bea? Oh my goodness, is it really you?"

William and Julia turned toward the door.

"Yes, my dearest Mary, it is!"

The two women embraced, and Mrs. Foster welcomed her visitor into the house. She turned to William and Julia. "Bea, this is Sir William Ramsey, baronet of Highland Hall, and this is my daughter, Julia." Mrs. Foster clasped Bea's hand. "Julia, this is my sister Beatrice, Lady Danforth."

Julia lifted her hand to her mouth. "Aunt Beatrice? Oh, how wonderful to finally meet you."

William nodded. "Lady Danforth." She looked slightly familiar, but he couldn't remember where or when they'd met. Mrs. Foster and her sister were obviously very fond of each other. Why hadn't Julia met her aunt before? But his questions would have to wait until another time. "If you'll excuse me, I'll be off to fetch the doctor."

Mary Foster extended her hand to William. "Thank you again, Sir William. We're very grateful for your kind assistance."

"You're most welcome." He turned to Julia. "Please send word and let us know how your father is doing tomorrow."

Julia nodded. "I will."

"Good night." He nodded to the other women, replaced his hat, and walked out the door.

The cool evening air chilled his face as he stepped off the small front porch and followed the moonlit path back to the car. Though the reason for his visit to the Fosters' home was not a happy one, he had been impressed by his time there. As soon as he had stepped through the door, he'd sensed the kind affection and warm family ties enjoyed by the Foster family.

How very different from his home in London, where strict rules and cool detachment were always the order of the day. He had spent very little time with his parents. His father traveled for months at a time on business, and his mother had given over his care to nannies and nursery maids, then tutors. How different his life might have been if his family had been close and loving like the Fosters.

Soft morning light streamed through the curtains of Julia's parents' bedroom. Julia yawned and stretched, then rubbed her tired shoulders. She had watched over her father since midnight, when she had finally convinced her mother to go and lie down for a few hours. For Julia, it had been a long night filled with tears and prayers, but with the new day had come acceptance and peace. She prayed God's grace would carry them through whatever lay ahead.

She rose from her chair at her father's bedside and scanned his face, searching for any signs of change. His cough and difficulty breathing had made it a restless night for him, but the last few hours he had seemed to sleep more peacefully, giving her renewed hope.

Her father slowly opened his eyes. "Morning, daughter." His voice was no more than a soft whisper, but it filled her heart with joy.

"Oh, Father." She leaned down and kissed his forehead.

"I didn't know you'd come."

His comment jolted her, since she had spoken to him several times during the night. She supposed the illness was causing his confusion. "I arrived last evening. Sir William brought me in his motorcar."

"Sounds exciting."

Julia smiled. "It was. I only wish we had come in the daylight. I would've loved to see the countryside speeding past."

He slowly reached for her hand. "It's good to have you here."

She squeezed his fingers. "Thank you, Father. It's good to be home."

His smile faded as he searched her face. "You look tired."

"I'm fine. Please, don't worry about me."

"I'm always concerned about you. I am your father." Fondness filled his eyes.

Her throat tightened, and she forced a smile for his sake. "And I am grateful for your concern. Now let me go and tell Mother you're awake." She started to pull away.

"Wait . . . There's something I must say."

She sat by his bedside again and tried to swallow

away the lump lodged in her throat, but it was useless.

"I know you feel a responsibility to stay in England and watch out for your mother and me."

She gave a slight nod. "We're family. Love binds us together."

"Well said. But we do not want to be a burden to you."

"Please don't say such a thing. You are not a burden."

"Nor do we want to keep you from God's calling."

Julia sighed. "I am sure God's calling for me today is to spend time here, with you and Mother."

"Yes, and I am grateful you've come. But when I'm gone, you and Mother must return to India and continue our work."

"Father, please, don't—"

He gripped her hand more tightly. "I'm not afraid to speak of my death. It opens the doorway to my heavenly home and the reward Christ has won for me."

Tears filled her eyes, and she reached for his hand again.

"I have followed the Lord faithfully for over fifty years, and I intend to remain faithful to Him until the end."

She leaned down and laid her head on his shoulder. "Oh, Father." It was all she could manage to say as her tears overflowed and coursed down her cheeks.

Fourteen

William pushed his breakfast plate away with a heavy sigh and stared out the dining-room window. A gray gloom seemed to have settled over the house since the calendar had turned to December. The days had grown shorter and the weather less agreeable. That must be the reason for his sagging spirits.

Lawrence entered the room carrying a small silver tray. "The morning post, sir."

"Thank you." William took the letter opener and three envelopes from the tray. He quickly scanned the return address of the first, and his stomach tensed.

Sarah set her teacup aside. "Who is it from, William?"

"Bixby, my solicitor." He put the letter aside to open last, since he was in no mood to read more about death duties or other legal affairs. He slit the second envelope and quickly scanned the brief paragraph. "This is from Mr. Henshaw."

"The art dealer you told me about?"

"Yes, he says he can take the train from London on the eighteenth to do the appraisal."

Sarah nodded. "And the final letter?"

William opened the third envelope. "This one is from David."

Sarah's eyes lit up at the mention of their younger brother. "Perhaps he's responding to our invitation to join us for Christmas."

William glanced at the first few sentences. "He says he'll arrive on the twenty-first and stay through the New Year." William shifted in his chair and read the rest of the brief letter, but it failed to lift his spirits.

He and David had never been close, at least not as close as William had been to Nathaniel. The four-year age difference between David and William may have been part of the reason. There were only two years between him and Nathaniel. David was eight when William had been sent away to school, so most of their childhood had been spent apart. As they grew older, a subtle rivalry developed between them, mainly spurred on by David's desire to prove that he was stronger, smarter, and more talented than William.

Buying out William's interest in the family business had been a boost to David's ego. But in his brother's eyes, it still didn't make up for the fact that William had been the one to inherit the title of baronet and Highland.

"I'm glad David is coming." Sarah sent William a pointed look. "It's important to be with family at Christmastime."

"Yes . . . I suppose that's true." He set his brother's letter aside and stared toward the window again.

"Really, William, I don't see why that should make you scowl."

"What?" He squinted across the table at Sarah. "Oh, I wasn't thinking of David. I was wondering why Miss Foster hasn't written."

His sister tipped her head. "We just received her letter on Wednesday."

"But she's been gone more than a week!"

"You're the one who told her she might stay as long as she was needed."

He huffed. "I had no idea she would stay away this long. And now that her father is improving, I thought she would set a date for her return."

She sent him a puzzled look. "I'm sure the children miss her, but they seem to be doing well."

"They are missing out on their schooling, and Andrew was caught in the pantry yesterday, helping himself to a slice of apple tart."

Sarah grinned. "I can see why he was tempted. That's my favorite as well. Why don't we invite the children to have luncheon with us? It would be a nice treat for them, and I'm sure the nursery maid would appreciate the break."

He nodded, still frowning. "I suppose."

"And after that, perhaps I should go to the village and visit the Fosters."

William straightened. "Yes. That's a splendid idea. And while you're there you can urge Miss Foster to return to Highland as soon as possible."

"I'll do nothing of the kind. I'll take them some provisions and let them know how relieved we are to hear that Dr. Foster is improving."

"Of course. That's what I meant. But if the opportunity presents itself, you might let her know we are anxious for her return."

Sarah's eyes glowed. "All right. I'll tell her, but only if I can do it without making her overly concerned about the children."

"Yes, of course." William tapped his finger on the table. Sarah was very tender-hearted and not likely to urge Miss Foster to leave her family any time soon. If he wanted that message delivered, he would have to do it himself. He laid his napkin on the table. "I have an idea. Why don't I drive you to the village, and we can both visit the Fosters?"

She rose from her chair. "That would be nice, but you must promise not to make Julia feel guilty for staying with her family."

"I shall be the perfect gentleman." William stood. "Oh, wait. Dalton asked to meet with me this afternoon."

Sarah froze and gripped the back of the chair.

"Mr. Dalton?" Her voice had suddenly gone light and breathless.

"Yes, he said something about discussing plans for the future. I certainly hope he's not planning to leave us. I rather like the man. He seems to have a sensible head on his shoulders, and I don't—" William stopped and studied his sister. "Sarah, are you all right?"

"Yes . . . I'm just feeling a little lightheaded. Perhaps I should go lie down."

"By all means. And if you're not up to visiting the Fosters, I can go on my own."

"I'll be fine."

"All right." He stepped closer and kissed her forehead. "You do look pale. Shall I send for Mrs. Emmitt?"

"No. Please don't bother her." She turned away.

William watched her go, his thoughts even more unsettled than they had been at the beginning of the meal. Something was definitely wrong. Sarah had not been herself lately. He hoped she wasn't seriously ill.

But if that were the case, he would take care of her. He had always watched out for her. Even when they were young children, he made sure no one taunted her about her limp or hand. And Sarah had always looked up to him and depended on him. They were as close as any brother and sister could be—or at least they had been until they'd come to Highland.

●●●

Sarah hurried down the backstairs and slipped past the kitchen. She could hear Chef Lagarde scolding one of the kitchen maids, first in English and then in French. The translation flew through her mind and sent a rush of heat to her cheeks. *Poor girl.* She hoped the maid did not speak French.

Mr. Lawrence stepped around the corner. "Miss Ramsey, is there something I can do for you?"

Sarah stifled a gasp. "No. I'm just . . . on my way to the greenhouse."

Mr. Lawrence's dark eyebrows dipped. "The greenhouse?"

"Yes, I want to speak to Mr. Dalton about . . . some flowers . . . for the dining room."

"I'd be happy to send a message with one of the footmen."

"No, thank you. I'd like to speak to him myself." She swallowed and nodded to him. "Please excuse me."

Mr. Lawrence narrowed his eyes but nodded. "Of course, miss."

Sarah fled out the back door and hurried across the courtyard. She glanced over her shoulder, then slipped under the arched entrance to the garden and ran down the gravel path.

With her heartbeat pounding in her ears, she pulled open the greenhouse door. "Clark? Are you in here?" No one answered, so she hurried down the center aisle, checking to the right and left, but she didn't see him working among the plants and flowers. When she reached the far end, she pushed open the back door and ran directly into Harry, one of the young under gardeners.

"Whoa." His hand flew up to keep his cap on his head. "I'm sorry, miss. I didn't see you coming."

"It's all right, Harry." She straightened her jacket. "Have you seen Mr. Dalton?"

"Yes, miss. He's down by the fountain, cleanin' up branches that came down in the storm last night. The wind must have really been howling up at the house."

"Yes, it was." She looked past him. "If you'll excuse me."

"Of course, miss." He tipped his cap and sent her a smile.

She nodded to him, then forced herself to walk at a slower pace. An icy breeze whipped past and stole her breath for a moment. She squinted against the wind and searched the gardens. Finally, she spotted Clark pushing a wheelbarrow full of branches. Lifting her hand, she waved.

He smiled, set the wheelbarrow aside, and hurried to meet her. "Sarah, this is a fine surprise. I didn't expect you until this afternoon." He searched her face, and his expression sobered. "Is something wrong?"

She bit her lip, wishing she had found the courage to speak to William about her feelings for

Clark. But she hadn't, and now she must make Clark understand why they had to wait. "William is in a very dark mood today."

"I'm sorry to hear it." He motioned toward his office. "Let's go inside. I don't want you to catch your death of cold."

"Thank you." She crossed her arms tightly and followed him through the door, glad for the warmth of the small wood stove that burned in the corner.

He offered her a chair, and she sat down. "Now tell me what happened."

"It's not just one thing. It seems a whole load of trouble has landed in William's lap, and he's just not himself."

Clark nodded, encouraging her to continue.

"He has decided to bring an art dealer from London to see about selling some of our paintings, but he doesn't know if that will be enough to solve our financial problems. I can tell they weigh heavily on him. And then today he received a letter from our brother David, saying he's coming for a visit over the Christmas holiday."

"You'd think that would cheer him up."

"I'm afraid not. William and David don't always see eye to eye. And since our father's death, issues about the inheritance and family business have pulled them even farther apart." She sighed. If only there was some way she could help her brothers mend their differences.

"I'm sorry to hear it. That's hard when family members are at odds with each other."

Sarah nodded. "He's also upset that Miss Foster has stayed away so long."

"She's still with her parents?"

"Yes. Her father seems to be on the mend, but she hasn't set a time for her return, and William has come to depend on her for more than just caring for the children."

Clark cocked his head. "Do you think he has feelings for her?"

"I suppose it's a possibility. He often invites her to sit with us in the evening, and they both seem to enjoy those conversations." She thought a moment more. "His face did light up when he saw her dressed so beautifully the night of Katherine's birthday dinner." Then she sighed and shook her head. "But I'm afraid William is very conventional. I can't see him pursuing Miss Foster, no matter how lovely and worthy she might be."

"It's a shame he would let her lack of money and position keep them apart."

Sarah bit her lip, then lifted her gaze to meet Clark's. "It's not just that. William hasn't been the same since his wife died three years ago in a riding accident."

"How terrible."

"It was a shock for us all." A painful lump rose in her throat as the memories came rushing back.

"He seemed to accept her death at first, but a few weeks later he sank into a dark depression that lasted well over a year. It changed him in so many ways."

"It would be very difficult to lose someone you love."

Sarah hesitated and then leaned toward Clark. "But that's just it. Love did not bring them together. Their marriage was arranged by our father and hers—joining the two families with the goal of expanding the business."

"But surely they grew to love each other, didn't they?"

Sarah slowly shook her head. "William tried. I know he did, but Amelia became more distant and unhappy with each passing year. Eventually she only stayed in London for the season. The rest of the year she visited friends in the country and rarely saw William and the children. She was in Yorkshire at the time of the accident, staying with Sir Charles Hollingsford . . . and there were rumors about him and Amelia."

Clark's brows rose, a question in his eyes.

Sarah nodded and looked away, her cheeks warming. "It's all terribly sad." She shouldn't have revealed such intimate details about her brother's unhappy marriage, but she wanted Clark to understand William's situation and how it might affect them.

"I'm afraid William has hardened his heart

toward love and marriage, and I doubt even Miss Foster can soften it." She clasped her hands and focused on him once more. "And that's why you must not speak to William today."

"What?"

"You mustn't tell him about us. Not yet. Surely it would be better to wait until after the Christmas holiday—when David has returned to London and William has had more time to resolve these financial issues."

One side of Clark's mouth rose slightly. "I don't like keeping a secret from your brother, but I hadn't planned to tell him about us today."

Sarah's eyes widened. "Oh, but William said you wanted to discuss your future plans, and I thought—"

"I meant expanding the greenhouse and gardens and planting more crops next spring. I need his permission to order the building materials and supplies. That's all."

"Oh, thank goodness." She rose from her chair and wrapped her arms around him in a fierce hug. The rough weave of his wool jacket brushed against her cheek. She closed her eyes and pulled in a deep breath, savoring the manly scent of earth and sandalwood and pines. The warmth of his embrace and the strong, steady beat of his heart were so comforting.

"I'm longing to tell your brother and the whole world how much you mean to me, but I gave you my promise to wait, and I intend to keep it."

The door swung opened, and William stepped inside.

Sarah gasped, and Clark stiffened.

William's eyes flashed. "Dalton! Take your hands off my sister!"

Sarah gripped Clark's coat sleeve.

William's face flushed. "What's the meaning of this?"

Clark turned to William. "I can explain, sir."

William glared at Clark, then shot a dark look at Sarah. "Go back to the house!"

Fire pulsed through her. "No, William. I'm not a child. You can't order me about."

"I am head of this family. You will do as I say!"

A fierce trembling shook her from head to toe. How could he treat her like this? Didn't she have a right to love and be loved?

"It's all right, Sarah." Clark's voice was calm but firm. "Do as he says and leave us."

"But I—"

"Please, let me handle this." Clark's tone brooked no argument.

"Very well. But there's one thing I must say before I go." She clenched her hands and faced William. "I love Clark with all my heart. If you dismiss him and send him away, I will go with him."

William stared at her, his eyes a stormy gray. "You don't know what you're saying."

"Yes, I do." Sarah swung away and marched out the door. But her strength only carried her a few more steps before she stifled a sob and ran back to the house.

Fifteen

Clark watched Sarah go, his pulse thudding at his temple. Her courageous declaration sent a new wave of strength through him. He straightened his shoulders and looked Sir William in the eye. "I'm sorry, sir. I know we should've come to you first, but now that you know how much we care for each other, I'd like to ask your permission to court your sister."

William's nostril's flared. "That is out of the question."

"But my intentions are honorable, sir. I want to marry her."

"Oh, I'm sure you do." William glared at him. "You think marrying my sister will provide you with an income for life. Admit it. That's why you wooed her in secret."

"No sir! That's not true. It makes no difference to me if Sarah has money or not. I've worked for my wages since I was twelve. I've no need of another income."

"Well, you won't be working here long if you continue to pursue my sister."

"We've no wish to leave Highland, sir."

"Stop! There is no *we!*"

Clark shot off a prayer for strength to control his temper. "I know this has taken you by surprise, but please don't make a decision right now."

"And why not? The possibility of you marrying my sister will look no better to me tomorrow than it does today."

"But I love her, sir, very much."

Sir William huffed out a disbelieving laugh. "You could marry anyone you wish, but you choose my sister. The fact that she's crippled and not likely to receive any other offers has nothing to do with it, I suppose."

Clark struggled to pull in a calming breath. "Her hand doesn't matter to me. It only makes me more determined to give her the comfort and love she deserves and make up for the losses she's experienced."

"What losses? My sister has been well cared for since birth. I have always seen that she has everything she needs."

"Everything except love and a chance to marry and have a family of her own."

"How *dare* you!" William jabbed his finger toward Clark. "You are forbidden to see Sarah or speak to her anymore! Do you understand?"

A heavy blanket of dread draped around Clark's

shoulders. "I understand what you've said, but I cannot fathom why you would hurt Sarah like this."

"I have no intention of hurting her. I am protecting her from making a terrible mistake."

Clark fisted his hands as the fire built within. *Help me, Lord.* Everything in him wanted to strike Sir William for those foul words, but it would only hurt Sarah if he did. He swallowed and reined in his burning anger. "I will pray you have a change of heart, for your sister's sake and your own."

William glared at Clark, then stormed out the door.

Clark sank into the chair and lowered his head into his hands. *Dear Lord in heaven, what am I to do?*

Julia wiped the back of her hand across her damp forehead and pushed a loose strand of hair behind her ear. Bending over the wooden tub, she scrubbed the sheet once more and dunked it in the soapy water. Her shoulders ached from doing another load of laundry, but at least she had spared her mother the wearisome task.

A cold wind whistled under the back door and sent a shiver down her arms. She plunged her hands in the warm water once more. Her feet might be freezing on this cold stone floor, but at least the rest of her was warmed by the steamy water.

Her thoughts drifted back to Highland as they had so often these last few days. What were the children doing this afternoon? Was Ann able to keep them happy and occupied? And how were Katherine and Penelope faring? Had they maintained the good habits she had tried to instill, or had they returned to their old routine of sleeping late, skipping Scripture reading and prayer, and ignoring their studies?

What had happened between Sarah and Mr. Dalton? Did he now call on her openly, or was their courtship still a secret?

And what of William? Was he spending more time with the children, or did he stay hidden in his gloomy library every day, poring over the estate's financial matters? Was he taking care of himself and finding strength to oversee Highland, his staff, and family?

Oh, how she missed him! How she missed them all.

Her mother stepped through the low doorway that led from the kitchen to the washroom at the back of the cottage. "Julia, we have a caller." She smiled and looked over her shoulder.

William ducked his head and followed her mother through the doorway.

A soft gasp escaped her lips. "Sir William." She nodded to him and quickly wiped her wet hands on her apron.

"Good afternoon, Miss Foster." With his hat in his hand, he frowned slightly as he looked around the dimly lit room.

"We weren't expecting you." Julia glanced at her mother.

"But it's nice of you to come," her mother added. "Sir William brought us a basket with some lovely meat, cheese, and preserves."

"That's very kind. Thank you."

Her mother's eyes glowed. "Well, I'll just go put on the teakettle." She returned to the kitchen.

"I'm sorry to interrupt you." He motioned toward the washtub.

Julia's cheeks warmed. "I'm almost finished. If I could just rinse and hang this last sheet, then I can offer you some tea in the parlor."

"Thank you. I would appreciate a cup of tea."

Julia returned to the laundry tub, her stomach fluttering. She couldn't imagine why her mother had brought William to the back room rather than invite him to sit in the parlor or at least the kitchen. What was she thinking? She must look a sight with her hair down, her sleeves rolled up, and her arms dripping with dirty wash water. Well, this was how she spent a good part of her day, and she ought not to pretend her life was any different.

She hefted the bulky sheet from the tub and began twisting out the water.

"That looks heavy. Let me help you."

"Oh no. It's fine. I'm used to it."

"I insist." He lifted one end of the sheet.

She stifled a groan and nodded her acceptance, though her face flamed. Together they wrung out the sheet and hung it over the line at the back of the room.

"How is your father today?"

"He seems to be regaining his strength. We're very grateful." She reached up and adjusted the sheet so it hung evenly over the line.

"I'm glad to hear it. That makes me feel a little easier about making my request."

Julia glanced his way, wondering what he meant, but his expression revealed nothing. "What request is that, sir?"

He glanced over his shoulder toward the kitchen, then back at her. "We've had a . . . bit of a crisis at Highland, and I'm hoping you might be able to return soon." His dark eyebrows drew together in a worried frown.

"Oh, dear. Has something happened to one of the children?"

"No, the children are fine, though they miss you terribly and ask every day when you're coming back."

That news warmed her heart. "I've missed them as well."

"This has nothing to do with the children or my cousins." He shook his head. "I'm sorry . . . It's difficult to speak of."

She clasped her hands. "Whatever it is, you can be sure I'll keep it in confidence."

He nodded and met her gaze. "It's my sister. It seems she's been carrying on a secret liaison with

Dalton, the gardener." His lips twisted as though the words left a bitter taste in his mouth.

Julia's heart sank. "Oh, I'm sure they haven't done anything improper."

"I caught them together this morning in his office. He has convinced her of his undying devotion." Sarcasm filled his voice. "But of course I know the truth."

"Which is . . . ?"

"He's willing to marry her in spite of her deformity because he has his eye on her inheritance."

Julia shook her head. "Oh, I don't think that's his motivation."

His eyes flashed. "You knew about this?"

She hesitated, remembering her promise to Sarah. "She did speak to me about it."

"Yet you said nothing to me?" He gripped his hat in his hand and looked away. "I would not have expected such disloyalty from you."

"Please, don't think of it as disloyalty. Sarah confided in me a few weeks ago, and I urged her to speak to you."

"But when she kept it from me, why didn't you come yourself?"

"She asked me not to tell anyone, and I gave her my promise. I thought she would tell you in time."

"Well, she didn't, and now she says if I dismiss Dalton, she'll run away with him."

Julia's knees suddenly felt weak, and she leaned

against the wall. "I'm sorry. I had no idea things had moved along so quickly. I thought there was time to do everything properly."

"Properly? You think I should agree to let my sister marry a gardener?" He shook his head. "A month or a year will make no difference. I would be the laughingstock of Berkshire and London if I allowed it."

"But surely you care more about your sister's happiness than the opinions of strangers."

"So you sympathize with her? You think I should let her go off and live in an old cottage as a poor man's wife?"

Heat flooded her face, and she lifted her chin. "A simple life in a cottage with a husband and children who love you is nothing to be ashamed of."

His stern expression faltered. "Of course not. Forgive me. I am not speaking of you or your family. I'm thinking of Sarah. She was raised in a privileged home and sheltered from the harsher realities of life."

"She may have been sheltered, but she knows her own mind, and she has set her heart on marrying Mr. Dalton."

"That's impossible. She would be throwing her life away."

"But Mr. Dalton is a sincere and honorable man. I believe he loves Sarah and would do everything in his power to make her happy."

"If she marries him, she'll become the focus of cruel gossip and lose her place in society."

"From what Sarah has told me, she has rarely been involved in society. I can't see how marrying Mr. Dalton would make any difference."

"But if I allow it, people will say I have not done my duty to protect and provide for her. I will be the one who pays for her mistakes."

"So that's your greatest concern: that it will reflect poorly on you?" She shook her head, stunned and disappointed. "I cannot believe you would take away your sister's one chance for love and marriage just to maintain your reputation."

His piercing expression darkened.

A warning rose in her heart, but she pushed past it. "Marrying to maintain wealth and position in society does not guarantee a happy future or godly contentment—as you well know."

His face reddened and became a stormy mask. "You have no right to speak to me in this manner. I have nothing more to say to you." He turned and strode past her out the back door.

Her legs began to tremble, and all the strength drained out of her. She grabbed the edge of the laundry tub. *Oh, Lord, what have I done?*

"Tea is ready." Julia's mother stepped through the doorway. "Where is Sir William?"

Julia swallowed, trying to find her voice. "He left by the back door."

"Goodness, Julia, you're as pale as a sheet.

Come and sit down." Her mother took Julia's arm and led her into the warm kitchen.

Julia sank into a chair and tried to still her trembling.

Her mother brought the teapot to the table and poured her a cup of tea. "For goodness' sake, what happened?"

"I'm afraid I spoke my mind too plainly, and I offended Sir William."

"Then you must make it right."

"But if he doesn't change his mind, he will hurt his sister deeply. How can I condone that?"

"You can apologize for the way you spoke to him without agreeing to his conclusions."

A surge of resistance rose in her heart. Sir William was wrong, and when her mother heard the details of the story, she would agree. Knowing her mother would keep the matter private, she told her about Sarah and Mr. Dalton, and then she explained how Sir William had discovered them. Her mother listened quietly, concern deepening in her eyes.

"So you can see why I expressed myself as I did." Julia shifted in her seat, feeling less certain of her stance than she had at first. What if she was wrong and Mr. Dalton's intentions were not pure? But hadn't Reverend Langford confirmed Mr. Dalton's character? Even so, she should not have spoken to Sir William as she had.

"I understand Sir William's concerns." Her

mother lifted her teacup and sat back. "It reminds me very much of the difficulties I faced when I decided to marry your father." Her gaze drifted toward the kitchen window, and her mouth tightened slightly. "The division it caused in my family has been very hard to live with at times."

"But you don't regret marrying Father, do you?"

"No. Of course not." She took a sip of her tea. "Two decisions have shaped my life. The first was following the Savior with my whole heart when I was seventeen, and the second was accepting your father's proposal two years later. I am eternally grateful I had the courage to do both. My life has been blessed as I've served the Lord, and I have enjoyed the love and devotion of a godly husband." Her expression softened. "But I do regret the pain I caused my family."

"That was not your fault. Your father is the one who refused to see you after you married."

Her mother nodded. "I had to fight a long battle in my heart to find forgiveness. But Christ has won the victory, and I am free of bitterness. Now, when I think of my family and all the years that have been lost, I feel sorrow rather than anger. I have accepted that my father may never change. Bea's desire to stay in touch and pass our letters on to my mother has been a great comfort."

Julia nodded, remembering their years in India and how much her aunt's letters had meant to her mother. The exchange of news had been carried on for many years without her grandfather's knowledge. Her grandmother often enclosed a note with her aunt's letters, and those words of love and encouragement had meant the world to her mother.

"But the point in all this," her mother continued, "is that you must make amends with Sir William so you can keep your position and encourage him and his sister to work out their differences. Marrying the person you love is important, but so are family relationships. And you, my dear Julia, may be the one the Lord wants to use to help them through these difficult days."

"I doubt Sir William will listen to anything else I have to say about it, especially now."

"But you still have influence with his sister. And if she will wait and give her brother time, perhaps he will come around and accept the idea of her marrying Mr. Dalton."

"I am not sure either of them can be persuaded to change their minds. Sarah might listen to reason, but Sir William is very proud and set in his ways. And he obviously disliked me giving my opinion today."

"Perhaps it was more the manner in which you shared it than the message itself."

Conviction washed over Julia's heart, and she looked down and smoothed out her apron. "I've done it again, haven't I? Failed to control my tongue when my emotions have been stirred."

She sighed. "I don't know why I so often assume I'm right and say exactly what I'm thinking. Later on I always regret I didn't pray and consider the timing or my words more carefully."

"Realizing our weaknesses is half the battle." Her mother smiled and set her teacup aside. "If you are going to be used by the Lord to help in this situation, you must cool your emotions and guard your tongue."

Julia nodded, knowing her mother was right.

"Sir William came here today, asking for your help." Her mother tipped her head, a question in her eyes. "That seems quite unusual, wouldn't you agree?"

"He knows Sarah and I have developed a friendship. I'm sure he thought I would help him convince Sarah to give up Mr. Dalton." Julia's heart ached as she thought of her friend. "I so want Sarah to be happy."

"Of course you do. But I must ask . . . Do you think there is some other reason Sir William came to see you today?"

"What other reason could there be?"

"Well, he has been very kind to you: driving you home in his motorcar, fetching the doctor, paying for the doctor's visit, and bringing that generous basket of food. And when he arrived today, he insisted on seeing you right away." A faint smile lifted her lips. "I wondered if there might be an attachment forming between you."

Julia quickly shook her head. "I'm sure Sir William doesn't think of me like that."

"But you mention him often. Have you grown to care for him?"

Julia's cheeks warmed. "Sir William is bound by the traditions of society. He would never become involved with someone on his staff."

"A governess is not the same as a housemaid," her mother added.

"No, but she would not be a good match for a baronet like Sir William."

Her mother gazed toward the kitchen window. "Perhaps, but there is something about his manner toward you that makes me wonder. He puts on a very valiant face, but I sense vulnerability in him, a need or some sort of wound that he tries to keep hidden."

"He has experienced several losses." Julia looked down, torn by her opposing feelings. "But he is a proud, opinionated man. His estate and position are much more important to him than his family or his faith. And for those reasons, I could never love him."

"Be careful, my dear. Pride does not afflict only the wealthy. A poor man or woman can struggle with the same vice for different reasons." Her mother laid her hand over Julia's. "It takes humility to put aside hurt feelings and see through to someone's heart." Wisdom and affection flowed from her mother's caring expression.

"Thank you, Mother. I'll consider what you've said."

"Good." Her mother's smile returned, and she gave Julia's hand a pat.

Julia refilled her teacup and stirred in a spoonful of sugar. Sir William might be set in his ways and determined to separate Sarah and Mr. Dalton, but she had been impulsive and spoken out of turn again. He had come asking for her help, and she had sent him away empty handed. That would never do. It was dishonoring—and almost as offensive as his opposition to Sarah and Mr. Dalton's attachment.

She took a sip of tea, a plan forming in her mind. Helping Sarah and Sir William resolve their differences was much more important than defending her wounded pride. She would write to him today, straighten out the matter, and ask to return to Highland as soon as possible.

Sixteen

William strode out of his bedroom the next morning, his mind churning with the unresolved issues between him and his sister. Following their confrontation in Dalton's office yesterday morning, she had fled to her bedroom and stayed there the rest of the day. He had hoped they could discuss the issue calmly at dinner, but Sarah had not come down. His cousins had been away dining with friends, so he had eaten alone.

Later, he had knocked on her door, but she had refused to speak to him any further. He instructed Mrs. Emmitt to bring her a dinner tray, but it had remained untouched in the hall.

His plan to bring Miss Foster home to help sort out the situation had failed miserably. His head began to throb as he recalled their conversation. How could she take Sarah's side and refuse to help him convince his sister to break off the romance with Dalton? He thought Miss Foster was sensible and loyal, but he had been disappointed by her response.

He supposed her youth and inexperience, along with her romantic ideals, made it difficult for her to understand the situation clearly.

She knew nothing of the scandal his late wife's unfaithfulness and death had caused him. He grimaced, thinking of the social snubs and cool dismissals he had faced. If a new round of gossip about his sister spread through London society, it would be much worse.

Perhaps he should not care what people thought of him and his family, but experience had been a harsh teacher. If Sarah ran away with Dalton, the ripples of disgrace would hang over them for years, and it would make it very difficult for his son to get into the right schools and for both children to find suitable mates. He growled under his breath as he crossed the gallery and headed down the main staircase.

He ought to dismiss Dalton, but that would only infuriate his sister, and there was a slim chance she might actually follow through on her threat to run away with him. If she did, he would never forgive himself for pushing her toward that choice.

When he reached the bottom of the stairs, he glanced at the line of servants waiting in the great hall for morning Scripture reading and prayer. Dalton stood near the end of the line, stone-faced, eyes fixed straight ahead, with the two under gardeners beside him. William set his jaw and shifted his gaze to the fireplace. Not one member of his family waited at the opposite side of the hall. His shoulders tensed as his butler approached.

"Good morning, sir." Mr. Lawrence nodded to him.

William pulled his pocket watch from his vest and checked the time. "Where is my family? Why haven't they come down?"

Lawrence leaned closer and lowered his voice. "It appears there is illness in the house, sir."

William frowned. "Who is ill?"

"One of the maids just informed me that Master Andrew and Miss Millicent are sick in bed."

Alarm shot through William, and he scanned the line of servants again, searching for his housekeeper. "Where is Mrs. Emmitt?"

"She has gone up to check on them, sir."

William glared toward the stairs and gallery. "What about Miss Ramsey and the young ladies? Are they ill as well?"

Dalton's head jerked to the left, and he shot William a panicked glance.

William ignored him and focused on Lawrence. "I have not seen them this morning, sir."

William huffed, his irritation matching his concern. He wanted to dash up the stairs and search out the situation himself, but the staff waited. "Very well. In light of the children's illness, we will dispense with Scripture reading this morning. Let us pray."

He waited while the servants bowed their heads and closed their eyes, then he followed suit. A dark foreboding pressed down on his heart. Though he was master of Highland and head of his family, he had no real control over what would happen to his children. Their health and well-being were in the hands of God.

"Dear heavenly Father, we come today acknowledging our dependence upon You." His throat tightened, and he had to swallow twice before he could go on. "We ask You to watch over our household and care for those who are ill. Please comfort and heal them, and give us wisdom as we carry out our duties to the best of our abilities. In the name of Christ our Lord we pray. Amen."

Lawrence stepped forward. "How can I be of service, sir?"

"We may need to send for Dr. Hadley. I'll go up to see the children and discuss it with Mrs. Emmitt." But he had no idea if the housekeeper was knowledgeable about such matters. Blast! Why wasn't Miss Foster here? She would know what to do.

"Very good, sir. I'll await your orders." Lawrence bowed slightly to William, then he nodded to the staff to dismiss them. They filed out, their mood somber.

William narrowed his eyes at Dalton as he passed, but the gardener stared straight ahead, his jaw set. There was no time to discuss matters with him this morning, and even if there were, William was not certain what he would say. He must settle things with Sarah before he spoke to Dalton again.

He hurried up the stairs and passed through the gallery. Sarah's room as well as the nursery and schoolroom were in the east wing, on the opposite side of the house from William's bedroom.

Mrs. Emmitt met him at the door of the children's room and ushered him in. Both children lay in their beds, their faces flushed, hair damp, and their breathing heavy. Lydia sponged Millicent's forehead while Ann stood by Andrew's bed, her hands clasped and a tired, worried expression lining her young face.

"What is wrong with the children?"

Mrs. Emmitt leaned toward him. "Ann was up with them all night. Both have fevers, chills, headaches, stomachaches, and sore throats." She glanced toward them with a weary sigh. "Their fevers are quite high. One of the kitchen maids is also sick with the same symptoms."

"Do you think that's how the children caught it?"

"I'm afraid so. We must be very careful and keep the others away so it doesn't spread through the house."

"I'll send for the doctor." William crossed to

the desk. Taking out a sheet of paper, he quickly penned a note to Dr. Hadley, asking him to come as soon as possible. While the ink dried, he turned and considered whom he should send. The nursery maid seemed the least busy, so he summoned her and sent her off to find Lawrence or one of the footmen.

William scanned the children's faces again. "Mrs. Emmitt, I'll leave you in charge here."

The housekeeper's eyes widened. "I am not a trained nurse, and I have other duties to see to."

Irritation burned in his chest. "You will stay until the doctor arrives or until I return with someone else to oversee the children's care. Do you understand?"

Her mouth puckered, but she gave a stiff nod. "Yes sir." She turned back toward the children's beds.

He strode down the hall to Sarah's room and knocked on her door. After two seconds of silence, he was through waiting. "Sarah, the children are ill. I need your help."

The door opened and she looked out, her eyes wide. "What's wrong with the children?"

His voice suddenly locked in his throat, and he turned his head away.

"William, what is it?"

He swallowed. "They both have fevers and sore throats."

She tipped her head, her expression easing.

"I'm sure they'll be fine. Children often catch—"

"No, this is serious. One look at them and—" His eyes suddenly burned, and he lifted his hand to rub them. Blast! He must get a grip on himself.

Sarah laid her hand on his arm. "It's all right. I'll go to them at once. You mustn't worry."

He straightened. "Thank you. I've sent for the doctor, but I'll feel better knowing you're there."

She sent him a reassuring look, then hurried off to the children's room.

William paced the hall. What would he do now? He didn't have the experience or temperament for sickroom duty. But driving to fetch Dr. Hadley would be much quicker than harnessing the horses and sending a footman in the carriage.

He ran to his room and grabbed his hat, coat, and gloves, then hurried down the main staircase and out the front door. As he rounded the corner of the house, he saw a woman crossing the park. Recognition flashed through him, and he lifted his hand. "Miss Foster!"

She immediately changed course to meet him. "Good day, sir."

"I'm glad you've come."

Her eyes widened. "I wrote you a letter, but as I prayed about it, I thought I should bring it myself." She took a letter from her coat pocket, then offered it to him.

"Thank you. I'll read it soon. But for now, I need you to go to the house and attend the children.

They're both quite ill. I'm going to fetch the doctor."

Concern filled her eyes. "Of course, sir. I'll go to them at once." She stepped away.

"Wait." He reached for her hand. "I just want to say . . . I'm very glad you've come back."

She smiled, and her eyes filled with warmth. "I'm glad as well." She glanced down at their clasped hands.

Relief rushed through him. He nodded and released her hand, then jogged off to the stables, hoping to catch the groomsmen before they harnessed the horses.

Sliding open the stable door, he hurried down the center aisle, searching the stalls. "Hardy! Gates! Are you here?" But no one answered.

Frowning, he pushed open the back door and scanned the rear stable yard. His car sat in the covered portico behind the stables. And there in the shade of the building stood one of the young groomsman, Peter Gates, and the nursery maid, Ann, clasped in a tight embrace.

"What the devil!" William marched toward them.

Gates dropped his arms and spun around. The maid gasped and stepped back, her face red and blotchy.

"I sent you with an important message!" He glared at the young maid. "But did you deliver it? No! I find you cavorting with the groom in the stable yard! Have you no conscience? No decency?"

Gates stepped in front of Ann. "There's no need to shout at her. She's upset after being up all night with your children."

William pointed at him. "You had better hold your tongue, young man, unless you want to be dismissed this instant."

The groom's face flushed red, but he clamped his mouth closed.

"I'm ever so sorry, sir." The maid's voice quivered as she stepped out from behind Gates. "I searched for Mr. Lawrence, but I couldn't find him. So I thought if I came out here and told Peter, he could go for the doctor."

"It doesn't look like either one of you were thinking one whit about my children or the doctor." He scowled at the maid. "Go back to the house. Report to Mrs. Emmitt. And don't let me catch you out here with Gates ever again. Do you understand?"

"Yes sir." She bobbed a quick curtsy, lowered her head, and ran back toward the house.

"And you, sir." He shifted his narrow-eyed gaze to the groom. "I should send you packing, but I don't have the time to deal with it right now. Go start my car."

Gates hustled off without a word.

William shook his head. What was this world coming to? Every time he turned around he discovered someone else carrying on a secret romance with no thought to the impact it would have on others.

Secret romances below stairs caused all kinds of trouble. He would have to speak to Mrs. Emmitt and Lawrence about the situation later. Right now he must find Dr. Hadley and bring him back to Highland to see the children.

He clenched his jaw as an anxious prayer formed in his mind. *Please watch over Andrew and Millie and restore them to good health. I have not been the father I should be, but if You will give me another chance, I will make an effort to change my ways. Please, Lord, I could not bear to lose them.*

Sarah looked up as the clock on the nursery mantel struck three. Late afternoon sunlight spilled across the floor and touched the head of Andrew's bed. She set his empty soup bowl on the bedside table. Surely, finishing his broth would help him regain his strength and fight off this terrible illness. She smiled down at him. "Why don't you just close your eyes and rest for a bit?"

"All right," he whispered and turned his head to the side. Poor lad. She had never seen him this ill.

The doctor's diagnosis of scarlet fever had struck fear in her heart and sent a wave of panic through the house. Dr. Hadley ordered the children to be isolated, and only Sarah, Julia, and

Ann were allowed in the nursery to care for them.

Sarah glanced at Ann as she put away one of Millicent's clean nightgowns in the closet. A basket of folded laundry sat at her feet. The girl was certainly faithful and a hard worker, but for once, Sarah wished Ann would leave the room so she could speak to Julia privately.

The last thirty-six hours had been an exhausting whirl, caring for the children and grieving over her brother's insistence that she must break off her relationship with Clark. If she wasn't so worried about Andrew and Millie, she would go downstairs right now and beg William to change his mind.

Clark was a fine, honorable man, worthy of her love and William's acceptance. Surely, there was some way she could persuade her brother to agree to their courtship.

Sarah closed her eyes and rubbed her forehead. Confronting her brother would have to wait until the children were out of danger and she had a little rest and could think clearly.

Across the room, Julia hovered over Millie, a spoon in her hand. "I know your throat is sore, dear, but please try one more little sip."

Millie whimpered, a pitiful look on her face. But she finally opened her mouth and accepted a spoonful of the chicken broth.

"That's a good girl. Now lie back and rest." Julia placed the half-empty bowl on the tray. "Ann, will you please take these dishes down to the kitchen?"

Ann nodded, looking as weary as Sarah felt. "Would you like me to bring up anything else?" she asked as she accepted the tray from Julia.

"Just some fresh water, please."

Ann nodded and left the room.

Sarah glanced at Millie, then checked on Andrew once more. Both children appeared to be resting quietly or asleep. She crossed the room to Millie's bedside and leaned closer to Julia. "I need to speak to you. And no one else must hear."

Julia nodded and led Sarah to the alcove across the room. "What is it?"

Sarah clasped Julia's hand. "William knows about my feelings for Clark. He discovered us alone together in Clark's office."

Julia lowered her eyes. "I know. He told me."

Sarah straightened. "He did?"

"Yes. He came to my parents' home that afternoon and asked me to return to Highland and try and convince you to give up Mr. Dalton."

Indignation surged through Sarah. "How could he think you would take his side and speak against Clark? Of all the prideful and self-righteous men in all the world—"

Julia laid her hand on Sarah's arm. "You must try to see things from his point of view. He loves you and is concerned for your future."

"If he truly loves me, then he ought to agree to our courtship instead of insulting Clark and . . .

and breaking my heart." Hot tears flooded her eyes, and she lifted her hand to her mouth. "Oh, Julia, what am I going to do? He has forbidden me to see Clark."

Sympathy filled Julia's eyes. "I'm so sorry."

Sarah sniffed and took a handkerchief from her pocket. "You should've seen him when he discovered us. He was so angry." She wiped her nose, and a tremor ran through her at the memory of her brother's fierce expression.

"What did he say to Clark?"

"I'm not sure. He insisted I leave. I didn't want to go, but Clark urged me to let him handle it."

"That was probably wise. I admire his courage."

"As do I, but before I left, I told William if he dismissed Clark and sent him away, I would leave Highland and go with him."

"Oh, Sarah." Julia searched Sarah's face. "That would be so painful for everyone."

"But I love Clark. There must be some way I can convince William to let us marry." She clasped her hands and paced a few steps away, her mind swirling with conflicting thoughts and emotions. Suddenly she spun around, hope rising in her heart. "Would you speak to William for us? Surely he'd listen to you."

"I tried that day he came to see me. And I'm sorry to say it did not go well."

Sarah moaned and sank down on the window seat. "Then what am I to do?"

Julia sat beside her. "You must pray about it and ask the Lord to guide you."

"I have prayed, and so has Clark. We've both been praying for a mate for years. And now we've found each other, and the only thing lacking is William's acceptance and blessing." She clasped her hand again. "Please, Julia, you must help me find a way to convince William that Clark and I should be allowed to marry."

Julia thought for a few moments, then turned to Sarah. "Here is what I suggest. Go to William and tell him what you've told me, then ask him to reconsider. But be calm and listen to whatever he says without argument. Perhaps if he feels you've heard his concerns, he might be more willing to hear what you have to say."

Sarah nodded, but she bit her lip, wondering how she would ever find the courage to face her brother and tell him everything in her heart.

"And be open to compromise."

Sarah frowned. "What kind of compromise?"

"Perhaps if you promise to wait a few months, that would give everyone time to adjust to the idea and see that you and Mr. Dalton are truly committed to each other."

"Do you really think that would help?"

"I'm not sure, but if waiting would resolve the issues between you and Sir William and allow him to give you his blessing, then it would be worth it."

Sarah sighed, her emotions rising and falling like the waves of the sea. "I can't imagine William changing his mind. He seems so set against us."

"Beyond all his objections, I believe your brother loves you and wants what's best. We must keep praying for him to have a change of heart."

"Yes, we mustn't give up hope." Sarah wrapped her arms around Julia and leaned her head on her shoulder. "Thank you, Julia. You are so dear. I don't know what I would do without you."

Seventeen

Julia folded the top edge of Millie's sheet over the blanket and smoothed it across the little girl's chest. "Time to rest, my dear."

Millie's forehead creased and anxiety filled her pale blue eyes.

"It's all right, Millie. I will be right here when you wake up." Julia gently ran her hand over the little girl's forehead. "Resting is the best thing you can do to regain your strength."

Millie's expression eased, and she released a faint sigh as her eyelids slid closed.

Julia scanned Millie's face, her heart aching for her. The prickly red rash seemed to be fading, but the sore throat, headache, and stomachache continued to make her miserable. Swallowing was especially difficult, so she resisted speaking and eating.

Julia sighed and straightened, her neck and shoulders aching from the long hours she'd spent caring for the children the last five days. It had been a wearying watch, with just Ann and Sarah giving her an occasional break for a few hours' sleep.

Sir William had heeded the doctor's warning and stayed away the first day. But the next morning, after breakfast, he arrived and announced he would not be kept from his children any longer.

Julia had been pleased by his refusal to follow the doctor's order and by his desire to spend more time with the children. Since that first visit, he had come three times each day to check on them and sit with them for a little while. Before he left, he always called Julia aside to discuss their condition and ask if there was anything she needed.

Her gaze drifted to the window as she recalled what he had said to her that first day. "I am placing you in charge of the children's care. You have much more experience with nursing than Sarah or Ann, and I trust your skills and good sense."

His confidence in her meant a great deal, and it had strengthened her determination to faithfully watch over Millie and Andrew through the worst of their illness.

Yesterday, when Andrew had improved enough to sit up and take a light meal, Julia asked William to read aloud a chapter from *The Prince and the Pauper.* Millie had listened for a few minutes, then fell asleep before the chapter's end. But

Andrew hung on every word and begged for a second chapter when William finished the first.

Julia smiled as she sank into a chair next to Millie's bed, remembering the animation in William's voice as he read the story and how the children responded and soaked up his attention. Caring for the children through this illness had been exhausting, but it seemed the Lord was using this time to draw William closer to his children. And that was a wonderful answer to prayer.

Sarah stepped through the doorway into the children's room, carrying her embroidery hoop and basket of thread. She set them on the bedside table. "Is Millie asleep?"

Julia yawned and nodded. "I think so."

"Why don't you go lie down?"

Julia shook her head. "I want to be here when the doctor comes."

Sarah sent her an indulgent smile. "All right. But at least put your feet up and close your eyes for a bit." She slid the padded footstool over in front of Julia's chair. "Go on. I'm perfectly capable of watching over two sleeping children." She nodded toward Andrew, who also rested peacefully in his bed.

Julia smiled. "All right. But wake me if there is any change in their condition."

"I will." Sarah took an extra blanket from the end of Andrew's bed and draped it over Julia.

"I'll just rest for a few minutes." The warmth of

the blanket weighed her down into the soft folds of the chair. She closed her eyes, and within seconds she drifted off to sleep.

William led Dr. Hadley up the main staircase and through the gallery. "I'm concerned about Millicent. She doesn't seem to be recovering as quickly as Andrew."

"Her health was not as strong as Andrew's before the illness. I'm sure that's the reason for her slow recovery."

William's shoulders tensed. "But she is out of danger, isn't she?"

His footsteps slowed. "It appears so. But scarlet fever can have some very serious complications —pneumonia or rheumatic fever, for instance. We must watch her very carefully until she is completely recovered."

William nodded, his resolve growing stronger. Millicent's poor appetite and persistent fever were nagging concerns. Miss Foster had asked the chef to send up broths, juices, and even ices to tempt his daughter, but she would only take small amounts.

"It's a stroke of luck you hired Miss Foster as governess. Her skills as a trained nurse are admirable."

The tension in William's shoulders eased a bit. "Yes, her years in India, assisting her father in the clinic, have given her some excellent nursing experience." But he knew it was more than that.

Spending time with Miss Foster these last few months had influenced him in many ways. And now he was sure it was divine providence rather than luck that brought her to Highland.

The doctor paused at the nursery door. "I think the children are going to be fine, but my examination today will give us a better idea how they are progressing."

William nodded and followed him through the doorway. The doctor paused and looked over his shoulder. "You understand, even at this stage, they may still be contagious."

"Yes, I understand."

"Very well." The doctor crossed the room to Andrew's bed. Sarah sat beside the boy, sewing and watching over him while he slept. She greeted the doctor in a hushed voice, then nodded to William. He moved to her side as the doctor took Andrew's hand and checked his pulse. The boy stirred and opened his eyes. He looked up at them with a sleepy smile.

William laid his hand on his son's shoulder. "How are you, Andrew?"

"Much better." He yawned and shifted in the bed. "May I have something to eat? I'm terribly hungry."

"How about some nice warm soup?" Sarah set her sewing aside and rose from her chair.

"I'd rather have something cool and sweet—maybe some ice cream?"

William grinned, glad his son's appetite was returning. "I'm sure we can find something agreeable." He glanced at his sister.

"I'll go down and speak to Chef Lagarde." Sarah smiled at William, relief evident in her eyes, then she turned and left the room.

While the doctor continued his quiet examination of Andrew, William crossed to Millicent's bed and checked on his daughter. Her face seemed less flushed and her expression more relaxed. A wave of relief coursed through him. Hopefully she had truly turned a corner, and the doctor would confirm it.

Miss Foster slept in the chair next to his daughter's bed. Her right hand rested on Millicent's pillow, as though she wanted to reassure her that she was close by if needed.

The sight of them both sleeping so peacefully touched him deeply. His gaze settled on Miss Foster. She looked so serene, with her long, dark eyelashes fanned out above her softly rounded cheeks. Her pink lips were slightly parted, and he noted the gentle rise and fall of the thin blanket covering her shoulders. A strand of dark brown hair lay across her ear and curved down her pale neck in the most appealing fashion.

He pulled in a sharp breath and averted his eyes. What was he doing? If she awoke and found him staring down at her, surely she would not be pleased. He took a step back and cleared his throat.

Julia stirred and blinked, then sat straight up. "Oh, I'm sorry, sir. I just shut my eyes for a moment."

"Please. Don't apologize. I'm glad to see both you and Millicent resting so peacefully."

She smoothed her hand over her hair and tucked behind her ear that one strand he had just been admiring. She glanced across the room. "When did the doctor arrive?"

"Just a few moments ago."

"What will he think of me, sleeping the day away?"

"He thinks you've done an excellent job caring for the children, and I quite agree."

Her ruffled expression faded and was replaced by a slight smile. "Thank you, sir."

Millicent's eyes fluttered open, and she looked up at him. "Papa . . ."

"Hello, Millie. Have you had a good rest?"

She nodded, a slight smile warming her expression.

"How are you feeling?"

"A little better," she said softly.

"Well, that's very good news." He leaned down and brushed his hand across her forehead, taking a closer look at her pale blue eyes and the sprinkle of freckles across her pert nose. "You must do all you can to get well, because I am making plans to go and cut our Christmas tree very soon."

Her eyes widened. "A Christmas tree?"

He nodded. "Mr. McTavish says we have some

very nice evergreens just west of the cottages, and you must come along to help me choose the very best one."

She pushed up to a half-sitting position. "Can we go today?" Her eyes brightened, but her voice still sounded strained.

William and Miss Foster exchanged a smile. "It's a bit too rainy today, but we'll go cut our Christmas tree very soon." He gently touched her shoulder. "Now lie down and rest. And you must listen to the doctor and Miss Foster and do everything they say so you can get well."

"I will, Papa. I promise."

"Did you say we're going to cut a Christmas tree?" Andrew called from his bed.

William turned. "Yes. Would you like to come along?"

"You know I would!" The boy's face lit up. "I'm sure we'll find a grand tree. And it will be much better than any we had in London."

William's hands fell to his sides. Their Christmas celebrations had been subdued the last two years since his wife's death. For the children's sake he must do better this year, and he would. "Do you think we should put the tree in the drawing room or the great hall?"

"The great hall," Andrew called, rising to his knees. "Then it can be very tall, and we'll see it every morning when we come down for Scripture reading and prayer."

"Oh yes, Papa, the great hall," Millie added.

The doctor patted Andrew on the shoulder. "There now, settle down, my boy. You don't want to strain your voice."

Andrew huffed and flopped back on the bed. "I'm feeling much better. I'm not sick anymore, not at all."

"I'm glad to hear it." The doctor slipped his stethoscope around his neck.

"When may I get up?" Andrew plucked at his covers. "I'm very tired of staying in bed."

"Soon." The doctor turned and addressed Miss Foster. "After twenty-four hours with no fever, he may get up for a short time. But he must take it slowly and not overtire himself."

Miss Foster nodded. "Very good, doctor. I'll see to it."

"And now let me see how this young lady is doing." He smiled at Millie as he approached.

William stepped back and motioned Miss Foster to join him by the door. He pulled his watch from his vest pocket and checked the time. "I need to go down. The art dealer from London is here, and he should be done with his appraisals soon."

He glanced at the children. "I'd like to hear the doctor's report about Millie."

"I'll come and find you after he's finished."

William nodded. "Thank you. I'd appreciate it."

"Of course, sir." A sweet smile lifted the corners of her mouth. "I'm glad to do whatever I can to ease your concern." She had obviously put their disagreement at her parents' cottage behind her and was ready to renew their friendship.

He returned her smile, knowing he should go, but he hesitated. Their gazes met and held, and a powerful sense of connection passed between them.

Just as quickly, a warning sped through his mind. He must not let his emotions overrule his good sense. He was grateful for Miss Foster's kindness and care toward the children. That was all. It couldn't be anything more. Emotions and feelings were not reliable, and he would not let them take the lead.

William drummed his fingers on his desk as he watched raindrops drizzle down the windowpane. He stretched and groaned. What he needed was a good hike across the fields, but rainy weather and concern for the children had kept him indoors for almost a week.

Lawrence stepped into the library. "Excuse me, sir. Mr. Henshaw has finished. Would you like me to show him in?"

William stood. The man might want to ask him about some of the paintings. "No. I'll come out."

Lawrence nodded. "Very good, sir. He wants to take the five o'clock train back to London. Shall I order the carriage?"

"Yes, have Gates bring it round and take him to the station when we've finished." William strode out of the library and met the art dealer in the great hall. "Mr. Henshaw, thank you for coming. I hope you were able to collect all the information you need for the appraisals."

Mr. Henshaw nodded. "Yes sir. Your man, Lawrence, has been most helpful." He glanced around the great hall. "You have a beautiful home and some very fine paintings."

"Thank you. I'm anxious to hear your estimation of their value."

Mr. Henshaw lifted dark eyebrows, surprise reflected in his eyes. "I want to give you an accurate appraisal, and that means I must do my research for comparable pieces and recent sales. I'm afraid it will take me a few weeks to find that information and write up my report."

"A few weeks?" Now it was William's turn to be surprised.

"Yes, and with the Christmas holiday coming, I don't believe I will be able to send it to you until well after New Year's."

William's shoulders tensed. "Mr. Henshaw, let me be frank. I am facing a deadline on the first of March to pay the death duties that were incurred when I inherited Highland. I need to know if the sale of these paintings is going to bring in sufficient funds."

"I see." Mr. Henshaw stroked his beard. "I'll do all I can to hurry the process along, but it takes time to make accurate appraisals. Then we must make arrangements to bring representative pieces to our gallery in London and put those on display. We also have to add your paintings to our catalog and be sure the information is published and distributed to prospective buyers. It's not a quick and easy process, not at all."

"I understand it won't happen tomorrow or next week, but with that deadline approaching, I need to know when I might expect to receive the proceeds of the sales."

"Well, it's hard to say. Most people who are redecorating or moving to new residences in London will do so in late winter or early spring so they can be ready to entertain guests during the season. But there are some"—he wrinkled his nose slightly—"Americans, for instance, who purchase artwork year round."

William lifted his brows. "Americans?"

"Yes sir, Americans and the *nouveau riche*—those who've made their money from industry, newspapers, or transportation rather than receiving it as an inheritance. They are the most likely buyers for these types of paintings."

William grimaced. "Yes, I suppose they have the money."

"Yes sir. And they like to line their walls with classic paintings by prominent artists to give the impression they have lived in their home for generations. But if you ask me, they fool no one but themselves."

"So you think our paintings might be purchased by someone like that?"

"Perhaps. But the process could also take months. There's really no way of knowing." He shifted slightly away from William. "I'm sorry. But I can't guarantee you will have the funds by the first of March."

"I see. So there's no way to know the amount we will receive or when we will receive it?"

"I can give you the appraisals soon after New Year's, but then we have to wait and see what sells."

"I don't suppose you would be interested in purchasing the paintings outright?"

"Oh, no sir. That's not how it's done. We act as your agent and representative, taking a commission only from the pieces that are sold."

William narrowed his eyes. "And just how much is your commission?"

Mr. Henshaw hesitated, his face coloring slightly. "Our commission is twenty-five percent for pieces up to fifty thousand pounds."

A shockwave jolted William. "Twenty-five percent?"

"Of course, the percentage decreases for those that sell for more than that."

He glared at Henshaw. "A quarter of the value goes to you simply for connecting me with a buyer?"

Mr. Henshaw straightened. "We do much more

than that, sir. As I said, we represent you and make sure you receive the highest price possible from each sale."

"Minus your commission."

Mr. Henshaw cleared his throat and lowered his gaze. "Yes sir. Minus our commission."

William blew out a deep breath. What did he expect? The man knew the market and had a decent reputation. William swallowed his irritation and nodded to Mr. Henshaw. "Very well. I understand. I'll look forward to receiving the appraisals and finalizing our agreement after the New Year's holiday."

"Thank you, sir." Mr. Henshaw smiled. "I promise we'll do our very best for you."

"I hope so, Mr. Henshaw."

The art dealer placed his hat on his head and reached out to shake William's hand. "A pleasure doing business with you, sir. A pleasure, indeed."

Sir William's voice rose from the great hall as Julia crossed the open gallery. Even though his words were polite, she could hear the tension in his voice. She frowned and glanced over the railing.

He stood below, conversing with a gentleman she assumed was the art dealer. As she descended the main staircase, he bid the man good day and Mr. Lawrence ushered him out the front door.

William looked up and met her gaze, his expression sober. "Miss Foster."

"You asked me to bring you the doctor's report about Millie."

"Yes." He motioned her to continue.

"Her fever has broken, and the rash is fading. He is pleased with her progress and says she is over the worst of her illness. He'll come again tomorrow afternoon to check on her."

"Very good." But the news did not bring him the relief she had expected.

"Is everything all right, sir?"

He glanced toward the door, his frown deepening. "No, I'm afraid it is not." He motioned toward the library. "There's something I want to discuss with you."

"Of course, sir." She followed him across the hall and into the library. She waited for him to offer her a chair, but he did not.

Instead, he paced to the fireplace, his back to her. "The art dealer has informed me it may take several months to see any income from the sale of the paintings." He turned and noticed she was still standing. "Please, be seated."

She took a chair and clasped her hands in her lap. "I'm sorry. I know you had hoped that would provide the funds you need."

"Yes. But stripping the house of these family treasures is becoming less appealing the more I consider it, especially knowing the hefty commission he wants to charge."

"How much is his commission?"

"Twenty-five percent." He released a disgusted huff.

Julia had no way of knowing if that was a fair commission or not, but Sir William certainly didn't seem to think so. "Is there some way you might sell the paintings without his help?"

He glared into the fireplace. "I doubt it. They've probably got a lock on the system." Clasping his hands behind his back, he crossed the room and stared out the windows toward the gray sky. "I must find some other way to raise those funds."

"I had hoped our efforts to economize would help."

His tense posture eased as he turned toward her again. "Your efforts are saving us a great deal of money, and I'm grateful. More important, they've allowed my sister to gain confidence and experience in running the house." Suddenly, his expression darkened again. "Although that has not led her in the direction I had hoped."

Julia looked down and pressed her lips together. She did not wish their conversation to become an argument.

He cleared his throat. "I know you don't agree with me on the matter of my sister and Mr. Dalton."

Julia opened her mouth, then thought better of it.

"I'll resolve matters with my sister in time. Right now we must find a way to raise the funds we need." He rested his hands on the back of the chair across from her. "And I hope discussing it with you will help me find a solution."

A pleasing warmth spread through her. Did he truly value her input even though they often clashed and came to opposing conclusions? Perhaps her mother was right, and the Lord had sent her to Highland to offer Sir William her encouragement and support through these difficult times. "I am happy to help you any way I can."

He studied her for a moment, his expression easing. "You are quite the mystery, Miss Foster."

"A mystery, sir? I don't understand."

"You have no experience running a large estate, but I find great comfort talking to you about these matters."

Her heartbeat quickened, and she looked into his eyes, trying to read the message behind his words, but he shifted his gaze away before she could decipher it. "I'm . . . I'm glad to hear it."

He sat in the chair opposite her, apparently unaware of her reaction. "An idea, Miss Foster. We must come up with a new idea."

She nodded, pushed down her emotions, and turned her thoughts into a prayer. A few moments later an idea formed in her mind. "Is there something else you might sell more quickly than the paintings? Rare books or jewels perhaps?"

"Sarah has a little jewelry, but it was given to her by our mother and grandmother. I wouldn't want to take it from her."

"No, of course not."

He glanced toward his bookshelves. "My late cousin was not a great reader. I'm afraid most of these are common books, and the same is true of our library in London, no first editions or books of special significance."

Julia nodded. "Do you have any other savings or investments that could be liquidated?"

"I sold my interest in our family business to my brother David before we left London. Most of those funds have already been used to make repairs here. The only other investment I have is our family home in London."

Julia straightened. "Why not sell the house and use the proceeds to pay the death duties?"

"I would have to convince my brother. He and I are co-owners."

"Does he live there?"

"No, he has his own residence across town."

"Do you think he would be open to selling?"

William frowned. "I doubt it. The house has been in our family since the 1840s. We're all quite attached to it, especially Sarah. David holds parties there a few times a year, and Sarah and I planned to stay there with the family when we go to town."

"Perhaps your brother would like to buy your half and have full ownership. Then the house would stay in the family, and you might still be able to use it on your visits to London."

William's expression eased. "That's a possibility. If the business is still going well, David might have the funds to buy me out."

Julia smiled, her heart lifting. "Sarah told me he is coming for a visit soon."

"He arrives on the twenty-first and plans to stay through New Year's Day." William rubbed his chin. "Yes, full ownership of our family home would appeal to David. He likes to feel he is in control."

"A financial agreement within the family could certainly be handled more quickly than the sale of the paintings."

"Yes, I believe you're right." He looked at her and smiled. "You see. I knew if we talked this through we'd come up with a solution. And I think this one just might work."

"I hope so, sir." Gratitude flooded her heart, and she thanked the Lord. If William's brother would agree to the plan, Highland would be saved, and everything would continue as it had.

But was that what she wanted: to continue on as governess? Or did she long for something more? And what about her dream of returning to India and serving the Lord there? For some reason, that dream didn't seem to shine as brightly as it had when she'd first come to Highland.

Was that because a new dream was forming in her heart, a dream that included the man who sat across from her?

Eighteen

Reverend Langford's wise and caring gaze rested on the congregation as he lifted his hand for the benediction. "The LORD bless thee, and keep thee: The LORD make his face shine upon thee, and be gracious unto thee: The LORD lift up his coun-tenance upon thee, and give thee peace. Amen."

Sarah rose from the pew, her queasy stomach fluttering as she turned and scanned the last two rows on the opposite side of St. John's Church. Several members of the Highland staff stood and prepared to leave, but she didn't see Clark Dalton among them.

She clasped Julia's arm as they stepped into the center aisle and walked toward the back of the sanctuary. William, Katherine, and Penelope followed. Sarah leaned closer to Julia and whispered, "Do you see Mr. Dalton anywhere?"

Julia glanced to the left. "He was sitting with the other members of the staff when we came in at the beginning of the service."

"Yes, but he's gone now." She searched across the sea of parishioners filing out the rear door, and her hopes fell. "I thought I might at least be able to see him and say hello."

"I'm not sure that's wise unless you've worked things out with Sir William." Julia sent her a questioning glance.

"Not yet." Sarah bit her lip and looked down, guilt squeezing her heart.

What must Clark think of her? It had been nine days since William had discovered them together. She had written Clark two notes and asked Ann to deliver them secretly, but he had not written back. Was he being honorable and obeying William's orders, or had he decided he didn't love her enough to risk losing his position? Sarah's heart throbbed, and she slipped her trembling hands in her coat pockets.

Sarah and Julia greeted Reverend Langford at the door, and then descended the steps to the churchyard.

Julia turned to Sarah with a gentle smile. "Why not talk to Sir William today?"

Sarah glanced around, her anxiety rising. "I'm not sure this is a good time. He has been so concerned about the death duties, the art dealer's appraisals, and David's visit . . ."

Julia smiled but sent her a doubtful look.

Sarah sighed. "All right. I admit it. I've put it off because I'm afraid of what he'll say." She looked back toward the church door as her brother stepped out into the sunshine and shook the reverend's hand. The two men exchanged a few words before William started down the steps. "What if he dismisses Clark?" Sarah whispered, her voice catching in her throat.

"He hasn't yet. Surely that's a good sign." Julia stepped closer and laid her hand on Sarah's arm. "Just talk to him. Tell him what's in your heart. He may not agree, but I'm sure he'll listen."

Sarah glanced over her shoulder as William approached. "Please stay with me while I speak to him."

Julia hesitated, but she nodded just before William joined them.

"Are you ladies ready?" He sent Julia a smile and then shifted his gaze to Sarah.

Sarah swallowed and slipped her handbag to the other arm. "I wondered if we might walk home so I could speak to you about . . . an important matter."

He lifted one eyebrow, glanced at Julia, and then Sarah. "If that's what you'd like."

"It is. And I've asked Miss Foster to stay with me, if you're agreeable."

"All right."

The tension in Sarah's shoulders eased a bit. "Thank you, William."

He spoke to Katherine and Penelope and sent them home in the carriage. Then he motioned toward the path. "Shall we walk?"

Sarah and Julia nodded, and they set off.

Sarah prayed for strength, then straightened her shoulders. "I'm sorry I didn't tell you about my feelings for Mr. Dalton. I know you were unhappy to find us together in his office, but I want to assure you that nothing improper happened between us."

"I should hope not."

"I should've spoken to you about it when you came to my door that day. But I was upset and afraid I would speak out in anger."

William nodded, looking thoughtful.

"I've had time to pray and think things through, and I want to say that I love Clark Dalton very much. And I'm convinced he is a good and kind man who would make a fine husband. But I'm prepared to listen to your concerns."

William cleared his throat. "Well, I appreciate that."

Sarah held her breath. *Please, God, soften his heart. Help him put aside his prejudices and see what's truly important.*

"If you had come to me yesterday, or even this morning before church, I would've given you a list of reasons why you should not become involved with Mr. Dalton, but, in the light of Reverend Langford's sermon this morning and the warning from James against judging a man by his social standing and outward appearance, I am rethinking my position on the matter."

Sarah blinked and almost missed a step. "What?"

"I'm not saying I have totally changed my mind," William continued. "But perhaps I was too hasty with my decision." He glanced at Miss Foster. "I've also given it a good deal of thought, and I would not want anyone to think I was not being fair-minded and considerate of your feelings and wishes."

Joy bubbled in Sarah's heart. "Oh, William." She threw her arms around him in a fierce hug. "Thank you!"

His stiff posture slowly eased, and he patted her shoulder before he stepped back. "I am not giving you permission to become engaged to Mr. Dalton. I don't believe either of us knows him well enough to make that decision yet."

"Oh, I'm sure once you spend time with Clark you'll see what a wonderful man he is."

"Yes, but we need to be cautious and certain of his character before there can be any agreement about the future."

Sarah pressed her lips together, barely able to keep her smile at bay. "Very well. I do so want your approval and blessing. I'm willing to wait."

"Miss Foster, you have been very quiet. I'm sure you have an opinion about Mr. Dalton that you'd like to share." There was a hint of challenge in his voice.

She glanced at him, looking as though she was

carefully weighing her words. "I have only spoken to Mr. Dalton a few times, but Reverend Langford says he is a wise and kind man who has a strong faith."

A look of surprise filled William's eyes. "You spoke to Reverend Langford about this?"

Sarah hurried to answer. "After Clark made his feelings known to me, I asked Miss Foster to make a few discreet inquiries about him."

"I see." He shifted his gaze back to Julia. "What else did you learn about Mr. Dalton?"

"People speak well of him in the village. Many admire the way he cares for his widowed mother and his young niece who came into his home after her parents died. He seems well liked by all the staff. Mr. Lawrence says he's diligent, and he treats those under him with fairness and consideration."

William clasped his hands behind his back. "My, you do seem to know quite a bit about him."

Sarah smiled. "You can imagine how pleased I was to hear these good reports. Knowing he is so well respected gave me confidence to move ahead."

"If you were so confident, why didn't you come to me?"

Her smile fell away. "I'm sorry, William. I was afraid you wouldn't approve, and it would cause a terrible rift between us."

"And it did for a time."

"But we are past that now. Thank you for reconsidering. It means the world to me."

He walked on a few more steps before he spoke. "We must proceed very carefully. I don't want to stir up a cloud of gossip and put a damper on Katherine's first season."

"No, of course not," Sarah said.

"Your actions must be above reproach. There can be no more secret meetings."

Sarah nodded.

"You may write to him," William continued, "and he may write to you. But you may only see each other a few times each week, with a chaperone. And there will be no final decision until this summer, after we return from London."

Conflicting thoughts swirled through Sarah's mind. Seven months was a long time to wait. What would Clark say? Did he love her enough to submit to William's plan? What if William had to sell Highland and return to London? What would happen to them then? But an even more important question rose in her mind: Was she ready to give up everything to become Clark's wife?

Assurance quickly flooded her heart, and she looked up at her brother. "I understand why you feel it's important for us to wait, and I hope Clark will agree."

"If he truly loves you, then waiting a few months should not be too difficult. It will give him an opportunity to prove he is sincere and eager to do things properly."

Sarah smiled at Julia, then turned to her brother. "Thank you, William. I'm grateful. I'll go and speak to Clark now."

"Sarah, would you please wait to see him until after luncheon? Perhaps then Miss Foster can act as your chaperone." He glanced at Julia.

"Of course. I'd be happy to."

Sarah leaned in and kissed Julia's cheek. "Thank you," she whispered, then set off, eager to get home and prepare to see Clark.

Julia watched Sarah hurry down the path, and relief flowed through her. Seeing Sarah and William come to an agreement about Mr. Dalton made her feel like a heavy weight had been lifted off her heart.

"You seem pleased," William said with a slight smile.

"I am. You've made your sister very happy."

"I hope we won't come to regret it." He watched Sarah disappear around the bend. "If she follows through with this and marries Dalton, she will live a very different life."

Julia walked a few more steps. "Yes, but marrying the man she loves will fulfill one of the deepest desires of her heart."

"You seem quite idealistic where love and marriage are concerned."

"I suppose that's because I was blessed to grow up in a happy home with parents who truly love each other."

"That is a benefit Sarah and I did not enjoy."

His admission surprised her. "I'm sorry."

"Oh, it's all right." He tried to look nonchalant, but she could tell it was a painful admission. "We leaned on each other through the years, and it drew us even closer."

She studied his pensive expression. "I think it will be hard for you to let Sarah go, no matter who she marries."

He sent her a half smile. "Yes, that's probably true."

"But if she marries Mr. Dalton, at least she'll stay at Highland, and you can see her often."

"If I can get my financial affairs in order and hold on to the estate. And I must so I can continue to provide employment for all the staff, including you, Miss Foster."

"I hope so. I've grown very fond of the children." She pictured their faces, and a bittersweet feeling filled her heart. "But if circumstances change, and I must leave Highland, I'm sure the Lord will provide for me and my family in another way."

William glanced off toward the distant hills. "I admire you . . . and your faith."

"My faith has very little to do with me and everything to do with my Savior."

287

He cast a curious look her way.

"What I mean is, the more I understand His character and the promises in His Word, the stronger my faith becomes."

"You make it sound so simple—you and Reverend Langford."

"Faith is not complex, though living it out in the face of challenging circumstances can be."

"I suppose your time in India had a great influence on your faith."

"It did, but not because things were always easy. We often faced dark days and very serious trouble."

"What kind of trouble?"

"Opposition from village leaders, superstition, and ignorance—they all made our work difficult."

"I had no idea. I always pictured you as victorious at every turn."

She shook her head. "Not at all. One time a young girl we rescued was taken away and returned to the temple. That was heartbreaking. Another time we made great sacrifices to help a high-caste Brahman woman when she was ill, yet she and her family remained hardhearted toward the gospel and later looked for ways to destroy our ministry. I cried out to God for justice in both those situations, but the circumstances didn't change."

"How did you hold on to your faith in the face of such disappointments?"

"God poured out His love and grace in our hearts, and He gave us many promises from His Word to sustain us. As I look back now, I believe my faith was strengthened more in the difficult times than it was when everything was going smoothly."

A shadow passed over his face, and pain filled his eyes. "I wouldn't say my faith has been strengthened by my trials—quite the opposite in fact."

"We have a choice to make when trouble comes. We can reach out to God and look to Him for strength and help, or we can doubt His love and purpose and allow our hearts to grow cold. It takes faith to believe that He can and will bring good out of those trials if we will only trust Him."

He pondered that for a moment, then nodded. "I'm afraid my faith has not been all it should be."

"Realizing you have a need is the first step in the right direction."

He nodded. "I believe you're right." Warmth filled his eyes as he looked her way. "I appreciate the way you look at life and circumstances through the eyes of faith."

Her heart lifted. She smiled up at him, sensing a new level of understanding between them. "Thank you. That's one of the nicest compliments I have ever received."

His grin spread wider, and they walked on together toward Highland.

• • •

Julia left Ann in charge in the nursery and crossed the hall, intending to go to her room and prepare her afternoon lessons for Katherine and Penelope, but the sound of someone running up the stairs stopped her at her door, and she looked to the right.

Katherine strode into the east wing with her head down and her shoulders sagging.

"Katherine, is everything all right?"

Katherine gasped, looked up, and brushed a tear from her blotchy cheek. "No, it's not, but why would you care?"

Julia pulled back, stung by the words. But seeing the misery in Katherine's eyes, she pushed her hurt aside and softened her voice and posture. "My heart goes out to anyone who is in distress."

Katherine's hard expression wavered, and her chin trembled. "We might as well cancel my plans for the season."

"Why would you say that?"

Katherine looked around, obviously debating whether she would continue the conversation.

With a prayer for grace rising in her heart, Julia reached out and touched Katherine's arm. "Do you want to tell me what happened?"

Katherine tensed, the struggle evident on her face. Finally, she released a shuddering sigh. "All right."

"Shall we go to my room?"

Katherine nodded and followed Julia. She crossed to the dressing table and sank down on the bench. "I can't go to London now. Everything is ruined." Her voice choked off and she lowered her head.

Concern filled Julia, and she took a handkerchief from the dresser and handed it to Katherine. "I'm glad to listen and help if I can."

Katherine sniffed and wiped her cheeks. "I went riding this morning with Margaret Covington. She seemed rather cool toward me, and when I asked her what was wrong, she told me Florence Burns and Elizabeth Tremble say I have deserted all my old friends and I care nothing for them."

"Why would she say that?"

"I suppose I have spent more time with Rosalind Sands and Emily Forester these last few months, but that's because they've both been presented and did the season last year. I thought becoming better acquainted with them would be helpful when I went to London."

"But Margaret and your other friends have been hurt by that?"

Katherine lifted her hands. "I suppose so. But I'm a year older than Florence and Elizabeth. They won't be presented until next year. It seems natural that I would seek out friends my age or older."

"What about Margaret?"

"She's also eighteen, and this will be her first season as well. We've been good friends all our lives. I can't believe she would side with Florence and Elizabeth against me."

"Perhaps she's not truly against you."

"It certainly seems that way."

"I know it's upsetting to have conflict with friends, but how can that impact your time in London?"

"Margaret's mother is very influential. If she feels I've snubbed her daughter and our friends, she'll make sure I'm not invited to the best parties and balls."

"But surely there's time to repair your friendships before the season."

"You don't know Margaret or her mother, and you've never done the season." Katherine brushed away another tear. "You wouldn't understand."

Katherine's dismissal stung, but Julia let it go. "It's true I haven't done the season, but I have faced a similar situation with some friends when I was your age."

"I thought you lived in India then."

"I did." Julia waited, hoping she'd piqued Katherine's interest.

Katherine looked up. "What happened?"

Julia sat in the chair opposite Katherine. "When we first arrived in India, we stayed at a large mission station in Bangalore to study the language and adjust to the culture. I met three girls there who were also daughters of missionaries, and we all became good friends.

"Then our family moved to Kanakapura to set up our clinic and begin our work in the village. My parents felt it was important to wear traditional Indian dress so we would be more easily accepted. That was a challenge for me at first, but I soon adjusted to it and enjoyed it.

"A few months later, when my friends from Bangalore came to visit, they were surprised to see how I dressed, because they all wore English clothing. It caused quite a stir."

"Why should they care how you dress?"

"They said I was throwing away my heritage and separating myself from them. They also thought I preferred spending time with the Indian girls who attended our Bible classes rather than with them, and they let me know it."

"How rude. I hope you told them they ought to pack their bags and go back to Bangalore."

"No, I ran off and cried buckets of tears. My mother came looking for me and patiently listened to my story, but she said I had hurt my friends, and it was up to me to make things right. Of course that stung my pride, and I resisted. But then she shared a poem that helped me see things more clearly."

"A poem?"

"Yes, I don't remember it all, but the first two lines have stayed with me ever since." Julia glanced toward the window, and her heart warmed as she recalled the words. "Make new friends, but keep the old, those are silver, these are gold."

Katherine's tense expression eased.

"You don't have to choose one set of friends over the other. Every friendship is important. And each friend needs our care and consideration."

Katherine wiped her cheeks and sighed. "I'm afraid it's too late to repair my broken friendships."

"You won't know unless you try. Why don't you write a note to each one, telling her you're sorry and explaining how much her friendship means to you?"

Katherine gazed at Julia and sent her a slight smile. "I suppose I do have a bit of experience with writing letters of apology."

Julia nodded and returned her smile. "Yes, you are quite an accomplished letter writer."

Julia glanced at her watch as she crossed the nursery. "Hurry, children. Your uncle David will be arriving any minute, and your father wants you downstairs to greet him."

Ann quickly finished tying a pink bow in Millie's hair. "There. Now you look very nice."

"Thank you." Millie smiled into the mirror at her reflection.

"I don't see why we must go down." Andrew tugged at his vest. "Uncle David has never cared much for us."

Julia straightened Andrew's collar. "I'm sure your uncle will be happy to see you."

"I don't think so." He looked up at Julia, a hint of painful confusion in his eyes.

She laid a hand on his shoulder. "Be pleasant and respectful."

Andrew sighed. "All right, but you'll see. He doesn't like us."

"If you greet him politely and act like a gentleman, I'm sure there won't be any problem," Julia added.

She guided the children downstairs to the great hall. Sarah waited for them there, along with several members of the staff.

Sir William exited the library and joined them. He frowned and glanced toward the stairs. "Lawrence, did someone send word to the young ladies?"

"Yes sir. Perhaps they've forgotten the time. I'll send a maid up to remind them." He turned away and quietly issued the order to Lydia, who quickly trotted up the steps.

Nelson walked in the front door. "Mr. Ramsey's car has just entered the gate."

"Very good." William led the family outside. The staff followed and lined up on the right, looking a bit like soldiers on parade, ready for inspection.

Julia, Sarah, and the children moved to the opposite side of the entrance. Julia adjusted Millie's hair bow and instructed Andrew to stand beside his father, then she slipped to the end of the line as the car approached up the gravel drive.

Sarah leaned toward Julia. "I am so looking forward to seeing my brother. It's been more than five months since our farewell dinner in London."

Julia smiled, glad to hear Sarah had a good opinion of David Ramsey, even though Andrew did not. Perhaps the boy had not spent enough time with his uncle to develop a strong bond. Hopefully, celebrating Christmas together would draw them all closer.

The car rolled to a stop. Nelson strode forward and opened the rear passenger door. David Ramsey stepped out, wearing a charming smile and an expensive hat, coat, and silk scarf. He resembled William, but he was a few inches shorter, with darker hair and eyes and a trim moustache.

"Welcome to Highland, David." Sarah offered him her hand.

He leaned forward and kissed her fingers. "My dear Sarah, it's so good to see you again." His expression dimmed slightly as he turned to his brother. "Thank you for inviting me, William."

"We're glad you've come." But William's stiff posture as he shook his brother's hand cast doubt upon that sentiment. He turned to the children, prompting them with a nod.

Andrew stepped forward. "Hello, Uncle David."

David shook Andrew's hand. "My, you certainly have grown since I saw you last."

Andrew glanced up at Julia, a silent question in his eyes.

She smiled and wished she could supply the polite words he needed to respond.

"Thank you," Andrew mumbled and stepped back.

Millie curtsied and smiled up at her uncle. "Papa said we had to wait until you came before we could cut our Christmas tree."

David chuckled. "I'm sorry I've kept you waiting."

"It's all right. I've been sick, but I'm better now." She looked up at William. "Can we go soon, Papa?"

"We'll go tomorrow morning if the weather is clear." He turned to David. "Shall we go inside?"

Before David could respond, Katherine and Penelope rushed out the door at the same time, jostling each other in the process.

Katherine shot a glare at her sister, then she straightened and turned toward their guest. As her gaze settled on David, her eyes brightened and her smile warmed several degrees. "Cousin David, how wonderful to see you again."

Surprise flashed in David's eyes. "Why, this cannot be our cousin Katherine, can it?"

"Yes, it is." She extended her hand to him.

"You were just a little girl the last time I visited Highland."

"That was several years ago. I'm eighteen now,

and I'll be going to London for the season this year."

"Well, I'm sure you'll have a parade of suitors eager to make your acquaintance."

Katherine blushed, obviously pleased by David's assessment.

William cleared his throat. "And this is our cousin Penelope."

The younger girl stepped forward and greeted him with a shy smile. "It's a pleasure to have you visit us again, Cousin David."

He nodded to her and smiled, though his response was not as warm as it had been for Katherine. "The pleasure is mine." He shifted his focus to Julia. "And is this another charming cousin?"

Julia pulled in a quick breath, and William glared at his brother.

Sarah took Julia's arm. "This is Miss Foster. She is the governess and has become a dear friend."

David lifted one eyebrow. "My, the children are certainly lucky to have such a lovely young woman oversee their education."

Julia's face warmed, and she shifted her gaze away. David Ramsey was certainly quick with compliments.

"Let's go inside." Sarah motioned toward the door. "Tea is ready in the library."

Mr. Lawrence dismissed the staff, and they filed around the side of the house, while the family, led by William, entered through the front door.

Julia hung back with the children, intending to go in last, but David waited for her under the arched portico. "I hope I didn't embarrass you by my comment, Miss Foster. That wasn't my intention." He seemed sincere, but there was a hint of humor in his eyes.

Her face flushed. "No, of course not." She glanced at the children. "We should go in."

"Yes, we don't want to keep everyone waiting." He smiled again and motioned toward the door. "After you."

Julia nodded, then took Millie's hand. "I hope you enjoy your visit to Highland, Mr. Ramsey."

"Thank you. I'm sure I will, especially now that we've met."

With her cheeks flaming, she ushered the children inside.

Nineteen

Ann hurried down the backstairs, Miss Ramsey's letter to Mr. Dalton tucked safely away in her apron pocket. If she took care of her errand quickly, she might be able to steal a few moments with Peter in the stables. She pressed her hand against her fluttering stomach and quickened her pace.

At least Miss Ramsey's letters weren't a secret anymore, and she didn't have to worry about being caught by Mrs. Emmitt. But even if the stern old housekeeper caught her, what could she say? Miss Ramsey was the mistress of Highland, and Ann was only doing her bidding.

She pushed open the back door and stepped out into the cool, misty morning. Rain rushed down the gutters and splashed on the paving stones of the back courtyard. She lifted her gaze, longing to see a bit of sun peek through, but the clouds hung low over Highland. Perhaps the mist would burn off by afternoon. Too bad she wouldn't be allowed out to see it. Unless, of course, Julia took the children out for a walk and brought her along. But Julia hadn't taken them outdoors since their bout with scarlet fever.

Ann crossed the courtyard, and her thoughts returned to the letter in her pocket. It didn't seem fair that Miss Ramsey and Mr. Dalton were allowed to carry on a courtship and she and Peter were not. But then, she was not an aristocratic lady, and Peter was not the head gardener. Still, even though she was only a nursery maid, shouldn't she have the right to follow her heart and experience love like anyone else?

"Psst! Ann!"

She gasped as her hand flew to her heart.

Peter stepped out from behind the stable door. He smiled and opened his arms. She ran to him, and he wrapped her in a warm embrace. She pressed her head to his strong chest and breathed in. My, he smelled lovely, like leather and hay and open fields.

"It's wonderful to see you, Ann. I've been worried about you."

"I'm sorry I haven't come down sooner." She stepped back and gazed up at his handsome face. "I've had more than my share of the load to carry lately."

"But you're all right?"

"Of course. Just a bit tired." She looked into his golden-brown eyes and sent him a weary smile. "Wouldn't it be nice to sleep in and not have to get up before the rooster crows?" She sighed and shook her head. That would never happen, at least not as long as she worked as nursery maid at Highland.

He clasped her hand. "Maybe that day is coming."

"What do you mean?"

"I overheard Mr. McTavish telling Mr. Hardy that Sir William has money troubles, and he may have to sell Highland."

Ann gasped. "What? How can that be? I thought he had loads of money."

"So did I. But he owes the government a huge sum for inheriting the estate. If he can't pay it by the first of March, he'll have to sell."

Ann stared at him, trying to sort it out in her mind. "What will happen then?"

"We'll be out of a job, that's what. Split up and searching for new positions."

Ann's legs suddenly felt weak, and she sank onto a crate. "Oh, that's terrible!"

Peter knelt before her. "But it doesn't have to be, not if we make our move first."

"What do you mean?"

"Give your notice, collect your reference, and come away with me."

Ann gasped. "I can't do that. My da would kill me."

"Not if you don't tell him."

"But I couldn't keep a secret like that. It

wouldn't be right." She wrung her hands while her stomach turned into a nervous pudding. "Even if I could, where would we go? How would we live?"

"My sister and her husband have a house in Oxford. I'm sure we could stay with them until we get jobs and find a place of our own."

"Oxford?" She'd never been farther than Fulton and the surrounding farms. What would it be like to live in a big university town? Staying with Peter's sister and her family might be respectable. It wasn't exactly the same as running away together. "Do you think they'd really let us live with them?"

"Sure they would. Their place isn't too big, but Sally would make room for us. Her husband, Charlie, works as a driver for a rich professor. Charlie knows everything there is to know about motorcars and driving. I'm sure he'd teach me, and in a few weeks I could be driving for a wealthy family."

"Would you like that kind of work?"

"Of course. Horses and carriages are on the way out. It's motorcars everyone wants now. And that means wealthy folks will need drivers."

"But what about me? What will I do?"

Peter scratched his chin. "I suppose you could work as a maid again." Then his eyes lit up. "Or maybe you could work in a shop. Wouldn't you like that better than wiping kids' noses and cleaning their boots? The hours would be better, and we could spend our evenings together." He grinned and winked.

She sighed. "It sounds lovely, but it would be a risk to leave Highland when we have no promise of work."

He stood and placed his hands on his hips. "Don't you trust me, Ann? I'll take care of you, I promise."

She bit her lip and looked away. He hadn't said anything about marriage.

Peter took her hand and gently pulled her up. "Listen to me, Ann. If Sir William can't pay his taxes, he's going to lose Highland. And if that happens, we'll have to find new positions, and there's no guarantee where we'll end up." He gripped her hand more tightly. "But if we leave now, we can start a new life, a better life . . . together."

"Oh, Peter." She looked into his eyes as questions rushed through her mind. If only he would propose and promise they'd marry as soon as they left Highland. But she couldn't force him to marry her. Those words had to come from his heart.

Julia's warning flashed through her mind: *If he truly loves you, he should do what's best for you, not just what makes him happy.*

But she loved Peter more than any other man she'd ever known. What should she do? How could she be sure of making the right choice?

• • •

Mrs. Emmitt pressed her back to the stable wall, her heart thumping in her chest. Surely Peter Gates was wrong. It couldn't be true. Mr. McTavish would never tell Mr. Hardy such a lie about Sir William. The boy must have made it up to try and convince Ann to run away with him.

What a scoundrel! Wait until Mr. Lawrence heard what had been going on. This would be Peter Gates's last day at Highland!

The wind shifted and blew a few raindrops across her cheek. She wiped them away. A sudden thought struck and snatched her breath. What if it wasn't a lie? What if Sir William was headed for financial ruin and planned to take them all down with him?

She pressed a trembling hand to her chest, trying to calm her racing heart. It would be hard to find another position at her age. Sixty-one wasn't ancient, but she had not aged well, and she didn't have much energy these days.

A burning sensation rose in her throat. How could this happen? She'd always thought she would work at Highland until she was too old to manage her duties. Then the family would give her a cottage and pension and take care of her until she died. She'd never dreamed she would be out in the streets, searching for another position at this point in life. It could not be borne!

She must speak to Mr. Lawrence. Surely he

would know if there was any credence to the story, and he should be the one to confront Peter.

"I'm sorry, Peter, but I have to go." There was no mistaking the lovesick tone of Ann's voice.

Mrs. Emmitt's lips puckered as though she'd bitten into a rotten piece of fruit.

"Just promise you'll think about what I said." Peter's voice sounded as smooth as honey.

Mrs. Emmitt pressed closer to the wall and strained to hear the girl's answer.

"All right. I promise."

Mrs. Emmitt pulled back into the shadows as Ann passed. Why was she headed toward the greenhouse rather than the back door? She listened for Peter's departure, and a few seconds later she heard the boy whistle a tune as his steps faded into the distance.

Mrs. Emmitt peeked around the corner and scanned the empty courtyard. Clutching her shawl around her shoulders, she strode back to the house.

She found Mr. Lawrence in the servant's hall, having a cup of tea. Lydia and Marie sat across from him at the table. "I need to speak to you . . . in private."

He lifted his dark eyebrows. "Very well."

She followed him down the hall and into the butler's pantry and shut the door.

"What seems to be the matter?"

"I've just overheard Peter Gates trying to convince Ann Norton to run away with him."

Mr. Lawrence eyes widened. "No!"

"Yes! And that's not all. He tried to sway her by saying Sir William might be forced to sell Highland to pay the inheritance tax."

Mr. Lawrence frowned. "Inheritance tax? Do you think he means the death duties?"

"I don't care what you call them. If it's true, you and I and everyone else who works here is in serious trouble."

Mr. Lawrence's scowl deepened. "I don't believe it. What would a stable boy know about Sir William's financial affairs?"

"He said he overheard Mr. McTavish speaking to Mr. Hardy."

Mr. Lawrence glowered at Mrs. Emmitt. "Where are loyalty and propriety these days? They should not be discussing the family's private matters among themselves, especially where others might overhear."

"Of course they shouldn't, but now that they have, we must use the information to our advantage."

"And how would you suggest we do that?"

"I'm not sure. We'll have to keep our eyes and ears open and see what we can learn." She fingered the keys hanging from her waist and tried to still her trembling hands. "Where would Sir William go if he sells Highland?"

"Back to London, I suppose. He has to provide a home for the children, Miss Ramsey, and his cousins."

Mrs. Emmitt nodded. "Do you think he'd take us with him?"

"He mentioned the possibility of me going with him to London for the season. But it was just a passing comment. I don't believe he'd truly given it much thought."

"What about me? Do you think he'd take me as well?"

"He has hardly had time to develop feelings of loyalty toward any of us."

"But Katherine and Penelope depend on me. I've overseen their care since their mother died."

"I'm sure the young ladies would want to keep you on, but Katherine is eighteen. She could marry within the year if things go well for her in London. Penelope's debut is only two years away. And they have Miss Foster to look after them now."

"Miss Foster indeed!" The burning sensation in Mrs. Emmitt's stomach flamed into her throat again. "So that's it? I'm to be thrown out like a bit of old rubbish after all my years of service to this family?"

"There's no need to be upset. This is all speculation. We don't know the truth yet."

"No. We do not. But I don't intend to stand by and let this all come down on our heads."

"I'm not sure we have any choice in the matter."

"Oh, I have a choice all right. And I'm choosing to keep my position and make my future secure."

Julia placed the jeweled comb in Sarah's hair and glanced in the dressing table mirror to check the placement. "How does that look?"

Sarah turned to the left and right and smiled. "It's perfect. Thank you, Julia. You always know just how to fix my hair." She adjusted her necklace and sighed. "With this hand of mine, it's nearly impossible for me to make it look the way I'd like."

Julie smiled at her friend, happy she could help. "Perhaps you should have a lady's maid now that you are mistress of Highland."

"I've thought about it, but I never had one in London, and since we're economizing, it doesn't seem wise to spend William's money that way."

"It's good of you to make that kind of sacrifice for your brother's sake."

"I don't mind. I want to live a simpler life." Her smile deepened, revealing a pretty pair of matching dimples in her cheeks. "Besides, it will make the transition easier when Clark and I are married."

Julia looked into the mirror and returned Sarah's smile. "I suppose Mr. Dalton was glad to hear Sir William has softened his stance."

"Yes. He's quite pleased, though we both wish

he hadn't asked us to wait so long to announce our engagement."

"But it will keep the family close, and you'll have your brother's blessing."

Sarah nodded. "I have to keep reminding myself of that so I don't grow impatient." She reached for an earring and held it out to Julia. "Would you help me with this?"

"Of course." Julia gently screwed the left earring into place, and then the right.

"I wouldn't fuss about my hair and jewelry, but since this is David's first dinner here, and Lord and Lady Gatewood are joining us, I thought I should make an effort."

"You look very nice. I'm sure it will be a lovely dinner."

A knock sounded at the bedroom door, and Sarah called, "Come in."

Katherine and Penelope entered. Both girls' cheeks were flushed, and they were still wearing their coats and hats.

"Aunt Louisa said to tell you she's bringing another guest for dinner tonight," Katherine announced.

It was certainly presumptuous of Lady Gatewood to add another dinner guest at this late hour, but then she often acted as though she was the mistress of Highland rather than Sarah.

"Another guest?" A slight line creased Sarah's brow. "And who would that be?"

Penelope's eyes lit up, and a playful smile lifted her lips. "Miss Alice Drexel of Philadelphia."

"I don't believe I've met her." Sarah rose from the dressing table bench and turned toward the girls. "How is she connected with your aunt?"

"Her father, Anthony Joseph Drexel II, is in banking, and he and Uncle Albert have business dealings together," Penelope said.

"I see. And have you met Miss Drexel?"

"She came with us today when Aunt Louisa took us for our dress fitting in Fulton." Katherine unbuttoned her coat. "She's twenty-four and quite attractive for an American."

Penelope slipped the scarf from around her neck and sighed. "I'd say she's positively regal. She's tall and blond and has the most unique green eyes, just like the color of moss growing on rocks by a stream. And beside all her outward beauty, she's the heiress to her family's fortune."

"Yes, in America, daughters are entitled to inherit rather than some distant cousin." Katherine's voice dripped disdain.

Pain flashed in Sarah's eyes, but she didn't respond to Katherine's jibe. "So what brings Miss Drexel to England?"

A look of delight filled Penelope's face. "Apparently Alice Drexel's younger sister, Olivia, was involved in some sort of scandal. Of course that reflects poorly on the family, and it has dimmed Alice's prospects for marriage in

Philadelphia, so they sent her here to find an English husband."

Katherine tipped her head, and a mischievous light filled her eyes. "One who would appreciate her fortune and doesn't mind a bit of distant American scandal."

Julia's stomach tensed. What was Katherine implying?

"Alice's mother died several years ago," Penelope continued. "So Aunt Louisa has taken Alice under her wing. She's intent on helping her find a suitable match."

"How long will she be staying?" Julia asked.

"She'll be at Bedford Hall with Aunt Louisa and Uncle Albert for at least a month, then she'll spend time in Bristol before she goes to London for the season."

"A month . . . with your aunt?" Julia swallowed. "That's quite a long stay."

"Well, it was quite a big scandal." Katherine glanced past Julia to the clock on the bedside table. "Oh, look how late it is. Come on, Penny, we have to go change for dinner." She sent her sister a teasing smile. "We wouldn't want to keep *anyone* waiting."

Penelope grinned. "No, we would not."

Katherine took a step and then turned back. "Oh, yes, Aunt Louisa said to seat Alice Drexel next to Cousin William."

Julia's breath caught in her throat.

"And David," Penelope added.

Katherine shot a glare at her sister.

"What's wrong?" Penny lifted her hands. "Aunt Louisa said to seat Alice between William and David."

Katherine huffed. "I don't remember her saying that at all. It was William she mentioned."

Penelope's brow creased. "No, I distinctly remember her saying—"

"Never mind, girls." Sarah motioned them toward the door. "I'll take care of the seating. Run along and change."

Katherine whispered something to Penny and tugged her sister toward the door. The younger girl giggled and nodded as they stepped into the hall.

Julia's concern grew as she watched them. There was obviously more going on than they were saying.

Sarah sighed as she turned back toward Julia. "I was going to sit between William and David tonight, but I suppose I should honor Louisa's request and rearrange the seating."

"You are the hostess of tonight's dinner. You can seat your guests wherever you'd like."

"But I would hate to upset Louisa and start the evening off on a sour note."

"I suppose so." Julia followed Sarah into the hall, but Sarah's words faded as troubling thoughts rose to replace them.

Would Alice Drexel be a good match for David or William? It seemed that was Lady Gatewood's intention by bringing her to Highland. David was an eligible bachelor, close to her age, and the more obvious choice. William was eight years older than Alice Drexel, and a widower with two young children. Surely the young heiress would not be attracted to William when she could have David. But William had a title and a grand estate—for the time being. And a wealthy bride might be just the answer to his financial problems.

Why did that prospect seem so troubling? If William remarried, the children would have a new mother, and he would have a companion to comfort him and meet his needs as only a wife could.

Her face warmed, and she quickly shifted her thoughts in another direction. Sir William's affections and private life were none of her business, although she couldn't deny the sadness she felt as that thought settled in her heart.

Before she could even scold herself for letting her mind drift in that direction, Lydia came running down the hall. "Oh, Miss Foster, you must come quick!" The maid's eyes darted to Sarah and she bobbed a quick curtsy. "Beggin' your pardon, Miss Ramsey."

Sarah nodded to her. "It's all right, Lydia. What's the matter?"

"Mr. Lawrence has sacked Peter Gates, and Ann is crying and carrying on down in the servants' hall. Mrs. Emmitt looks like she's ready to pop her cork, and I'm afraid she'll sack Ann too if she doesn't stop. Won't you come down, Miss Foster? I know Ann will listen to you."

"Of course."

"I'll come with you," Sarah said.

Julia lifted her skirt and hurried down the backstairs, with Sarah and Lydia close behind. When they reached the bottom floor, the sound of voices raised in a heated argument reached her ears. She dashed around the corner and came to a halt.

Peter stood at the end of the hall, across from the grim-faced Mr. Lawrence. Mrs. Emmitt stood next to the butler, her face set in a stern scowl. Ann clung to Peter's arm.

The housekeeper drew herself up and narrowed her eyes. "Peter Gates, you have been deceptive and led this young woman into all kinds of trouble."

Peter lifted his chin, defiance in his eyes. "We've done nothing wrong! You've no call to dismiss me."

"I have a very good reason, and I've no intention of arguing the point." Mr. Lawrence held his gaze steady and stood his ground like a commanding general. "You will pack your bags and leave first thing in the morning."

Ann bit her lip. "Please, Mr. Lawrence, don't send him away."

"I've spoken to Sir William, and the decision has been made."

Peter glared at the butler. "All right. If that's the way it stands. I'll be more than glad to be done with the whole lot of you."

"Oh no, Peter, don't go!" Ann cried. "Please, talk to Sir William. I'm sure you can work things out." She dropped her hold on Peter and turned to Mrs. Emmitt. "We only met a few times. Nothing bad happened. I promise."

"Stop! That's enough! I won't hear any more of this." Mrs. Emmitt shifted her glare to Peter. "And don't even think of appealing to Sir William. No false words or hypocritical apology will make any difference."

Peter gripped Ann's hand. "These people care nothing for you. You're just a slave to them. Get your things, Ann, and come with me."

Mrs. Emmitt gasped, and Mr. Lawrence's eyes grew as round as saucers.

Tears filled Ann's eyes, and her chin trembled. She looked at Peter and then Julia, clearly torn.

Julia pressed her lips together. *Please, Lord, help her make the right decision.*

Twenty

William walked downstairs, his footfalls soft on the plush red carpet, and his mind on the conversation he needed to have with David. He had thought through his approach, but he wasn't certain about the timing. Would it be better to allow his brother to settle in for a few days, or should he speak to him tonight after dinner?

The question was not simply whether David had the funds to buy William's half interest in their London home. The real issue was, would he be willing to part with the money to help William?

The sound of a woman crying and raised voices stopped him at the bottom of the grand staircase. He turned to the left, following the sounds. Two maids stood clustered at the open green baize door leading down to the kitchen and servants' hall.

William cleared his throat. The maids gasped and stepped back.

"Beggin' your pardon, sir," the little blonde said, clutching her dusting cloth to her chest. "We didn't mean to be listenin' in, but we weren't sure if we should go down now with all that goin' on."

He frowned as he crossed to the open door and cocked his head.

"These people care nothing for you."

That was Peter Gates's voice if he was not mistaken. But to whom was he speaking? "You're just a slave to them. Get your things, Ann, and come with me."

William drew himself up. Impudent man! How dare he try to convince that young girl to run away with him. William strode past the maids and marched down the stairs. "What is going on here?"

Mr. Lawrence, Mrs. Emmitt, Ann, Sarah, Miss Foster, and Peter all turned his way. Peter fisted his hands at his side and glared at William.

Mr. Lawrence met him at the bottom of the stairs. "I am sorry, sir. We didn't mean to disturb you."

"It's all right."

Mrs. Emmitt scowled at the groom. "Peter is just leaving, and I've a mind to send Ann with him."

William glanced at Ann, who was weeping in Miss Foster's arms. His sister stood beside them, patting the young maid's back. Miss Foster lifted her gaze to meet his, her eyes filled with sympathy and a plea for mercy.

A ripple of surprise traveled through him. He knew exactly what she wanted him to do, and it was the complete opposite of his housekeeper's wishes. He considered it a moment more, then faced the groom. "Peter Gates, you have disappointed us with your deceptions and reckless actions. Mr. Lawrence will not be writing a reference for you."

Peter's eyes registered shock, but the rest of his expression remained unchanged. "You might be master of this house, but you don't own me. I'll be glad to leave this place. No more bowing and scraping to the likes of you!"

William clenched his jaw. "We have nothing more to say to you. You will leave the house immediately."

Spiteful fire burned in Peter's eyes. He spun away and stormed off, banging out the back door and striding away into the night.

Mrs. Emmitt lifted her chin, her expression like granite. "I believe the girl should go as well. It will only cause problems if she stays."

Ann looked at him, a pleading expression on her tear-stained face. "Please, sir, don't send me away."

The silent appeal in Miss Foster's eyes remained unchanged, and he could not ignore it. He pulled in a deep breath and slowly blew it out. "I'll consider the situation." He nodded to Ann. "You may go upstairs."

Mrs. Emmitt's eyes blazed, and she shot a heated look at Mr. Lawrence.

The butler stepped closer and lowered his voice. "Sir, perhaps it would be best if Mrs. Emmitt and I—"

William straightened. "I will let you know my decision."

Mrs. Emmitt's silent fuming was unmistakable as she spun away and marched off toward her parlor. Sarah and Miss Foster gathered around Ann and guided her toward the backstairs.

"Miss Foster," William called. "May I speak to you for a moment?"

She sent Sarah and Ann on and rejoined him. "Yes sir?"

A kitchen maid carrying a basket of potatoes walked past, and one of the footmen strode toward them with a tray of glasses.

"Come with me, please."

William led her upstairs. When they reached the great hall, he crossed to the fireplace and she joined him there. "I hope you understand why I had to let that young man go."

"Yes sir, and I think it was a wise decision. He was not willing to admit his mistakes or commit to changing his ways."

Her agreement warmed his heart, and he nodded.

"But I hope you will consider keeping Ann on. I'm afraid if you send her away now, she'll run straight into Peter's arms."

He didn't like the sound of that.

"She has made some poor choices, but she is a hard worker, and she doesn't want to lose her position."

"So you feel she should have another chance?"

"Yes sir. And if she is given guidance and time to mature, I think she'll become a fine young woman. I'd like the opportunity to help her."

"You would keep an eye on her and encourage her to make better choices?"

She nodded. "I would, sir."

He glanced away. Mrs. Emmitt would not be pleased, and Lawrence would not agree, but he could not deny Miss Foster's request. He focused on her again. "Very well. Ann may stay."

Miss Foster's eyes widened. "She may stay?"

"Yes."

A smile burst across her face, and she laid her hand on his forearm. "Oh, thank you, sir. This means so much to me."

He returned her smile, and his chest expanded as warm feelings coursed through him. To see her so happy and pleased with his decision filled him with deep satisfaction.

"Well, you both certainly look happy." David crossed the great hall toward them.

Miss Foster dropped her hand. She stepped back and lowered her gaze.

"Miss Foster, it's a pleasure to see you again. Are you joining us for dinner?"

Did her hand tremble slightly as she smoothed

out her skirt? Was she embarrassed by his question or by the fact she was obviously not dressed for dinner, since she had not been invited?

She looked up, her expression serene and giving no hint to her true feelings. "No sir, I will be dining with the children."

"What a pity. I was hoping we might have a chance to get better acquainted." David smiled and lifted one eyebrow.

William clenched his jaw.

"If you will excuse me." Miss Foster nodded to William, then to David.

David watched her cross the great hall and start up the stairs, then he chuckled under his breath. "My, she is lovely. Too bad she is the governess."

William shot a quick glance at Miss Foster. Had she overheard David's remark? He certainly hoped not. He stepped toward his brother and lowered his voice. "That's quite enough."

David pulled back, a glimmer in his eyes. "What's the matter, William? Has the pretty, young governess caught your eye as well?"

Julia stifled a gasp and almost missed the next step. She straightened her shoulders and continued climbing, pretending she hadn't heard David's comments.

She listened for William's reply, but she heard nothing. Her throat tightened, and she blinked against her stinging eyes. What did she expect? David's assessment was correct. She was a paid member of the staff, and her lack of wealth and position created a huge gulf between her and William.

She could never cross that gulf, and he would never choose to do so.

The sorrow of that thought sent a painful tremor through her. When had she allowed her heart to begin to hope for something more?

Had it started at her parents' cottage when her mother suggested the possibility? Or was it before that, when he took her into his confidence and asked for her input concerning his financial struggles? No, if she was honest, it went even farther back, to the day she had challenged him to spend more time with his children, when he had listened and looked at her with that hint of acceptance and admiration in his eyes. Her heart had been drawn to him then, and those feelings had only grown stronger over time.

How could she have let it happen?

When they first met, she thought he was a brooding, selfish man with little true concern for his children or anyone else.

But now she knew he was a strong, confident man who thought deeply. He loved his children and his sister and took his responsibilities very seriously. And though she didn't always agree with his decisions, they were based on his desire to do what he thought was right and best for his family and staff. He was an honorable man, a noble man.

Her understanding, admiration, and affection had grown so subtly she hadn't even been aware of it. Or if she had, she had pushed it aside.

But now that the truth was clear, there was only one choice before her.

She must cast off those thoughts and double the guard around her heart. That was the only wise and prudent choice. But knowing the right thing to do and doing it were two different matters.

When she reached the gallery, the footman announced the arrival of Lord and Lady Gatewood and Miss Alice Drexel.

The desire to see Miss Drexel from a discreet distance tugged her toward the banister, and against her better judgment, she peeked over.

William and David walked forward to greet their three guests, and Lord Gatewood introduced Miss Drexel to William.

Miss Drexel was a lovely, tall blonde, and she wore a stunning silvery-blue evening dress. The beads decorating the lace overdress shimmered as she smiled and offered William her hand. "Thank you for inviting me to Highland. You have a very beautiful home."

He took her hand and nodded. "It's a pleasure to meet you, Miss Drexel." He turned to David. "This is my brother, Mr. David Ramsey."

David bowed to Alice, swept up her hand, and kissed her fingers. "Miss Drexel, it's a delight to meet you. I detect from your accent that you are an American."

She nodded, looking pleased. "Yes, I'm from Philadelphia, but I've been longing to visit your wonderful country for many years."

"We're glad your wish has finally come true." He tucked her hand into his arm and walked with her toward the drawing room.

Lady Gatewood removed her cape and handed it to the footman, then she turned to William. "What must we do to impress on the girls how important it is to be present when their guests arrive for dinner?" She glanced up the stairs.

William followed her gaze. "I'm sure they will be down soon."

Julia gasped and stepped behind a pillar. Had she been seen? She certainly hoped not.

What was the matter with her? If she'd caught Katherine or Penelope sneaking around like this, she would've given them a lecture about proper manners and respecting others' privacy. Rather than eavesdropping on her employer and his friends and family, she ought to be more concerned about setting a good example and living out her faith.

With that warning in mind, she slipped down the hall to find Katherine and Penelope and let them know they were late for dinner again.

• • •

Sunlight filtered through the trees, spreading a touch of warmth to the cool, clear morning. William pulled in a deep breath, savoring the scent of cedar, moss, and soil as he strolled down the wooded path with Miss Foster, Andrew, and Millie at his side. It was wonderful to be outdoors again. It always amazed him the way spending time in nature made him feel refreshed and alive.

Up ahead, Clark Dalton and Sarah led them on their search for the perfect Christmas tree. Katherine, Penelope, David, and Alice Drexel followed a short distance behind. The young women chattered away about the upcoming holiday, Katherine and Penelope describing past Christmases at Highland and Alice explaining American traditions.

Millie sighed and looked up at him. "Papa, my feet are getting tired. Are we nearly there?"

"This has been quite a long walk for you, hasn't it? Why don't I give you a lift?" He reached down and picked her up. Millie sighed happily and laid her head on his shoulder. She was surprisingly light, and he found he quite enjoyed holding her close like this. Her soft breath warmed his neck, and he smiled. It had been a long while since he had carried his daughter in his arms.

Too long.

Miss Foster glanced across at them, her eyes

glowing with a happy light. "I don't think it's much farther, Millie."

"I don't mind." Millie snuggled in closer. "As long as Papa carries me."

"It's a good thing you're light as a feather pillow," he added.

Millie giggled. "Oh Papa, I weigh more than a pillow."

"Not much more." He glanced at Miss Foster, and they exchanged a smile.

This was the kind of outing they both enjoyed, and he could tell she was pleased he had included the children. And he was pleased as well. With Miss Foster's encouragement, he had been spending time with the children each day at tea or after. A renewed fondness warmed his heart as he thought of them now, and it melted away some of the pain from the past. His gaze shifted to Miss Foster, and gratefulness warmed his heart. She was bringing them all closer and helping him in so many ways.

"Look, there's a good tree!" Andrew ran ahead to a large evergreen that stood proud and tall at the edge of a clearing. "Isn't that grand?" He dashed back and motioned for them to join him.

Dalton stood to the side, his saw in hand as everyone else gathered around the tree.

William carefully set Millie on the ground next to Miss Foster, then lifted his hand to shade his eyes and inspect the evergreen. "Dalton, what type of tree is that?"

"I believe it's a spruce, sir."

William nodded. "How tall would you say it is?"

"At least fourteen feet, maybe fifteen."

His brother strode around, checking the back. "It has a nice shape. No problems on this side." He glanced at Alice. "What do you think, Miss Drexel?"

Her eyes widened for a moment. "Oh, it's a lovely tree." She shifted her gaze to William, her smile warming. "It's quite tall, but you certainly have room for one that large in your great hall."

A ripple of unease traveled through William. Alice Drexel was a beautiful young woman, skilled in social graces and conversation, but there was something about her that didn't quite ring true. Perhaps it was just that she was an American and much more free-spirited than most English women.

Since her arrival last night she had continually complemented him and Highland, remarking on how large and lovely the rooms were, how exquisite the paintings and furnishings, how beautiful and rare the antiques. She asked him about the history of the estate and wanted to know more about his family and connections in London. The conversation made him a bit uncomfortable, but he couldn't very well refuse to answer. After all, she was a friend of Lord and Lady Gatewood's and his dinner guest.

When Sarah mentioned the outing to cut the Christmas tree, Lady Gatewood maneuvered the conversation so that they had no choice but to invite Alice to come along and spend the day with them.

William took Millie's hand. "What do you think, Millie? Does that Christmas tree meet your approval?"

She nodded, her eyes sparkling. "Yes, Papa. It's beautiful."

"Very well." William signaled Dalton. "Let's cut it down."

"Yes sir." Dalton moved toward the tree. Andrew was eager to help, so Dalton asked him to hold back the branches and give him more room to work. Sarah and Miss Foster stood with Millie, Katherine, Penelope, and Alice and watched from a safe distance.

David joined William. He crossed his arms and nodded toward Sarah. "Country life seems to agree with our sister."

"Yes, I believe Sarah is very happy here."

"That wouldn't have anything to do with that fellow Dalton, would it? What is he—the gardener?" David asked with a skeptical lift of his eyebrows.

William straightened. "He is head gardener, following in his father's footsteps."

"Well, he certainly has his eye on Sarah, and it looks as though she is doing nothing to discourage him—quite the opposite in fact."

William set his jaw and looked away. He had

forgotten how arrogant his brother could be. But hadn't those been William's exact thoughts not long ago? It shamed him now, hearing them repeated by his brother.

"I hope you'll keep things under control. We wouldn't want Sarah to do anything that would tarnish the family's reputation here or in London. That would reflect poorly on us both."

"No, we wouldn't want that." Sarcasm tinged William's voice, but David didn't seem to notice.

David's gaze shifted from Sarah to Miss Foster, and a slight smile lifted one side of his mouth. "Discreet affairs with someone of a different social class are acceptable for men like us. But society takes a very dim view of aristocratic women who choose that path."

Irritation flashed through William. "Sarah would never be involved in an affair."

"No, I suppose not. She's lived a sheltered life, and she's always had you as her protector." David smiled as though that was particularly amusing.

"Affairs—discreet or otherwise—are the devil's trap. Anyone who takes that path is a fool and courts his own destruction. I want nothing to do with them, and neither should you."

"My goodness, William. I didn't realize you were such a paragon of virtue."

William clamped his mouth closed. This was neither the time nor the place for an argument with his brother, especially on this topic.

"This is the twentieth century, William. Times are changing."

"What is right will never change. Chastity before the wedding and faithfulness after, that is the only way to assure a happy and long-lasting marriage."

David smiled. "Yes, I suppose it's time I began to think more seriously about the prospect of marriage." He stepped closer and lowered his voice. "So, what do you think of Miss Drexel?"

What was David asking him? Did he mean to imply he was interested in pursuing her, or was he suggesting William should? He huffed and adjusted his jacket. "I don't really know her well enough to say."

"I wasn't keen on the idea of an American wife, but perhaps I should reconsider. She has enough beauty to tempt me, and when that fades, there would always be her fortune to keep me happy."

William shook his head. "If that's your attitude toward marriage and selecting a bride, you are apt to be very disappointed."

David chuckled and slapped him on the shoulder. "William, old boy, you're always so brooding and serious. You look like you're carrying the weight of the world on your shoulders. Why don't you relax and enjoy life a little?"

William crossed his arms and looked away. Perhaps if he didn't carry the painful memory of his wife's unfaithfulness or the current weight of his struggle to save Highland, he might be less brooding. What was wrong with David? How could he forget the shame and sorrow Amelia's affair and death had caused William?

"Stand back everyone!" Dalton called. "The tree's coming down!"

William quickly surveyed the scene, making sure his family, Miss Foster, and Miss Drexel were in a safe place, then he nodded to Dalton. The gardener made the final cut, and the tree crashed to the ground as the children cheered and the women clapped. Sarah hurried to Mr. Dalton's side and thanked him. She squeezed his hand and sent him a bright smile.

The muscles in William's neck and shoulders tensed. He wanted Sarah to wed and be happy. Getting to know Dalton better had eased his fears—to a degree. But David was right about one thing: the more time Sarah and Dalton spent together, the more obvious their feelings for each other would become.

He studied his sister and her beau again, and the truth was undeniable.

Soon the staff would be discussing it, and then the whole village would know. Was he ready to deal with the repercussions? He had better get ready, because they were coming.

Twenty-One

Evergreen garlands decorated with red bows and cinnamon sticks hung on the banisters of the grand staircase, filling the air with a fresh, spicy fragrance. Julia waited near the bottom step, holding hands with Andrew on one side and Millie on the other. Across the hall, the lofty Christmas tree stood between the fireplace and the library doorway.

Mr. Dalton emerged from beneath the lowest branches and dismissed his two young assistants who had helped him bring in the tree and secure it in place.

Sarah hurried to his side. "Thank you, Mr. Dalton. That's the perfect spot."

He brushed off his hands. "I've added extra weight to the base. That should hold it steady."

"We've never had a tree quite this large." She looked up and smiled. "It's beautiful."

He nodded, a twinkle in his eyes. "I'm glad you're pleased, miss."

She looked back at him. "I am pleased. Very pleased, indeed."

The exchange appeared to be normal conversation between a diligent head gardener and a grateful mistress of the house, but Julia could see the silent ebb and flow of affection between them, and it warmed her heart. Sarah deserved this happiness after so many years of buried hopes and isolation.

Andrew tugged on Julia's hand. "Can we decorate the tree now?"

"Yes, we've been waiting ever so long!" Millie looked up, her eager expression making Julia smile.

Sarah motioned them closer. "Come and help me open the boxes."

Andrew and Millie ran to Sarah, and Julia followed, eager to join in. Although her family had celebrated Christmas in India by giving gifts and singing carols, it had been twelve years since she had decorated an evergreen Christmas tree.

Sir William stood by the fireplace with his brother beside him. "Dalton, we'll need a ladder to reach those higher branches. Can you bring one in?"

"Yes sir. I'll fetch it now." Mr. Dalton strode off.

Millie reached in a box and pulled out the first ornament—a handblown glass bird painted green and gold. "Oh, look at this one, Papa. Isn't she pretty?"

"Very nice." He smiled. "I remember hanging it on our Christmas tree when I was a little boy."

Millie's eyes grew round. "Really?"

William chuckled. "I know it may seem hard to believe, but I was your age once." He motioned toward the box. "And most of these ornaments have been in our family for many years."

"Then I will put this one in a very special place." Millie reached up and gently hung the golden bird on a sturdy branch.

"I hope you haven't started without us." Katherine descended the stairs with Penny and Alice. Two footmen carrying a large trunk followed them. "Our family ornaments were put away upstairs."

Sarah sent Julia an anxious glance and then crossed the hall to meet Katherine. "You're just in time. The children are anxious to get started. Come and show us what you've brought down."

The footmen placed the trunk on the floor near the tree and lifted the lid. Penny folded back the tissue paper to reveal a layer of exquisite glass ornaments. Julia stepped closer, intrigued by the beautiful designs: flowers, stars, bells, fruit, fish, musical instruments, baby Jesus, Mary, Joseph, and the wise men on camels, each one delicately painted.

"Aren't they lovely?" Penny looked around the group with an eager smile.

Katherine took a rose-shaped ornament from the

trunk. "Most of these are from Germany. They were brought here by our mother's family."

Sarah stepped closer and peered into the trunk. "What a wonderful collection. I'm so glad you brought them down. I was worried we wouldn't have enough ornaments for a tree this size, but putting them all together will solve that problem very nicely."

The decorating began in earnest as they took ornaments from the trunk and boxes and placed them on the tree. Soon the lower half of the tree was covered with a bright array of beautiful decorations.

Mr. Dalton returned with the ladder and set it up. He glanced around the group and turned to Sarah. "Would you like me to hold the ladder for you?"

Sarah paled and shook her head. "I'm afraid I've never cared for heights or climbing ladders." She bit her lip and slipped her withered hand into the fold of her skirt.

Julia sent her an understanding look. Sarah's fear of heights made sense. The weakness on the right side of her body and her crippled hand and arm limited her strength and agility. Thankfully, she could depend on others to tackle any tasks that required climbing a ladder.

"I can decorate the top. I'm good at climbing." Before anyone could stop him, Andrew charged up the ladder's narrow steps.

Mr. Dalton grabbed hold to steady the ladder.

"Careful, Andrew," William called.

Julia's heart lurched to her throat, and she hurried toward them.

"I'm all right. Hand me an ornament." Andrew leaned back at a wild angle and held out his hand.

"Two hands!" his father shouted, dashing toward his son.

Andrew jerked back and almost lost his grip.

Julia gasped and reached out, preparing to catch him if he fell.

The boy swung back and grabbed hold. "Goodness, Papa. You scared me."

William gripped the ladder on the opposite side from Mr. Dalton. "I could say the same to you." He looked up. "Please slow down, Andrew, and think about what you're doing."

The boy glanced around at everyone's startled faces, and his expression sobered. "Yes sir. I'm sorry."

"It's all right." Sarah passed Andrew a wooden ornament carved in the shape of a crescent moon. "How about finding a nice place for this one?"

Andrew nodded and hung it on a nearby branch. Then he climbed down, apparently content to do the rest of his decorating from the ground.

Mr. Dalton offered to climb the ladder. Sarah thanked him, and they worked together to decorate the higher branches.

Alice took out an ornament that looked like actual ram's horns and smiled at William. "There must be a story behind this one."

He nodded, looking pleased at her selection. "That belonged to one of my uncle's prized rams." He grinned at David. "Remember that? I believe we added it to our collection when I was twelve."

His brother grimaced. "Yes, after we ate that tough old ram for Christmas dinner. It's one of my more painful childhood memories."

William chuckled and shook his head.

"You certainly have some interesting family traditions." Alice sent William a teasing smile.

Julia tensed as she watched Alice continue her conversation with William. Her laughter and smiles might be considered flirtatious, but she offered the same lively responses when she spoke to Katherine or Penny. Perhaps that was just her way of interacting with everyone once she became better acquainted.

A half hour later, Julia stood back with the others and admired the finished Christmas tree. Red bows, cinnamon sticks, toffees, and bunches of mistletoe had been added around the ornaments. Small white candles were clipped to the end of several branches, though they would not be lit until Christmas Eve.

William lifted his gaze and gave a satisfied nod. "Very good work, everyone. I've never seen a finer tree."

"It is beautiful." Alice added, her smile bright as she turned to William. "Now that we've finished that project, I wonder if you'd give me a tour of your library. Lady Gatewood said you have a fine collection, and you might allow me to borrow a book or two if I asked you very nicely."

A muscle in William's jaw flickered before he nodded. "Of course. I'd be happy to loan you as many books as you like." He motioned toward the library.

"You're so kind." She smiled and slipped her hand through the crook of his arm as they walked into the library.

Julia's eyes widened, then she quickly shifted her gaze away. There was no doubt in her mind now. Alice Drexel was definitely flirting with William.

Ann appeared at her side. "Shall I take the children upstairs?"

Julia nodded. "Thank you, Ann. It's time for me to meet with the young ladies."

The nursery maid nodded and led Andrew and Millie up the steps. Mr. Lawrence directed the footmen to remove the trunk and boxes from the great hall. Sarah left to discuss dinner details with Mrs. Emmitt.

Julia approached Katherine and Penny. "We have an hour until tea. Shall we meet in the drawing room for a French lesson?"

Katherine and Penny exchanged a quick glance, then Katherine turned to Julia. "Penny and I have a Christmas project we need to finish and some gifts to wrap, so we were hoping we might skip our lessons today."

Julia searched Katherine's face. Were they actually making preparations for Christmas, or was this just another excuse to avoid their studies? She chose to give them the benefit of the doubt. "All right. We'll set aside our lessons."

The girls exchanged happy smiles and hurried up the stairs.

Julia gazed at the tree again and smiled. Preparing for Christmas seemed to be drawing the family closer. She noticed the little golden bird Millie had placed on the tree first had fallen off and landed on the carpet. She picked it up and hung it on the tree again.

"Well, it seems you and I are the only ones left to enjoy all these splendid decorations." David crossed the hall and joined her.

An uneasy sensation prickled through Julia. She reached out and adjusted one of the red bows on the tip of a branch. "It is a beautiful tree."

"Yes." He tipped his head and studied her. "Beautiful." A slow, suggestive smile eased across his features.

She stepped to the left, intending to walk past him. "If you'll excuse me, I need to go check on the children."

He matched her steps, blocking her path. "Won't you stay and spend a little time with me?"

She swallowed, her mind searching for an

excuse. "I'm sorry, but I have some duties I need to attend to."

"But this is our chance to get to know each other." When she didn't answer, he chuckled. "What's wrong? You're not afraid of me, are you?"

She raised her chin, meeting the challenge in his eyes. "No, but I think it's best if we end this conversation now."

His charming smile cooled. "You would not want to displease me, Miss Foster. I have a great deal of influence with my brother. And I'm sure you don't want to risk losing your position."

She locked gazes with him. "Unless you move out of my way, I will tell Sir William exactly what you've said, and I don't believe he will approve."

David laughed, but he stepped back. "My, my, you're certainly not afraid to speak up for yourself, are you?"

She shot him a heated glance, then spun away and marched up the stairs. His laughter followed her as she passed the landing. She gripped the railing and continued on, determined to put as much distance between herself and David Ramsey as possible.

William walked into the library with Alice by his side. The way she had slipped her arm into his seemed a bit forward, but perhaps that was an America custom. Still, it left him ill at ease and unsure of what she would say or do next.

"I'd love to learn more about British history." She glanced at the shelves and then looked back at him, her eyes bright. "Is there a book you might recommend?"

He took a step away, removing his arm from hers. "I'm sure we have several, but I must say I am a bit surprised. I would've thought you'd ask for a novel or a book of poetry."

"You mean because I'm a woman or because I'm American?"

His face warmed. "I'm sorry. That was rude of me to make an assumption about your interests."

She laughed softly. "Please, don't apologize. Most women would prefer a novel or poetry, but my father is a great scholar, and he passed his love for learning on to me. History, philosophy, literature—I enjoy them all."

William nodded. "Science and nature are my preferred subjects, but I do enjoy historical biographies. There's much we can learn from the great men and women of the past."

"Yes, as they say, those who cannot remember the past are condemned to repeat it." She smiled and cocked her head, a question in her eyes.

"That's a Spanish philosopher, isn't it?"

"Yes, George Santayana. My father and I recently began reading *The Life of Reason*. She laughed softly. "There are actually five volumes. I'm not sure we'll get through them all, but it's quite interesting. Have you read it?"

"No, I'm afraid not. But I agree with him about the importance of learning from our past mistakes." His wife's face flashed through his mind. He pushed the image away and focused on Miss Drexel. "We must take those difficult lessons to heart and not repeat them."

"That's good advice." She looked at the shelves again. "So, what shall I read? I want to understand the English and be well informed when I go to London in the spring."

"I wish I could convince my young cousins to take their education more seriously. They seem to be continually distracted by dress fittings, riding lessons, and calling on friends."

"Oh, they're young. I'm sure their interests will expand in the next few years."

"I hope so." He scanned the shelves and pulled out a thick leather-bound volume. "Here we are, *Hardwick's History of the British Empire*." He held it out to her. "That should do the trick."

Her eyes widened. "My goodness. It looks quite heavy."

"It is, but it's a classic . . . and a concise history."

"Thank you. I'm sure I'll enjoy it." She accepted the book and placed it on the settee. Her gaze shifted to a small table nearby, and she smiled. "What an unusual table." She leaned down and inspected it more closely. "Why does it have so many drawers with letters painted on them?"

"It's called a rent table. My ancestors used it to collect the money owed them by their tenant farmers. The alphabetized drawers kept everything in order."

She smiled up at him. "How clever."

David strode through the doorway, his face flushed. "That little governess of yours is quite the flirt."

A shock wave jolted William. "Excuse me?"

"Oh, never mind." David straightened his jacket and brushed off his sleeve. "It's not important."

Irritation flashed through William. "If a member of my staff has acted in an inappropriate way, I want to be informed."

David huffed. "No need to worry, William. I've set her straight. She won't try that again, at least not with me."

William studied his brother. The accusation seemed out of character for Miss Foster. She had never been flirtatious with anyone at Highland. At least he had never seen it.

But he was not the best judge of character, especially where women were concerned. His late wife had kept her unfaithfulness secret for more than a year. He had not believed the rumors until he found the love letters from Sir Charles Hollingsford two months after her death. Pain twisted through him, and he gripped the back of the chair.

David turned to their guest. "So, Miss Drexel, what have you and my brother been discussing?"

"Please call me Alice. All my friends in Philadelphia do."

David nodded. "We're glad you consider us your friends, and we'd be happy to call you Alice. And you must call us David and William."

"All right. Thank you, David." She sat in a chair near the center of the room. "You know, before I left home, everyone told me the English were cold and unfriendly, but that's certainly not true. You've all been so terribly kind. I adore Katherine and Penelope, and your sister Sarah is one of the sweetest women I've ever met."

"I'm quite fond of her as well," David added with a grin.

Alice laughed. "They also said the English have no sense of humor, but that's not true either."

"I'm glad we can challenge those dreadful myths and set the record straight." David took a seat across from her. "I'd hate to think we'd all been painted in such broad, negative strokes."

"Well, I will sing the praises of the English wherever I go." She turned to William. "It's quite a treat for me to visit you at this time of year and experience a real English Christmas."

"We're glad you could join us." William's thoughts shifted to his plans for Christmas Day. Lord and Lady Gatewood, along with Alice, would join them for a special holiday dinner, and he planned to include the children and Miss Foster as well.

Thoughts of Miss Foster brought David's comments to mind again, and his shoulders tensed. Could it be true? Had Miss Foster flirted with David? His brother's easygoing personality always had charmed the ladies. But that was no excuse. It was improper for any of the staff to flirt with family members. But if he were honest, what bothered him most was that Miss Foster might prefer David to him.

With that revelation came another wave of clarity. He didn't just admire Miss Foster or appreciate the way she cared for his children. He had grown quite fond of her. His chest tightened and felt as though someone had wrapped heavy bands around it, making it difficult for him to draw in a deep breath.

How could he have let this happen? When had he dropped his guard?

"I hear you have something called crackers, and everyone wears colorful paper hats. It sounds quite merry." Alice tipped her head and smiled at him. "Is that right?"

William blinked and quickly replayed her words. "Yes. Christmas is always a special time."

But he couldn't quite bring himself to smile. With Highland's uncertain future heavy on his mind and the unsettling awareness of his growing feelings for Miss Foster, the possibility of a merry, carefree Christmas seemed to have vanished like mist rising off the pond.

Twenty-Two

Julia checked her reflection in the children's mirror and released a soft sigh. Though it was Christmas Eve, she wore a plain navy skirt and white blouse, as she did most days. But honoring the Lord and celebrating His birth didn't depend on how one was dressed. It was a matter of the heart. Still, she couldn't help wishing she had something nicer to wear. She owned only one piece of jewelry, the gold cross necklace her parents had given her on her eighteenth birthday. So she had put that on this morning, hoping it would brighten up her plain outfit.

"Do you think Papa will like our present?" Millie lifted the small gift-wrapped box by its bright red ribbon.

"Don't drop it!" Andrew scowled. "A compass is no good if it's broken."

"I'll be careful." Millie adjusted her hold on the box.

"Maybe I should carry Papa's present, and you

should take Aunt Sarah's." Andrew pushed the other gift across the table toward his sister. "There's no chance you could break a shawl."

Millie sighed, but she handed their father's gift to Andrew and took the other in its place.

Julia lifted the basket of cards the children had made for the staff, then held it out to Millie. "Would you like to carry this down or shall I?"

"I can do it. It's not heavy." Millie took the basket.

Julia's heart warmed as she thought of how the children had put so much creativity and effort into making the cards and choosing and wrapping the gifts for the family. They seemed to have taken her encouragement to heart and were as excited about giving gifts as they were about receiving them.

The clock struck three, and Julia collected the presents for Katherine and Penny. "Time to go." She guided the children downstairs to the great hall where they were to meet the rest of the family. As soon as everyone was assembled, they would all go down to the servants' hall for the staff Christmas party. All the indoor and outdoor staff, as well as their families who lived on the estate, had been invited.

"Put your gifts over there with the others." Julia pointed across the hall to a cloth-covered table by the Christmas tree.

Andrew's eyes widened. "Look at all the presents! Do you think some of them are for us?"

Julia laughed softly. "I'm sure there are a few for you and Millie."

Andrew and Millie peeked at the tags, searching for gifts with their names on them. Julia placed Katherine's and Penelope's presents on the table. She hoped they would like the leather-bound journals she had helped the children choose for them.

Her relationship with the girls had been slowly improving over the last few weeks, ever since the children's bout with scarlet fever. She hadn't won Katherine over completely, but at least they were able to get through their lessons most days without too much resistance.

Penny had definitely softened toward Andrew and Millie. She often stopped in the nursery to see them, and she'd even stayed to read them a story last week. Katherine had joined her that day, and Julia was pleased that she also seemed to be forming a closer attachment to the children.

Andrew turned and looked up at her. "Will there be any other children at the party?"

"I believe Mr. Dalton's niece, Abigail, is coming. She's about Millie's age."

Millie's eyes lit up. "I saw her in the garden when we first came to Highland."

"No boys?" Andrew crossed his arms.

Julia held back her smile. "I believe I heard Mr. McTavish has two sons. But I'm not sure how old they are."

"I don't much care their age, as long as they're boys."

Julia smoothed down his wavy red hair. "I'm sure they will be happy to meet you."

Sarah walked down the stairs. "Hello, my dears. Are you ready for the party?"

"Aunt Sarah, we have a gift for you!" Millie ran to meet her at the bottom of the steps.

"Not now, Millie," Andrew called. "We don't open gifts until after dinner tonight."

"I know. I just want to show Aunt Sarah her present." Millie took Sarah's hand and led her to the table. "It's that one, right there." She pointed to the gift.

"How thoughtful." Sarah bent and kissed Millie's cheek. "I'll look forward to opening it later."

"Miss Foster took us shopping in the village last week, and we bought presents for everyone." Millie twirled and spun toward the tree, and Andrew joined her.

Taking the children to Fulton in the governess cart had been a fun adventure for them all. They finished their Christmas shopping in less than an hour, so Julia took them to her parents' cottage for a short visit. Her parents had been delighted, and her mother had served them tea and ginger cakes, then sent them off with oranges as a treat for the trip home.

Julia's brother, Jonathan, was due to arrive

home today, and she could hardly wait to see him. She would love to be there to greet him, but that was not possible. She would see him and her mother at church on Christmas Day. Then she hoped to see her family on Boxing Day.

Sarah approached Julia. "How do I look?" She ran her hand down the skirt of her dark green dress. It was made of a lovely silk fabric with a subtle stripe that gave it a pleasing texture. The small ruffles around the double collar and at the bottom of the skirt added a special touch to the design. "Is this is too elegant for the servants' party?"

"No, you look lovely."

Sarah leaned closer. "I'm going to meet Clark's mother and his niece for the first time."

Julia smiled. "I'm sure you will make a very good impression."

Sarah squeezed her hand. "I hope so."

Katherine and Penny walked down the stairs. Katherine's royal blue dress highlighted her fair complexion and golden brown hair. Penny's light green dress with ivory lace insert at the neck looked pretty as well. Both girls seemed in good spirits and ready to enjoy the holiday.

William walked out of his library. The children ran to greet him, but his expression remained sober while they chattered about the Christmas gifts.

Julia's concern grew as she watched him. She loved celebrating Christmas, and she couldn't imagine why he would be downcast on such a special day. A sudden thought struck, and her heart clenched.

Was he thinking of past Christmas celebrations and remembering those who were no longer with him: his parents, his older brother . . . and his wife? Sympathy flooded her heart. If only she could reach out and comfort him.

But she could not, and that truth pierced her heart. She needed to banish those thoughts and concentrate on the children. She had been hired to care for them, not their father. She must remember that. But it was becoming more difficult every day to ignore how much she cared for William.

He took his watch from his vest pocket. "I suppose we should go down."

Julia glanced around the group. "Shouldn't we wait for David?"

He swung toward her, and his eyes narrowed. "David?"

Immediately she realized her mistake. "Forgive me. I meant Mr. Ramsey."

Sarah placed her hand on her brother's arm. "It's all right, William. We all call him David."

"It's not the proper way for her to address him." His troubled expression hinted at something more behind his words.

Julia swallowed. Certainly she'd crossed the lines of propriety, but even so, it seemed odd for him to be so upset about her mistake.

"Honestly, William"—Sarah gave his sleeve a gentle tug—"please don't take offense. Most of these rules of address are out of date. It's Christmas Eve, and time we were all on more friendly terms."

His expression eased, but his eyes still held a trace of . . . what? Mistrust? "Very well. We don't want to keep everyone downstairs waiting." He turned and strode off.

Swallowing the sudden lump in her throat, Julia gathered the children and followed the group past the green baize door.

Piano music and laughter flowed out from the servants' hall, but as soon as William and the others walked through the doorway, the music stopped.

Mr. Lawrence approached and nodded to Sir William. "We're glad you could join us, sir."

"Thank you, Lawrence. Happy Christmas to you all." William motioned toward Lydia, who sat at the piano. "Please, continue playing."

Lydia smiled and turned back to the piano, but she chose a softer tune, and the conversation among the servants became more subdued.

Holly, pine branches, and oranges decorated the center of the large wooden table laden with cookies, pastries, tea, and punch. In the corner of the room, on a side table, a stack of wrapped gifts and a basket of gingerbread men sat, waiting to be distributed to the servants and their families.

William and Sarah walked around the room, stopping to greet each servant. Katherine and Penelope came after, shaking hands and wishing each one a happy Christmas.

Chef Lagarde picked up a tray of pastries and held it out to Julia and the children. "*Joyeux Noël,* my friends. Please, help yourselves."

Andrew's eyes lit up, and he scooped up two of the pastries. Millie took one and thanked the chef. Julia raised her eyebrows and sent Andrew a glance.

"Thank you, Chef Lagarde," Andrew mumbled past the pastry in his mouth. "These are very good."

The chef laughed. "You are most welcome." He moved on, offering his treats to the others.

Millie touched Julia's arm. "Look, there's the little girl I met in the garden. May I go and see her?"

Julia glanced across the room just as Mr. Dalton introduced Sarah to his mother. Mrs. Dalton looked to be in her late fifties and wore a warm smile as she took Sarah's hand. Relief filled Julia. Surely Mrs. Dalton was a kind woman who would welcome Sarah into her heart and family.

Millie tugged in her hand. "Miss Foster? May I go, please?"

"Oh yes, you may."

Andrew took another pastry and followed Millie, then changed directions when he saw Mr.

McTavish and his two sons near the piano. One boy looked a little younger than Andrew, and the other was just a toddler, but Andrew seemed happy to join them.

Julia glanced around, feeling a bit awkward. Her position as governess left her strangely in the middle—below the family and above most of the other servants except for Mrs. Emmitt and Mr. Lawrence. She and Ann got along well in the nursery, but Ann had joined the group at the piano, watching Lydia play.

"Would you like some punch?" Nelson held out a glass toward Julia. His teasing smile and the tilt of his eyebrows made her slightly uncomfortable, but she didn't want to be rude.

"Thank you." She accepted the cup.

He seemed to take that as an invitation to join her. "It's nice to see you downstairs with us for a change. We're not a bad lot. You should come down and take a meal with us more often." He lifted his cup to her in a toast. "But be that as it may, Happy Christmas."

Her face warmed, but she forced a small smile and raised her glass to touch his. Just as she did, William turned and looked her way. She saw surprise in his gaze . . . and something more.

Displeasure? Disappointment?

Both?

Julia's stomach dropped. What had she done now? Wasn't the purpose of the party for the staff and family to enjoy Christmas Eve together? Why shouldn't she accept a cup of punch and a toast from Nelson? William had no right to scowl at her as though she had broken some rule.

The compassion she felt for him earlier evaporated. He might be her employer, but he did not have a right to spoil her Christmas Eve with his gloomy mood and dark looks. She had done nothing wrong.

She turned away from William and focused on Nelson. "This is delicious. Thank you."

"Have you tried the pastries?" Nelson lifted a tray and held it out to her.

She chose a small round one with raspberry filling. "So, Nelson, how long have you worked at Highland?"

"I've been here three years. Before that I worked for Sir James Martindale in Chelmsford."

Julia tried to pay attention as Nelson went on, but her gaze drifted to William, watching him make the rounds and greet each servant. Would he stay in a gloomy mood all day and spoil the holiday for the children? She certainly hoped not. It was one thing to scold her, but it was quite another to steal the children's Christmas joy.

David walked into the servants' hall and glanced her way. She shifted her gaze back to Nelson and nodded as though she were absorbed in what he was saying. Nelson might be a bit obnoxious, but she would rather spend an hour with him than a single moment with David Ramsey.

William sank back in the overstuffed chair and released a heavy sigh. The Christmas tree shimmered with candlelight reflecting off the tinsel and ornaments. Flames leaped and crackled in the fireplace, while the scent of wood smoke, evergreens, and candle wax hung in the air.

Katherine and David sat across from him engaged in conversation about the best sights to see in London, their opened Christmas gifts beside them. Sarah, Penelope, Miss Foster, and the children completed the circle that Christmas Eve.

William drummed his fingers on the arm of the chair as he stared into the fire. He should be enjoying this time with his family gathered round. His gifts had all been given, and the evening was coming to a close, but something undefined weighed down his spirit.

He glanced across the room at Miss Foster, and his mood sank a few more degrees. She had distanced herself from him today. Was it because of their clash that afternoon? Or was there another reason? Had she truly used his brother's given name by mistake, or did it confirm she had deeper feelings for him? The thought of her falling in love with David made his stomach knot.

His brother had never been faithful to one

woman, nor was he serious about marriage, especially to someone of a lower class.

William closed his eyes, trying to block out Miss Foster's image and quiet those disturbing thoughts. David would return to London next week, and hopefully that would put an end to it. Everything could go back to normal.

Opening his eyes, he glanced at his brother. He still needed to have a conversation with him. He should do it tonight, while David seemed to be in a good mood, thanks to all the attention Katherine had focused on him today.

William pressed his lips together. That concerned him too. Katherine and David ending up together was not a happy thought. He would have to speak to his brother about that as well.

Millie approached, holding her treasured Christmas gift. "I love my new doll, Papa. Thank you for giving her to me."

"You're welcome, Millie." Sarah had chosen the doll, and he felt a bit sheepish taking the credit, but his sister wouldn't mind.

Millie walked over and sat beside Miss Foster. "Isn't she the prettiest doll you've ever seen?"

Miss Foster smiled and placed her arm around Millie's shoulders. "She's lovely, and I hope you'll take very good care of her."

Millie nodded. "I will. She can sleep right beside me when I go to bed tonight."

Andrew picked up an arrow from his new

archery set. "Papa, can you take me out tomorrow and show me how to shoot?"

"We'll see. We're attending church in the morning, and then Lord and Lady Gatewood and Miss Drexel will be joining us for Christmas dinner at two."

Andrew wrinkled his nose. "After that? Please? I really want to try them out."

"I said, we'll see."

At his gruff tone, Miss Foster glanced his way, a question in her eyes.

He shifted in his seat. She was right to question him. There was no need to snap at his son just because his thoughts were far from happy. He managed to offer Andrew a smile. "Perhaps there will be time for an archery lesson after dinner, if the weather holds."

Andrew's face lit up, and he lifted the arrow into the air. "Yes! Thank you!"

William nodded to his son. "Remember, those are real weapons, and you must handle them with care and respect."

"Yes sir. I will." Andrew replaced the arrow in the quiver and tested the strength of the bow-string again. William wasn't sure the archery set was the wisest purchase, but it had been Miss Foster's suggestion. He hoped it would help Andrew learn to focus his energy and attention.

He looked across the room and studied Miss Foster. Was she pleased with the gift they had given her? Sarah had chosen some silky, blue material that could be made into a dress. After Miss Foster unwrapped it, she had thanked William and Sarah, but her response seemed a bit subdued.

He frowned. Why hadn't he selected something nicer? But Sarah had handled most of the Christmas shopping, and it would not have been proper for him to choose an extra gift for Miss Foster. Still, it would do his heart good to see her as delighted with her gift as the children were with theirs.

The clock struck nine, and Miss Foster rose from her chair. "Come along, children, it's past time for bed."

Andrew groaned. "But it's Christmas Eve . . . Can't we stay up a little longer?"

"We've had a lovely day, and there are more special things planned for tomorrow. Let's have a grateful heart and bid your family good-night."

Andrew sighed and rose to his feet. "Thank you for my gifts."

William nodded to his son. "You're welcome, Andrew."

Millie kissed her aunt and offered hugs to everyone else. She embraced William last, lingering in his arms for a moment. "Happy Christmas, Papa. I love you."

William wanted to reply with the same sentiment, but his throat tightened, and he patted her back instead. "Thank you, Millie."

Miss Foster took Millie's hand and met his gaze. "Thank you for a pleasant evening." But he couldn't miss the trace of sadness in her eyes.

"You're welcome." He wished he could tell her he was sorry for his cross words earlier and the distance it had put between them, but that wasn't possible with the whole family gathered around.

"I should go too." Sarah yawned and stood. "Good night, everyone."

Penny rose from her chair and looked at her sister. "We should go up as well."

"You go ahead. I'm not tired yet."

"But Katherine, you always say you need your beauty rest. And you wouldn't want to be cross and irritable on Christmas Day, would you?" A silent challenge passed between the sisters.

Katherine sent her sister a heated glance, but she rose from her chair. "I'm sure I'll be well rested and ready to celebrate the holiday tomorrow." She nodded to David and then William, wished them good night, and strode past her sister.

Penny shrugged, a slight smile on her lips. "Good night, all. I hope you sleep well." She took a candle from the side table and followed Katherine up the stairs.

David chuckled. "I can't believe this country life. Nine o'clock and the whole family is off to bed."

William turned toward his brother. "I don't mind staying up a bit longer. In fact, I was hoping there'd be an opportunity for the two of us to talk."

"Well, now's the time. What's on your mind?"

William shifted in the chair. "Moving to Highland has been quite an adjustment for me."

"Yes, I can imagine how trying it must be, with this huge house and estate to occupy your mind." David's tone carried a hint of sarcasm.

William leveled his gaze at David. "Running the estate does take a great deal of thought and planning, and that's what I wanted to discuss."

David settled back. "All right. I'm listening."

"I've received an updated assessment of the death duties, and they're much higher than I anticipated."

"Really?" A hint of amusement lit his eyes.

William forced down his irritation. "Yes, and I must pay the full amount by the first of March, or a large fine will be added."

"How dreadful." David propped his feet up on the ottoman.

"Really, David, can you be serious and try to put yourself in my shoes for a moment?"

His brother's expression sobered. "I've always walked in your shadow, William, but I've never been too skilled at stepping into your shoes."

Surprise rippled through William, and he studied his brother. David had never admitted the feelings of rivalry that existed between them.

William had hoped time and distance would ease that strain. Apparently it had not.

But he had no choice. He had to press on. "The truth is, I'm in a bit of a financial bind. The estate provides an income, but not nearly enough to pay the death duties along with the other expenses. I've explored several options to raise the funds, but I haven't found one that will make the money available in time."

"And what does that have to do with me?"

"I wondered if you might be interested in becoming the sole owner of our London home."

David pursed his lips. "You mean, buy you out—the way I bought out your interest in the family business?"

"Yes, that's what I was thinking."

David rose to his feet, a slight smile lifting his lips. "Well, now, I don't know."

"I thought we might have a professional assess the value of the house and furnishings, and then we would have a fair way to set a price for my half interest."

"And where do you suppose I would get the money to buy your half?"

"From the business we inherited from our father and from your other investments."

David's face colored slightly. "Ramsey and Sons has not been as prosperous as I'd hoped. In fact, we've had quite a downturn these last few months."

William frowned. "How can that be true? When I left last summer, we had a huge backlog of orders waiting to be filled."

David turned and paced a few steps away. "We've had several challenges since then. One of our ships went down in November, carrying a full load of cargo."

"You have insurance to cover that kind of loss."

"Yes, but it's taking a long time for the claim to be processed. I haven't seen one shilling yet. Then Milton Braggs resigned last month over some silly misunderstanding, and I haven't been able to replace him." David lifted his hand. "It's just been one thing after another. I can't believe how difficult it is to run the business."

"So . . . what are you saying?"

David turned and faced him. "I'm sorry, William, but I don't believe I have the funds to bail you out this time."

William studied his brother, disbelief turning his stomach. "So you won't help me?"

"I don't think it's fair for you to expect me to solve your financial problem. If you don't have the income to run the estate, then you'll just have to swallow your pride and let it go."

Heat flashed through William. "That's your answer?"

David shrugged. "I wish I could give you the money, but I don't think that would be wise."

William rose and faced his brother. "I'm not

asking you to *give* me anything. I'm offering you total ownership of our London home in exchange for the funds. You could keep the house as an investment or sell it. I'm only asking that you pay me a fair price for my half."

The muscles in David's jaw rippled. "I suppose I can discuss it with my solicitor, but I can't promise you the funds."

William clamped his jaw against the reply rising in his throat. He did not want to destroy the slim chance that his brother might still help him. "Very well. I'll wait to hear from you after you speak to your solicitor."

The sound of footsteps on the stairs drew William's attention. He glanced to the left as Miss Foster reached the lower landing.

David turned her way as well, and a slight smile replaced his guarded expression. "Miss Foster, you decided to rejoin us?"

She hesitated and sent David an uncomfortable glance. "No sir. I would like to speak to Sir William."

"Well, don't let me interrupt. I was just going up." David crossed the hall and met her at the bottom of the steps. "Good night, Miss Foster." His voice lowered to an intimate tone. "I hope your sleep will be sweet."

Irritation burned in William's stomach.

"Thank you," she murmured, but she shifted her cool gaze away and stepped far out of his path.

Relief welled up in William. Perhaps she was not enamored with David after all.

"I'm sorry to disturb your conversation with your brother." She crossed to meet him.

"It's quite all right. I don't have any more to say to him tonight." He glanced past her, up the stairs, but David had already disappeared. "Are the children tucked in for the night?"

"Yes sir, although I'm not sure how quickly they'll fall asleep considering all the excitement and sweets they enjoyed today." She sent him a slight smile, as though testing his mood.

"Yes, we did indulge them a bit, but Christmas comes only once a year. I'm sure they'll be fine in the morning."

"I wasn't being critical. I was very glad to see everyone enjoying the day together. They'll treasure these happy memories for a long time . . . as will I."

Her pleasant words and sweet smile soothed his spirit, and the burning in his stomach eased. "I'm glad to hear it."

She pressed her lips together and glanced toward the fire.

"Is there something you wanted to say?"

"Yes sir. I know I usually take my half day on Sunday afternoon, but I wondered if I might take the twenty-sixth off instead."

"Boxing Day?"

"My brother is visiting, and my aunt Beatrice

has arranged for us to see our grandmother."

He frowned slightly, thinking of Sarah's plans to take gifts to their tenant farmers that day. He thought he would go along and bring the children and Miss Foster, but without her it wouldn't be the same.

"I was wondering if I might leave at ten, after Scripture reading and prayer. I understand the trip to London will take at least two hours.

"Will you go by train?"

"No, my aunt's chauffeur will drive us."

"I see." His frown deepened. He didn't like the idea of her traveling that far with the weather so questionable this time of year.

"I know it's inconvenient for me to be gone all day, but I've never met my grandmother, and I'd like to have that opportunity."

His eyebrows rose. "You've never met her?"

"No sir, I haven't."

"Why is that?"

She lifted her gaze to meet his. "My grandfather disapproved of my parents' marriage. He cut off all contact with them after their wedding."

"That seems harsh."

"Yes sir, I'm afraid it was. But my mother and her sister exchanged letters over the years, and those were passed on to my grandmother."

"And your grandfather allowed that?"

"He didn't know." She hesitated a moment, then continued. "He passed away earlier this month."

"I'm sorry." He sent her a questioning glance. "You never mentioned wanting to attend his funeral."

"There was no funeral, at his request."

"It sounds as though he wanted to control things even after his death."

She nodded. "But we can close that chapter now and look forward to being reunited with my grandmother."

He nodded. "Very well. You may go. I wish you safe travels and a happy day."

"Thank you." She looked up at him. Her lips parted, and her eyes glowed with appreciation— and a hint of something more.

His heartbeat quickened, and his gaze traveled over her upturned face, taking in the soft blush on her cheeks and her full pink lips. He swallowed hard.

"Good night, sir." She averted her gaze and stepped toward the stairs.

"Wait. There's something else I want to say."

She turned, a look of expectation in her eyes. "Yes?"

"I believe I overreacted this afternoon when you called my brother by his given name."

"Oh, no sir. That was my mistake. I know you like people to be addressed properly, especially when the children are present."

"Yes, I do . . . But giving people the benefit of the doubt and offering grace to cover their mistakes is more important than proper address, and I failed in that regard. I apologize."

Her expression warmed. "Thank you, sir."

"So we are friends again?"

"Yes, of course, friends always." She dipped her head, then headed up the stairs.

Longing rose and filled him as he watched her go. He closed his eyes, trying to ease the ache, but her image lingered before his mind's eye, and the ache throbbed through him more powerfully.

Foolish, stupid man. He must not think of her that way. It wasn't right. She was committed to leaving him and returning to India, and he had promised himself he would not marry again. He was only torturing himself with thoughts of her.

And it had to stop.

Twenty-Three

The chauffeur opened the rear passenger door of Aunt Beatrice's luxurious motorcar, and Julia stepped out. She gazed up at her grandmother's large brick home—and her eyes widened.

Her brother, Jonathan, climbed out after her. "Did you grow up here, Mother?"

"Yes, I did." Julia's mother took the chauffeur's hand and joined Julia and Jonathan. Aunt Beatrice stepped out last.

Jonathan slowly shook his head. "My goodness, I had no idea your family was so . . ."

"Wealthy?" Aunt Beatrice supplied with a slight smile.

Jonathan's face colored. "Yes, I suppose that's what I was thinking."

"It's all right, Jonathan." Aunt Beatrice inclined her head. "It's your family as well, and it's time you and Julia became acquainted with your grandmother."

Jonathan looked at Julia, surprise and a bit of

apprehension reflected in his eyes. She couldn't blame him. She felt much the same. They turned and followed their mother and aunt up the steps to the front door. The butler immediately ushered them inside and took their coats, then showed them into the drawing room.

The house was not nearly as large as Highland, but the beautiful furnishings and expensive décor were just as lovely. Potted palms, heavy drapes, and rich color schemes gave the home a luxurious atmosphere.

Aunt Beatrice turned to the butler. "Higgins, will you please tell Mrs. Moorefield we'll speak with Mother before we have luncheon?"

"Yes, m'lady." The butler bowed and retreated from the room.

Julia's mother clasped her hands and turned to her sister. "Do you think I ought to go up first? That might give Mother time to prepare before she meets Jonathan and Julia."

"There's no need. Mother is quite anxious to see you all."

Julia's mother leaned closer to Beatrice and lowered her voice. "But you know how Mother can be, and I don't want her to say anything hurtful to them."

"Don't worry. You'll find her quite changed. The years have softened her in many ways."

She nodded, still looking uncertain as she turned to Julia and Jonathan. "Are you ready?"

"Of course." Jonathan sent her a confident smile. "I'm quite looking forward to it."

Julia took her mother's arm. "We've prayed to be reunited with your family for many years."

"Yes, that's true. I only wish your father could be here with us."

Julia nodded. Her father had wanted to come, but Dr. Hadley felt the trip would be too strenuous for him. He had stayed home and assured them he would lift them up in prayer all day.

Beatrice led the way upstairs and knocked on the first door on the right.

"Come in," a frail voice called.

They followed Beatrice into the large bedroom, and Julia tightened her hold on her mother's arm. The scent of lemon oil and camphor floated on the air.

Her grandmother rested in a large canopy bed with heavy gold drapery tied back at each corner. She peered at them as they drew closer, her wrinkled face pale and her skin papery thin. A ruffled nightcap covered most of her hair, except for a few white curls in front. Several pillows supported her while a plump gold coverlet lay over her.

Her grandmother extended a bony finger toward Julia's mother. Her chin trembled, and tears filled her watery blue eyes. "Mary?"

"Yes, Mother, I'm here." Julia's mother hurried toward the bed and embraced her mother. They exchanged greetings, and then both wiped away their tears.

"I want you to meet your grandchildren." Julia's mother turned and smiled at them with shining eyes. "This is Jonathan and Julia. Children, this is your grandmother, Henrietta Shelburne."

Jonathan stepped forward. "Grandmother, I'm very happy to meet you."

"My, what a tall and handsome young man you are." She held out her hand to him.

He grinned, took her hand, and kissed her fingers. "Thank you. If only my good looks could carry me through my medical training, but alas, that's not the case. I must work doubly hard to prove I'm not just a handsome face."

Grandmother smiled. "I'm pleased to hear you have a fine sense of humor as well. Why aren't you married?"

His eyes widened, but he smiled. "Oh, I thought I should finish my training first, and then I must find someone who is willing to return to India with me."

"Do you have someone special in mind?"

"Not yet. I am focusing on my studies right now."

Grandmother nodded. "That's very wise." She turned to Julia. "And what about you, young lady? I understand you are working as a governess?"

Julia smiled. "Yes ma'am. I am."

"Are they good people?"

"Oh, very good, ma'am."

She glanced at Beatrice. "Do we know them?"

Beatrice nodded to Julia.

"I am employed by Sir William Ramsey, baronet of Highland Hall, near Fulton in Berkshire."

Grandmother considered that. "Ramsey . . . I knew a Charles Ramsey many years ago." She shifted her gaze to Julia again. "Tell me about the family."

"Sir William is a wise and caring man, a widower with two young children. His son Andrew is nine and Millicent is six. He is also the guardian of his two cousins. Katherine will be coming to London for her first season this spring, and Penelope turns sixteen soon. I oversee the care and studies for all four of them."

"What happened to his wife?"

Julia hesitated, surprised her grandmother would ask for such details, but she supposed someone who was elderly and cut off from society by poor health enjoyed hearing about the lives of others. "She passed away three years ago."

"I see." Her grandmother settled back against the pillows. "And are you happy there? Is it a good situation?"

Julia nodded. "Yes ma'am. I am grateful and quite content."

"But what about your own prospects for marriage?"

Julia's face warmed as Sir William's face rose in

her mind. "I am twenty-seven and well past the age when most young women marry."

Her grandmother's silver eyebrows dipped. "You look much younger than twenty-seven, and there is no reason why you shouldn't marry. The problem is you've been hidden away in India all these years, and now you're toiling in seclusion in the country, overseeing someone else's children, when you ought to be out in society meeting your prospective husband."

Julia's mother took a step closer. "Julia is a loving daughter who has made many sacrifices to serve the Lord and help our family. We are very proud of her."

"Of course you are, as you ought to be." Her grandmother shifted her gaze to Julia. "I'm sorry, my dear. I didn't mean to offend."

"It's all right. You haven't offended me." She swallowed and forced a small smile. "The Lord knows my circumstances, and if He wishes me to marry, He'll bring the right man into my life. If not, then I'm content with that prospect as well."

Her grandmother shook her head. "I've always believed we must do our part to make those connections possible, and then we give the good Lord something to work with." She sighed. "The spinster life may be fine for some, but I don't believe it is the best path for you."

Julia's mother sent her an apologetic glance, then focused on their grandmother. "Please tell us how you're feeling. Has your doctor been to see you recently?"

That shift in the conversation occupied her grandmother for several minutes as she described her aches and pains and numerous complaints. Julia listened patiently, but soon her mind drifted to her grandmother's comments about her lack of marriage prospects. Was Grandmother right? Should she still hope for marriage and do more to make that possible? But how could she with her duties as governess?

"Julia?" Her mother touched her arm.

Julia blinked. Oh dear. She'd lost track of the conversation. "Yes?"

"Your grandmother has a gift for you." Her mother pointed to the envelope on the nightstand.

"Oh, thank you." It was traditional to give gifts to the poor on Boxing Day. Was that what had prompted her grandmother, or was it simply a gesture of love meant to draw them closer? She took the envelope with her name written on the front. Jonathan took his as well, then passed the third envelope to their mother.

"They're just small gifts," Grandmother said.

Julia glanced at her mother. Should they open the envelopes now, or wait until they were out of her grandmother's presence?

"Thank you, Mother. It's very kind of you to think of us." Julia's mother slipped the envelope into her skirt pocket.

Julia started to do the same, but her Grandmother pointed a trembling finger at her. "Go ahead. Open them now."

Julia carefully tore open her envelope and found a ten-pound note inside. What a wonderful surprise! This would provide a nice cushion for her. "Thank you, Grandmother."

"You're welcome. I wish it could be more. Perhaps when Mr. Holloway, our solicitor, settles the matters with your grandfather's will—"

"Mother." Aunt Beatrice sent her a warning glance. "Please, don't make any promises."

Grandmother sighed. "Yes, I suppose you're right. Mr. Holloway says there is no guarantee what will be left after he settles the debts and pays all the taxes and duties."

"Of course, Mother. We understand." Julia's mother smiled. "These are generous gifts. Thank you so much."

Julia nodded, then released a soft sigh. It would be wonderful if her grandmother could relieve her family's financial burden, but it didn't seem likely.

Somehow that realization didn't disappoint her as much as she thought it would. Experience had taught her that God would supply their needs. He had done so during those twelve years they were in India, and He would watch over them now.

After all, He was the giver of every good gift. He had blessed her in so many ways. She would not doubt Him now.

• • •

William adjusted his goggles and steered the car around a rough section of road. The cold wind blowing through the open window ruffled the hair beneath his cap and numbed his ears.

Alice tossed the veil covering her large hat over her shoulder and smiled his way. "I think it's wonderful that you drive yourself."

He smiled. "You do?"

"Yes. It's very exciting." The ends of her veil fluttered in the breeze. She turned toward him, her green eyes bright.

"I like it too, Papa," Andrew called from the back where he sat with Sarah and Millie.

William glanced over his shoulder, checking on the children. They looked warm and happy, wearing heavy coats and sitting close to their aunt with a blanket over their laps. He focused on the road again. "I thought about hiring a chauffeur when we came to Highland, but I enjoy driving, and we have the groomsmen and carriages when we need them." He slowed and turned left at the crossroads.

Millie leaned forward. "Where are we going now, Papa?"

"I want to stop at the cottages and deliver those last three boxes." They had already visited their tenant farmers and given each family a box containing sweets, nuts, dried fruit, tea, sugar, flour, and spices. He wished it could be more, but with the financial pressures he faced, it was all he could do this year.

"Who lives in these cottages?" Alice brushed her veil back.

"Some of the old servants who used to work for the family."

She nodded, a slight line appearing between her slender golden eyebrows.

William pulled the car to a stop in front of the first of the three stone cottages, and Andrew jumped out. "I can carry the boxes." He reached in and took a gift-wrapped box from the rear bench seat.

"I want to carry one." Millie climbed down and took a second box.

Sarah passed the last box to Andrew with a smile. "Careful now."

Andrew nodded and slowly adjusted the two boxes so they were balanced.

William smiled, pleased to see Andrew showing some caution.

"I'll take those." Alice lifted the boxes from Andrew's arms. "We wouldn't want you to drop them and spoil the gifts."

Andrew looked as if he was about to object, so William squeezed his shoulder. "Thank you, Alice."

Andrew scowled and trudged off with Sarah and Millie.

A ripple of unease traveled through William.

Though Alice continually offered him bright smiles and witty comments, her lack of patience with the children was wearing on them all. But she was young. Perhaps she didn't have much experience dealing with children.

William put that thought aside and knocked on the front door of the first cottage. A few seconds later, an elderly man, puffing on a pipe, opened the door. He wore a heavy green sweater and tweed pants with a red winter scarf wrapped around his neck.

"Good afternoon, Mr. Morrison. How are you today?" William had met Mr. Alfred Morrison, the former groom, the first week he had arrived at Highland, when Mr. McTavish had taken him on a tour of the estate.

"Very well, thank you, sir." He smiled, but his gaze hesitated when he noticed Alice. "What brings you all to my door today?"

"We have a gift for you." Millie stepped forward and offered him the box.

His eyes lit up. "Well, now, isn't that a nice surprise."

"We visit all our friends on Boxing Day and give them presents," Millie added with a delighted smile.

"Boxing Day, you say?" He chuckled and winked at William.

"Yes sir," Millie said. "It comes every year, the day after Christmas."

"Well, that's very kind of you to remember me. Would you like to come in? We could have a cup of tea, and you could sit by the fire and warm yourselves."

Millie looked up at her father with an eager smile, and Andrew did the same.

Before he could reply, Alice shook her head. "No, thank you. That's kind, but we don't have time today."

The light faded from the old man's eyes, and he slowly nodded. "Of course, m'lady."

"Why can't we go in, Papa?" Impatience filled Andrew's voice.

Alice's expression hardened, and she sent Andrew a cool look. "We have several others to visit, and I promised Lady Gatewood I'd be home in time for tea."

Andrew frowned at Alice, then shifted his irritated gaze to William.

William turned to Mr. Morrison. "We hope you'll enjoy the gift, and we wish you a happy new year."

The elderly man nodded again, a touch of sadness in his expression as he closed the door.

Sarah sent William a disappointed glance, as did Millie. But Alice took his arm and smiled up at him. "Thank you, William." She released a shuddering breath. "I couldn't imagine drinking tea in that old man's dreadful little cottage."

"I'm sure it would've been fine."

"But who knows what it's like inside. You wouldn't want to expose me or the children to filth or disease."

"No, I would not, but I doubt Mr. Morrison's cottage contains either."

"Well, I appreciate your deferring to me. I don't mind giving gifts to the poor, but I'm not comfortable having tea with them."

William swallowed the firm reply rising in his throat. He would not argue with Alice, especially in front of the children, but he did not appreciate her attitude. As the baronet of Highland, he had a responsibility to care for those who lived and worked on the estate. It was his duty to treat them with respect and kindness.

Apparently that was something Alice did not understand.

Twenty-Four

Julia skated to the side of the pond and turned to catch a better view of William, Andrew, and Millie. Lifting her hand, she squinted against the bright sunlight reflecting off the snow-covered landscape.

Andrew flew past, his skates mere extensions of his feet as he raced across the icy pond. His face glowed pink beneath his freckles, and a few strands of flaming hair escaped from the back of his blue knit hat. Freedom and joy radiated from his face.

William glided toward Julia at a slower pace, holding hands with Millie, who was still struggling to catch the rhythm of skating. But she looked up and smiled at Julia, obviously delighted to have her father's full attention.

Julia grinned and waved as they passed. "That's the way, Millie. Keep going."

"What about me?" William called, his eyes shining.

Julia laughed. "You're doing very well."

He sent her a dashing grin, and her heartbeat sped up. How handsome he looked when he smiled that way. She shifted her gaze to Katherine and Penny.

They were both experienced skaters who enjoyed being on the ice, and David had no trouble keeping up with them. His teasing laughter rang out across the pond as he sped past the girls and dared them to join him in a race.

Sarah and Clark came around next, holding hands and skating at an easy pace, happiness lighting both their faces. Sarah had been floating on a cloud since William had agreed Clark could join them on today's outing. It was a thoughtful gesture on William's part, and Julia was pleased he had eased his stance on keeping their relationship a secret.

Alice caught up with William and Millie and skated around once with them, then she cut across the pond and glided to a stop next to Julia. Her flushed cheeks and bright smile highlighted her lovely features. "Goodness, I haven't skated like this since I was a little girl."

Julia smiled. "You look as though you are enjoying it."

"I am, but I'd be glad to take a break for a few minutes. Would you like to sit down?" Alice motioned toward a wooden bench at the side of the pond.

A slight ripple of unease passed through Julia. Alice usually acknowledged her with a nod or a smile, but this was the first time she had initiated a conversation. She scolded herself for hesitating and smiled. "Yes, thank you."

"William tells me you were a missionary before you came to Highland."

Julia nodded. "My family and I served in India for twelve years."

Alice tipped her head, her gaze fixed on Julia. "Yes, that's what he said."

Julia shifted and looked across the pond at the skaters. Why had William discussed her background with Alice? It seemed odd, but perhaps Alice had asked him.

"Our church in Philadelphia has sent out several foreign missionaries—some to Africa and others to China, but we don't have anyone serving in India."

Julia forced a slight smile.

"The reason I mention it is that my father is quite a philanthropist. He's always looking for a good cause to support. And I thought if you were returning to India, he might be willing to give a generous gift toward your work."

"Oh, that would be very kind. I'm sure my parents would be happy to write to him and tell him more about our mission."

"Are they still in India?"

"No, my father became ill last summer and

needed medical treatment. That's why we returned to England."

"I'm sorry to hear that. How is he doing now?"

"He's had a difficult time, but he finally seems to be improving."

Alice's face brightened. "So you'll be returning to India soon?"

Julia glanced across the pond at William and the children, and her heart clenched. "That is our hope, but I'm not sure of the timing. There are several things to consider."

"Well, you mustn't worry about William and the children. I'm sure he can find another governess to replace you. If you're called to serve the poor and suffering and bring them the gospel, then you must go." She reached for Julia's gloved hand. "I admire you so much. And I'd be more than happy to speak to my father about your work. I'm sure he'll be very generous with his support."

A tremor passed through Julia. "Thank you."

David whizzed past. "Alice, come join us!"

"I'll be right there." She turned back to Julia and smiled. "You will keep me informed about your plans, won't you?"

Julia's reply lodged in her throat, so she nodded and forced another smile.

Alice stood and pushed off across the ice, leaving Julia alone on the bench.

Searching across the pond, she looked for William. Millie had taken a spill, and he lifted her to her feet again, their laughter ringing out across the pond.

The thought of leaving him and returning to India made her heart heavy. Would it be wrong for her to stay here? Did she have to go halfway around the world to prove her faithfulness to God and her commitment to following His will? Couldn't she serve the Lord right here by caring for William and his family?

But that might not be possible for many reasons.

Her gaze shifted to Alice, and she bit her lip. In the last few days Alice's interest in William had become quite clear, but it wasn't as easy to determine if he returned her feelings. He'd been polite and seemed to enjoy their conversations, but Katherine or Sarah had been the ones to suggest Alice join them in their activities.

Julia closed her eyes and tried to still her spinning thoughts. She must pray and commit all these things to the Lord, then trust that He would lead her, but her faith felt weak and wavering.

What shall I do, Lord? What do You want from me?

She waited for an answer, but no clear impression or specific directions came to mind.

Opening her eyes, she looked across the pond. William and Alice now skated side by side with Andrew and Millie following close behind. They looked perfect together, very much like a happy family.

She pressed her lips together, her hopes sinking. Wasn't that what she wanted for William and the children?

But in her heart, she knew the truth. She wanted to be the one who captured his attention and filled that role in his heart and life.

"I don't see why we must go to bed now when everyone else is staying up until midnight." Andrew's mouth twisted into a scowl.

Julia smoothed the covers over Andrew's chest. "Everyone else is an adult."

"I'm not an adult," Millie piped up from her bed across the room.

Julia smiled. "No, you are not, and that's why you are also going to bed now."

"But it's New Year's Eve," Andrew said. "I think I should be allowed to stay up with the others."

Ann picked up Millie's shoes. "Your papa made the decision, not Miss Foster, so you should be a good lad and stop complaining." She set the shoes in the closet and closed the door.

Andrew sighed. "All right. But next year I'm staying up until midnight with everyone else. I'll be ten then, and that's certainly old enough."

Julia brushed the hair off his forehead. "We'll see. Now it's time for prayer."

"Millie should go first," he said, still looking vexed by his early bedtime.

"All right." Julia turned to Millie.

The little girl folded her hands and closed her eyes. "Dear God, thank You for today and for Papa and Aunt Sarah and Miss Foster and Ann. Please keep us safe while we sleep, and don't let us have any bad dreams. Amen."

Julia added her own thanks for the day, then turned and nodded to Andrew.

"Dear God, please let Papa take me out to practice archery again tomorrow. Thank You for everything, and please let me stay up until midnight next New Year's Eve. Amen."

Julia's heart warmed as she listened to their prayers. She kissed them both on the forehead, then turned down the lamp. "Good night, my dears. Sleep well, and I'll see you next year."

"What?" Millie looked up at Julia with a confused expression.

Andrew huffed. "Don't you understand? Tomorrow morning will be next year."

"Oh yes." Millie yawned. "That's right. Good night, Miss Foster. Good night, Ann."

Julia closed the door partway and followed Ann into the hall.

The nursery maid stopped and wiped her hand across her forehead. Her shoulders sagged as she poked a strand of blond hair back into her cap.

"Are you all right, Ann?"

The maid slowly shook her head. "I can't stop thinking about Peter and wondering what he's doing, especially tonight."

Julia reached out and touched her arm. "I'm sorry."

Her eyes grew misty. "I haven't heard from him since he left. Not even one letter."

Sympathy filled Julia's heart. "I know that must be hard." Ann's painful news confirmed Julia's impression that Peter had little true concern for Ann or what was best for her. Still, Ann cared for him, and she needed consoling.

"I don't know how I'll ever get past it."

"Losing touch with someone you love is never easy. But the pain will ease if you give it time."

"I don't see how it could. I love Peter, and I always will."

Julia slipped her arm around Ann's shoulder, wishing there was more she could do. "Are you going down to the servants' party?"

Ann shook her head. "I don't think so. I'd just spoil the fun for everyone else."

"But it might take your mind off your troubles."

Ann bit her lip, looking torn.

"What if I went with you?"

Ann's eyes widened. "Would you?"

"Of course." Julia sometimes felt out of place in the servants' hall, but if going down to the party would help ease Ann's broken heart, then she would make the effort.

"All right." Ann's face brightened. "I'll just go up and change."

"Knock on my door when you're ready." Julia

glanced down at her plain skirt and blouse, wishing she had something special to wear to the party.

"I'll be right back." Ann hurried off toward the stairs.

Julia hoped she would not regret her decision. Staying up until midnight and ushering in the new year with a toast and some revelry wasn't the usual way she spent New Year's Eve. The footmen had been joking about the party, making it sound rather wild. But surely Mr. Lawrence and Mrs. Emmitt would be there and see that things did not get out of hand.

She chuckled and shook her head. She had no doubt about that.

William glanced at the clock in the drawing room and took a seat next to Sarah on the couch. He sat back, thankful he could soon bid everyone good night. He was tired of parlor games and trite conversation, but it would be rude to leave before the clock struck midnight and he wished everyone a happy new year.

Alice, Katherine, and Penelope sat opposite him, while Lord and Lady Gatewood were seated on his right. David stood by the fireplace, a drink in his hand. William frowned—that was at least David's fourth drink since they'd left the dining room.

William had lifted the ban on alcohol for the

evening because Lord and Lady Gatewood had sent over a special selection for New Year's as their gift. Unfortunately, David's drinking had loosened his tongue and caused a few uncomfortable moments during their game of charades.

Between Katherine's flirting, David's bragging, and Alice's playful banter, he longed to call it an evening. It wouldn't have bothered him so much if Lady Gatewood hadn't been watching him and Alice so closely. He could practically see the matrimonial wheels turning in her mind, and it grated on his nerves.

"Let's play one more round." Alice smiled across at him, her green eyes dancing. "I love charades."

"I'm not sure we have time." William checked the clock again.

"Then why don't we play Alphabet Minute? That doesn't take long."

David took another glass from the silver tray. "Sounds like a grand idea. I can converse at length on any topic." He smiled and downed the amber liquid in his glass.

William narrowed his eyes at David. "Yes, but can you think clearly enough to start each sentence with the next letter of the alphabet?"

"Of course I can. My mind is as sharp as a sword and as strong as . . . as strong as it needs to be to play Alphabet Minute."

William shook his head. "I think you've played enough games tonight."

"Whas wrong with you, William?" David's words slurred. "Why are you always so serious?"

Heat flooded William's face, and he clenched his jaw. He'd had enough of David's surly comments.

Sarah stood. "Why don't we just enjoy conversation for the next few minutes?" She turned to Mr. Lawrence. "Will you please prepare the champagne for our midnight toast?"

"Yes, miss." The butler moved to the far end of the room where the champagne waited on ice.

Sarah joined Penelope and Katherine and engaged them in conversation.

William stared into the fire, his mood sinking lower. What would the new year hold for him? If David wouldn't buy his half interest in the London house, would he agree to sell it? Could they even find a buyer in time? If the house did sell, where would they stay when he took his family to London? He'd assured Katherine she would have her debut this April. Lady Gatewood would have a fit if he canceled those plans after all the effort and expense she had borne in the preparations.

What if he sold the London house, and then ended up losing Highland as well, where would he go? He had to provide a home for his children, sister, and cousins. He sighed and closed his eyes, his concerns feeling like a four-stone weight bearing down on his shoulders.

"Why the long face, William?" Alice sat beside him.

"It's nothing, at least nothing for you to be concerned about."

"All right." She smiled and patted his arm. "But if you ever need a friend to listen to your troubles, you can count on me."

He nodded but didn't reply. Somehow the prospect of talking to Alice about his concerns didn't seem nearly as comforting as sharing them with Miss Foster.

He glanced toward the open door leading to the great hall. Had Miss Foster enjoyed being included in the family's New Year's Eve tea this afternoon? Where was she now, up in her room? Perhaps he should go check on her. He shook his head. That wouldn't be appropriate, especially not this late in the evening.

"William?"

He turned back to Alice. "Yes?"

She searched his face, her brows drawn together. "I don't think you heard a word I said. It's almost midnight." She nodded toward the clock, a look of impatience in her eyes. "Shouldn't you gather everyone for the toast now?"

Irritation coiled in his stomach. Alice was sounding a great deal like Lady Gatewood, and he didn't appreciate her tone. He rose to his feet and nodded to Lawrence.

The butler carried the tray of champagne flutes around the room, serving each guest. They all stood and formed a loose semicircle in front of the fireplace.

The clock struck midnight, and William lifted his glass. "Happy New Year, everyone."

"Happy New Year," they all responded, then exchanged smiles and took sips of champagne.

As the clock continued to strike, Sarah turned to David and kissed his cheek. "Happy New Year, David. I'm very glad you're here with us."

Penelope and Katherine exchanged a kiss on the cheek, and Lord Gatewood kissed his wife.

Alice looked up at William with a smile.

Heat flushed his neck and face. A kiss at midnight was traditional. It wouldn't mean anything special. "Happy New Year, Alice." He leaned toward her intending to kiss her cheek, but at the last moment she turned, and her lips met his. Her mouth was soft and warm, and she responded with unguarded enthusiasm.

Surprise shot though him, and he pulled back.

She smiled, her green eyes sparkling. "It's all right, William. It's New Year's."

His brother slapped him on the shoulder. "Bold move, William. You're making me jealous."

Alice laughed softly and kissed David on the cheek. "Happy New Year."

David slipped his arm around Alice's shoulder and grinned. "I've decided I love American women, truly I do." His hand shook slightly as he lifted his champagne flute and nodded to William. "I told my brother you were a beautiful woman the first day we met. Any man who marries you will be very lucky. Isn't that what I said, William?"

William took hold of David's arm. "That's quite enough. You don't want to embarrass yourself."

"No, that's what I said. I remember it all very clearly."

William pulled him closer and lowered his voice. "Keep silent. You're making a fool of yourself."

David pulled his arm away and glared at William, then crossed to the piano, turning his back on everyone.

Sarah moved the group to the great hall and William followed. They bid Alice and Lord and Lady Gatewood good night. Alice sent William one last smile as she stepped out the door.

Sarah sighed and turned to William. "I'm off to bed. Good night." Katherine and Penelope climbed the stairs with her.

William paced into the library. Though the hour was late, he would not be able to sleep until he calmed the troubling thoughts swirling through his mind.

• • •

The servants' hall buzzed with conversation and laughter as the staff gathered to enjoy their New Year's Eve celebration. Chef Lagarde, the kitchen maids, and Mrs. Emmitt had baked all afternoon, and now the table was loaded with sweet and savory treats for the staff to enjoy.

Julia took a cup of cider and a piece of shortbread from the tray and found a seat next to Marie, one of the maids. They had just finished a rousing game of Forfeits, and she was glad for a break. Thankfully, she had not been asked to perform a song or tell an amusing story to regain the handkerchief she had placed on the table at the beginning of the game.

When Nelson suggested they play, Julia thought about excusing herself and going upstairs, but Ann seemed eager to take part, so Julia stayed. She looked across the room and spotted Ann sitting with Lydia by the piano, a smile on her face. Julia's spirits lifted. It was good to see Ann enjoying herself again.

Nelson slung his arm around Betsy's shoulder. "I think Betsy should sing another song for us." Several of the servants clapped for the kitchen maid who had already entertained them with one song during the game.

"I'll play the piano, if you like," Lydia added with a smile.

Betsy grinned, her rosy cheeks glowing. "All

right. I'll sing, but only if you'll all sing along."

Hearty agreement rose from the group, and soon Betsy was leading them in "Sweet Rosie O'Grady." Then she taught them "By the Light of the Silvery Moon," and finally they sang "Meet Me Tonight in Dream Land."

Heat flooded Julia's cheeks as they sang the chorus. She was used to singing hymns and sacred songs, and it didn't seem proper to sing about spooning and cuddling in the moonlight. She glanced around the group during the next verse, but they all joined in without hesitation, even Mr. Lawrence and Mrs. Emmitt.

"Come on, let's sing the chorus again," Betsy called.

"Meet me tonight in dreamland,
under the silv'ry moon;
Meet me tonight in dreamland,
where love's sweet roses bloom.
Come with the love-light gleaming,
in your dear eyes of blue.
Meet me in dreamland,
sweet dreamy dreamland,
there let my dreams come true."

As Julia sang, a vision of William's handsome face and deep blue eyes filled her mind. A warning echoed through her heart, and she tried to banish the image. It was foolish to let the words of the song sway her emotions. But when she sang the chorus a third time, her thoughts returned to William, and the longing in her heart grew stronger.

If only he would think of her in such a tender and loving way, take her into his heart, and cherish her, how happy and grateful she would be. Her throat tightened, choking off her voice, and her eyes stung from unshed tears.

She swallowed and glanced toward the door. Perhaps she should leave before someone asked her what was wrong. She could never admit she grieved for William and the love and life they could never share.

But she didn't want to spoil the party for Ann. She glanced across the room again. Ann leaned against the side of the piano as Lydia played. One of Clark's young assistant gardeners stood beside her. Ann glanced at him with shining eyes, and they exchanged a smile and continued singing.

Ann didn't need her. No one needed her—especially not William. Not since Miss Drexel had arrived at Highland.

Lowering her head, she stood and walked toward the door. Marie and Mrs. Emmitt glanced at her as she passed, but no one questioned her or urged her to stay.

She stepped through the doorway and hurried down the passage toward the back staircase. Cool air flowed in from a partially open window by the back door leading to the courtyard. She pulled in a deep breath and straightened her shoulders.

What would her parents say if she confided in them about her struggle? How would they counsel her? The heavy weight of conviction settled over her heart.

Self-pity was not an admirable quality, and she should not indulge in it one moment longer. But changing her feelings was easier said than done.

She headed up the stairs, her heart aching. She passed the ground floor, climbed to the first, then turned down the hallway toward her bedroom. As she approached her door, she heard footsteps and then a loud bump farther down the hall.

She cocked her head and listened, and someone issued a muffled groan. She pulled in a sharp breath. Could it be William? Had he fallen? Her heart lurched, and she hurried down the hall.

In the gallery at the top of the stairs, a man lay slumped on the floor, moaning. The light was so dim she couldn't see him clearly.

Julia's mind raced as she hurried to his side. "Are you all right, sir?"

The man slowly lifted his head, and recognition flashed through her.

David's eyes drooped to half-mast, and his mouth hung open in an odd smile. "Miss Foster?"

"Yes sir. Are you ill? Shall I call someone to help you?"

"No, I'll be all right, if I can just get to my feet." He pushed up to his knees, then stood and swayed.

She gasped and reached to steady him. His stale breath washed over her, and she clamped her mouth closed against the awful smell. "Why don't you sit down, sir? There's a chair right here. I'll ring for someone to help you to your room."

"No. I don't want to trouble the servants. Just walk with me." His slurred speech and foul breath made it clear he was not ill at all . . . but inebriated.

Julia glanced down the hall, wishing someone else would appear to help them. Even if she did ring for a servant, they were all downstairs at the party and not likely to hear the summons.

He took hold of her arm. "Come on. We can do it."

She debated another second. But this seemed to be the only answer. He'd already fallen once, and she couldn't very well leave him on his own. "All right."

He leaned against her, and they started down the hallway. The farther she walked away from her own room, the more uneasy she felt.

When they'd almost reached the end of the west wing, he stopped and motioned to a door on the left. "Here we are. This is my room."

"Then I will bid you good night, sir." She started to pull away.

But he gripped her arm. "Don't go. Not yet."

Alarm flashed through her. "I must."

"It's all right. Why don't you come in and keep

me company." He leaned closer, and his liquor-laced breath washed over her. "No one will know."

She pulled back. "No sir. I cannot."

He grabbed her other arm. "Oh, come on. It will be fun."

"Please, let go. You're not thinking clearly." But he tightened his hold. A thousand frightening thoughts raced through her panicked mind as a scream rose in her throat. Without warning, he pushed her against the wall.

She gasped, but he stifled the sound as he pressed his mouth over hers in a burning, punishing kiss.

William took a candle and climbed the stairs, weary to the bone, although he doubted sleep would come any time soon. The distant sound of piano music floated up from the servants' hall below. There would be some sleepy-eyed maids and footmen in the morning, but he wouldn't begrudge them a little New Year's celebration.

When he reached the gallery, he heard voices in the west wing hallway. One of them sounded feminine. That was odd. Only he and David were staying down this hall. All the women in the family had rooms in the east wing.

Had his brother talked one of the housemaids into joining him in his room? A burst of indignation filled his chest, and he strode down the hall. He would not allow it. Not in his house!

Holding his candle aloft, the flickering light revealed a couple kissing by David's door.

"What is going on?"

David pulled back, revealing the woman in his embrace.

A shockwave jolted through William. "Miss Foster!"

David swayed and lifted his hand. "Now, William, there's no need to be upset."

William grabbed his brother by the shirt front. "What are you doing?"

David pulled away. "We're just two lovers kissing good night."

Miss Foster gasped. "That's not true!"

"It's no use pretending, my dear. He has discovered our secret."

Miss Foster shook her head, a look of disbelief and revulsion on her face. She was either a very good actress or his brother was a bald-faced liar.

David closed his eyes and swayed again. "I'd love to stay and chat, but I'm suddenly feeling . . . very ill." He raised his hand to his mouth, then turned and lunged into his bedroom, slamming the door behind him.

Miss Foster turned to him. "Please sir, you must believe me. I never . . ." Her voice choked off.

"Then what are you doing all the way down at the end of this wing?"

"I was helping Mr. Ramsey to his room."

"And why would you do that?"

"He fell at the top of the stairs." She pointed past his shoulder. "I was coming up from the party in the servants' hall, when I heard a noise. I went to investigate and discovered Mr. Ramsey sprawled on the carpet, moaning. He asked me to help him back to his room."

"Surely you know it's not appropriate for you to come down here with him. Why didn't you ring for a footman or Mr. Lawrence?"

"The servants were all at the party. The singing was quite loud when I left. I didn't think they would hear the bell." She looked at him, her expression earnest, but he clenched his jaw and looked away. He would not be swayed by innocent looks or deceived by a far-fetched story. Not in his own house by someone he had trusted.

She lifted a trembling hand to her throat. "You must believe me, sir."

"Well, it's very hard when I discover you wrapped in my brother's embrace, kissing a man you barely know."

"He stole that kiss!"

He stared at her, trying to make sense of it, but he couldn't keep the doubt and disgust from twisting his expression.

Her eyes glittered, and her mouth firmed. "Very well. If that's what you think of me, I give you my notice. I'll leave in the morning."

"Now wait a minute! I am in charge here. I will decide if you are to stay or go."

"No sir. I cannot work for someone who doubts my word and questions my character." She stepped past him.

"Miss Foster!"

She turned back, her gaze piercing. "I have never lied to you. I've always been faithful and true in my heart and in my actions, and if you do not believe that, then I cannot stay." She left him and fled down the hall.

Painful doubts tore through him as he watched her go. What if he was wrong? What if she was telling the truth and she was the victim rather than the culprit? If that was the case, she needed him to be her protector and defender, not a judge and jury. But he had not come to her defense. He had let his past influence the present, and he had condemned her because of it.

The weight of his harsh words pressed down on his heart, and he blew out a deep breath. He started to follow her down the hall, but as he reached his bedroom door, his steps slowed. It was late. They were both tired and upset. Surely it would be better to wait until morning and let their emotions cool. Then they could think more clearly and resolve their differences.

With a weary heart and load of guilt weighing him down, he opened his bedroom door and entered his room.

Twenty-Five

A sob rose in Julia's throat as she fled down the hall. How could William believe she would welcome a kiss from a drunken cad like David Ramsey? She wasn't sure which made her angrier—David forcing himself on her or William suspecting she was a willing partner to it. Both were insulting and outrageous.

She jerked open her bedroom door, rushed inside, and shoved the door closed behind her. With her head pounding, she dropped onto her bed and let her tears flow.

How could this have happened? Why didn't William believe her? Would she really have to leave in the morning? *Oh, Father, what a terrible, terrible mess. Please help me sort this out.*

For several minutes she poured out her heart to the Lord. When her tears finally slowed, she grabbed a handkerchief from her nightstand and blotted her hot cheeks. It was too late to make sense of it tonight. When morning came, she would pray again and somehow find the strength and direction she needed.

With a heavy sigh, she rose and changed into her nightgown, then blew out her candle and climbed into bed.

Closing her eyes, she took several slow, deep breaths, trying to calm her thoughts, but the dreadful events of the evening continued to parade before her eyes.

Finally, she drifted into a half-dreaming state, but a faint sound in the hall roused her. Squinting toward the door, she listened for a few seconds, then told herself she was being silly. There was no one in the hallway. With a huff, she rolled over and tugged on the blankets, but they had become twisted, so she sat up and shook them out.

A whiff of smoke drifted past her nose. She stopped and sniffed the air.

Surely it was just the scent of ashes from her bedroom fireplace carried down the chimney by the wind. Still, she ought to be certain.

Tossing back the covers, she climbed out of bed. Faint moonlight flowed through the window, illuminating her path to the fireplace. Bending low, she took the poker, examined the charred wood, and sniffed the air.

The fire had gone out long ago, and there was no scent of smoke. She rose and walked toward her bedroom door, and the smoky smell returned. A tremor raced up her back, bringing her more fully awake.

She eased the door open, and a hazy wave of smoke poured in. Stifling a gasp, she shoved the door closed. She must warn William and rouse the rest of the family and staff, but her first priority was the children. With a trembling hand, she lit a candle, then grabbed her shoes and shoved them on her feet. There was no time to change, so she grabbed her dressing gown, pulled it on, and tied the sash.

She started toward the door, then turned back and grabbed her cross necklace from the dressing table and stuffed it in the pocket of her dressing gown.

Lifting a silent prayer for courage, she opened the door and ran across the hall. Glancing to the right, a shaft of fear pierced her heart. Just a few feet down the hall, flames leaped up the wall and across the ceiling.

"Fire! *Fire!*" She ran into the nursery and slammed the door behind her. Jerking the cord several times, she rang the bell to summon someone downstairs. There was no hall boy on duty, but perhaps the scullery maid would hear it and alert Mr. Lawrence. But she had no time to wait for help to arrive. She must take the children to safety before the fire reached their room.

"Andrew, wake up!" She shook his shoulder.

He stirred and squinted up at her.

"There is a fire. You must put on your shoes and coat."

His eyes widened. "A fire?"

"Yes. Now hurry and do as I say."

Andrew sprang from his bed and darted to the closet.

Julia rushed to Millie's bed and woke her. "Andrew, get Millie's coat and bring it here."

The little girl rubbed her eyes and sat up. "What is it? Why do I need my coat?"

Julia grabbed Millie's shoes and knelt before her. "There is a fire, and we must dress quickly and go outside."

Millie's chin quivered, and she began to cry.

"You must be brave." Julia's mind raced as she helped Millie with her coat, then grabbed her hand. "Come with me."

Andrew ran to the door.

"Wait!" Julia rushed after him. "Let me check first." She touched the doorknob, and searing heat singed her fingers. She gasped and jerked back. "Don't touch it!"

Panic pulsed through her. How could the flames have reached the door so quickly? She spun and searched the room. The only other exit was the window.

She dashed across the room and unlatched the window. Cold wind blew in, chilling her face and neck.

Andrew ran to her side. "Maybe we can climb down."

Julia leaned out, peering into the darkness, searching for footholds, but even with the moonlight, it was difficult to see clearly. "It's too high."

Andrew knelt on the window seat and looked down. "It's not so high."

"It's at least thirty feet, if not more."

Andrew's eyes widened, and he gripped her arm. "I read about some boys who tied sheets together and used them to climb out a window."

Julia shook her head. "That's too dangerous. Millie could never climb down."

"But I'm strong. I could do it. Then I could wake the others and get help."

Millie's cries grew louder. Julia clenched her hands, her mind spinning as she searched for another answer, but there was none. "All right." She ran to Millie's bed, tore off the sheets, and tied the ends together. Andrew jerked the blankets off his bed and brought her his sheets.

Millie's sobs turned to coughs as the stinging smoke and fumes seeped under the door and a smoky haze began filling the room.

Julia tossed a blanket toward Millie. "Go and lay it in front of the door to keep the smoke out." Millie picked up the blanket and scampered across the room.

With Andrew's help, Julia pushed the heavy oak

dresser closer to the window and tied the end of one sheet to the leg. She tugged on the fabric, testing the strength of her knots. She would never forgive herself if Andrew fell and was injured. Maybe she should be the one to climb down and take the risk, but she couldn't leave Millie.

There was no other choice. Andrew must go.

Satisfied that her knots were secure, she tossed the sheets out the window. Andrew joined her on the window seat and gazed down again.

The sheets dangled and swayed several feet above the ground, and Julia's heart fell. "It's not long enough."

She started to pull the sheets up, but Andrew stopped her. "It's all right. I can jump the last few feet."

Julia wiped her stinging eyes and checked the distance once more. It looked as though Andrew would have to jump at least six feet. She turned and gripped his shoulders. "Look at me."

Andrew lifted his face, his gaze intense.

"You must climb down very carefully. Take your time and be sure of each move. When you reach the ground, run to the back door and pound hard. If no one answers, run to the stable and wake the groomsmen sleeping upstairs. Tell them they must wake the rest of the family before they fight the fire. Do you understand?"

"Yes." His voice came out a choked whisper, and he threw his arms around her neck.

She hugged him tight. "You are a brave boy, Andrew. I know you can do this." She held him a second more, then kissed the top of his head. Millie's chin trembled as she watched Andrew crawl across the window seat, grab the sheet, and lower himself out the window.

Julia held on tightly to the sheet, wanting to send her strength to Andrew as he climbed down. Her eyes burned and her throat tightened. *Oh, Father, please keep him safe and bring help soon.*

Someone grabbed his shoulder. "Sir, sir! You must wake up."

William blinked, trying to clear the heavy fog of sleep from his head. "What is it?"

Lawrence leaned toward him, his face flushed and his eyes wide. "There's a fire in the east wing!"

Alarm shot through William. "The children!" He threw back the blankets and jumped from his bed.

"Master Andrew is safe. He climbed down from the window and ran to wake us."

"He climbed down? Good heavens, how did he do that?" William pulled on a pair of pants.

"I'm not sure, sir."

"What about Millie, Sarah, and the girls—and Miss Foster?" William shoved on one shoe.

"I woke Nelson and Patrick and sent them up the backstairs."

A plan of action formed in William's mind as he

jerked on the second shoe. "Go wake my brother and the indoor staff. Get everyone out to the back courtyard for safety. Send someone to wake the grooms and gardeners. Then we'll organize the men to fight the fire."

Lawrence gave a grim nod and tightened the belt of his robe. "Very good, sir."

"I'll see to the women and Millie." Stuffing his nightshirt into his pants, William dashed out his bedroom door, with Lawrence running behind him.

The sound of pounding feet and voices in the hallway above reached his ears along with a strange crackling noise. Smoke hung in the air and grew thicker as he hustled through the gallery toward the east wing. His eyes burned, and he raised the front of his nightshirt to cover his mouth.

As he rounded the corner, a wall of fire halfway down the east wing stopped him cold. Flames leaped and danced up both walls, cutting off his access to the nursery and the rooms beyond. He squinted against the stinging smoke, but he could not see what lay past the flames. He would have to try reaching them from the servants' stairs.

He raced down the main staircase and through the great hall toward the back of the house. When he reached the rear hallway, someone shouted from above. He stopped and looked up.

His first footman, Nelson, thundered down the stone stairs, with the second footman, Patrick, close behind. "We can't get through this way."

Patrick pushed past Nelson. "Let's try the main staircase."

William grabbed his arm. "It's no use. I've already tried."

The panting footmen exchanged anxious glances and then looked back at William. "What shall we do, sir?"

"Go to the rear courtyard. Report to Mr. Lawrence. We'll gather the men to fight the fire and try to reach them."

The footmen hurried downstairs, and William followed, his mind swimming through a thick haze of fear. There had to be some way to reach Millie and the women. He rushed out the back door, and a blast of cold wind whipped through his nightshirt. He strode across the cobblestones, searching for Lawrence.

The maids stood to one side, huddled together with Mrs. Emmitt. The grooms and under gardeners ran toward him from stables, carrying buckets and an extension ladder.

"Papa!"

William spun around as Andrew dashed toward him. His son leaped into his arms and held on tight. A muffled sob broke from the boy's throat.

"Andrew." He wrapped his arms around him, and the first wave of relief flowed through William. "How did you get down?"

Andrew pulled back and wiped his cheek. "Miss

Foster helped me tie some sheets together. But she and Millie are still up there."

William's heart clenched. "Bring that ladder!" he shouted as he set Andrew down. "Lawrence, take the men and do what you can to put out the fire. But no one must risk his life to save the house. Do you understand?"

"Yes sir." Lawrence turned and shouted orders, sending some men to gather buckets and others inside to carry water upstairs.

The two young gardeners approached with the ladder.

"Follow me!" William ran around the side of the house to the east wing. Smoke curled out the open window where the rope of sheets hung almost to the ground. But no one looked out at them. Sick dread poured through him.

"I don't see them." Fear choked Andrew's voice. "Millie! Miss Foster!"

William placed his hand on Andrew's shoulder. "It's all right." But his own throat closed, and he could say no more. He directed the men to raise the ladder and lean it against the wall of the house.

"Shall I go up, sir?" The young gardener turned, awaiting his order. He looked strong and able, but William would not trust the lives of those he held most dear to anyone else.

"No. I'll go. Hold the ladder." William launched up the wooden rungs. *Please, God. Let me be in time.*

• • •

Julia crouched on the floor, trying to stay below the smoky cloud filling the room. Acrid fumes stung her nose and throat as she tried to blink away her stinging tears. She placed her arm around Millie's shoulder and pulled her closer, wishing she could shield her from the smoke.

Millie coughed. "Where's Andrew? Isn't he coming back?"

"Help is coming, Millie. Don't worry." *Please Lord, let that be true.* She glanced toward the door. How much time did they have before the fire burned through?

She could climb down the sheets and jump to the ground, but she could not leave Millie to face the fire alone. *Please, God, have mercy on us for Millie's sake and for William's. He could not bear the loss of his daughter after all the other losses he has endured.*

A shout sounded below the window.

Julia gasped and stood up. Millie sprang up beside her, coughing and waving the smoke away from her face.

"Millie! Miss Foster!" William's head rose into view, his frantic eyes searching for them through the haze.

"Papa!" Millie scrambled onto the window seat and jumped toward him.

"Whoa, my darling." He clutched the window-sill.

Julia grabbed hold of Millie's waist to stop her from pushing her father backward off the ladder.

William took hold of his daughter's shoulders. "Can you climb down the ladder with me?"

Millie's face crumpled. "Oh, Papa, I can't. It's too high."

He shot a silent question at Julia.

An idea flashed through her mind. "Can you carry her on your back?"

He sent her a grateful nod, then climbed a step higher and braced his hands on the window seat. "Help her on."

Julia boosted Millie onto her father's back, and the little girl wrapped her arms around his neck and her legs around his waist.

William shifted her a bit, trying to balance her weight. It was a risky decision, but they had no other choice. "You must hold on tight, Millie."

"I'm afraid, Papa!"

"It's all right." Julia touched Millie's arm. "Just close your eyes—trust your father."

William focused his intense gaze on Julia. "I'll be back for you."

Julia glanced over her shoulder at the smoky room, her throat burning. "There's no time. I'll follow you down."

He shot her a desperate look. "All right. But be careful."

"I will." She gave William a few seconds head

start, then knelt on the window seat and backed out.

Gripping the sides of the ladder, she slowly lowered her foot, searching for the rung. The cold wind whipped around her, numbing her cheeks and hands. She glanced toward the ground, and her stomach plunged.

Please, Lord, help me.

She forced herself to look up and took the next step. Smoke swirled around her, stinging her nose and eyes. She pressed her lips together and slid her trembling hands down the sides of the ladder, taking one step and then another.

A cheer rose from the crowd below as William and Millie reached the ground.

Thank You, Lord.

A sudden explosion blasted from the open window above. Julia gasped. The ladder swayed. The maids screamed.

"Hold tight!" someone shouted from below.

Julia squeezed her eyes closed and clung to the ladder. A second passed, then someone gripped her ankle, guiding it to the next rung.

"That's the way." William's strong, deep voice sent a comforting wave through her, but her knees felt like jelly. He leaned in, pressing his shoulder against her legs, steadying her.

"Oh, William." Her voice trembled.

"It's all right. Just keep going."

She looked over her shoulder at him. He nodded and urged her on. She refocused and continued down. William reached the ground, then placed his hands around her waist and lifted her down beside him. Another cheer rose from the maids as they rushed forward to surround them. She looked up at William, her throat tight and her heart flooded with gratitude.

He pulled her into his embrace, crushing her to his chest. "Thank You, God," he whispered in a choked voice. She melted against him, her own heart echoing the prayer.

Andrew and Millie wrapped their arms around them both.

"Help us!" Katherine shouted, leaning out her open bedroom window. Penelope stood next to her, frantically waving her arms.

"Hurry! Move that ladder," William called. "We've got to reach Sarah as well."

The men whisked the ladder away and leaned it against the wall below Katherine's window. Flames shot from the children's bedroom window, lighting the night. Harry, the young gardener, hustled up the ladder to help Katherine down.

Julia met Katherine at the bottom of the ladder and embraced her. Katherine choked back a sob and held on tight for several seconds.

Finally, Julia stepped back and watched Penelope descend with Harry's help.

Clark Dalton ran around the side of the house and across the grass toward William. "Where's Sarah?" he shouted, his eyes wide.

William clenched his jaw and pointed to the fourth window. "That's her room."

Julia looked up at Sarah's dark window, and a shiver raced down her back. Surely the blast would have awakened her. Why wasn't she at her window?

Clark rushed over to the base of the ladder as Penelope reached the ground. William joined him, and they quickly moved the ladder to Sarah's window.

Determination lined Clark's face as he sprinted up, calling Sarah's name. When he reached the top, he banged on the glass and leaned closer to peer inside.

"Can you see her?" William called.

"No." Clark yanked on the window, but it was locked.

"Find something to break the glass," William shouted.

One of the young gardeners brought a rake. William grabbed it and carried it halfway up the ladder to meet Clark. Then Clark raced to the top again.

Julia bit her lip, her heart pounding in her throat. *Please, Lord . . .*

Millie grabbed her hand. Penelope, Katherine, and Andrew moved closer as they all fixed their gaze on Clark.

He steadied himself at the top of the ladder. "Watch out below!" He swung the rake toward the window. It shattered, sending pieces of glass raining down on the bushes below. He shouted to Sarah again as he broke the jagged glass around the edges of the window, then dropped the rake and climbed inside.

The crowd stilled. Julia held her breath and tightened her hold on Millie's hand.

A few seconds passed, then Clark and Sarah stepped up to the open window.

A murmur passed through those waiting on the ground. William flashed a relieved glance at Julia, and she returned the same.

Clark tried to coax Sarah out the window and onto the ladder, but she shook her head and pulled back, sobbing. Then she buried her face in his shoulder.

Julia's thoughts flashed back to the day they had decorated the Christmas tree: Sarah feared heights!

Clark wrapped his arms around her. "I'm taking her out the other way!"

William lunged forward and grabbed hold of the ladder. "You can't!"

Clark shook his head, then turned away and disappeared from view.

William turned to Julia, his eyes wide, his expression stunned. "They'll never get through. It's a wall of flames." He whirled away and set off at a jog toward the back of the house. The two young gardeners ran after him.

Julia, the children, and the maids hurried around

the house to the rear courtyard, where they gathered by the open stable door. Lanterns had been hung to bring more light to the courtyard.

A flatbed wagon pulled by four horses rolled around the side of the house, and several men jumped from the back.

Mrs. Emmitt clasped her hands. "It's McTavish and some of the tenant farmers."

William shouted instructions to McTavish and the men, but as he turned back toward the house, Clark dashed out, pulling Sarah by the hand.

Julia ran toward Sarah. "Oh, Sarah, are you all right?"

Sarah nodded as she coughed and placed her hand on her chest. "Give me a moment, please."

William looked her over, concern lining his face. "I was so worried."

Sarah's cough quieted, and she clasped Clark's hand. "I'm fine, thanks to Clark."

"Good heavens, man, how did you do it?" William stared at Clark, eyes wide.

Clark held tight to Sarah's hand. "I'm not sure exactly. I just prayed like mad, then we ran through the hall and down the backstairs."

William shook his head. "But the footmen said they couldn't get through."

Clark glanced back at the house. "A few of the men are up there now with your brother, trying to put out the fire. Perhaps the Lord used them to open the way, or maybe we're like Daniel's three friends in the fiery furnace, and God shielded us from the flames."

William placed his hand on Clark's shoulder. "Thank you. That took a lot of courage. I'm grateful."

Clark looked at Sarah. "I'm just glad Sarah is all right."

William nodded and glanced toward the house. "I'm going back in. I could use your help, Dalton."

"I'm with you, sir."

He sent the gardener a grateful nod, then turned to go.

Julia reached for William's arm. "Please, be careful."

He looked into her eyes, and his stern expression eased. A surge of emotion passed between them, and her heart lifted.

He gave her a brief nod, then strode toward the house with Clark by his side.

Twenty-Six

Early the next morning, William looked at the burned-out cave at the end of the east wing as questions cycled through his mind. How had the fire started? Where would he find the money to repair all that had been destroyed?

He pulled in a shallow breath and clamped his mouth closed against the smoky stench. How long would it take to rid the house of that dreadful smell? At least the damage had been limited to two floors in the back half of the east wing, and more important, no lives had been lost.

"Where shall we sleep now?" Katherine slipped her hands into the pockets of her pale-blue dressing gown and joined William, Penelope, Sarah, and Miss Foster as they walked away from the east wing.

"There are plenty of bedrooms in the west wing." William nodded in that direction. "You may choose any room you like."

"What about the maids?" Penelope asked.

"Where will they sleep?" The fire had burned through the ceiling of the nursery and Miss Foster's room and damaged several of the maids' bedrooms on the floor above.

William glanced at his sister. "Sarah and Mrs. Emmitt will have to sort that out."

Sarah nodded. "I'm sure we can find new rooms for everyone. But first we must have some breakfast. It's been a long night, and we have a busy day of cleanup ahead."

As they reached the gallery, David strode out of the west wing dressed in clean clothes and looking well rested. "Morning, all."

Julia took a step closer to William and sent him a questioning look.

William studied his brother. "Where've you been?"

"What do you mean? I was fighting the fire with everyone else."

William narrowed his eyes. "I haven't seen you for several hours."

"Well, when it looked like you had everything under control, I went up to wash and change."

Doubt swirled through William's mind. His brother always seemed to find an excuse to avoid hard work.

David's face colored slightly, and he shifted his gaze to Sarah. "Are we having breakfast? I'm quite hungry."

"Yes, we're just going down." Sarah said.

"Although I'm not sure what Chef Lagarde has prepared. He's spent most of the night fighting the fire along with all the rest of the men."

"But I'm sure David's well aware of that," William muttered under his breath.

David's gaze turned cool. "Perhaps you'll be glad to know I'm leaving this morning."

"Oh, David." Sorrow clouded Sarah's eyes. "I thought you weren't leaving until Saturday."

David flicked an unseen piece of lint from his sleeve. "Unfortunately, country life is not all I hoped it would be." He glanced at Miss Foster, his expression hardening. "It's time I returned to London."

Julia's cheeks flushed, and she averted her eyes.

"Perhaps that's best." William gave a slight nod, barely able to restrain himself from saying more.

"There's no need for you to leave." Sarah sent William a hurt look, then took David's arm. "Come and have breakfast with us. We can talk about this after." Sarah and David walked downstairs. Katherine and Penelope followed. Miss Foster hesitated, her cheeks still stained pink.

William waited, wanting to be certain David and the others were out of range. He turned to Miss Foster. "I feel I ought to apologize for my behavior last night."

She looked away, but he could see she knew exactly what he was referring to.

"When I found you in the hall with my brother,

I should have come to your defense instead of questioning you. I know David. And I'm quite certain I misjudged you. I hope you'll forgive me."

"Of course, sir." But she still carried a trace of hurt in her eyes.

He straightened, determined to explain his reaction and make things right. "You see, my late wife, Amelia, carried on a secret affair for over a year before her death."

Her face paled. "I'm sorry. I didn't realize."

"Neither did I, and that's the worst of it. Not only was she unfaithful, she was also deceptive, and I'm afraid her actions have tainted my view of people."

"That must have been painful for you."

His throat tightened, and he looked away for a moment. "Yes, painful and humiliating. Half of London knew of her affair, and the other half heard about it after her death . . . everyone, that is, except me. I didn't learn of it until two months later, when I found letters she had hidden in her room."

Sympathy filled Miss Foster's gaze. "Thank you for telling me. It helps me understand."

"What? That my wife had no trouble leaving me behind for another man?"

"No sir," she said softly. "It helps me see why it's difficult for you to trust and believe that someone could love you and be devoted to you."

He stilled, and a tremor traveled through him. Was she speaking in general terms or about herself?

She looked him in the eyes. "I hope one day you'll find someone who is worthy of your love, and with her help, you'll rebuild your broken trust and all that has been lost will be restored to you."

His heartbeat sped up as he searched her upturned face. Surely she was not saying she wanted to be the one to help him rebuild his life, was she?

He stepped closer and reached for her hand. It was soft and small and fit perfectly in his, such a sweet and caring hand that spread comfort and love to whomever she touched.

Her lips parted as she looked up at him, a touch of wonder in her eyes.

Voices and a commotion rose from the great hall below, and they stepped back. Her hand slipped from his, and regret swept through him like a powerful wave.

Mrs. Emmitt slipped behind the pillar at the end of the gallery and cocked her head to listen. Sir William and Miss Foster stood together at the top of the stairs, engaged in what appeared to be a very cozy conversation.

"You see, my late wife, Amelia, carried on a secret affair for over a year before her death."

Mrs. Emmitt raised her hand to her mouth and

stifled a gasp. His wife had been unfaithful? She could barely hear Miss Foster's soft reply, but her tone was obviously sympathetic—and maybe something more.

A burning sensation rose in Mrs. Emmitt's throat. Why would Sir William tell Miss Foster such intimate details about his life? She was just the governess. She should not be the one to console Sir William.

She turned, intending to slip away down the hall, but then she heard Miss Foster's reply: "I hope one day you'll find someone who is worthy of your love, and with her help, you'll rebuild your broken trust and all that has been lost will be restored to you."

Why, that little hussy! So *that* was what she was after—not a footman or a groom, but the master himself. How dare she even consider such a thing! Did she think she could just cast a line, hook one of the most prestigious men in the county, and reel him in like a fisherman caught a trout?

She had no rank, no place in society, and definitely no money.

Mrs. Emmitt shook her head. It couldn't be borne. She would never take orders from the likes of her!

Voices one floor below in the great hall caught her attention as Mr. Lawrence announced the arrival of Lady Gatewood and Miss Drexel.

Ah, now *there* was a real lady. Miss Drexel had

connections and style, and it was rumored in the servants' hall that she was an heiress who possessed a fortune—enough money to secure the future of Highland and save them all.

She might be an American, but she would still make a fine mistress for Highland. No doubt Miss Drexel would want to run an English household properly, and she would look to Mrs. Emmitt to be her teacher and guide. And that was a role she was more than ready to resume.

If only Sir William would take his eyes off Miss Foster and focus his attention on Miss Drexel, then the future would be secure, and everyone would be happy.

Everyone except Miss Foster, but that could not be helped. Highland must be preserved. And Mrs. Emmitt would make sure no one stood in the way.

"Oh, William, we heard about the fire!" Alice Drexel swept across the great hall and met him at the bottom of the stairs. She reached for his arm. "Are you all right?"

"Yes, we're fine." But he glanced at Miss Foster and noted her pale face and the gray smudges beneath her eyes. She looked exhausted. He must be sure she took time to rest.

Alice's hand tightened on his arm. "Thank goodness. I was so worried. We were all very worried, weren't we, Louisa?"

"Of course. Are the girls all right?" Lady Gatewood looked past him.

"Yes, we're fine, Aunt Louisa." Katherine crossed the great hall from the dining room, with Penelope close behind. "How kind of you both to come." Katherine kissed her aunt's cheek and then Alice's. Penelope did the same.

Alice's gaze darted from Penelope to Katherine. "My goodness, you're all still in your dressing gowns."

"I know, isn't it dreadful?" But Penelope's eyes sparkled as she spoke. "We had to climb out Katherine's window, and a gardener had to help us down a ladder to escape the fire."

"How frightening!" Alice sent William another anxious look. "Did you escape out your window as well?"

"No. The fire was confined to the back half of the east wing. We were able to put it out before it spread further."

"We're sorry to greet you dressed like this, but our clothes were all destroyed," Katherine said.

"Except for a few things that were in the laundry," Penelope added with a smile.

Lady Gatewood took off her coat and handed it to the footman. "Thank heaven your new wardrobe for the season is still at the dressmakers. That would've been a terrible loss."

William stifled a groan. Highland had nearly

burned down, and Lady Gatewood was concerned about the girls' dresses?

"Have you had breakfast?" Katherine asked.

"No, we came over as soon as we heard the news."

"Why don't you join us?" Penelope smiled again. "Then we can tell you all about the fire."

Alice turned to Lady Gatewood.

"Go ahead, dear. I'll be there in a moment."

Alice slipped her arm through Katherine's as they walked toward the dining room. "It's so kind of you to offer us breakfast after all you've been through."

"It was rather exciting, really." Penelope took Alice's other arm, then looked back. "Miss Foster, you're welcome to join us."

Miss Foster hesitated and glanced at William. He nodded. She sent him a tired smile, then followed the girls into the dining room.

His gaze lingered on her as she walked away. It was a good thing their conversation in the gallery had been interrupted. Emotions were running high this morning. No doubt that was what prompted him to share the sordid story about his wife, and it was why she had responded with such sympathy. He must not assign any more meaning to it on his part—or hers.

He turned to Lady Gatewood and motioned toward the dining room. "Shall we join them?"

"In a moment." She looked toward the stairs. "How extensive is the damage?"

"Quite extensive, I'm afraid. Six bedrooms and the hallway were all gutted. There's also damage to the maids' rooms on the floor above, and some water damage on the main floor in the music room."

"Oh my." Lady Gatewood pursed her lips. "What will you do?"

He did not want to discuss his plans with the butler nearby. "We'll rebuild, of course."

"But how can you afford to do that?"

He stepped toward her and lowered his voice. "I don't believe you need to be concerned."

"But I am very concerned."

Why couldn't the infernal woman lower her voice?

"Highland has always been my nieces' home, and I do not want them cast out into the countryside with nowhere to live."

"That's ridiculous! No one is going to be cast out."

"Well, how can you afford the repairs when you can't pay the death duties?" She lifted her hand toward the upper floors. "Do you have some new plan to save Highland that I'm not aware of?"

"I have two months before I must pay the duties, and I'm looking into selling our family home in London."

"You believe you can accomplish that before March?" Her arched eyebrows communicated her doubts.

"I don't seem to have any other alternative."

Lady Gatewood's expression mellowed. "Ah, but there is another solution, and you may find it quite agreeable."

"And what is that?"

She glanced toward the dining room, then looked back and smiled. "Alice has grown quite fond of you, and if you were to woo her and propose marriage, I'm sure her father would give you a very generous wedding gift that would more than cover those expenses."

He scoffed. "That's out of the question. I've no intention of proposing marriage to someone I barely know."

"Then get to know her. She is a lovely young woman, and I'm sure she would be very pleased to deepen the friendship."

"Please, don't encourage her."

"Why not? I think you and Alice would be a perfect match. And with her family's fortune behind you, your financial problems would be solved. Highland would be on firm footing for years to come."

He shook his head. "That's not the answer."

"Think of your children, William. They deserve to have a mother."

"They are well cared for."

"But don't you want Millicent to have a place in society and marry well when the time comes? And what about Andrew? Shouldn't he be master of this estate some day?"

"Yes, yes, of course! But I'm not ready to marry again."

"Even to save Highland?"

He shot a glance at Lawrence. The butler stared straight ahead at the far end of the hall, no doubt hearing every word. "Please, let's say no more about this now. Come and have breakfast."

"All right. But Alice leaves for Bristol on the eighteenth. She'll only be there for a few weeks, then she is off to London to prepare for the season. And you can be sure, with her winsome personality and handsome fortune, she'll receive a proposal in no time."

"No doubt." Sarcasm laced his voice, but Lady Gatewood didn't seem to notice.

"My advice is to strengthen the bond between you and come to an understanding before Alice leaves the county. Otherwise, someone else will snatch her up, and it will be too late."

William stifled a growl and strode off toward the dining room.

Mrs. Emmitt poured herself a cup of tea and sat down to rest a moment in her parlor. What a wild night it had been, escaping the fire and then helping with the rescue efforts. Heavens, it had all been so frightening. For a time she thought the whole house would be consumed by the flames. But thanks to the efforts of the men and the good hand of providence, the fire had been put out.

Of course now she would have to oversee the cleanup and set up new rooms for everyone who had been burned out of the east wing, as well as handle all her regular duties. She sighed and shook her head. How in the world would she ever get it all done?

A knock sounded at her door. "Come in." She set aside her teacup.

Mr. Lawrence stepped through the doorway, his expression sober. "Do you have a moment?"

"Of course."

He quietly closed the door. "You know I am not one to pass on gossip, but I've just overheard something I thought you should know."

"And what would that be?"

"Lady Gatewood is trying to convince Sir William to propose to Miss Drexel."

"Really?" She smiled.

Mr. Lawrence lowered his gray eyebrows. "You would be happy to see him marry an American?"

"If her money can secure our positions, then yes, I'd be very happy indeed." She leaned forward. "I'd tell him to marry a China doll if she had a fortune that would save Highland."

Mr. Lawrence sniffed and tugged at his waistcoat. "Well, I certainly would not."

"Then 'tis time you stopped being so particular and started thinking about the future—yours and mine, to be precise."

He sat in the chair opposite her. "I suppose

you're right. His marriage to Miss Drexel may be a necessity."

Mrs. Emmitt cocked her head. "What do you mean?"

"The rumors about Sir William's financial troubles are true. Lady Gatewood confirmed it. He must pay a large sum in death duties by the first of March, and now with the expenses incurred from the fire . . ." He shook his head. "He seems to have no other choice but to pursue Miss Drexel and her fortune. At least that's Lady Gatewood's opinion."

"Did he agree?"

"He was hesitant to discuss it, perhaps because Nelson and I were present."

Mrs. Emmitt adjusted her glasses. "I'm afraid there is another reason."

Mr. Lawrence frowned. "What do you mean?"

"Miss Foster has set her cap for Sir William, and he's tempted by the idea."

"Miss Foster! Why, that's more outrageous than him marrying an American heiress." He held up his hands. "No. I don't believe it. Sir William would not lower himself to marry a governess. He is a gentleman and much too dignified to do something unseemly like that."

She pursed her lips and looked up at him. "I'm sorry to say it, but you're wrong."

"How can you be sure?"

"Because I overheard the two of them talking

in the gallery, and her tone was very sweet and alluring, if you ask me."

Mr. Lawrence's face grew red. "Then she ought to go."

"It's not that simple."

"And why not? We are in charge of the staff. If we believe she is acting in an improper manner, then we should dismiss her."

"I don't believe Sir William would allow it. If she's to go, it must be her own decision."

"But why would she do that?"

"I'm not sure, but we must think of a way to convince her it is her duty to leave." Mrs. Emmitt stood, the weight of the situation pressing down on her. "If we don't act soon, Highland will be lost, and we'll all be out on our backsides before the snow melts."

Twenty-Seven

Julia walked into her new room carrying the two outfits Lady Gatewood had sent over to replace her burned wardrobe. Both dresses were wrinkled and worn, and they looked as if they had been pulled from the bottom of a missionary barrel— and she was all too familiar with how clothing looked when it came out of a missionary barrel.

She chided herself for her ungrateful attitude. The dresses would be fine as soon as they had been washed and pressed. She also had a skirt and blouse and some undergarments that had been hanging on the line in the laundry the night of the fire. Still it was hard to be thankful after she saw the lovely dresses Alice Drexel had sent for Sarah, Katherine, and Penny. Some would need to be altered a bit, but at least they wouldn't have to wear their dressing gowns until new clothes could be ordered in Fulton.

She glanced around and released a soft sigh. This guest room was much larger than her former quarters. The soft green-and-gold color scheme gave it a pleasing, feminine touch. But it had not been used for quite some time, and it was in need of a good cleaning. The maids were all busy, so she had offered to see to it herself. She didn't mind. She was used to caring for her home and family.

She laid the dresses on the chair near the fireplace and crossed to the window. Opening the shutters, she looked out across the snow-covered parkland. The golden sun dipped low, ready to slip behind the rolling hills in the distance. Several massive cedars, dusted with snow, stood like dark giants stationed around the park. A few other trees lifted their bare, black branches in sharp contrast to the pale lavender sky.

Highland was beautiful in the winter. What would it look like in the spring? Would she be here to see nature come back to life, to stroll across the hills and fields with Andrew, Millie, and William?

Her heart ached as she thought of the letter she had received two days earlier from her mother. Her father was regaining his strength, and he spoke every day about returning to India. It was good news, really. She ought to be glad. But she sighed and turned away, uncertain how she would ever leave William.

"May I come in?" Mrs. Emmitt stood in the open doorway, carrying a stack of folded sheets and pillow covers. "I brought these up for you."

"Thank you. That's kind, especially when you have so much to do today."

"I hope the room is adequate."

"It's lovely. I'm quite content." She forced a smile, though her heart was heavy. She was probably just tired from the emotional strain of the fire and having been awake most of the previous night.

Mrs. Emmitt placed the sheets on the end of the bed. "I don't want to trouble you, but there is something we should discuss."

A slight feeling of apprehension rose in her heart, but she nodded.

"It's a delicate matter. I'm not quite certain how to begin."

"Whatever it is, I'll try to help you if I can."

"Yes, I know you will." She glanced at the chair. "Shall we sit down?"

"Yes, of course." Julia sat on the bench at the dressing table, and Mrs. Emmitt took the chair next to it.

Mrs. Emmitt clasped her hands in her lap. "I'm very concerned about Sir William."

Julia's heart lurched. "What do you mean?"

"I'm afraid he's in danger of losing Highland."

Julia glanced away. The financial matters William had shared with her were confidential. She couldn't very well reveal what she knew to Mrs. Emmitt. "Why do you say that?"

"I'm not sure if you're aware of it, but when someone inherits an estate like this, the government requires them to pay a very large percentage of its value in death duties."

"Yes, I understand death duties."

Mrs. Emmitt's eyes widened, but only for a second. "With an estate as large as Highland, the duties will be extremely high, and from what I understand, Sir William is having a difficult time raising the funds he needs."

Julia looked down, not wanting to confirm or deny what she knew.

"If Sir William can't pay the death duties by the first of March," Mrs. Emmitt continued, "the estate will have to be sold. If that happens, Sir William will not only lose his house and land, he'll also lose his position in society and his reputation. A baronet without land is . . . well, it would announce to the world that he is a failure." The housekeeper lowered her chin and looked at Julia over the top of her glasses. "Do you understand?"

Julia nodded. "Perhaps that's why he wanted to simplify the menus and have Miss Ramsey oversee the purchasing."

Mrs. Emmitt pursed her lips, looking as though those changes were still painful. "Simplifying the meals and trimming expenses may have helped a bit, but now with the damages from the fire, he must pay for those repairs as well as the death duties, and that has backed him into a corner."

Julia swallowed. Where was Mrs. Emmitt going with this conversation?

"I believe Sir William invited his brother to Highland with the hope that he would help him out of these financial difficulties." Mrs. Emmitt shook her head, looking grim. "But I doubt that will happen. I don't know why, but when Mr. Ramsey left this morning, it was clear he and Sir William were not parting on good terms."

Dizzy waves of regret flooded Julia. This was her fault. Her foolish choice to walk David to his room had driven a wedge between the brothers and destroyed William's chance to receive the funds he so desperately needed. "I'm so sorry."

"There is still a chance to save Highland, and you must be the one to make it happen."

Julia looked up. "What can I do?"

"There is an opportunity for Sir William to come into a great deal of money if he were to marry Miss Drexel."

Julia's heart clenched. She rose to her feet and turned away. Lifting a trembling hand, she rubbed her throbbing forehead.

"Please, listen to me, Miss Foster."

Julia slowly turned and faced the housekeeper.

"Sir William is hesitant to propose to Miss Drexel, and I believe we both know the reason why."

Julia stared at Mrs. Emmitt, her hands suddenly ice cold.

"I'm afraid you have captured his attention, and as long as you remain at Highland, he will not be interested in anyone else."

Her mouth fell open. "But I didn't intend to attract his attention."

"Of course you didn't. But you are young, and he is a man—a lonely man at that." She adjusted her glasses and looked Julia over. "I suppose he couldn't help himself."

A guilty wave poured over her, and her face flamed.

"He cannot marry you. You are merely a distraction, and that is the problem."

Mrs. Emmitt's words sliced through her heart.

"I can see that you care for him, and that makes the situation all the more difficult."

Hot tears stung Julia's eyes, but she blinked them away, determined to control her emotions.

"It would be best for everyone if you give your notice and leave as soon as possible."

Julia shook her head. "But I can't do that. Who will watch over the children and see to the young ladies' education?"

"It will only take a few days to find another governess."

Julia's legs trembled, and she sank down on the bench. Of course, she could easily be replaced. Someone else could fill the position and care for them all.

"I'm sorry, Miss Foster. I don't like to be the one

to put this unhappy choice before you. But if you care about Sir William and his family, then you will go quietly and give him no hope of convincing you otherwise."

Julia closed her eyes and pulled in a ragged breath. She loved William with all her heart, but Mrs. Emmitt was right. There was no future for them, and if she stayed at Highland, it would only lead to loss and heartbreak for them both.

The choice was clear.

And somehow she must find the courage to make it.

William stared at the telegram in his hand and read it once more, his heart sinking like heavy stone.

SPOKE TO SOLICITOR. NO FUNDS AVAILABLE. HE ADVISES AGAINST SELLING LONDON HOUSE. APOLOGIES. DAVID.

"Sir, would you like me to gather the staff for Scripture reading and prayer?"

William looked up and blinked at Lawrence. "What?"

"Do you want to proceed as usual this morning with Scripture reading and prayer?"

"Yes. I'll be there in a moment."

"Very good, sir." Lawrence nodded and left the library.

William tossed the telegram onto his desk and stared toward the window. He should have known his brother would not help him. When William questioned David yesterday morning about the incident with Miss Foster, he'd laughed it off and said William was overreacting. But William had not backed down, and David left in a huff, without apologizing for the despicable way he had treated Miss Foster.

He shook his head. What a fool he'd been to think his brother would stand with him through these trials.

The sound of everyone gathering in the hall roused him from his discouraging thoughts. He picked up his Bible from the desk and walked out to meet them, his mood sinking lower.

The staff lined up across the hall. Sarah, Katherine, and Penelope waited for him by the fireplace, but Miss Foster and the children were missing. The grandfather clock at the end of the hall struck nine, and he glanced up the stairs.

Miss Foster came into view as she crossed the gallery with the nursery maid and children. Andrew bounded down the stairs, but Miss Foster did not call him back as she usually did.

William frowned at his son, and Andrew slowed his pace as he crossed the hall.

"Sorry, Papa. We didn't mean to be late, but we had some trouble with our clothes." Andrew looked down at his mismatched outfit. Apparently someone had given the children clothing to replace what had been burned in the fire, but Andrew's pants looked too short and his shirt was several sizes too large.

William frowned and tried to catch Miss Foster's eye, but she stared straight ahead as she slipped into her place beside the children. Her face looked dreadfully pale, and her eyes appeared to be red, as though she had been crying. The drab gray dress she wore hung on her like an old sack.

His frown deepened. "Miss Foster, are you ill?"

She glanced at him and pressed her lips together, then quickly looked away. "No sir."

He stepped in front of her and lowered his voice. "I mean no offense, but your dress and appearance are quite . . . unusual."

"Most of my clothes were destroyed in the fire. Lady Gatewood sent over this dress for me."

"Where did she find it—in the rag bin?"

Miss Foster's pale face flushed pink. "I don't know, sir."

He huffed. "I'm sorry. I'm out of sorts." He turned to Sarah. "Can you please find Miss Foster something else to wear? And Andrew as well?"

Sarah nodded, but her unhappy expression warned him that his tone and actions could be considered hurtful.

He faced the staff and found all eyes focused on him. Lawrence sent a stern glance down the row, and they quickly lowered their gazes.

William opened the Bible, painfully aware that he had spent no time reading it for several days, and he had not prepared a passage for this morning.

He turned to Psalms, which so often soothed him. The page fell open to Psalm 112, and he began reading. "Blessed is the man that feareth the LORD, that delighteth greatly in his commandments. His seed shall be mighty upon earth: the generation of the upright shall be blessed.' "

Andrew looked up at him with a question in his eyes.

William wished he could acknowledge Andrew's interest and explain the verse, but this was not the time. "Wealth and riches shall be in his house." The phrase caught him by surprise, and his voice faltered.

Sarah sent him a concerned look.

He cleared his throat and continued. "His righteousness endureth for ever. Unto the upright there ariseth light in the darkness: he is gracious, and full of compassion, and righteous. A good man sheweth favour, and lendeth . . ."

His brother's refusal to lend the needed funds rose in his mind, churning his thoughts. He clenched his jaw and focused on the page again. "Surely he shall not be moved for ever: the righteous shall be in everlasting remembrance. He shall not be afraid of evil tidings: his heart is fixed, trusting in the LORD."

The psalm continued, but his throat felt so tight he could not go on. He closed the Bible, bowed his head, and tried to steady his emotions. But conviction pressed hard upon his heart. How could he expect the Lord to bless his home and family when he had given little thought to trusting Him or asking Him to guide and direct?

Things had to change, and he would start with an honest prayer.

"Father, we come to You today, asking forgiveness for our lack of trust and for the times we have pushed ahead without consulting You. Forgive us for losing sight of what is most important.

"We thank You that no lives were lost in the fire and no one was seriously injured. Thank You for the way everyone worked together, risking their lives to save Highland and rescue those we love.

"We ask for Your mercy and grace. Please help us be worthy to carry Your name and spread Your light through our household and our world. We lift this prayer in the name of Jesus Christ, our Lord and Savior. Amen."

He looked up, and his gaze connected with Julia's.

Her pain-filled eyes glistened with tears.

His chest tightened. He'd never seen her so distraught. Had she received some terrible news from home? Or was she still upset about the fire?

He had no idea, but he intended to find out as soon as he had a quiet moment with her.

He waited while Lawrence dismissed the staff. Ann took the children upstairs. Sarah, Katherine, and Penelope walked into the drawing room.

Miss Foster turned to him. "May I speak to you in private, sir?"

A wave of relief passed through him. "Yes, of course."

He led the way into the library, shut the door, and motioned toward the chair. "Please sit down."

She averted her eyes. "I prefer to stand."

The muscles in his shoulders tensed. "Very well."

She raised her chin and fastened her blue gaze on him. "I must give you my notice."

"What?" He stared at her, stunned.

"I'm resigning my position. I would like to leave as soon as possible."

His mind spun. "Has something happened to your family?"

"No sir."

"Then what is it?"

"I'm sorry, sir. I cannot say."

"You cannot say?" He strode to the fireplace, heat flushing his face as he turned to her. "Do you have another offer? Someone willing to pay you more?"

Hurt filled her eyes. "No sir."

"Then I don't understand." Pain pierced his heart, but he pushed it away and let his anger build to cover it. "You told me if you were leaving, you would give me several months' notice. How can you walk in here and tell me that you want to leave as soon as possible?"

"I'm sorry. I know it's . . . inconvenient."

"Inconvenient? No, it's uncaring toward the children and disloyal to me." He lifted his hand. "How can you give me no warning—no time to find a replacement?"

She looked down, and her silence hung between them like a heavy curtain.

"Why?" His voice rose. "Why would you do this?"

She lifted her face, her eyes pleading with him. "Please, sir. I cannot say."

"So that's it?" He shook his head as painful memories washed over him. What a fool he'd been to think that she was different. "Once again I have been deceived by someone I trusted."

She clasped her hands. "I would never deceive you, sir."

"Well, that's exactly what you've done. You made me believe I could count on you for loyalty and support. But I see I was wrong." He set his jaw and nodded toward the door. "If that's what you want, you may go."

She lowered her head again, her shoulders sagging.

His heart wavered, but he steeled himself against it. "Collect your pay from Mrs. Emmitt on your way out, then do not return to Highland. Do I make myself clear?"

"Yes sir." She looked up, and this time, her face was set like stone. She turned away and strode out the door.

Tears blurred Julia's eyes as she left the library. Sarah's and Katherine's voices floated out from the drawing room. Penny's merry laughter followed. Julia pressed her lips together, fighting back her tears as she passed the open doorway. She could not say good-bye. Not to them, and not to the children. Doing so would only make a scene and cause more hurt.

Her stomach swirled at the thought of facing Mrs. Emmitt, so she slipped through the music room and out the side door, even though it meant she would leave behind her final month's pay.

The icy wind stung her hot cheeks and nearly jerked the door from her hand, but she managed to push it closed. Wrapping her arms around herself, she started down the gravel path. Dark clouds scuttled past overhead, and she hurried around the corner of the house.

Clark walked toward her across the back courtyard. He smiled and lifted his hand, but as he drew closer, his expression sobered. "Miss Foster, where are you going?"

"I'm leaving." She could barely force the words past her tight throat.

"To visit your family?"

"No. I've given my notice. I'm leaving Highland . . . and once I walk out the gate, I'll not be allowed to come back."

His eyes darkened, and concern lined his face. "You must be freezing. Come with me." He nodded toward the greenhouse.

A cold shiver raced up her back. She had no coat, and she was in need of the kindness of a friend. She nodded and walked across the courtyard and past the greenhouse with him. He ushered her into his office and gave her a chair by the wood stove.

"Now tell me, why would you leave us when you know we all love you?"

His gentle tone and kind words brought a fresh wave of tears to her eyes. "I don't want to go, but I must."

He shook his head. "I'm sure Sarah won't agree, and neither will the children."

She bit her lip. "I wasn't able to say good-bye, not to Sarah, or the children, or anyone. Will you do that for me?"

"Yes, of course, but . . ." His face suddenly darkened and he leaned toward her. "Has Sir William done something improper? Has he hurt you?"

She pulled in a sharp breath. "Oh no! Please,

you mustn't think that. He has always been a gentleman and treated me with kindness and respect." Her eyes filled. "This is my decision, not his."

Clark's gaze softened and he nodded. "You love him, don't you?"

Her gaze darted to meet his. How had Clark discovered her secret?

"Does he feel the same about you?"

"No, and you must promise not to tell him about my feelings for him."

"But if he knew, perhaps he would—"

"No. Trust me. If I don't go, everyone on staff will lose their jobs, and Sir William will lose his home and his position in society."

Doubt filled Clark's expression. "How could your staying on at Highland make all that happen?"

"I am a distraction." She had to swallow hard to get past that bitter word. "But if I go, and he forms an attachment with Miss Drexel, they can marry. Then his financial problems will be solved, and he won't lose the estate."

"So you love him, but you're leaving so he can marry Miss Drexel and with the hope he can hold on to Highland?"

She sat up straighter and nodded. "Yes. Sometimes love demands a sacrifice."

Clark rubbed his chin and nodded. "That may be true, but is the Lord calling you to make that sacrifice?"

She closed her eyes, her heart lifting the same question in a silent prayer. She waited and the answer settled over her with a painful but calm assurance. "Yes, I believe He is, and I am willing, though it breaks my heart to do it."

He pondered that for a moment. "Very well, then. If He's called you to it, I won't try to dissuade you."

She rose from the chair. "I should go before the rain starts."

He glanced toward the window. "I can give you a ride in the wagon."

"No, I can walk. I'll be fine."

Concern filled his eyes. "Then take this." He shrugged off his jacket and handed it to her. "At least it will keep you warm."

She hesitated, then allowed him to help her slip it on. "Thank you." She started to say she would return it, but that was not possible. "I'll send it back."

He gave her a sad half-smile. "I'll explain things to Sarah, and we'll pray for you."

"And I will pray for you and everyone at Highland." With that she turned away and walked out into the cold morning.

Twenty-Eight

William could not stand being indoors one more moment. He rose from the card table and strode out of the drawing room.

Alice hurried after him. "William, wait. We haven't finished our game."

He clenched his jaw, holding back the retort rising in his throat. He'd had quite enough of silly card games and boring conversations about who would be going to London for the season and what parties and events they would attend. The rain had passed, and the temperature was rising. Perhaps a walk would clear his head and lift his sorry mood.

Lawrence approached.

"Please bring me my coat and hat. I'm going for a walk."

"Very good, sir." Lawrence nodded and set off to retrieve them.

Alice's golden-brown eyebrows dipped as she glanced toward the front door. "I suppose I could join you. But it looks awfully cold."

He wanted some peace and quiet, not a companion. "You're right. It's much too cold. There's no need for you to go with me."

"But I can tell you're upset. Wouldn't you like a friend to come along?"

"Alice, I know you mean well, but there are times a man needs room to think and breathe."

A wounded look filled her eyes. "I didn't realize I was preventing you from breathing."

"I'm sorry. I don't mean to be rude." He glanced away, trying to come up with an explanation. "Everything has been in an upheaval since the fire. I'm just not in the mood to socialize."

It was more than that, much more, and he knew it. Miss Foster's leaving had shaken him deeply. Nothing had been the same since she had walked out the door five days ago.

Sarah had been hurt and hinted he was to blame. Katherine and Penelope, who had never wanted a governess, were now complaining that they would not be ready for the season without Miss Foster's help. Andrew had gotten into mischief several times and driven the poor nursery maid to tears. Millie had woken up with night-mares twice, and today she had a stomach-ache and was not able to eat anything. As for William himself, he had a nagging headache that would not leave, and he could barely force down his meals.

The only one who seemed unaffected was Mrs. Emmitt, who assured him they would find a new governess within the week, though she had not brought him one candidate.

But Miss Foster's departure was not his only problem. Time was running out to resolve his financial issues. With his brother's refusal to buy out his interest in the London house and the need to repair the fire-ravaged east wing, there seemed little choice but to at least consider the possibility of marriage to Alice Drexel. There might be no other way to save Highland. He clenched his jaw and tried to push away the uneasy feeling tightening his chest.

Lawrence returned with William's coat and helped him put it on. Then he handed William his hat and gloves. "Will there be anything else, sir?"

Alice looked at William with a slight smile and a question in her eyes. She would be leaving for Bristol in a week and half. Was that enough time to make such an important decision? He'd never know unless he opened himself up to the possibility. He tugged on his glove and nodded. "Please bring Miss Drexel's coat as well."

Her smile warmed. "Thank you, William. I'm sure a brisk walk is just what we need."

William swallowed a sigh. It would take more than a jaunt across the park with Alice Drexel to ease his troubled mind.

Julia dipped her hands in the hot, soapy water and wiped the mixing bowl clean. A crackling fire burned in the wood stove, sending cheerful warmth into her parents' cozy kitchen. The tempting scent of meat pies and steaming applesauce hung in the air, promising a good supper.

Her father stepped into the kitchen. "I'm sorry, but here's another cup to wash."

"I don't mind." She looked over her shoulder, and her heart lifted. His color had improved, and his face looked fuller under his neatly clipped silver beard. "How are you feeling, Father?"

"Better all the time." His eyes shone as he handed her the cup.

"I'm so glad." Julia had slipped back into her role as dutiful daughter, assisting her mother with cooking and cleaning as well as answering correspondence and discussing Scripture with her father. It was as if nothing had changed, and yet everything was different.

Her time at Highland and, more important, her love for William and the children had changed everything.

She forced those thoughts away and focused on scrubbing the tea stains from the cup. If she wanted her wounded heart to heal, then she must keep a check on her thoughts and emotions. But that was not an easy task.

Her mother entered the kitchen carrying an envelope and sniffed the air. "My, it smells wonderful in here."

"The meat pies should be done soon." Julia wrung out the dishcloth and hung it on the hook. She glanced out the window at the fading light, and her thoughts drifted back to Highland once more.

"What are you thinking about, my dear?" Mother's gentle voice stirred Julia from her thoughts.

She turned and forced a slight smile. "How glad I am to see Father so much improved." She had been thinking that only moments before, and she hoped the Lord wouldn't mind her keeping her thoughts about William to herself.

Father smiled. "It's an unexpected blessing."

Mother's eyes grew misty. "One we're very grateful to receive." She shifted her gaze to Julia, and a shadow crossed her expression. "But I'm worried about you, Julia."

"I'll be fine, Mother." Julia reached for a towel and dried her hands. "I just need time to adjust to . . . the changes."

Her father and mother exchanged a concerned glance, then her mother sat down and opened the envelope.

Julia laid the towel aside. "Who is the letter from?"

"Your aunt Beatrice." Mother read the first few words and then gasped.

"What is it, Mary?" Father's silver eyebrows rose.

"The issues with my father's will have been resolved, and we are all going to receive a portion of the inheritance."

"Really?" Julia crossed to her mother's side and looked over her shoulder.

Mother read the letter aloud, and when she came to the section listing the amounts that were to be given to each of them, her mother and Father exchanged stunned looks.

"But how can it be true?" Julia sank down in the chair next to her mother. "I thought Grandfather cut off all connection with you and Father when you married."

"He did, and he drew up a will that left me out. But he must have regretted it later and changed his will to include us."

"When we visited Grandmother, she said they didn't expect to be able to help us financially."

Her mother turned the letter over and scanned the rest of the message on the back. "She says there were legal questions that needed to be resolved first, and she didn't want to raise false hopes."

Father chuckled. "I think she wanted to be sure she approved of you all before she released the money."

"Now, Phillip. You mustn't speak ill of my mother."

"You're right, dear. This is a wonderful blessing, and I'm very grateful." Father rose from his chair.

"Our needs will be met now, and Julia will be freed from her duty to work and support us." He smiled at Julia. "And best of all, it will allow you to return to India and resume our work."

Mother's eyes brightened. "And you won't have to wait to raise the funds, you have what you need. In fact, you'll have more than enough for the rest of your life, if you're wise and you manage it well."

Julia stared at them, still trying to take it in. With this money she would be a free and independent woman. She could go where she wanted and do whatever she pleased. But as she pondered that thought, her heart sank. The only place she truly wanted to go was back to Highland, but she could never go there again.

Father studied her, and his expression sobered. "What's wrong, Julia?"

"I'm thankful we won't have to worry about our financial needs, but I'm not certain about returning to India."

"What makes you hesitate?" Father asked.

"I do love our friends there, and the work is very fulfilling, but . . ." Julia bit her lip and looked down at her clasped hands. She had told her parents why she'd left Highland, but she had only hinted at her true feelings for William. Perhaps it was time to be totally honest with them. "I'm afraid my heart is still with those I care for at Highland."

Father's brow creased and he crossed his arms.

"I'd like to tell Sir William Ramsey what I think of the way he treated you."

Mother laid her hand on his shoulder. "Now, Phillip, don't say anything you'll regret."

"I'm glad you left," Father continued. "Knowing he would let you go to save his estate makes me certain he is not worthy of you."

"Please, Father, he doesn't know how much I care for him, and it's much more complicated than that."

"It doesn't seem complicated to me. If he were an honorable man who knew what was most important, he would value your godly character and realize you are a treasure worth far more than a thousand Highlands."

His words soothed her heart, and she leaned over and kissed his forehead. "I know you love me, but you see things from the perspective of a protective father, not as Sir William sees them. You must give him the benefit of the doubt and forgive him as I have."

Father sat back and released a sigh. "I suppose you're right, but it's not easy when I can see how much he hurt you."

"That was not his intention. I'm sure of it."

Mother watched Julia closely. "If he had asked you to stay, what would your answer have been?"

The question cut Julia to the heart, and she looked away. "He did not ask, so there's no point in answering."

"But if you were given the choice between returning to India or staying here and marrying Sir William, what would you choose?"

Her throat swelled. "Of course I would stay," she whispered. "But it's foolish to even speak of it. That door is closed." She straightened her shoulders. "I must make new plans, and receiving this inheritance seems to indicate I should return to India."

Father nodded. "Very good, my dear. I quite agree."

But a loving look of concern clouded her mother's eyes.

Twenty-Nine

William slipped his hand into his jacket pocket and felt the small velvet ring box hidden there. He'd carried it with him for the last three days, but he hadn't found the right moment to speak to Alice. He huffed and shook his head. That wasn't true. There had been plenty of opportunities. The real issue was he lacked the conviction to make a declaration of love and ask Alice to become his wife.

He strode downstairs and into the great hall to await his dinner guests. Tugging at the neck of his shirt, he loosened his white tie a bit. Lord and Lady Gatewood and Alice would be arriving soon. Alice would be leaving for Bristol tomorrow morning on the nine o'clock train, and Sarah had planned this farewell dinner in her honor.

If he was going to propose, it would have to be tonight. How he wished his heart were in it.

Sarah and Dalton walked into the great hall from the dining room.

Dalton nodded to him. "Good evening, sir."

"Dalton." William returned the nod.

"Clark brought in some lovely roses for the table." Sarah smiled at the gardener, her eyes shining.

"Thank you," William said.

Dalton's warm gaze remained on Sarah. "I hope you'll enjoy them."

"I'm sure we will," she added.

William watched them, wishing he understood how they could be so happy and comfortable together. It seemed as though they had known each other for years rather than months. Would he and Alice develop a strong bond and grow to love each other in that same way? Doubt flooded him, and his face fell into a brooding frown.

Sarah turned to him. "William, what's wrong?"

He rubbed his forehead and sighed. "I'm sorry. I don't mean to cast a pall on the evening. I'm just not myself tonight."

Sarah exchanged a glance with Dalton. When she looked back at William, he could easily read the worry in her eyes.

"All right, not just tonight." William sighed. "Go ahead. Say what's on your mind."

Sarah clasped her hands. "All right, I will. You've been in a dreadful mood since Julia left, yet you refuse to discuss it."

"What is there to discuss?"

"She was more than a member of the staff. She

was my friend, and she was a good friend to you as well."

"Friend?" He huffed and shook his head. "I don't think so. What kind of friend deserts you at the first opportunity?"

Sarah started to reply, but William held up his hand. "I have no desire to discuss anyone who is so disloyal."

Sarah's eyes flashed. "William, that is not true, and you know it."

"What else would you call someone who leaves without notice or explanation? She gave no thought to how that would hurt those she left behind."

He had taken Julia into his confidence and shared his private struggles, even telling her about his wife's unfaithfulness and how that had almost destroyed him. And what was his reward? She had marched out the door without a back-ward glance. His heart still ached because of her decision, but he pushed those feelings away and set his mouth in a firm line.

"She left because she thought it was best for you." Sorrow filled Sarah's voice.

"How could it be best to run off like that? I trusted her, but she let me down in the worst way."

Dalton's face flushed, and he looked as though he would burst.

Sarah turned to Dalton. "If you won't tell him, I will."

"Go ahead. You didn't promise her your silence."

Sarah focused on William again. "Julia left because she loves you."

William pulled back, certain he had not heard her correctly. "What?"

"She loves you, William, with all her heart. And I can't believe you could be so blind that you didn't see it."

"But she never said . . ."

"Of course not. What do you expect her to do? Pour out her heart and beg you to marry her?"

"No, but why would she go then?"

"She was convinced if she stayed she would be a distraction and prevent you from proposing to Alice and saving Highland."

William stared at Sarah, while he struggled to piece that information together.

"Was she right? Do you want to marry Alice?"

William searched his heart, still seeking an answer. "I thought I could for the sake of the estate, but how honorable would it be to propose marriage to Alice when my main reason would be to benefit from her fortune?" The truth became clear. He shook his head, disgusted with what he had almost done. "That was Father's goal when he arranged my marriage to Amelia, and look at what that did to us."

"So what will you do, William?" Sarah watched him closely. "Is holding on to this house and estate what truly matters most to you?"

William's gaze traveled around the great hall. He lifted his eyes to the ceiling arched high overhead, and his sister's question echoed through his mind. He had only lived at Highland a short time, but it represented the history and prestige of his family. Becoming baronet and master of Highland had helped him regain some of the self-respect he'd lost when his wife betrayed him, but—

"If you ask me," Sarah continued, "inheriting Highland has proven to be more of a burden than a blessing, especially since it separates you from those you love. And I believe you do love Julia. If you didn't, her leaving would not have hurt you as much as it did."

The truth of Sarah's statement sank into his heart, but the question remained. Was he willing to give up Highland? Could he let it all go for the one he loved?

Julia kissed her mother's soft cheek, and the fragrance of lavender floated around her, bringing back pleasant memories. Then she leaned into to her father's strong embrace. Closing her eyes, she pressed her face against his warm wool sweater and lingered a moment. Oh, how much she loved them, how much she would miss them.

"Are you sure you don't want us to go to the station with you?" Mother clasped her hands together, looking close to tears.

Julia pressed down her own emotions, looked in the mirror by the door, and adjusted her hat. "There's no need for you to wait out on that cold platform. I'd rather say good-bye here at the house."

Her father took her hands in his. "You can still change your mind, you know. I don't want you going back to India just to please us."

Julia swallowed, her determination wavering. Her travel arrangements had come together so quickly it seemed a confirmation that this was the right path. Still, her heart ached at the thought of leaving England and all those she loved.

She reached for her handbag. "The decision is made. I'm packed and ready to go."

"We'll follow as soon as we can." Father's voice was strong, but the confidence in his eyes wavered slightly.

Julia nodded and forced a smile, but she knew the future was uncertain for her parents. Dr. Hadley didn't believe her father was strong enough to travel overseas or work in a tropical climate, and he might never be.

"Mr. and Mrs. Wilson will meet your train in Southampton." Mother followed her to the door. "They'll take good care of you and help you board the ship on Thursday."

Julia nodded and looked into her mother's eyes.

Mother lifted her hand and touched Julia's cheek. "We love you, my dear, so very much."

"And I love you." She swallowed and forced out her words. "Now I must go, or I'll miss my train." Then she turned away before they could see her tears and hurried out the door. "Good-bye. I'll see you soon."

"Good-bye," her parents called as they watched from the cottage doorway.

Their neighbor Hiram Johnson had loaded her trunk onto the back of his wagon with the help of his son. Mr. Johnson nodded to her and offered her a hand. She stepped up and took a seat on the wooden bench at the front of the wagon.

He climbed up beside her, and picked up the reins. "Ready to go, Miss Foster?"

"Yes, thank you." Julia waved to her parents once more, then turned and faced the road, blinking away tears. The wagon lurched forward, and the morning fog swirled around them. But as they rounded the bend and came into a clearing, the sunlight broke through.

"Looks like it'll be a nice day after all." Mr. Johnson smiled and clicked to encourage the horses to quicken their pace.

The ride to the train station took less than ten minutes. Julia thanked Mr. Johnson as he helped her down. He and the porter wrestled the large trunk down from the back of the wagon and onto a rolling cart. The porter tagged her trunk, then set off across the platform.

She took a deep breath of cool morning air and

lifted her eyes to the blue sky. Two larks swooped past, and she watched them disappear into the trees beyond the station. Slipping her hands into her coat pockets, she let her mind drift to the first day she had arrived at Highland, and a bitter-sweet smile formed on her lips.

Memories flooded back, and a strong yearning rose in her heart. How she wished she could see Katherine enjoy her first season and perhaps meet her future husband. And what a delight it would be to watch Penny continue to grow into a beautiful young woman.

Andrew came to mind next, and her smile spread wider. What a dear rascal he was, with his boundless energy and a deep longing to please his father. She hoped he would grow into a wise young man with strong, godly character. And dear Millie, she was just beginning to blossom like a delicate little flower. How that darling girl had stolen her heart. Who would cherish her and teach her all she needed to know as she grew up? Would she learn to love the Lord and follow Him with her whole heart?

Julia released a sigh as she walked the length of the platform and found a spot out of the wind.

She tried not to think of William, but all they had shared rose and filled her mind. The sadness of parting from him returned like a crushing weight, and she could barely pull in her next breath.

Would he find happiness and contentment in his marriage to Alice? With Highland's future secure, would he pursue some other worthy goal? She hoped he would enjoy a long and happy life, filled with the love of family and meaningful service to God and his fellow man. She prayed he would have all of that and more.

Her hand trembled as she pulled her train ticket from her pocket and read the words once more. Was this truly God's will? Had she listened to His voice, or was she simply running away from the pain of a broken heart?

She closed her eyes and focused her thoughts. No, this was the right decision. She must not listen to those doubts. Her heart might not be in it yet, but if she stepped out in faith, her feelings would follow in time.

The bell sounded, announcing an oncoming train. She looked down the tracks, and in the distance, a dark engine approached, puffing smoke and pulling several passenger cars behind.

"Miss Foster!"

Her breath caught in her throat, and she turned, knowing his voice before she saw his face.

William ran across the road, jumped up at the end of the platform, and dashed toward her, his face flushed and his breathing heavy. "I was afraid I would be too late."

She stared at him, unbelieving. "How did you know I was here?"

"I went to your parents' home." He pulled in a breath. "They told me you were leaving."

"Oh." Confusion swirled through her mind.

The train pulled in, its brakes screeching and steam billowing up around them.

"Well, it's kind of you to come and see me off." It was too painful to continue looking at him, so she turned away. "This is my train. I should go."

"Miss Foster—Julia, please wait."

She slowly turned, her heart beating loudly in her ears. *Julia* . . . He'd called her Julia!

He took off his hat and held it in his hands. "I misjudged you and drove you away with my foolish words and hurtful actions. And I would understand completely if you decided to board that train and put half a world between us, but I'd like you to come back to Highland."

She searched his face. "As the governess?"

"No." He groaned "Blast! I'm not doing this very well. Not as the governess. As my wife."

Julia gasped. "But . . . I thought you were going to marry Alice."

He shook his head. "I don't love Alice. And it would be unfair to marry her just to save my estate." His eyes warmed with a hopeful light as he watched her response. "What are houses and land when you cannot share them with the one you love?"

A smile rose from her heart to her lips.

He stepped closer. "I may not have a home or land to give you, but I do love you, and I promise I will do all I can to provide for you."

"You would give up your chance to save Highland to marry me?"

He nodded. "You are worth that, and so much more. I was a fool not to see that from the first."

She soaked in his loving words, letting them strengthen her heart.

"All aboard!" The conductor glanced her way. The train hissed and released another cloud of steam.

William reached for her hand. "I know I'm asking a lot, with my future so uncertain, but will you stay? Will you be my wife?

Julia felt like her heart would burst. She tightened her hold on his hands and looked into his eyes. "Yes, I will."

He pulled her into his arms and held her close. She closed her eyes, savoring his nearness and the wonderful words he had just spoken.

He stepped back and looked at her, a serious question in his eyes. "But this is a huge sacrifice to give up your calling to India. Are you sure?"

The answer rose in her heart, and she nodded. "My highest calling is to love the Lord with all my heart, soul, and strength, and I want to always be true to that. But there are many ways to serve Him and many seasons in our lives. And I believe I can serve Him here, as your wife and as Andrew and Millie's mother. It's a gift, a treasure, and I'm grateful to receive it."

His smile spread wider. "Very well said."

She looked up at him, her heart overflowing. "And I have a gift I want to share with you."

He cocked his head. "A gift? What do you mean?"

"I've received an inheritance from my grandfather . . . It's more than enough to pay the death duties and all the other expenses at Highland."

He stared at her. "An inheritance?"

She laughed. "Yes, it's true. We can save Highland together, and it can remain our family's home for generations to come."

"Oh, my darling." He shook his head. "I don't know what to say."

"Say you will accept it, and thank the Lord with me, because He is the giver of every good gift."

He nodded, his eyes shining. "Yes, and we'll thank Him every day of our lives."

She smiled, inviting him closer. He slipped his arms around her, leaned down, and brushed his lips across hers with the softest touch. Her eyelids fluttered closed, and the last of her doubts faded as he held her close and kissed her tenderly. Joy flooded her heart, and her sweet thanks rose to heaven.

Thirty

On a bright and clear morning, the first Saturday in April, wedding bells rang out from the stone tower of St. John's Church in the village of Fulton. A happy crowd of Highland staff, friends, family, and villagers gathered on the front walk of the church following the lovely ceremony.

The guests were smartly dressed, the men in their best suits and the women in their finest spring dresses and hats. Lining up on both sides of the walk, they waited to cheer the bride and groom as they left the church and boarded the carriage that would take them to Highland for the wedding luncheon.

Millie, wearing a pretty pink dress with many ruffles, stood on tiptoe, searching past the crowd, then she turned and clasped Julia's hand. "Why aren't they coming?"

Julia smiled down at Millie. "They'll be out soon. They must sign the registry first."

Andrew tugged at his necktie and shifted his

weight from one foot to the other. "I hope they hurry. I'm getting hungry."

William placed his hand on Andrew's shoulder and smiled at Julia. She returned the smile. How handsome he looked in his morning coat with the white rosebud pinned to his lapel. It had been a very touching wedding ceremony, and Julia had been seated close enough to see the tears in William's eyes when he kissed his sister's cheek and gave her away to Clark Dalton.

He leaned down and whispered in her ear. "Only five more months . . . Then we will be celebrating our own wedding."

She nodded, hope and expectation rising in her heart. They had decided to take that time to get to know each other better and prepare for their marriage. In two weeks they would travel with the family to London for Katherine's first season. Guiding her to make the best plans for the future was a priority for both William and Julia.

"Here they come!" Millie called.

Sarah and Clark stepped through the arched doorway, and a cheer rose from the crowd. Sarah looked elegant in her satin-and-lace wedding gown. She took Clark's arm and walked toward Julia and William. Her train flowed out behind her, and the beading around her neck and sleeves sparkled in the sunshine. The fragrance of her pink rose bouquet drifted on the breeze. Clark, looking very dashing in his morning coat, a pink rosebud pinned on his lapel, beamed proudly as he escorted his new wife down the walk.

Millie reached into her basket and tossed pink rose petals in the air. Clark's niece, Abigail, giggled and joined her on the other side of the walk.

Amid the shower of petals, Sarah stopped to kiss William's cheek. "I love you," she said softly.

"As I do you." He sent her a brave smile, then shook Clark's hand. "Take good care of her."

"I will. I promise."

Sarah turned to Julia, her eyes shining. "Thank you. Without you, none of this would have been possible."

Julia shook her head. "The Lord has blessed us all." She leaned in and kissed Sarah's cheek. "God be with you, my dearest."

"And you as well." Sarah squeezed Julia's hand, then she turned to Clark.

"Are you ready, Mrs. Dalton?" Clark grinned.

"Yes, I am." Happy light danced in Sarah's eyes as she took Clark's arm again.

"We'll be off then." Clark turned to William. "We'll see you at Highland."

"Yes." William nodded. "We'll see you there."

Clark helped Sarah board the carriage, then climbed in beside her.

William took Julia's hand and wove his fingers through hers as the carriage pulled away. The crowd cheered again, and Julia lifted her hand to wave.

As the carriage rounded the bend, William released a sigh and smiled down at Julia. "What a happy day."

"Yes, one of the happiest."

His tender gaze lingered on her. "Thank you for loving me and my family."

Julia's heart lifted as she looked up at him. "I do, so very much."

He lifted her hand to his lips and kissed her fingers. "And my love will always be yours."

The church bells rang out again, sending a message of hope and joy throughout the village, across the hills—and echoing all the way to Highland Hall.

Readers Guide

1. Education was quite different in the Edwardian Era than it is today. What do you think of Julia's approach to teaching and working with Andrew and Millie? How do you think being taught by a governess would compare to the various types of education children receive today? What would be the benefits or drawbacks?

2. William was haunted by memories of his wife's unfaithfulness. How did this impact him in the story, and how would you advise someone who has experienced that kind of wounding as he or she moves on?

3. Why did Katherine struggle with the idea of having a governess? Were her objections reasonable? How do you think Julia was able to help her grow and change in the story?

4. William and David struggled with sibling rivalry in their relationship. Why do you think that happened, and how did it impact them? Adult sibling relationships can be complicated. Share what you believe is the best method of conflict resolution within these close connections.

5. Sarah's handicap was caused by a stroke when she was an infant, and it limited her use of one hand and arm. Clark helps her see that God can bring good into our lives through our handicaps and struggles. Can you share a difficult experience or limitation you've faced in your life and a way God used it for good?

6. William thought inheriting the title of baronet and overseeing his family's estate would help him regain his feelings of self-worth. What are some other ways a person could regain a sense of self-worth and experience healing after they have been hurt or betrayed?

7. Katherine was preparing for the London social season and her debut in society where she hoped to meet her future husband. What do you think of these methods of finding a mate? Were they too shallow, or do we overthink it today, relying less on family connections?

8. Sarah and Julia enjoyed a special friendship. What do you think drew them together? What are some of the blessings you have enjoyed in your friendships?

9. Andrew had a hard time controlling all his extra energy. What are some ways Julia helped him deal with that challenge? Do you find

children with Andrew's challenges receive greater empathy and resources today or not?

10. At the beginning of the story, Julia felt her family was called to serve the Lord in India, but in the end she changed her mind and decided to stay in England and marry William. What do you think of her choosing a different direction in life? Have you ever sensed the Lord directing you to serve Him in a particular way? Have you ever changed course and gone in a different direction?

11. Sarah asks Julia to keep information about Clark from William. Do you think she was right in doing so, and was Julia, as William's employee, right to keep the secret to herself?

12. When the story opens William has a formal and distant relationship to God. How did it change over the course of the story, and what brought about those changes?

Acknowledgments

There were many people who provided support, information, and encouragement in the process of bringing this book to life. In the research and writing of *The Governess of Highland Hall*, I am deeply grateful to

- Cathy Gohlke, fellow author and friend, who helped me brainstorm the original ideas, loaned me research books, and gave me constant encouragement throughout the writing and revision process. This book would not have been possible without your love, friendship, and support.
- Steve Laube, my literary agent, for his wise counsel and guidance, and for being an anchor and a tireless advocate. I feel blessed to be your client.
- Terri Gillespie, Claudia Gentile, Katy Dovgala-Carr, and Ella Furlong, my friends and fellow authors, for providing helpful brainstorming and thoughtful critiques.
- Iola Gulton and Evangeline Holland, for their help with English customs, dress, and language, and for general knowledge of the time period. As an American writing a historical novel set in England, I definitely needed their input and assistance.

• Shannon Marchese, Karen Ball, Laura Wright, and Rose Decaen, my gifted editors, who helped me revise and polish this story so readers might truly enjoy it.

• Kristopher Orr, the talented designer at WaterBrook Multnomah, and Mike Heath, of Magnus Creative, for their work on the cover that so beautifully portrays the mood, heroine, and setting of the story.

• Amy Haddock, Ashley Boyer, and the whole team at WaterBrook Multnomah, for their outstanding work with marketing, publicity, production, and sales, and to each one there who played a part in bringing this book to you.

• Scott, Josh, Melinda, Melissa, Peter, Ben, Galan, Lizzy, Megan, and Shirley, for their love and belief that I could write something worthwhile. It's a joy to share the journey with you!

Most of all, I thank my Lord and Savior, Jesus Christ, for His constant love and watch-care over my family and me. I am grateful for the gifts and talents He has given, and I hope always to use those to bring Him glory and honor.

About the Author

Carrie Turansky has loved reading since she first visited the library as a young child and checked out a tall stack of picture books. Her love for writing began when she penned her first novel at age twelve. She is now the award-winning author of eleven inspirational romance novels and novellas. Carrie and her husband, Scott, who is a pastor, author, and speaker, have been married for more than thirty-five years and make their home in New Jersey. They often travel together on ministry trips and to visit their five adult children and three grandchildren. Carrie also leads women's ministry at her church, and when she's not writing she enjoys spending time working in her flower gardens and cooking healthy meals for friends and family.

She loves to connect with reading friends through her website, www.carrieturansky.com, and through Facebook, Pinterest, and Twitter.

Center Point Large Print
600 Brooks Road / PO Box 1
Thorndike ME 04986-0001 USA

(207) 568-3717

US & Canada:
1 800 929-9108
www.centerpointlargeprint.com